The Dark Angel Chronicles
Book II

Daemon Lord

By Brian K. Stoner

Martinsville, Indiana
www.BookmanPublishing.com

To the fondest memories of my father,
Kevin M. Stoner,
who taught me that I must try to be aware of everything,
but defeated by nothing.

Prologue

It was early evening, and business was good at The Sleeping Dragon. Balon Trush, the inn's owner, was having one of his most profitable days. He bustled about, his largish frame moving with the sureness of familiarity from table to table. Balon believed that people worked better if their boss worked with them, and as if to prove it, his serving maids had always been among the most efficient—and most well-liked—in all of Green Haven.

"Our entertainment for the night still hasn't arrived," came a familiar voice from behind him, more hopeful than concerned.

Balon turned to find his only daughter, Lilly, looking up at him. Far from worried, she was hoping to *be* the entertainment. She was good at it, and she loved doing it, but they always played this game of dutiful employee to employer while at work. "See what you can find," he said with a smile. "If all else fails, I'll dust off the old flute, and you can give us a dance." The flute would hardly require dusting— Balon played every night before he went to bed—but he hadn't performed in the common room himself for nearly two years. His daughter danced frequently, though; it was one of her greatest joys. Lilly smiled and disappeared through the kitchen door to change. Her room lay just beyond the kitchen, across from Balon's own. If the promised entertainment didn't show up soon, it would be one less expense to pay. Tonight would be very profitable indeed.

At that moment, a rowdy-looking bunch of soldiers stumbled into the common room. They were mercenaries, by the look of them, and already more than a little drunk. Balon motioned for Rolf to keep an eye on them. Rolf had been working for Balon nearly five years now, and the big man's mere presence was usually sufficient to discourage any trouble from the rougher patrons. The soldiers took seats in a corner, ordering ale immediately. They were a little too free with their hands, but Sara, the serving maid, handled it well. She simply backed out of their reach, maintaining her courteous smile, and moved off to fetch their drinks. The Sleeping Dragon usually didn't attract such men, but they were still far from unheard of. Balon followed Sara back to the cellar. He would serve these men himself.

When he returned, smiling inwardly at the disappointed looks on the soldiers' faces as he served their drinks, the inn's door opened again, admitting a creature the likes of which Balon had never seen in all his life. She was easily the most beautiful woman he had ever laid eyes on, with fiery red hair flowing nearly to her waist, and strangely sharp eyes that, oddly enough, drew a man's attention entirely away from the moderately generous display of bosom her dress afforded. Clad in an ornate black and red gown that in no way inhibited her movement, she might have been royalty, save that she smiled respectfully at the serving maids, as if she considered them equals. A hush fell over the common room when she entered, and she blushed slightly, clearly embarrassed by the attention. Quickly, but with a grace that made her seem not to hurry at all, she took a seat three tables down from where the mercenaries sat.

After serving the soldiers, Balon moved to where the strange visitor was seated. "I am Balon Trush," he said politely, "the owner of this inn. Would you like any refreshments?"

She looked up at him, her kind smile a sharp contrast to her fierce eyes. "May I have a glass of red wine, please?" she asked, and Balon nearly forgot to respond, so surprised he was by her voice, a voice so unlike any other he had ever heard that it made him wonder if his mind were playing tricks on him. If innocence and malevolence could intertwine, they would form the voice that escaped those ruby lips. "I prefer new over old."

"At once, m'lady," he stammered, uncertain how to address her. He was so shocked at her voice—and her very appearance in his inn; lords and ladies seldom came here—that he forgot to so much as wonder at the strangeness of her request. Before he could move to fetch her drink, she held out a golden coin to him, though he did not see her reach for it. That much was understandable, considering the state he was in. He took the coin, bowing respectfully and moving away. By the time he reached the cellar, he had regained his wits enough to look at the coin, and his eyes widened. The gold in his hand was worth at least ten times the cost of the drink she had ordered. He would need to find her some change after she was served.

When he returned with the newest red wine in the cellar—only now wondering why anyone would order new wine—one of the mercenaries was talking to the mysterious Lady. She seemed confused by what he was saying, though not at all frightened. Still, Balon felt a growing uneasiness, and from the way the man was looking at her, it was entirely justified. Quickly he signaled Rolf to follow him, and he headed for the table.

"Is there a problem, m'lady?" he asked tentatively as he set her glass down, hoping to avoid any trouble, but it was the mercenary who answered.

"No problem, friend. Just move away. The wench and I are talking."

"Wench?" the Lady asked, appearing genuinely confused.

"I think, sir," said Balon, "that perhaps you should return to your table." He nodded to Rolf, and the big man stepped between Balon and the mercenary. Balon did not see the dagger until it was too late. One moment the soldier had begun to turn away, and the next he was spinning. Before Rolf had moved a muscle, blood was flowing from his neck as he fell.

The mercenary laughed contemptuously. "Never send a strong-arm against a trained soldier," he sneered. "Now turn away. The wench and I are going upstairs."

"I believe I would prefer to remain here," the Lady said calmly. "Please leave me, and I will see what I can do for the wounded man."

The mercenary laughed harder now. "The wench thinks she has a choice." The other soldiers laughed coarsely, sharing his mirth. He grabbed the Lady's arm, wrenching her from her seat.

Before Balon could move, fire exploded around the man's entire arm. The Lady extended her hand apparently without effort, and the mercenary was flung halfway across the common room. He did not move again. Balon's mind raced even as fear froze his muscles in place. She was a witch! A witch had come to his inn! As if nothing terribly untoward had happened, she rose calmly.

"I am very sorry for this," the witch said to Balon. She moved toward him, holding something out in her hand, and he backed away in fear. What would she do to him? Lowering suddenly moist eyes—what could drive a witch to tears?—she set the object down carefully on the table, and quickly walked out the door. After a few moments, Balon recovered himself enough to look down at whatever she might have left, probably an evil talisman. To his astonishment, he found that it was a large purse, filled to overflowing with gold coins.

Chapter 1

Night was falling as they approached the volcano, the setting sun staining the sky a bright crimson. Serana wondered grimly how much of the land would be stained crimson as well, before the Daemons were through. It had taken only three days to travel this far, the elementals gliding effortlessly through the land as if born to nature. Perhaps they were, at that. Allaerion ran easily, his feet barely touching the soft earth beneath him, as if the wind itself carried him along. Alier had disappeared from time to time, coming into view again just over the next hill, or from behind a tree; she never appeared hurried, but was always a few paces ahead of the rest whenever she showed herself. Serana was not certain exactly *how* Seleine traveled—the Ice Witch would only smile secretively with a murmured "later" whenever asked—but she, too, arrived at whatever campsite they selected at roughly the same time as the others. Though not an elemental herself, Serana was well enough acquainted with their magic to travel as one of them, using bits and pieces from what each of them were doing. In the beginning, she had simply run as Allaerion did, but Alier was teaching her to meld with the earth, and to use the unique life force of each thing that grew to find her way before emerging again at the surface. Serana could not yet remain earth-melded—that was what Alier called it—as long as the Earth Enchantress, but she was improving slowly. She had spent so much time on elemental magic now that she felt as if she should somehow belong among their races, though to no one in particular.

It was odd, truly. Serana did not feel that she should be an Air Wizard, a Fire Warlock, an Earth Enchantress, or an Ice Witch, but rather that she should belong to all four, a being in tune with all of nature and... still something more. She was a Sorceress, but she was alone, with no others to teach her what she should become, what directions her gifts should take. The Dark Angel—the Serian—had helped as he could, and so had Rillian and the elementals, but without another Sorceress to learn from, Serana was concerned that she would never truly master the magic that was her heritage.

When she pushed through the last clump of trees, the volcano came into view, and Serana stared in shock at what she saw. A massive boulder blocked the mouth of the volcano, obviously the work of Daemons. Besides them, only the Serian could have managed the feat, and he certainly never would have done so. If Blackfang and the Guardian had been inside when the boulder was put there, they must surely be dead.

"Well, there's only one way to find out," Seleine said quietly, as if reading her thoughts. Together, the four pressed on as night descended like a cloak of doom over the land.

When they reached the volcano, they could tell immediately that the caves had collapsed. "There is no way in or out," said Allaerion, returning from a circle of the mountain. "If the dragons were in there, they must certainly have starved to death."

"He is right," Alier agreed. "That boulder was put there some time ago, far longer than a dragon could go without food."

"I will not accept that there is nothing we can do," Serana said as calmly as she could, not really sure where the vague plan forming in her mind would take them. "Alier, with our combined strengths, can we move the boulder?"

"Not unless you are at least twice as strong as I in Earth," the Earth Enchantress replied flatly, "and you aren't."

Serana nodded, taking on the Serenity to clear her mind. "But why must we only use Earth? I could melt parts of the boulder with Fire, and Allaerion could help me guide away the fumes with Air. Seleine, you could freeze the lava in place, after Alier and I move it to where we need it. We don't need to simply move the boulder; we can reshape it."

Alier blinked. "Very impressive, Serana. I would not have imagined such a feat possible with only the four of us, but it might just work."

"I think it will," Serana decided. "We should start immediately."

"Wait a moment," Seleine cautioned, holding up her hand. "Your plan may work, but not if we don't work as a unit. I need to know exactly where to freeze the lava, and unlike you and Alier, I can't see the shape of the boulder from the patterns of Earth energy."

"And I need to know what directions to channel the air," put in Allaerion.

They were right. The problem would be difficult, as they would need to shift the energies a great deal during the process. They needed to work as one...

"Will you trust me?" Serana asked suddenly as the solution came to her. "Will you trust me to take control of your energies? If we work that way, I'm certain we'll succeed."

"Serana," Seleine said gently, "I would trust you with my life, but you are talking about taking the life-forces of three elementals at once. I don't think..."

"No, that's not what I mean," Serana interrupted. "I don't need to take the energy out of you, but merely control it. I think I know a way to link us, so that I can direct everything myself."

Allaerion laughed, and Seleine soon joined him. Alier simply shook her head. "Once again, Serana, you point out the obvious solution before you've even seen it," she said. "I would wager everything I own that you have just conceived the very way their parents linked to charge the Armor of the Elements."

Everything was ready quickly. Serana's plan turned out to be a bit different than what the elementals had probably used, but not a great deal. When the Armor of the Elements was charged, the elementals must have formed a mesh of energy from all four elements, and used it as a focus to weave around them all. The main difference was that when the Armor was made, each elemental would have retained equal control. Because she could wield all four elements, Serana simply used herself as the focus, bringing the other three in contact with her, and granting her control over their power.

As soon as the linking was complete, Serana set to work. Earth magic granted her a detailed picture in her mind of how the boulder was situated, so she worked with her eyes closed, depending entirely on those senses. Using Fire in thin streams, she melted away a small section of the rock, a part that was not supporting anything, creating a small hole. The rest would be tricky, but Serana felt more than ready for the challenge. If the dragons might possibly be alive, she would find them, and if they weren't… Well, she did not like to consider that yet.

***

Blackfang looked about the cavern, his eyes well attuned to the darkness after his weeks of captivity. The Guardian lay sleeping beside him, and he watched her silently. If not for her, he would most certainly be dead by now. Not even a human was small enough to crawl out of the mountain, blocked as it was, but the Mist could go anywhere. The Mist had provided food and breathable air, and though it could not lift the boulder, it had sustained them, at least physically.

The Guardian was also responsible for Blackfang's continued sanity. In all his life, he had never once been captive, and claustrophobia was driving him mad. If not for her calming presence and her seemingly endless ways of distracting him, he would surely have lost his mind. He might still, if they did not find a way out soon.

A sudden sound brought him from his thoughts. He looked around, searching for the source of the rumbling and hissing, but to no avail. Suddenly, a ray of light broke through from above, and Blackfang was nearly blinded, so accustomed he had become to the darkness.

As his eyes slowly regained their focus, he realized that a small hole had formed in the huge rock that blocked them in. He watched in fascination as the rock seemed to melt of its own accord, becoming lava that flowed—unbelievably—*upward!* It soon stopped, and froze beneath a layer of ice that quickly melted away in the heat, leaving hard stone behind. More holes began to form, small at first, but growing continually. The process was slow, but after an hour or so had passed, all that remained of the boulder was a huge web of stone, each strand no thicker than one of Blackfang's arms. Who or what could have performed such a miracle was beyond him, but hope surged through his entire being.

"What has happened?" asked the Guardian, rousing from her slumber. She closed her eyes briefly, then reopened them. "I understand now," she said softly.

"Well, I don't, but I certainly am not complaining," Blackfang replied.

"It is the Sorceress," the Guardian explained, "along with three elementals."

Blackfang snorted derisively. "Impossible. Only the Serian possesses enough strength to do this, and he would have simply lifted the rock."

"It is the Sorceress" the Guardian insisted. "I told you that she would be necessary."

It was then that another voice reached them, a voice that seemed to emanate from the air itself. "Back away from the center," said the voice. "Keep to the walls."

The two dragons obeyed wordlessly, understanding what was to happen, and no sooner had they reached the walls than the web of stone came crashing down to the floor. Without waiting a moment longer, Blackfang spread his wings, leapt into the air and flew to freedom.

As he circled his volcano, he saw four tiny figures at the base of the mountain. The Guardian had already landed near them, and appeared to be speaking with them. Blackfang flew down to join her.

As he drew near, Blackfang heard the voice again, but it now came not from the air, but from a young girl in a green dress, a Sorceress High Priestess. So the Guardian had been right...

"When the Daemon Lords attacked us," she was saying, "the Serian of Music was trapped, unable to wield his Power. I need to know how that happened, and how we might prevent it in the future."

The Guardian closed her eyes as Blackfang alighted beside her. "I do not know how it was done, Serana. It was the first time any such thing has happened. I do know that it was you who saved the Serian, and that a part of the final answer will come from you." The crystal dragon was silent for a moment before speaking again. "I can tell you this much... The Daemon Lords may only trap the Serian if they number seven. If there were two Seriani, fourteen Daemon Lords would be required. If there were three, there is not sufficient energy in the world to sustain the number that would be needed."

"The Serian of Music admitted to me that there is a way for him to create more of his own kind," said Serana suddenly. "Please tell me how. I volunteered myself, but he would not transform me."

The Guardian regarded her sadly for a moment before speaking. "I cannot tell you, for that knowledge is his to give. I can only advise you to never try to possess him. He is not to be yours."

The Sorceress appeared surprised and confused, but she nodded. "Thank you," she said simply.

The crystal dragon nodded. "For those who saved my life, and Blackfang's, I only wish I could do more."

Blackfang spoke tentatively, feeling rather awkward. "I, too, would like the chance to repay you. For a very long time, I would have welcomed death, but now I have reason to live." He glanced at the Guardian. "I do not have the Mist's knowledge, but if there is any feat I may perform for you in repayment, you have but to name it."

The High Priestess stared at him in surprise, but her expression soon turned thoughtful. "There is one thing," she said quietly.

Chapter II

The battle was not going well. Three days ago, the Daemon army had attacked, and it was obvious to everyone that without the support of the elves and vampires, Rhanestone would have fallen on that first day. Now, during a small respite after yet another Daemon charge, Rillian was beginning to wonder if they could hold out through another night. He was exhausted, but he dared not sleep. The Daemons could attack again at any moment, and the huge stone that had been moved to replace the ruined gate would not hold for long, even strengthened as it was by his magic. Half of the Elite Guard lay slain, and though the Rhanestone army was still strong and their allies steadfast, everyone was beginning to tire... everyone, that is, except the Daemons.

Relentlessly, they attacked day and night, falling back only when boiling pitch and arrows dipped in Dragon's Tears drove them away. Ella had improved Rillian's exploding arrows, and even found a way to mix extract from Dragon's Tears into the explosive, killing up to three Daemon Scouts with a single shot, but supplies were running low, and the Daemon army showed no sign of slowing.

Worse yet, the infernal creatures had seemed to learn battle tactics overnight, attacking in stealth wherever Rhanestone's defenses were weakest. If not for the elven archers and vampire spies, the Keep would surely have been overtaken already. No one was particularly happy about the vampire presence, but Lord Alexander had been speaking to everyone of their merits, a complete turn-around from his former attitude—the change was not surprising, if the beautiful vampire woman who followed him everywhere truly had given herself as *yamin'sai*; Rillian had been more than surprised at *that* announcement—and Duke Rhanestone continually pointed out that they had saved the defenders more than once. It was true; they had. Rillian wondered at the way enemies could become friends—or at least mutually tolerated allies—when faced with a common threat.

Perhaps at least something good would come of this war, if any of them survived to remember it…

Rillian continued to grow younger, his endurance and vitality strengthening steadily with each passing day. Tonight, however, he felt as old as he had ever felt, exhausted and worried. He had not slept at all since the attacks began, and it was becoming more and more difficult to keep his eyes open. Walking along the wall to watch for the next attack, he suddenly slipped and fell backwards, but strong hands caught him.

"Rillian, I am relieving you of duty," came Duke Rhanestone's voice. "Get some sleep."

Rillian tried to look alert. "Sir, if they attack again…" he began.

"Old friend," the Duke said softly, "no one has been more loyal and true to Rhanestone than you have, but you are mortal, and you cannot continue without rest forever. Sleep, or you'll be no use to anyone."

Rillian nodded, resigned. Duke Rhanestone had had no more sleep himself, but he was not as old as Rillian, and he had always been among the strongest of men. Stumbling slightly, Rillian made his way back to his room and collapsed on the bed. When he awoke, it was morning, and from the sounds outside, Rillian knew the battle raged on. Not bothering to stop at the kitchen for food, he rushed to the wall, where he found the Duke shouting orders.

The Daemons' latest plan was simple. They were throwing themselves at the front gate, determined to break down the stone that held them back. Looking down, Rillian saw Ella stride purposefully into the courtyard below, and his stomach constricted in fear. "Ella!" he shouted. "Get out of there! They're trying to break it down!" If she heard him, she gave no sign, but he soon saw that she was not alone. Three elves, dressed in white robes, accompanied her.

Not waiting to see what was to happen, Rillian rushed down the stairs, bounding down to the courtyard. When he reached them, they had already begun… something. They were using magic, but Rillian had no idea what they were doing. Ella was working as efficiently as the elves—priests, Rillian decided—but it was no magic that he had ever taught her. She must have been studying with them as well.

Suddenly, the stone cracked under a ferocious blow from the other side, but the girl and the elves continued working, oblivious. Rillian opened his mouth to cry out to her, to make her come away, but the words never took voice. In astonishment, he watched as the stone melded itself together again seamlessly, as if it had never been cracked. Rillian reached out with his own senses, and suddenly understood. "Earth magic," he breathed.

Ella and the elves lowered their hands, turning away from the stone. "It should hold better now," she said, smiling to Rillian.

"When did you have time to learn that?" he managed.

"Whenever I wasn't studying with you or Valaran," she replied with a shrug. "If I'm going to learn magic, I may as well learn as many different things as I can."

"Very true, Ella," he agreed. "In fact, I would very much appreciate it if you would take me with you when you go to your next lesson from them."

Before she could reply, Duke Rhanestone's voice rang down from the wall. "Rillian, we need you up here!" Rillian ran up to join the Duke, and his mouth went dry at what he saw. There was a man among the Daemons, *commanding* them!

The man, dressed in black robes that were vaguely reminiscent of those the Seriani wore, strode forward purposefully. If his attire was like unto the Seriani, the resemblance ended there. Where the Serian of Music seemed to glow with peace and light to any with enough magical sense to feel it, this strange man exuded cruelty and death. The man, surrounded by Daemons that seemed to be bowing and scraping with each step, extended a hand, pointing at the stone blocking the gate, and in moments it shattered inward, as if from a terrible blow. Rillian's heart nearly stopped as he saw wave upon wave of Daemons surge forward toward the now-open passage into Rhanestone. The strange man was still standing where he had been, with his arms crossed, and satisfaction written upon his face. Duke Rhanestone, at Rillian's side, had gone white with horror. After so many generations of standing steadfast, Rhanestone Keep would fall. There was nothing left to be done, except to take as many Daemons with them as they could...

As the first wave approached the gateway, Rillian began to pray to the Power. He prayed as the black swarm drew nearer, prayed as he had never prayed in his life… and to his astonishment, his prayer was answered. Fire from heaven rained down on the Daemons, two mighty pillars of flame that engulfed the creatures, destroying them utterly. The next wave halted, turning around to run, but not before the flames engulfed them as well, turning scores of Daemons to ash. The strange man was nowhere to be seen. Rillian stared, unable to believe what was happening, as yet another wave of Daemons perished in burning agony. He looked upward slowly, and his shock deepened as a shadow fell over him. The flames had not come from heaven after all, but from two great dragons, one black as night and one that shimmered with every hue of the rainbow.

Rillian glanced at Duke Rhanestone, but the other man was simply staring at the sky in wonder. As the Battlemage of Rhanestone Keep cast his gaze over the walls, he saw that every other soldier was doing the same, transfixed by a sight that was as improbable as it was wonderful. Rillian did not know how long the dragons would continue to fight for them, but for tonight at least, Rhanestone would be safe.

When the Daemon army had begun to flee in earnest, the dragons circled back, heading for the Keep. For a horrible moment, Rillian feared that they might attack, killing humans, elves, and vampires as quickly as Daemons. Instead, they flew over the stone walls, landing gracefully in the courtyard—at least, the black dragon landed gracefully; the other stumbled and nearly fell, but regained balance quickly. Oddly, it was this second dragon, obviously the younger of the two, who spoke, her voice resonating throughout the Keep.

"Defenders of Rhanestone," she said, her voice unmistakably female, yet as inhuman as any voice Rillian had ever heard, "I am the Guardian of Mist. We come to aid you in your hour of need." If there had been clumsiness in her landing, there was no trace of it in her bearing. She turned her huge head, taking in the soldiers on the walls, her being invested with a majesty rivaled only by that of the Serian of Music. "We were trapped in Blackfang's volcano, but were rescued by Serana, High Priestess and last remaining member of the Sorceress race. In repayment of our debt to her, we have come to fight at your side until the Daemon army is defeated."

Stunned silence answered her, but within moments, Duke Rhanestone's voice came clearly from the wall. "Then we welcome you, and offer whatever hospitality we have to give," he said.

The black dragon, which could only be Blackfang, stirred at this. When he spoke, his voice held none of the majesty that the Guardian's had, but it was powerful and inhuman nonetheless. "Your hospitality we may need soon, but only insofar as that you allow us the use of this courtyard to feed and rest in safety. I will hunt when we aren't fighting, so worry not about your food supply." He stretched his wings, seeming to relax slightly. "As for our debt to the Sorceress..." Blackfang paused a moment, as if searching for words. "While it is true that we owe her our lives, I, for one, would kill these Daemons simply for sport, whether this... structure... were here or not. I won't be satisfied until every last Spawn of the Black Void is hunted down and wiped from existence!"

Dangerous and legendary as the dragon was, it was Blackfang's attitude that won over the Rhanestone soldiers. Anyone who hated Daemons so thoroughly had a place in their hearts, and the cheers that erupted from the walls lasted several minutes before the Duke began shouting orders to have the gateway sealed again. Moral was high as the soldiers set to work; it seemed as if the Power itself had infused the men with renewed energy. With Blackfang and the Guardian of Mist on its side, Rhanestone Keep would drive back any army of Daemons! Rillian only hoped it was true.

Chapter III

The young vampire was waiting when he appeared, huddled on her narrow bed in the tiny room of the inn, as if trying in vain to hide from her fate, from the nature that was thrust upon her. When she saw him, she rose shakily to sit on the edge of the mattress, tension draining from her as water drains from the trees after rain… slowly. The Serian of Music smiled, and kept his voice gentle. "I am sorry that I am so late in returning to thee."

"I had feared," she whispered, "that you were part of a fanciful dream, my mind's way of hiding from me the act of killing an innocent person to satisfy my monstrous hunger." She smiled, the first real smile he had seen touch her face. "Now I see that it was real, that I have not yet murdered to survive."

"I have returned to see that thou shalt never need do so." He extended his hand to her. "Come, and I will take thee to those who would aid and teach thee." She stood, and came to him with a trust born of desperation. As soon as her hand touched his, he transported them to Rhanestone, to the midst of raging combat.

She clung to him, trembling, as they stood atop the north wall of Rhanestone Keep. "All will be well," he whispered, soothing her with music in her mind while his attention remained on the vast army surging toward the walls. Engaging himself directly in the battle was not possible, of course—the Book of Dream had warned him against it; his battle, the larger battle, would be fought elsewhere, with the mysterious maiden foretold to him—but he could not resist a small aid in the short time he could allow himself here.

The dragons were here, of course, the Guardian of Mist guarding the gate as Blackfang rained fiery death on the Daemons below, but there was a Lord approaching with deliberate, deadly purpose, and even the two dragons together could never hope to defeat so powerful an adversary. So long as he did not directly kill…

Dark shapes soon appeared around him, and he gave the young vampire over to the care of her brethren. "Take care with her," he told them. "She was turned improperly, and knows nothing of thy ways." The vampires nodded wordlessly and led her away.

Drawing deeply on the Power, the Serian unfolded his wings, allowing himself to shine as a beacon to the warriors of Rhanestone. Focusing on the earth before the gates, he called forth Dragon's Tears. Hundreds of blossoms sprang from the soil, creating in seconds a great garden that stretched spans beyond the gate, and still further within, a protective barrier that no Daemon could cross, at least for a time. It was all he could do... for now.

Folding his wings, he moved on, to continue his search.

***

The vampire followed numbly where the others led. She had a name, or thought she did, but somehow she could no longer remember it. She had been a farmer's daughter, or at least, she had spent a great deal of time on a farm, a green place with trees and large, open clearings, where she could still remember running through the fields with no thought beyond the joy of freedom, the feel of the wind on her face and the sun on her skin. Surely it had to have been a farm. She remembered four men, a father, two brothers, and someone whom she couldn't place. None of their faces were clear to her any longer.

Now she was a vampire, a creature of evil, whatever the beautiful Dark Angel had said. He was the first to show kindness to her since she had been changed, the first to offer her anything more than threats and anger. Now he was gone, and in his place...

She shuddered involuntarily as one of the dark-cloaked figures touched her arm. It was a light touch, seemingly meant only to guide her to the stairway at her left that led down off the thick wall of stone where the Dark Angel had brought her, but it sent a wave of revulsion through her entire body.

"Take this," whispered a tall, dark-haired man—he looked like a man, at least, but she knew better—as he wrapped a dark cloak around her shoulders. She wanted to throw the garment away, to fling it as far from her as she could, and the evil it represented with it... but she had no will to fight. She herself was more evil now than any mere piece of cloth, and the cloak would help keep her warm.

"Where are you taking me?" she managed, though she found it difficult to care.

"To Morganna, our leader," replied a young woman—a creature who *looked* like a young woman. "She will want to meet you, before we begin your instruction." So, she was to be instructed, trained in wickedness, as if her very existence were not vile enough.

Oddly, the people around her seemed somehow different than any had before. Despite her revulsion, she felt a strange… kinship with the vampires—the *other* vampires. The humans seemed to glow faintly, or at least "glow" was the first word that came to her mind. There was no light; it was more a sensation, unlike anything she remembered feeling before. It was a little stronger in the elves, a brighter… glow.

The small group—there were eight, she knew without looking; the feel of kinship made each distinct—led her in through a door from the courtyard, down a narrow passage, and into a large room at least four times the size of the one where the Dark Angel had found her. There were more vampires here. She felt an urge to run, but it would have been a useless effort. They had her now.

A golden-haired woman rose gracefully, stepping down from the raised chair that her bearing made seem a throne. "Our new member has come home," she said with a slight smile. "Welcome to you. I am Morganna. What is your name?"

"I… don't remember," the young vampire said hesitantly. The name was there, somewhere in the back of her mind, but she could as easily capture mist as remember it.

Morganna took her hands, studying her eyes intently, and a small shiver went through the younger vampire. It felt as if the golden-haired woman had peered into her very soul… "You were hurt," Morganna said softly, and for a moment her face darkened. It was no more than a moment; calm seemed a part of the creature as surely as her piercing eyes. After a long pause, she spoke again, loudly enough for all in the room to hear. "Until you remember your name, you will be called Reilena, which means 'remembrance' in the Ancient

14

Tongue." She smiled again, a bare curving of her lips, but strangely it seemed to touch her eyes nonetheless. "You are one of us now, Reilena. Make yourself at home among us. We will speak again when you have had time to settle."

As Morganna glided away, Reilena—it *was* a pretty name, regardless that it was given by an evil creature—let herself be led to still another hallway, smallish and lined with plain wooden doors. Her guards—she was sure they were guards, to keep her from escaping— showed her into a room behind one of the doors. As soon as she was through the door, the tall man—vampire; he was not a man—nodded as if to himself. "I will be in the next room on the right," he told her. "Please let me know if there is anything you require. I will return after you've rested, to take you back to Morganna." Before she could form a reply, he had slipped out and closed the door behind him. Wondering why a vampire would care whether she needed anything— would evil creatures care even for each other?—Reilena turned to look around her new quarters. It was a comfortable, cozy little room, and if the bed was a bit narrow, it was soft, and the sheets were clean.

Reilena sat down on the bed, her mind still numb. Things had happened so quickly in the last few hours that she still scarcely believed her senses. Only last night she had been praying to the Creator for death, and instead, a Dark Angel had rescued her, only to deliver her into the hands of the very evil which had ruined her life, the evil which she had become. Perhaps moments past as she sat there, unmoving, or perhaps it was hours; Reilena did not know. Eventually, though, there was a knock on the door, and when she opened it, the tall vampire stood waiting to take her back to his leader.

"What will she do with me?" Reilena asked, surprised that she still cared. She was evil herself now, after all. It would be better if she died, and if the others did as well. She knew it would be better, but she wanted to live… Perhaps the evil was already taking root within her, that she would wish it to survive.

"She will speak with you, to learn of your past. It will help her to decide how you would best fit in among us." He did not look at her as they walked. His eyes remained ahead, yet somehow it seemed he was watching her, gauging her reaction to his words. He gave no sign as to whether or not he was pleased by what he saw.

"Why do you want me to fit in?" she asked. Why would they not simply destroy her? Surely that was what evil did... destroy. Of course, it also spread; leaving her alive meant more wickedness in the world.

He did look at her then, a slightly quizzical expression on his face. Reilena realized that all the vampires' expressions were slight, as if they remained always reserved, never truly passionate about anything. "You are a vampire," he said, as if that should explain everything. They walked on in silence then, but they did not return to the large room where Morganna had been the previous day. Instead, the tall vampire led Reilena to a door almost identical to that of her own room. He knocked once, and without waiting for a reply, opened the door, motioning her to enter.

Morganna was sitting in one of two chairs, reading. Reilena had never considered that vampires might read—what use were books in killing the innocent?—but the greater surprise was the room itself, almost identical to the one Reilena had slept in. Odd, that the leader of the vampires would have no better accommodations than a new recruit. The tall vampire did not follow her in; he closed the door behind her as soon as she had entered.

"Did you sleep well?" asked Morganna without looking up.

"I did not sleep," Reilena replied. There was no reason to lie.

The golden-haired vampire did look up then, marking her place with a strip of leather and setting the book aside. "You were left for five hours. Were the rooms uncomfortable for you?" There was concern in her eyes—slight concern, as all vampires' expressions were slight, but it was there. Reilena was confused.

"Why do you wish me to sleep?" she asked carefully.

Morganna tilted her head slightly, as if puzzled by the question. "While it is true that our kind need not sleep so often as humans, we still do require rest, and you have been through quite an ordeal. Do you require something in particular for your comfort?"

"I don't understand," said Reilena. "Why do you care that I am comfortable? Am I not your prisoner?"

"Prisoner?" the vampire leader asked incredulously, her eyes widening as she rose. "You think yourself a prisoner?" Folding her arms and tapping a finger on her lips lightly, she was the picture of a woman trying to solve a difficult puzzle. "Yes," she said finally, "I suppose I can see why you would come to that conclusion." For a moment, Morganna seemed to struggle with herself, but she quickly recovered her control. "Please, sit," she said softly, indicating the other chair. Suiting her own words, she gestured to the other chair again when Reilena didn't move.

Reluctantly, Reilena moved to sit across from the vampire—the other vampire; she had to remember that—watching carefully for any sign of hostility. What had the golden-haired creature struggled with?

"Let me begin by explaining something to you," said Morganna, her voice surprisingly gentle. "You are not a prisoner here, nor are you a guest. You were given into our care by the Serian of Music because he found you, improperly turned, and knew that we could care for you, teach you what you must know in order to survive. Beyond that, we can offer you a home, a clan, a place among us."

Reilena hesitated. Morganna seemed sincere, but since Reilena had entered the room, images had begun flashing in her mind, images of walking along the forest at night, of being knocked to the ground by a dark figure. The room began to fade... What room? She was outside, walking home as she had done many times. The dark figure... what dark figure? There was no one there, of course. She had always had an overactive imagination. From the corner of her eye, she caught a flicker of movement in the trees, likely some night animal she had startled. A shadow moved from the forest toward her. Shadows didn't move that way... No creature could move so quickly! Before the thought was complete, he was upon her, knocking her to the ground, her breath leaving her in a rush. She could no longer move, no longer see, no longer even feel, except... There was pain, sharp pain in her neck as blood—her blood—flowed down her dress. She was dying. She tried to struggle, but her limbs may as well have belonged on the corpse she was quickly becoming. She was dying, dying... In her mind, she screamed. *Dear Creator, I'm dying!*

"Calm yourself, child," said a voice from somewhere. "You are not dying." Had she somehow managed to speak aloud? The pain was gone, and sensation was returning slowly. There was light from somewhere, and feeling. She was sitting on something... a chair. Yes, it was a chair. There was a hand on hers, offering comfort. Comfort? Who would offer comfort? Had her father found her? No, his hands were larger, more calloused. Sight returned finally, the light taking form as the room returned. A pair of dark, almost black eyes filled with concern looked into hers searchingly, framed by golden curls. Morganna... her name was Morganna.

"What... happened?" Reilena asked. Reilena? Was that her name? She could almost recall having another, but the vague impression was gone as soon as she tried to focus on it.

"Apparently, you remembered something of what happened to you," the other woman said softly. No, not a woman... she was a vampire. Morganna was a vampire... a vampire! Reilena sprang from the chair, backing away in horror. Reilena, that was not her name... it was only given to her because... She was a vampire! She had become...

There were arms around her, holding her gently, helping her into a chair. She couldn't see. Everything was blurry, vague, indistinct. Something was touching her face... a moist cloth? No, a handkerchief, moist from... tears? She was crying...

"You are safe now, child. He cannot hurt you again," said the soft voice... Morganna's voice. Suddenly her mind snapped into focus. She was sitting in a chair, the other vampire—the leader of the vampires—kneeling beside her with an arm around her, dabbing gently at her face with the other hand, drying her tears. "Please calm yourself. All will be well now."

"I've become the monster that killed me," Reilena said thickly. She felt numb, barely able to move any part of her body.

The arm around her stiffened a bit, but only for a moment. "You are not a monster," Morganna said. Her voice was soft, but it held steel. "We are not monsters."

"But the creature that killed me..."

"*Was* a monster," finished Morganna. "Yes, he was a monster, a grotesque and twisted perversion of all we stand for." Her voice held a passion Reilena had never heard from any vampire yet. She could almost believe... but everyone knew that vampires are evil.

"Few know half of what they think they know, particularly of our kind," the golden-haired creature said in disgust. Had Morganna read her thoughts, or had she spoken aloud again? The passion was gone now, replaced by weary determination, but her eyes never left Reilena's. "We are nothing like the filth that did this to you," she said finally. "We will help you, if you will let us."

Slowly, tentatively, Reilena held out her hand. When Morganna took it, she willed herself not to flinch. She almost succeeded.

"It will take time," the other vampire said, "but I will be here, as will the others."

Reilena had to swallow before she could speak. "Thank you," she managed. Morganna's hand squeezed gently on hers, and to her surprise, she felt her own hand squeezing back.

Chapter IV

Ilsa stood beside the tethered horses, her heart pounding. The men had found a large stone with a deep depression, very defensible, and prepared to face the Daemons. They were arrayed at the opening, armed with a few of the weapons that the High Priestess had enchanted. Trisan held a pair of thin blades that glowed faintly red, while Olsever hefted a huge war hammer that emitted tiny sparks every few seconds, more when he moved it. It had been his before the High Priestess enchanted it, and for some reason she'd seemed reluctant to try, but he'd insisted, and eventually she had done as he asked. Jarek and Jarel had staves, Jarek's sparkling with a faint sheen of frost, despite the warm air, and his brother's red as Trisan's blades. They all stood alert, watching the trees ahead for signs of the approaching Daemons.

Ilsa's task was to keep the horses calm, and to back up the soldiers with her magic wherever possible. The first was easy enough; a simple charm held the animals at peace, and would keep them docile even if the forest were burning around them. Her magic was not yet as strong as it should be, but it was far better than it had been at any time since the Daemons took her. She could be some help, at least.

The first of the Daemon Scouts emerged from the forest directly ahead of them, advancing warily. Its huge, gaping maw dripped saliva as it drew near, and the powerful muscles in its legs rippled with anticipation. Its entire being exuded a frightening hunger, as if it could devour them all and never sate its need. Trisan moved forward from the group calmly, his glowing blades held ready. The Daemon snapped at him, but one of his blades grazed its muzzle, and the huge beast howled in pain, smoke rising from the wound. As if the howl were a signal, three more Daemons sprang from the woods at a run, closing in on the man, but Olsever, Jarek, and Jarel were beside him at once. Olsever's hammer crushed the first Daemon's head with a single blow, and a bolt of jagged lightning lanced from the impact to one of the newcomers, hurling it back into the trees. The remaining two did not last much longer. Jarek's staff connected with the side of a Daemon's head, and the beast's body suddenly froze in place, covered in a thin layer of ice. Another blow shattered the body like glass. Jarel's opponent lunged, to crush the man by sheer weight, but the soldier sidestepped swiftly, bringing his staff up into the creature's side, searing the coarse, black fur and the flesh beneath. The Daemon howled, but before it could move, Jarel slammed his staff into the wound like a spear, driving it through the beast's heart. The stench of roasting flesh filled the air, but it was gone in moments, swept away by a sudden wind. Ilsa had never even had time to think of using her magic.

The forest was silent when the wind died. No birds sang. No insects chirped. Nothing moved. The Rhanestone men watched the trees warily, but there was nothing to see. Slowly, Ilsa became aware of a faint sound, a distant boom, something like thunder, but regular, slowly repeating in the distance, and gradually gaining in strength. The soldiers glanced uneasily to each other, then put away their weapons and ran for the horses. "We're leaving," Trisan said shortly.

"But why? What is it?" asked Ilsa apprehensively.

"A Captain," Olsever rumbled gruffly. "We'll be alright once we get back to the Keep. You and Rillian together could surely drive it off, and we'll have more soldiers to use these enchanted weapons."

"We'll be safe in the Keep," agreed Jarel, smiling reassuringly. "It's only a few more days away."

Days? It would still be *days* before they reached safety, and something these men feared was behind them? "What..." she began, but then had to stop to work moisture back into her mouth. "What is that sound?"

Trisan glanced at her, but remained silent for a moment before answering, his body flowing easily with the movement of the horse beneath him. When he finally spoke, Ilsa's heart nearly stopped. "Footsteps."

***

The Serian of Music had never broken a promise in all of his existence—none of his kind had—and he could not do so now, regardless of the cost to himself. He appeared in the Temple of the Arts, in the room where he had left the Priestesses. It was now empty, save for Avaelar, the High Priestess of the Order. She looked up from the book she'd been reading, and smiled. "You've returned to us," she said warmly in greeting. "One of us has kept watch at all times, but I am honored that it is I who am allowed to greet you."

He felt slightly awkward when she spoke in such ways. The Seriani had never required or desired worship of any kind, and he felt still less worthy of it than the others had been; he had taken more lives than all the rest combined, even if those not belonging to Daemons were not directly by his hand. "I must ask a question of thee, Avaelar. There is no need to disturb the others."

The old Priestess laughed softly, shaking her head. "The others would never give me a moment's peace if I spoke with you myself without even letting them know you're here. I will summon them, and then together we shall try to answer your question."

The Serian sighed inwardly. He had very much hoped to avoid any further contact with the girls, for they would no doubt insist yet again—quite innocently, of course—that he betray his heart. Living would never be easy again.

In minutes, seven girls stared up into his eyes from where they knelt around him, and Avaelar had returned to her place in the chair again. Liliandra was missing. Hoping to stave off any further insistence on their part, Music spoke quickly. "The Book of Dream spoke of Daemon Lords in detail, but not of their ability to render one of my kind vulnerable, unable to touch the Power... trapped in whatever form he or she was occupying at the time of the entrapment." Seven pairs of innocent eyes widened in horror, and seven pairs of hands reached out to touch his shoulders, his arms, his knees, his feet, as if trying to lend him their strength. Avaelar did not react, save to nod. She watched him impassively, taking in everything he said without forming conclusions yet.

"Dream knew that I would be the last," he continued. "How he knew is a mystery even to me, but that he knew is an undeniable fact. I am mentioned specifically in the text."

"And you are to raise us," the youngest-looking of them all said with certainty. Her bright blue eyes gazed up at him earnestly from her pale face, framed by hair so fair as to appear nearly white.

The Serian shook his head slowly. That they would be raised was indeed foretold, but it remained possible, if his suspicions were correct, that he would not be the one to perform the raising. How that could be he did not yet know, but it was possible. "The issue at hand," he said, "is that the Daemons possess a weapon which, if Dream was not mistaken, could destroy even me. I have considered and rejected the possibility that this weapon is a combination of seven Daemon Lords, for it seemed a single entity. That, and I rather doubt that a single Sorceress, however talented, could defeat this weapon as she defeated the Daemon Lords." He was forced to pause here, and relay the events concerning his capture, and his escape at Serana's hands. How she had done that was something of a mystery, but not a great one. She was very powerful in her own right, and likely the vast majority of the Daemons' strength was directed to holding him in their trap. "My question to all of thee is whether or not thou hast possession of other texts, outside the Book of Dream, which mention such a weapon."

The seven young Priestesses had all edged closer to him as he told his tale, worry for him plain on their innocent faces. Avaelar, fortunately, was still thinking clearly. "Many other texts have come into our possession over the years," she said thoughtfully, "but none mention a weapon beyond the Daemons' dark magic itself. I have read them all, some of them several times, and I am certain there is no mention of any such weapon."

"Then I must continue my search," he said quietly. "Fare thee well."

"Wait!" a dark-haired young Priestess cried. "You must raise us first!"

He disappeared quickly, before she could continue. She would one day be raised, impossible as that notion seemed, but he hoped it would not be by him. He appeared a few miles from Green Haven, the closest city in the world to the Barrilian Mountains, outside Rhanestone Keep. It had once been known as Ereanthea, the city of the Earth Enchantresses, but few now remembered that time or that name. Summoning his black horse, he rode into the city. He'd felt close to something during his stay in the nearby town, where he'd met Liliandra, but he was not certain what. Perhaps he would find it in the city itself.

Green Haven was still called the Garden City by many, for plants of all kinds thrived in its soil with very little care, even if they would surely have died elsewhere. The Serian of Music could still see the complex, subtle energies of Earth flowing through the land on which the city stood, the last remnant of what was once a monument to the people of Ereanthea.

As he approached the city gates, his senses detected an unusual amount of unrest, concentrated not far from the gates, and he took steps to shield his own energy. If there were a mystical being of some sort causing the difficulty, it would be best to have the element of surprise at his side. No single being could stand against him, but his encounter with the seven Daemon Lords had left him wary.

He passed through the gates unchallenged; Daemons were not at all difficult to spot, and other races tended to prefer that Green Haven remain neutral. It was, after all, the one city remaining where no traveler seeking food and rest would be turned away.

The commotion he'd sensed centered round a small inn. There was fear in the air, and a residue of something the Serian found quite impossible. A dark-cloaked figure hurried away from the Inn, and he followed, wary but curious. He sensed very little from this figure, yet his instincts told him to learn more. The figure wove through the crowd effortlessly, and disappeared into another inn down the street. Leaving his horse to a stable boy, along with a silver penny, the Serian of Music stepped into the inn, disguising his energy completely, making himself appear no more than a human in a dark cloak.

The cloaked individual had taken a seat in a corner of the inn, alone, and was staring at the table, motionless. Music seated himself across the room, where he could watch easily without appearing to.

24

When the inn's owner came by, he ordered Sorceress' Nectar, a drink the locals insisted was found in the ruins of the Sorceress village twelve years ago. In reality, it was a blend of juices squeezed from fruit that grew only in Green Haven. Long ago, before any other being alive would remember, it had grown in other places as well... but the Serian could not afford such reminiscence now.

He watched as the innkeeper moved to the table where the cloaked figure was seated. The innkeeper seemed very much surprised by what he was hearing, and stared wordlessly for a moment. The figure drew back its hood then, to look up at the man, and the Serian nearly gasped in surprise himself. The face was that of a beautiful young woman with fiery red hair, but that was of no consequence. The hair was wrong, as were the eyes—they flickered between dark brown and dull red—but the face was unmistakable. Understanding and compassion shone from it like light from the sun as she gazed up at the startled innkeeper, repeating her order, but there was something more, a wrongness that the Serian could not grasp, particularly not in conjunction with that face. The man recovered himself with an effort, giving her a hasty bow before all but running to fulfill her request. Music had not heard what was said; the Power used to listen would have revealed him to any with the proper senses—that, and the shock of what he was seeing had rendered him temporarily immobile. He caught himself staring after a few moments, and tore his eyes away from the all-too-familiar face, but quickly saw that it didn't matter, and returned them. All other eyes in the inn were turned toward her too, though she seemed to be doing her best to ignore them; the slight flush of her cheeks as she stared down at her table was the only indication that she was aware of the attention. She had to be the one he sought, for even now he sensed the wellsprings of power within her, concealed somehow, but not entirely, not from him. She had to be the one, and yet... He would make no move yet; he could not have trusted himself even if he'd known what to do. For now, he would wait, and watch.

Keeping his senses alert, in case she moved, he tore his eyes away again, keeping them on the table in front of him. He had to think. Surely she must be the one he sought, yet he did not believe he could make himself destroy her. Perhaps she could be kept from Serana, to grant the Sorceress some safety... He was rationalizing, and he knew it. His mission was to destroy her, for if he did not, she would surely destroy Serana, and hope would be lost, if it were not already... He could not bring himself to transform the Sorceress, even upon her request, and her transformation was key to all, as the Book of Dream stated. It also stated, however, that he would not be made to betray his heart, and that, at least, gave him hope, a tiny spark of hope in a universe of darkness. He'd been so certain that he could destroy even a creature of the Power, for the greater good, if only he could find her, yet now, when he sat in sight of her, he could not act. Fate, it seemed, was crueler even than the Daemons, to put that face on the one whom he must kill.

"Please don't cry," a voice said from beside him. Dimly, he realized that his cheeks were moist with tears, but the sound of that voice drove every other thought from his mind. If all the innocence of the first moments of Creation could blend seamlessly with all the hatred of the Daemons, the result would be the voice that now echoed in his ears. He was shocked to the core that such a voice could even exist, particularly without his knowledge, but more so that its owner could have crossed the distance between them without his sensing it, even overwhelmed as he had been by emotion. He looked into her face again, only barely keeping his features smooth, but he could not summon voice to reply. "I am Lady Firehair," she said softly, her piercing eyes filled, almost in contradiction to their sharpness, with concern.

"I am the Lord of Eridan," he managed, surprised that his voice remained steady.

"May I join you?" she asked. She took a seat across from him when he nodded, placing her cup—filled with the same juice he had ordered—on the table in front of her. "Why were you crying, sir?"

There was really no reason to lie. "My tears are shed in mourning for one who has passed long ago."

"I am sorry," she said gently, compassion filling her beautiful face once more. "If I could bring her back for you, I would."

"Thou art far too kind," he whispered.

"Nay, dear sir." She shook her head slightly. "Methinks perhaps thou dost mourn without cause."

Had he a physical heart, it would have stopped. Only when she slipped into it herself had he realized that he'd reverted back to his usual speech patterns. "Without... cause?" he managed, pressing his hands to the table to stop their trembling.

"If her passing was long ago," she continued, appearing not to notice his shock, "then perhaps she would prefer that her life be celebrated, rather than her death mourned."

"It is... not so easy as that," he said softly, recovering himself in the sorrow of his loss; it had defined him for two centuries.

"Please stop," she whispered, and he looked up sharply. Her eyes were fixed on his, concern for him radiating from her, overpowering even the vague wrongness he had sensed before. "Thou art mourning again already, wrapping thyself in pain. No creature of such beauty should cling so tenaciously to grief."

He stared at her, unable to speak. Those had been Shape's words, after Dream had passed, when the loss of one of his kind had nearly undone him. It would have undone him, if not for her, since he had not yet sworn his oath. What had happened after...

"Let me help thee," she said softly, reaching across the table to him. When her hand touched his, a shock went through his entire being, as lighting speeding through him, not harming, but awakening him. She felt it as well, it seemed, for she withdrew her hand immediately, staring at him as if she'd never seen him before. "Thou art..." she breathed, gazing at him as if she'd never seen him before that moment. In moments, however, she seemed suddenly frightened. "I must go," she said quickly, rising and walking out the door without pause. He followed, but when he reached the door, she was gone, leaving no trail even to his senses.

***

Lady Firehair hurried home. Her uncle had summoned her, and she dared not be away when his servants came to fetch her. She was not supposed to be out in the world, among other beings, but she could not help herself. Her family's company was never pleasant, though she felt guilty for saying it even within her own mind. She needed to escape from her home sometimes, to be among other people, to see them laugh and love, to feel the joy in their hearts when life was kind to them. She needed to feel the wind in her face, the sun on her skin, sometimes the feel of cool water flowing through her fingers as she dipped her hand in a stream. Most of all, more than anything else, she needed the music, and the one who made it.

She'd never spoken with him before. Oh, she'd whispered words to him when he was nowhere near, and she'd watched him from a distance when he was, but she'd never had a conversation with him, basked in the radiance of his presence. She knew him on sight, and even if her senses had told her today that he was merely human, she knew that he was much more. The brief touch of his hand confirmed that, if she'd needed any confirmation. She couldn't trust her senses with him, in any case; emotion often overwhelmed them where he was concerned. How she'd wanted to hold him when he'd cried, to banish his tears and bring a smile to his face once more! It was not to be, of course. She was a disgrace to her family, and unworthy to be wed to anyone, least of all him. Perhaps, though, now that she'd spoken with him, she could ask him for help. Her uncle had given her a task to help redeem her, though nothing could redeem her fully. It was a very difficult task, something she had no idea how to accomplish. Perhaps she could ask the strange creator of music for help… if only she could find something to offer him in return.

She reached her room quickly, well before her uncle's servants arrived to fetch her. She always arrived before them; she traveled quickly, and they were incompetent fools, often taking time for their own amusements before retrieving her. None of them liked to look at her, and she'd spent the first fourteen years of her life believing that she was ugly beyond measure. Given the alternative, she might almost have preferred the ugliness, for she'd been disillusioned by a band of soldiers who found her attractive, and wished to use her for their perverse pleasures… whatever they were. She only knew they were perverse pleasures because the old woman she'd found a few days later had told her so. She'd killed one of them by accident, a reflex to the fear that had come with being yanked to him by the arm. The others had fled her, and she'd been unable to bring back the one she'd killed. She'd tried for nearly an hour before giving it up as impossible, she'd made it a rule to avoid being seen by people of all races, to hide among them unnoticed instead. Only recently had she broken that rule, and it had resulted in two more deaths. When she'd finally given up trying to bring the man back, she went to the stream nearby to wash the blackened blood from her hands and the tears from her eyes. The stream ran into a little pool where she enjoyed swimming, and it had been calm that day. When she'd looked down into the water, she saw her reflection for the first time in years—she'd avoided it since childhood, not wanting to look on her ugliness. She had transformed! She was no longer a child with wisps of tangled red hair sticking out in all directions from her dirty face. She saw a beautiful girl, approaching womanhood, staring up out of the lake at her.

Since that day, she'd gone back to the pool many times, marveling at how she changed, slowly but surely, into the woman she now saw. It had been years now since her appearance had altered any further, but she still went back from time to time, wondering what had happened to make her beautiful, where before she had been ugly. Whatever it was, her uncle's servants never noticed. They'd stopped looking at her when she was a child, and seemed not to notice how she'd grown. She was glad that they hadn't noticed; her uncle's servants liked to hurt women who were beautiful, hurt them in some way that Lady Firehair didn't know, and didn't want to know. Perhaps it had something to do with the same perverse pleasures the soldiers had wanted to use her for, all those years ago, but she could not be sure.

"Your uncle wishes to see you," rasped one of the servants at her door, not opening it. They all had horrible, ugly voices, not like the man who made the music. His voice was beautiful and enchanting. Her uncle's voice was not like those of his servants either; his was deep, powerful, commanding… but not beautiful. She never told him any of these things, of course, for he would want to know what she'd compared the voices to, and she couldn't let him know she'd been away again. Her punishment for the first time was enough that she would never let him know again.

"I will go to him," she answered through the door. She waited until the servants left before moving quickly through the dark, smoky halls to her uncle's chambers. When she reached them, she knocked once on the door, and called inside, "I am here, my Lord." He always required that everyone called him "my Lord," and since she was his niece, she received the title of Lady. In truth, Lady Firehair did not know exactly what her uncle was Lord of; she only knew that when he required something, it was best to see that he received it.

"Come in," his deep voice commanded. Steeling herself for another unpleasant visit, she opened the door and went inside.

Chapter V

The boots were located in what Allaerion claimed was once an Air village, located on a mountain top that had been flattened by friendly Earth Enchantresses long before he was born. The village hadn't been heard from since his childhood, so Allaerion was fairly certain that it had been long-abandoned. Though technically two separate items, the boots apparently counted as one piece to the Armor of the Elements, according to Alier. Serana didn't really understand why the elementals had divided the magic that way, particularly when the gauntlets and arm pieces were separate, but she hoped to learn when the entire suit was assembled.

Serana was finally beginning to master Alier's strange way of traveling; she could remain earth-melded nearly as long as the Earth Enchantress now, though she couldn't yet travel quite so quickly that way. Alier claimed that her progress was nothing short of miraculous, particularly for a Sorceress, but Serana knew her own flows of Earth magic were slow and cumbersome compared with the Weaver's. She'd considered the possibility that her pregnancy might be effecting her performance, but Alier claimed it was still too early for that to happen, and even after she started showing, the changes would be subtle, nothing to hinder her magic significantly.

She didn't always travel earth-melded, of course. She practiced Allaerion's wind walking, as he called it, nearly as often. Seleine still hadn't taught anything of her own methods of travel yet, instead focusing their lessons on combat and self defense. Serana could now throw a jagged bolt of ice up to sixty paces, further if she used Air magic to speed it along, and she could freeze a Daemon Scout's blood with little more effort that it took to throw the Arrow of Light.

When the flat-topped mountain came into view, sunset was fast approaching, and the four of them decided to make camp for the night. Allaerion continued his lessons in swordplay, as he did every evening. Serana was becoming nearly as proficient as he, particularly since she had begun using Air to speed her movements. She'd actually disarmed him once, two nights before, but it remained her only victory over him.

Surprisingly—or perhaps not, considering their age difference—Alier's skill with a staff easily surpassed even Allaerion's with a blade. The Weaver of Earth was more graceful in her deadly dance than anyone Serana had ever seen, and her mastery of her element was literally legend. She was a difficult teacher, but Serana learned quickly. There was a rhythm to the energies of the earth beneath her feet, something Alier called the heartbeat of life, and the secret to an Earth Enchantress' fighting skill was learning to dance with it. There had been a few in the Sorceress village who had learned the technique, and they were easily the greatest hand-to-hand fighters in the area, with or without their weapons. Even the fabled Elven Priests, who practiced a limited form of Earth magic, but who excelled in unarmed combat, had not surpassed them. Serana was only beginning to hear the heartbeat of life, or at least she thought she was, but Alier promised that in time, it would sing to her.

The Earth Enchantress, one of the oldest beings alive, possessed a wealth of knowledge even outside her mastery in the arts of magic and hand-to-hand fighting. Serana spoke with her whenever she could, drinking in the stories she told, learning the histories of various peoples in the world, some of whom no longer existed. Alier was born more than a thousand years ago, in a world of peace and prosperity, where the nine Seriani governed all with wisdom, understanding and compassion. She'd been a child when the first of them had died, and she'd watched the world they'd built and loved crumble into ruin as they disappeared from it, until only Music and Shape remained. They did not give in to despair, the only thing that could kill one of their kind, because their love for each other sustained them. When Shape died, two hundred years ago, Music was broken. He wasn't seen in the world for nearly fifty years after that, and even after he reappeared, he had been reclusive. Alier did not know why he survived, for surely the losses he'd suffered should have destroyed him utterly, but she said the world was fortunate indeed that he did.

"He never took another mate," the Earth Enchantress said wistfully, her eyes filled suddenly with sharp longing. "He exists now in sadness and solitude, at once the most beautiful and the most miserable creature alive."

"You're in love with him," Serana whispered.

For a moment, she thought she'd made a mistake, speaking so rashly, but Alier merely remained silent, gazing off into the night. When she finally spoke, Serana felt as if an echo of the Serian's solitude whispered through the words. "Many women have fallen in love with him, over the years. I have merely been alive to love him longer." With that, she rose, and withdrew into her tent to sleep. Serana knew better than to follow.

Before they set out the next morning, Alier announced that she had a confession to make. "The village is not abandoned," she said quietly.

"You've scouted ahead in the night?" asked Allaerion. "That is dangerous, even for you."

Alier snorted. "I could escape a Daemon Lord, if I were well-rested, but that isn't the point. I never left camp last night. I know the village isn't abandoned because I've lived there for the past few centuries, since not long after I disappeared and everyone presumed me dead. I must admit that I didn't expect to venture there again, least of all so soon. How could a piece of the Armor have been hidden there without my knowledge?"

Allaerion appeared too stunned to speak, though Serana couldn't fathom why, so Seleine answered for him. "Probably because it was hidden there by a Sorceress High Priestess who didn't want it found."

"Leliah," Alier breathed. "That one could have done it. If she did hide it, I would have been hard-pressed to find it even if I were looking." She glanced at Serana with a small, speculative smile. "You, on the other hand, might find it little more than a mild challenge."

"What could I do?" asked Serana, bursting with curiosity for anything having to do with her grandmother.

"Leliah loved using her own blood signature to disguise her work, so that only she would be able to see it once it was done. As her granddaughter, you could act her part. The spell wouldn't be able to tell the difference.

"If the village is not abandoned," said Allaerion slowly, "why have they not been heard from in so long?"

Alier smiled sadly. "Because they have forgotten their heritage. Not long before I left, the most competent of them was no more powerful than you, who have never really studied."

Serana was a little confused by the sheer horror that crossed the other two elementals' faces, but she said nothing. She'd been around her companions long enough to know that there were a few issues on which they could be extremely touchy, and that when it came to those issues, it was best simply to observe.

"Don't worry about it," Alier said with a grim smile. "I'd imagine there have been a good many changes since I left. The Serian of Music paid that village a brief visit to enlist my help, and he put a few other things to rights while he was there."

The four of them continued on to the mountain in silence, each lost in his or her own thoughts. The climb to the top would have been difficult for Serana if not for Alier's lessons in earth-melding, but Allaerion and Seleine managed easily enough. Though neither was a match for Serana in raw power, they both were far more experienced in their respective elements than she. Serana still wanted to know how Seleine traveled; she was going to experiment on her own soon, if the Ice Witch wouldn't show her.

When they reached the flattened mountaintop, they stopped, staring. There was a new building under construction, the groundwork sparkling in the late morning sun. "It looks like crystal," Serana breathed.

"Use your other senses, not just your eyes," Seleine chided. "It's not crystal; it's ice."

Serana flushed with embarrassment, and shifted her senses, watching the patterns of energy dance and weave around the structure. "It's being built with magic," she said at once.

"Most of it was done with Air," agreed Allaerion, "though they definitely have some Ice Witches working for them as well. Alier, I thought you said they were incompetent."

"I also said that there have probably been a good many changes since I left," she said softly, staring as much as any of them.

"There have been," said a new voice from behind them. "I didn't expect to see you again so soon, Alier, but I couldn't be more pleased."

"Aeron!" cried the Earth Enchantress, rushing to embrace the newcomer warmly. Serana nearly gasped when her eyes fell on the young Air Wizard. His strength in his element nearly matched Alier's in hers.

"A Sorceress!" he exclaimed in delight, extending his hand to her in greeting. "If I'm not mistaken, the High Priestess herself. Please, be welcome in our village, and take my warmest wishes to your people when you return."

Serana blinked in confusion, but before she could respond, Alier cut in. "Aeron, you learned volumes from that library, but some of those books are years out of date. The Sorceress village was destroyed sixteen years ago. Serana is the sole survivor."

"My humblest apologies, High Priestess," the Air Wizard said shakily, taking her hand and squeezing gently. "I had no idea."

Uncertain what else to do, Serana nodded and squeezed his hand in return. It seemed to be enough, for he immediately turned to welcome Seleine and Allaerion, inviting them all to come closer, and see the construction of the new School of Magic, of which he would be the Headmaster.

It was still more wondrous up close. Serana's senses drank in the flows of energy, her mind filing away the patterns to be studied and used later. The ice was strengthened by both Water and Air magic, and would remain solid and hard even in summer, if summer ever came at this altitude. There were young Air Wizards all over the structure, and a few Ice Witches here and there, weaving the energies almost in unison. It took Serana a moment to realize that they couldn't see each other's flows, and she asked Aeron how it was possible for them to work in unison that way.

"Look again," he said with a small smile, unable to keep the pride from his voice.

She did so, and suddenly realized that they'd employed a technique very similar to what she'd used with her friends to free the dragons. There was a very faint mesh of energy, both Air and Water, encompassing the entire construction site, and each worker was linked to it. Serana suspected that she herself would be linked as well, if she were merely to step within range of the spell. "Very impressive," she complimented him. "Your idea, I'd imagine." None of the others even approached his strength, though the weakest wasn't terribly far behind Allaerion's—Allaerion could have been far stronger, had he actually studied magic. Watching the way they wielded the flows, however, she imagined few of them possessed the Warrior's skill, whatever their strength.

"They're learning quickly," said Aeron, smiling proudly, "but it will take time before they reach their potential. The building of this school is wonderful practice for them."

"Could I help for awhile?" Seleine asked suddenly.

Aeron smiled in understanding and gestured toward the building, inviting her to do as much as she pleased.

"I believe I will as well," said Allaerion unexpectedly, an oddly distant look in his eyes. He followed the Ice Witch down to the site, where they added their own skills to the work. Serana noted that the mesh took them in just as she'd suspected when they crossed its boundaries.

"It has been a long time since either of them have seen others of their own kind," Alier explained, noting the mild confusion on Serana's face. "There is something in each of us which longs to work the magic with our kindred."

"I can understand that," Serana said quietly, "but aren't we in a bit of a hurry?"

The old Earth Enchantress shrugged. "A day or two here will not make much difference one way or the other. Besides, the Serian of Music will not allow Rhanestone to fall before we reach it."

"In that case," Serana said tentatively, "could I help as well?"

Aeron bowed deeply. "You do us too much honor, High Priestess."

Working on the School of Magic was the most fun Serana had had in ages. The flows of magic were alive to her, and within the mesh, she was connected to every other worker, could feel what they were doing. The plans for the building were embedded in the mesh somehow—a brilliant idea, in Serana's opinion—so everyone knew exactly what needed done; they had only to pick a place and start working. Serana chose a spiral staircase that needed to climb up the center of the school to the highest tower, where students would practice weather control. She gathered snow from the nearly endless supply on the side of the mountain, and shaped the water with Air, freezing and strengthening it using both elements together. There were no specifics in the design about the style of the staircase, other than a vague idea that the railing should be some sort of intricate lace, so Serana chose vines and flowers to be carved in the ice, a climbing path of frozen greenery. A young Ice Witch approached her soon after she'd begun, looking nervous but curious.

"Pardon, High Priestess," she said with a small curtsey. "My name is Illiese, and I am a little confused. May I ask a question about your magic?"

Wondering if she'd done something wrong, Serana nodded, pausing her work to listen.

"I've been studying about Sorceresses in the library, and I learned that they often have a branch of elemental magic in which they're strongest. When I saw the water molding itself for you, from a distance, I thought you were using Air quite proficiently, but when I drew nearer, I saw you hardening and strengthening with Water magic, and I can feel your power. Your gift is obviously Water, but I couldn't seem to find the Air Wizard who was helping you earlier. None of them were close enough, you see... Only Aeron is strong enough to have shaped the water for you from a distance, and he hasn't worked on the school in days, so that the rest of us can practice." Illiese blushed and lowered her eyes when she was finished, as if embarrassed about having spoken so much to a High Priestess. Serana would never quite get used to that.

"I didn't have an Air Wizard helping me," she explained gently. "For reasons unknown to me, I seem to be equally gifted in all four elements. I have passed a Rite of Oneness in Water, Fire, and Earth."

The young Ice Witch's eyes widened at the idea of a Sorceress using all four elements. "You should speak with Aeron." She blushed again but continued determinedly. "He could stand for you in the Rite for Air. You could be the first magic-user ever to complete all four

Rites!" She lowered her eyes again. "Could I perhaps ask a favor of you?"

Serana smiled. "Of course. What is it?"

"I have studied very hard for most of my life, though only openly since Aeron came into power..." She trailed off, fidgeting with her hands.

"Go on," Serana said encouragingly.

"I've never taken the Rite of Oneness," Illiese said breathlessly. "Would you consider... standing for me?"

Serana blinked in surprise. "I..." She had never considered the possibility of standing for an Ice Witch, or any other elemental, for that matter. *Could* she?

"I understand if you won't." Illiese lowered her eyes sadly. "I'm sorry for bothering you."

"It isn't that," Serana said quickly. "I just don't know whether or not I'm qualified."

Illiese stared at her for a moment as if she were mad, but a new voice cut in before she could speak.

"You're as qualified as I am," Seleine laughed, coming to stand beside them. "And this girl is definitely ready for her Rite." Noticing Serana's look of confusion, she went on. "Serana, all that is required to stand for someone in a Rite of Oneness is successful completion of your own Rite in the same element. Since you passed—with flying colors, I might add—then you're ready."

"In that case," Serana said, somehow unable to stop smiling now, "I would be honored to stand for you, Illiese."

The young Ice Witch beamed with delight. "Oh thank you, High Priestess! Thank you so much!"

Serana laughed, a little taken aback. "Please, call me Serana. We'll perform the Rite tomorrow morning."

Illiese hugged Serana impulsively, then murmured something about telling Aeron, and ran off.

"I think you have a fan," Seleine told her with a grin. "It only takes a sight of you working elemental magic to impress any number of elementals, you know."

"What do you mean?" Serana asked uncertainly, and her friend laughed.

"What I mean is that you are more skilled in each of the four elements than many elementals are in their own. Just trust me when I say that's very rare indeed, so rare as to be unique, even."

Now it was Serana's turn to blush. It seemed to be a day for blushing. When Seleine left, she went back to her work, now uncomfortably aware that many of the elementals around her were staring.

Chapter VI

"You can't be serious!" exclaimed Aeron, but it was clear his old friend was entirely serious. "All *four* elements?"

"All four," affirmed Alier. "I do not know exactly how it was done, but I gather that the Serian of Music had a hand in it."

"Where that one is involved, I'll believe nearly anything," admitted Aeron, remembering his own brief encounter with the dark-cloaked being. "So what is it you want me to do?"

"Stand for her in a Rite of Oneness," the Earth Enchantress replied.

"She is certainly strong enough in Air."

"She has already completed the Rites in the other three elements. I stood for her myself in Earth, and I was harder on her than on any Earth Enchantress I've ever stood for."

"Be careful with that," Aeron warned. "You could kill her if you're not gentle during a Rite." He'd read extensively about Rites of Oneness during his time in the library, and like everything else he'd read in those three weeks, the knowledge was ingrained in his mind, as if he'd earned it through long experience.

Alier actually laughed as if he'd made a joke. "Kill *her*?" she cackled. "She nearly killed *me*!"

"That is impossible," Aeron said flatly. During a Rite of Oneness, the student is entirely under the will of the teacher, the one standing. The student will experience anything and everything the teacher wishes, having no power to escape the reality imposed by the teacher's will. More importantly, any magic the student wields during a Rite can only effect the fabricated world, not the real one. It is for that reason that a teacher must always take care to protect the safety of a student during the Rite, for the student's safety is literally in the teacher's hands entirely.

"It is impossible for an elemental," Alier corrected him. "The Sorceress race possesses a magic elementals cannot wield, a magic that manipulates the energies of life itself. Serana was about to fall into a pit of lava and die, in her Rite, but she called the power of her heritage to save her."

"I don't follow." Aeron was becoming more confused by the moment. How could life energy save anyone from boiling lava, even in a Rite?

"Life energy is far more potent than elemental energy, Aeron. Serana took the molten rock, the poisonous fumes, even the air around her, and converted it all to pure life energy. Since she was in the world of a Rite of Oneness, that energy all came from her teacher, me.

Aeron was stunned. "She actually *drained* you?"

"Almost completely," Alier nodded gravely. "Had she drawn any more, even my body would have faded away and disappeared."

"How is it that you're still alive, then?"

The Earth Enchantress shrugged. "She put most of the energy back. She hasn't learned to control the power yet, not really, but her potential is frightening even to me. Don't be easy on her when you stand for her Rite. Don't be gentle with her." Alier paused a moment, as if considering. "However," she said finally, "if you don't want to risk your life, don't force her to drain you."

"Aeron!" cried Illiese, bursting into the room. When she saw Alier, she lowered her eyes apologetically and offered to wait outside.

"No, please go on," Aeron told her. He didn't think Alier would mind, and besides, the Ice Witch seemed extremely excited; he wanted to know what had happened.

"I'm going to take my Rite of Oneness tomorrow morning!" she said breathlessly.

It was very good news. Illiese had been ready to take her Rite for some time, but there was not a sufficiently competent Ice Witch in the village to stand for her. Aeron had technically never taken one himself, but the knowledge the Serian had provided him made it unnecessary. "That's wonderful, Illiese. The Ice Witch who came into town with Alier, Seleine… Is she to stand for you?"

"No, the Sorceress High Priestess!" Illiese nearly squealed with delight.

Alier blinked in surprise, but her expression turned thoughtful an instant later. "She could do it," the Earth Enchantress said slowly. "In fact, she could probably do it at least as well as Seleine could. I would like to speak with her before you begin, though."

This was almost too much for Aeron to handle. "Is she a Sorceress or a Serian?" he asked faintly.

"She has a long way to go before she reaches *that* kind of power," Alier assured him. "Still, I don't believe there has ever been a Sorceress with more potential."

The following morning found Aeron, Alier, Illiese, and the Sorceress High Priestess standing in the village center. The Earth Enchantress drew the Sorceress away briefly, speaking quietly enough that Aeron could not hear without magic, and he didn't care to eavesdrop. When they were finished, the Sorceress moved over to where Illiese stood, a little apart from the others.

"Are you ready," she asked, and the young Ice Witch nodded.

"Then we begin." Both women closed their eyes, and Aeron knew the magic had begun, though he couldn't sense it. It was more than a little disconcerting to know that Water magic was being wielded with that much proficiency by an individual who radiated strength in Air.

"You'll be standing for her this evening," Alier said quietly from beside him.

"That's insane!" Aeron whispered harshly. "You know as well as I do that a Rite drains the teacher as much as the student."

The Earth Enchantress smiled faintly. "Don't forget that she had drained each of us, though the others to a lesser extent than myself. She held so much energy at the end of each Rite that she had difficulty sleeping, and was ready for another Rite the very next day."

"Even so," Aeron persisted, "She should not be draining Illiese while standing for her. The task should tire her at least as much as it does Illiese."

"It should," Alier agreed, "but it won't. She has reserves of energy that surpass even my own. Don't forget that she wields five different types of magic, and all proficiently." The Earth Enchantress' lips curved into a small, mischievous smile. "Would you like to place a wager on it?"

"What kind of wager?" Aeron asked warily.

"If she is remotely near as tired as Illiese when it is done, I will do you a favor of your choice. If she isn't, you must do me a favor of my choice, in addition to standing for her in the Rite this evening."

"You have a deal," he said with a smile of his own. No one could stand for a Rite without being drained significantly. "And if she is up to it, I will stand for her this evening." He suddenly realized that he'd missed Alier more than he had thought.

"Thank you, Aeron." Alier placed a hand on his shoulder, and he smiled, enjoying the contact. Though she wielded a completely different element from his own, she was more his mentor than anyone else had ever been. He craved her approval even after advancing as far as he had, and he would do much just to see her smile. Awkwardly, he placed an arm around her as they watched, and she didn't pull away. It was good to have her back, even if only for a little while.

***

Illiese stood in a snowy forest, looking around anxiously. The three Daemon Scouts that had already attacked her lay dead some distance behind her, frozen by her magic. Something else was stalking her now, though, something much bigger, much more terrifying. She could hear its footsteps rumbling like thunder, always closer, no matter how fast she ran. She knew that she would have to face it eventually, but the prospect filled her with fear.

Suddenly it burst from the trees ahead of her. How had it circled around her? Its horrible red eyes were fixed on her as it advanced on legs like huge tree trunks, the joints backward. Its skin resembled the bark of a tree, but it was black. The terrible claws at the ends of its long arms flexed in anticipation as it advanced, hunger written in its very presence. It wanted her.

Illiese screamed and backed away, but she knew there was no escape. Summoning the energy around her, she froze its giant legs in place, but the Daemon—it had to be a Daemon—paused only a moment before ripping free. Desperately, she called up the snow around her, forming hundreds of razor-sharp shards of ice and hurling them at the creature. The shards sliced through the bark-like skin, and the creature howled in pain, a sound that chilled the Ice Witch's blood. In moments, though, it was coming again, faster than before. Concentrating, she melted the snow beneath it, and froze it again, creating a thick layer of slippery ice. The Daemon lurched and went down, but it was up again in moments, lumbering toward her, crawling on all fours. Its claws bit deep into the ice, providing the grip it needed. While it was slowed, Illiese ran.

The thing had to be a Captain, one of the huge Daemons Aeron had told her about from his readings. She hadn't wanted to believe that such things could exist, but he'd insisted that they did. He was right.

Frightened as she was, Illiese wasn't running blindly. She knew what she sought now, though she didn't know if it would be enough. The steady boom of thunder from behind told her that the creature was moving again. It would catch up to her soon, and she had to be ready.

She soon found what she'd been looking for, a large lake she'd seen before the Scouts attacked her. Hardening the already-frozen surface, she ran to the lake's center, and a little past, her footing sure on her element. She ran until she reached the center of the lake, then stopped and turned just in time to see the Captain burst from the trees. When it saw her, it screamed in rage, a sound that reminded Illiese of nothing so much as hundreds of souls crying out in agony. Focusing to keep her thoughts clear, she waited. Soon, the Daemon stepped onto the ice, moving slowly but purposefully, its red eyes glowing dully with ravening hunger. When it was halfway to her, she struck.

The ice beneath the Daemon suddenly broke, and the creature went down into the freezing depths, but Illiese didn't stop. She froze the water above it, hardening and strengthening the surface of the lake, trapping it inside. When she was finished, she let out the breath she'd been holding in a sigh of relief. She'd won.

Before she could take her first step toward the lake's edge, the ice beneath her cracked as if from a terrible blow. A moment later, it shook and cracked again. Illiese ran, but the shaking ice beneath her sent her tumbling down face-first. She looked back, and a huge claw broke through the ice where she had been standing. Illiese wanted to panic, but Aeron had told her in one of the lessons at the school that calm was the key. What school? It didn't matter; she had to be calm. At once, the answer came to her.

Illiese closed her eyes, focusing on the flows of energy in the lake. She could *feel* the Daemon, the black intruder in the water's depths. A quick search revealed the creature's wounds from her shards. She directed the water into those wounds, forming jagged knives of ice that ripped them open further. Pouring her entire being into the task, Illiese drew the knives toward each other, then away sharply, tearing the massive body apart. She froze the water around it then, a giant sphere of ice beneath the surface, and held it solid for several minutes. She listened with her senses for the Daemon's heartbeat, and only when it had stopped entirely did she relax, drained. She had never been so exhausted in her life, and she fell back onto the thick ice beneath her, the world spinning into darkness.

***

Serana opened her eyes. Illiese was lying on the ground, in a deep sleep, and Aeron and Alier were still standing, watching.

"It's over, then," said Aeron, watching her carefully. "How did she do?"

"Very well," Serana told him with a smile. "She killed a Daemon Captain, and that's not an easy task. Believe me; I know."

Aeron looked to Alier uncertainly, but the Earth Enchantress' expression was unreadable. "Well, we need to put Illiese to bed, then. You might want to rest as well, High Priestess."

Serana rose from where she sat—she didn't remember sitting down—and found that she was indeed tired, but she could feel her strength returning slowly. Calling Air magic, she lifted Illiese gently and turned to Aeron. "Where shall I put her?"

The Air Wizard's eyes were wide with surprise, and Alier was laughing softly behind him. "What is it?" asked Serana, confused.

"N…nothing," Aeron managed. He seemed to visibly take control of himself. "It appears that I've just lost a wager."

Serana brought Illiese to her own home, following Aeron and Alier. The two were conferring quietly ahead of her, too quietly for her to hear. Serana felt a little put-off that they didn't include her, but she imagined they had things of their own to speak of, considering how long they'd known each other. By the time they arrived at Illiese's house, Serana was feeling almost completely recovered. She wished it didn't take so long for her energy to replenish itself, but there was no help for it.

"Will you be up to facing your own Rite this evening?" asked Aeron once they'd seen the young Ice Witch safely to her bed. It was the first he'd spoken to her since just after she'd finished standing for Illiese, and Serana was a little surprised by the question. A quick glance to Alier explained his foreknowledge, though; the Earth Enchantress would want her to complete her last Rite as well.

"Certainly," Serana answered him with a smile. "I would be honored if you would stand for me, Headmaster." Alier had undoubtedly already asked him, but Serana thought it best to be polite, and ask for herself.

Aeron surprised her again by bowing deeply. "The honor, High Priestess," he said gravely, "would be entirely mine."

Serana spent the day working on the construction site, despite Alier's advice that she get some rest. Working with elemental magic was refreshing; so long as she didn't try to do too much at once, she doubted she could tire from it any more than from walking. Her spiral staircase was finished, up to the highest point of the school already built. She didn't want to make it climb any higher until the rest of the building caught up a little, since a lone staircase climbing into the air would look rather awkward. Instead, she worked on the great hall, where the students would gather for large assemblies. It was a tremendous room—or would be when it was finished—with rows of sculpted ice seats lined with feather cushions. None of the ice would ever melt, of course—well, not unless an angry Fire Warlock stormed through the school, at least—so she could afford to be as creative as she wished on their design. She created comfortable arms and backs, and designed elevated levels, so that students could easily see the front of the hall, where the Headmaster would be standing to deliver any announcements he had. The seats themselves were slow work, of course, since there were so many, but Serana took her time, carving intricate, fanciful creatures into the arms and legs of the chairs, and making the backs seem filled with ocean waves, like the ones she'd seen in the pictures in books from the Vault at Rhanestone. Serana dreamed of seeing an ocean one day; so much water in one place would be truly fascinating.

"High Priestess, w... what are you doing?" asked a young Air Wizard she'd not seen before. Serana checked the mesh again, to be sure her work was in accordance with the design, and it was.

"I'm making the seats for the great hall," she told him uncertainly. She'd completed about twenty, just a tiny fraction of the three hundred in the plans. The School of Magic was being designed with growth in mind.

"Forgive me, High Priestess," he said shakily, fidgeting with his hands and not meeting her eyes, "but the seats... well, they're supposed to be uniform."

Serana ran a critical eye over her work, confused. "But they *are* uniform," she said quizzically. There was not a single difference in any of them; even the ocean waves were identical from one seat to the next.

The young Air Wizard seemed even more nervous now. "Well, it isn't that, High Priestess," he stammered. "It's just... well... I've talked with a few of the Ice Witches... and most of the Air Wizards too, and... well... ah..."

"What is it?" Serana demanded, more than a little concerned that she'd made some error she was unaware of.

"None of us could duplicate those chairs!" he finished in a rush. He flushed with embarrassment and lowered his eyes.

Serana stared. She'd never even considered that possibility. "Well," she said slowly, "I could teach you."

The Air Wizard's eyes shot up to hers, and he blinked, then hastily lowered them again. "You would... teach us?" he asked, his voice filled with such awe that Serana had to laugh.

"Of course!" she managed between giggles. "Bring a few of your friends, some Ice Witches and Air Wizards both, and I'll show you how to make the chairs. You'll have to work together, taking turns."

"Together..." he said softly, as if it were a word only recently learned, but before she could respond, he'd run off with shouts of "The High Priestess is going to teach!" Serana was completely taken aback.

Within minutes, what must have been the majority of the workers on the site were gathered around her, watching curiously. She'd not expected nearly so many, but there was nothing to do now but go on. "First, the Ice Witches need to gather the water, and form it into the general shape of the chair," she said, using Air to make her voice heard throughout the crowd. Many of the Air Wizards watched the flows curiously, and she explained them briefly, for their benefit, before demonstrating the gathering of the water for the Ice Witches.

"Next," she went on, "the Air Wizards need to carve the creatures on the arms and legs." She demonstrated, but most of the spectators seemed hopelessly confused. She tried another chair, going much more slowly, and they seemed to catch on, at least a little, as she finished the chair, alternating between the elements. Next, she broke them up into groups, one Ice Witch in each—there were far fewer Ice Witches than Air Wizards—and set them to practicing.

Serana walked among the groups, making suggestions and corrections as they worked. She was surprised by how quickly they caught on, but then, they *were* elementals, after all, however poorly they'd been trained in the past. By the end of the day, nearly two thirds of the chairs in the great hall were finished, and Serana was confident the others would be done without her.

"Impressive," Aeron said softly, appearing at her side. "I couldn't have taught them so quickly myself. Still, you should not have exerted yourself so, if you are to participate in your own Rite this evening. Would you prefer to wait until morning?"

Serana eyed him quizzically. "Whatever for?" she asked, genuinely confused. "I hardly spent any energy at all here; the students did most of the work."

Aeron blinked, but didn't answer her. "This way, then," was all he said as he turned away, heading for the center of the village. Allaerion, Seleine, and Alier were already there, waiting for her. They had all come to support her; it made her smile. "Are you ready?" Aeron asked, and she nodded. "Then we begin."

Chapter VII

Serana stood on a mountaintop, between two rocks roughly twice her height. The chill wind whipped her gown back and forth around her legs, making her shiver almost instantly. There was little point in not being comfortable, at least, so Serana cast a quick spell of Fire, using Air to hold it in place, to warm herself. She buffered herself against the wind, so that her dress hung properly. Once she was satisfied with her work, she took a look around. There appeared to be a path behind her leading back through the mountain, but a massive boulder blocked the way. The thick snow on the wind made it difficult to see very far, but she thought there was a black shape in the distance, just beyond her vision. Whatever it was, it was large, and it was growing closer. Instinctively, Serana crouched lower between the rocks, intent on having whatever cover she could.

The shape suddenly burst through curtain of snow, and Serana stared in wonder. It was a great blue dragon, not so large as Blackfang, but sleeker, probably faster in flight. She knew the dragon wasn't real, that it was only part of the world Aeron was creating for her, yet still tears came unbidden to her eyes, that such magnificent creatures no longer roamed the mountaintops in the real world.

Wiping her tears hastily, she tried communicating with the dragon, using Air to amplify her voice, so that she could be heard over the wind. Rather than answering her, the beast screamed in rage, drawing back its head in preparation to strike. Not knowing what else to do, Serana threw up a wall of Air to block its fire, but it wasn't fire that shot from the huge mouth; it was lightning. Her shield held, but the bolt bounced to one of the rocks beside her, and it began to fall inward. There was no time to move; in moments she would be crushed. Quickly, Serana melded with the earth, slipping just beneath the surface of the mountain, to emerge a few feet from the rocks. The blue dragon spotted her instantly, but this time she was ready. Powerful streams of air smashed into the beast's wings, driving it into the mountainside with an audible crunch. It recovered in moments, though, and raced up to her, intent on trying its teeth where its breath had failed.

Killing the dragon would have been a simple matter—a razor-thin sliver of Air could have severed its head from its body—but Serana didn't *want* to kill it, even in this fabricated world. Instead, she wrapped a thick coil of air around its neck, and another around its body, binding its wings down, making them useless for flight. The coil at the neck she attached to the other, rendering the beast barely able to move its head. When she was satisfied, she used Air again to strengthen her voice. "Why did you attack me?" she asked.

"You have violated my territory," the dragon's voice, distinctly female, answered sharply. There was a pause, and then "Why did you not kill me?"

"I don't want to kill you," Serana said simply. "You are beautiful."

"I admit defeat," the dragon said, her voice filled with a profound sorrow. "Release me, and by the ancient law, I will leave this mountain in shame."

"Why would you leave?" asked Serana in confusion. "I don't want your territory; I'm only here to practice, to better my skills in Air magic."

The huge head swung as far as it was able to regard her. "You would… let me stay?"

For answer, Serana dissolved the bonds holding the dragon in place. Instantly, the huge body lunged into the air and flew away. "I will not forget you," the inhuman voice whispered on the wind.

No sooner had the dragon gone than another scream ripped through the air, one that filled Serana with terror. The boulder blocking her exit exploded, and she threw up another shield of Air to protect herself from the shards, but the creature that came through wasn't the Captain she'd expected. It looked like a captain, but it was larger, more powerfully built, and unless Serana was completely mistaken, it commanded a crude sort of magic, a magic that was black as life energy was white. "A General," Serana whispered to herself, backing away as far as she could.

The Daemon lumbered forward, the rock beneath its feet crumbling with each step, its pulsing red eyes fixed malevolently on the Sorceress. Serana hadn't wanted to kill the dragon, but she had no such qualms about Daemons. She sent a razor-sharp stream of air slicing through the huge neck, and the creature stopped... but nothing happened. The head didn't come off. Instead, it melded itself to the body seamlessly, not leaving even a scar.

Serana threw the Arrow of Light at the creature's chest, intent on knocking it back through the pass, but a huge hand came up, and caught the magic, drawing it to the gaping mouth. Serana watched in horrible fascination as the Daemon fed on her spell, absorbing the energy in moments. Then it was heading toward her again. There was no time for thought, no time for anything but action. Summoning Air magic to the full extent of her ability, she slammed a violent wind into the General's side. Just as it struck, the rock beneath the beast's feet exploded in razor-sharp shards. The Daemon lost its footing and went down, but Serana didn't stop. Using a trick she'd learned earlier that very day from Illiese, she gathered the snow from the air, creating hundreds of jagged shards that sliced through the creature's thick skin, powered by her terrible wind. She used Earth magic to plant spores inside the wounds, growing the poisoned mold Alier had told her of during their long talks before reaching the Air village. None of it was enough.

The General regained its footing in moments, if somewhat shakily, and started forward again. Serana focused, putting more power into the wind, but she was near her limits, and she could feel herself beginning to tire slightly. In desperation, Serana drew energy from the air, the snow, the rocks beneath her, anything she could find to sustain herself for one last attack. She could have drawn far more, but she was conscious of the fact that whatever she took came from Aeron, and she didn't want to hurt him as she'd hurt the others. Air and Water woven in unison... She could picture in her mind what she was about to do, and she focused every ounce of her being into the task, drawing deeply on her reserves for the necessary strength. When all was ready, she struck.

There were storms Serana had heard travelers speak of, back in Alon Peak, storms made from wind that spun, forming giant funnels that sucked up and destroyed all in their wake. Even the rain driven by these storms was said to be deadly, so great was the force that powered it. At Serana's command, one of these storms reached down from the sky, centered on the Daemon General. Serana summoned more shards of ice, letting the powerful winds drive them to slice the creature to ribbons. She could no longer see the General—the storm hid everything—but she could *feel* it, a malignant intruder on the mountainside, still very much alive even within her storm. Serana's energy was draining fast, but with a last, desperate surge of power, she collapsed the side of the mountain where the Daemon was standing, and let her storm push it from the now-nearer edge.

She fell to her knees as the General's soul-wrenching scream echoed into silence. Her storm died, and her protective heat spell dissolved, leaving her exposed to the harsh wind that still remained. She crawled to the stones where she'd stood when the Rite began, taking what small shelter they still afforded. Soon she would pass out from sheer exhaustion, if the Rite didn't end, but for a moment nothing happened. There was a distant groaning, seeming to come from everywhere at once, then silence. The groan came back, stronger, and suddenly Serana realized in horror what was happening, though she had no idea what to do about it. Aeron had known what he was doing when he designed this mountaintop. It was weaker than most, and when she'd collapsed a part of it to kill the General, she'd unwittingly weakened it enough that the rest would fall, at least the part where she sat.

Fighting to stay conscious, Serana crawled toward the pass. Had she the strength, she'd have earth-melded, but she doubted she could have even healed a simple cut at that moment. Aeron would know exactly how weak she was, yet he did not relent. She didn't know what she'd done to make the Air Wizard dislike her, but she no longer cared. Whatever he did, she would *not* fail this Rite! Gathering her depleted strength, she drew energy from her surroundings, absorbing it into herself, preparing to save herself when the mountain collapsed beneath her. Before she'd more than begun, though, the ground gave way beneath her, and she was falling. The two large rocks were going to smash into each other during the fall, with her in between, and she was forced to use what energy she'd gathered to push them away.

Dimly, through the blackness that was encroaching on her mind, she became aware of another sound, a now-familiar cry she'd not expected to hear again. Before she knew it, there were blue scales beneath her, and powerful wings beating on each side as she soared away from the crumbling mountaintop on the blue dragon's back. "Thank you," she whispered to the dragon, just before the world went black.

***

Serana opened her eyes, but when she tried to sit up, she fell back immediately. She was still in the village center, in the spot where she'd stood to begin the Rite, and it was very dark.

"Don't move, dear," Seleine said. "You're finally having a normal reaction to a Rite of Oneness." The Ice Witch hesitated a moment, then added, "Well, mostly normal."

"Mostly?" asked Serana, turning her head to watch her friend's eyes.

"The fact that you're awake isn't normal," Alier told her with a smile, appearing beside Seleine. "I can't say that I'm terribly surprised, though. Thank you for not draining Aeron any more than you did."

Serana looked away. "I tried to… The mountain was collapsing, and I didn't know what else to do, but he stopped me."

"He was forewarned," the Earth Enchantress said gently. "Besides, he is almost as skilled as I am." There was a note of pride in her voice. Perhaps Alier had played a part in training Aeron, despite their completely different elements.

"What was it like?" asked Allaerion curiously, kneeling beside where she lay. The Air Wizard's gaze was unusually intense.

Serana told him everything she could remember. There was a sort of haze over some of the details, but if she thought a moment, they all came to her. Allaerion and Seleine shared a glance that contained volumes of meaning—meaning that Serana could not interpret—at the mention of the blue dragon, and all three elementals' eyes widened when Serana told them about the Daemon General. When she'd finished, they all shared a nervous glance before looking down at her again. It suddenly occurred to her that none of them had made any

53

move to carry her off to bed, as they had wanted done with Illiese. Allaerion may not have Aeron's ability, but he was certainly skilled enough to lift her on a cushion of Air, as she had done for Illiese.

"He shouldn't have used a General," Alier said finally. "That was dangerous."

"He did seem to get its strength right, though," Seleine mentioned, and the others glanced sharply at her. "I had help when I fought one," she said hastily. "We didn't go *looking* for it or anything." That seemed to make them relax. Allaerion and Alier both seemed to think Seleine was entirely too ready to jump into danger. Serana only found it endearing. She felt that she would always be there to protect her sister. Whatever their blood, they were sisters in every way that mattered.

"How is Aeron," Serana asked. None of them had mentioned his condition.

"He'll be fine in a few days," Alier told her. "He's very strong, but you did wear him out." She smiled fondly. "I told him you would."

Suddenly realizing that she'd been lying in the snow, Serana shivered and sat up. Only after she'd done so did she realize she couldn't have a few minutes ago. Allaerion and Seleine appeared surprised, but Alier merely smiled and offered her hand to help Serana up.

Once on her feet, Serana felt a little dizzy, but it passed. She was tired, though... extremely tired. "I think I need some sleep," she said, surprised that her voice didn't tremble. She couldn't remember ever having been so thoroughly exhausted in her life.

"You can have my bed for tonight," Alier said with a reassuring smile. Allaerion put an arm around her for support, and the four of them made their way to the Earth Enchantress' home. Once there, Serana collapsed on the bed and immediately fell into a deep sleep.

When she woke, it was late morning. The sun shining through the window was well above the housetops. She sat up experimentally, and found that she was quite refreshed. No doubt she'd lost a day, since it was common to lose two or three after a Rite of Oneness. She found Seleine in the next room, curled up in a chair with a book.

"You're up already?" the Ice Witch exclaimed. "It's only been a few hours, Serana. Are you sure you're alright?"

"I'm fine," Serana said with a shrug. "I wouldn't want to face another General anytime soon, but I think I could handle a Captain without any problem."

Seleine laughed. "Yes, you're fine. Would you like some breakfast?"

The next two days passed uneventfully. Serana spent most of her time working at the construction site, teaching lessons of some sort almost every time she went. It was great fun using magic for building, creating rather than destroying, but she was beginning to worry that they had spent entirely too much time here in the village. Rhanestone was under attack even now, and without the Armor of the Elements, the keep might fall. Whenever she asked the elementals, though, they always said something vague about waiting until Aeron recovered. Serana liked Aeron well enough—though since her Rite, she wondered whether or not he liked her—but she'd examined him herself, once she'd recovered, and he was in no danger; he only needed rest.

Illiese was on her feet again just two days after Serana, if not yet up to her full strength. At Alier's direction, the young Ice Witch began taking over Aeron's duties while he recovered, directing the building of the school—not that it required a great deal of direction anymore; the students were learning a great deal from Serana—and addressing the concerns of the older citizens, many of whom still couldn't quite accept that magic was not merely a matter of willpower. Serana had learned a little of small-town politics from watching her father, the mayor of Alon Peak, and it seemed to her than Illiese knew what she was doing. She had a gentle, yet confident manner that seemed to calm even the most aggravated citizens in moments, and her answers to their questions were always clear and to the point. As far as Serana could see, the Ice Witch was nearly as adept at Aeron's duties as Aeron himself. She lacked the raw power that he exuded, the air of command, but she made no pretenses of being able to summon terrifying storms or bolts of lightning, and no one expected it of her.

It had been nearly a week since the Rite by the time Aeron got out of bed, and he was anxious about the lost time. After wolfing down a very large breakfast, he was off to the construction site. Serana went with him, watching curiously. She'd stayed either at the school or with Illiese most days, and she'd assumed that the gradual recovery the Ice Witch had displayed was normal, since no one had indicated otherwise. Aeron, however, seemed fully recovered already; his energy levels were as high now as they had been when she'd met him. Of course, he'd been asleep far longer than Illiese.

"Thank you for accompanying me," he said suddenly, still looking ahead as he strode down the street toward the school. "I'm told you've done a remarkable job with the students, and after what I observed before the Rite, I can't say that I'm surprised. I just want you to know that I truly appreciate your help."

"It was my pleasure," Serana said uncertainly. He didn't *seem* ill disposed toward her.

"As you've no doubt guessed," he went on, "the Rite you undertook was well beyond what I believe any Air Wizard, including myself, could have passed."

Serana felt too shocked to respond, but he didn't look at her, so he didn't see the expression on her face.

"I should say that I'm sorry for putting you through all of that, but the truth is that I'm not at all. You have more raw ability than any elemental ever has, probably more than any Sorceress, from everything I've read." He did slow now, and look into her eyes. "I have read quite extensively; believe me." His expression changed then, a mild confusion entering his eyes. "Why do you look so surprised?"

"Why would you put me through a Rite that no Air Wizard could pass?" she blurted out. "You could have killed me!"

He actually laughed. "Killed you?" he managed between chuckles. "Killed *you*?" He shook his head, obviously trying to bring his mirth under control, but with only moderate success. "My dear girl, you nearly killed *me*!"

Serana stared at him in horror. "But I was careful!" she exclaimed. "I didn't draw much, and you stopped me before I'd more than begun!"

Aeron didn't laugh this time. He studied her in silence, his eyes suddenly curious and intense. "You were aware that you were in a Rite," he said finally, as if to himself.

"Of course I was aware of it!" Serana snapped in exasperation. What did *that* have to do with anything?

Aeron blinked, and stopped walking entirely. "Were you not aware, High Priestess, that while a student is undertaking a Rite, he or she is completely unaware that the dream world of the Rite is not reality? It is only afterward that the difference is apparent." When Serana didn't respond, he went on briskly. "The fact that you *were* aware indicates that either you were not fully in the world of the Rite, or that your perceptions cannot be so easily contained. After standing for you, I know that you were indeed fully in the world, so I can only assume that the second explanation is correct. Unfortunately, there have been very few Sorceresses gifted enough to undertake a Rite of Oneness, and even fewer records of those who have. Nothing I've read suggests that members of your race would be fully aware, as you were, but neither does it suggest that they would not. In either case, it is curious, don't you think?"

Serana had never considered the possibility that others might *not* be aware they were within a Rite the entire time. "Does that mean it didn't work?" she asked.

"Absolutely not," Aeron assured her. "A Rite of Oneness both boosts and refines the flows of energy for its element within the student who undertakes it. If you require proof, then test yourself. You are still not my equal in Air magic, but you are not far from it in raw power, and not terribly far in skill either. You are significantly closer than you were when you arrived here." After a moment, he smiled. "Alier asked me to be hard on you, Serana, and I trust her judgment further than I trust anyone else's. The more difficult the Rite, you see, the more the student gains from having completed it."

"Then you haven't taken a disliking to me?"

Aeron appeared entirely baffled. "Is this one of those questions women ask to confuse men?" What was he talking about? Men were the ones who asked confusing questions. Everyone knew that! Aeron shook his head, then started walking again before he continued.

"Serana, I barely know you. What I do know is that you have helped train the students on the construction site, and you've done a wonderful job of it. I also know that you are not only the High Priestess and last surviving member of the Sorceress race, but also talented beyond what any record I have available suggests is even possible. I assure you, I have no reason whatsoever to dislike you." He glanced at her warily, as if afraid she might misconstrue something he'd said. Serana was beginning to think that even if she lived as long as Alier, she might never understand men.

When they arrived at the site, the students were busy at work. They were organized in groups, as Serana had suggested, each group consisting of ten members, at least one of which was an Ice Witch. Because there were so few Ice Witches compared with the Air Wizards, Serana had decided that they must be taught to utilize the Water magic as efficiently as possible, else the work would go very slowly indeed. The majority of the building was done with Air magic, of course, but it was far easier to gather and shape the ice with Water, leaving the detailed work for the Air Wizards. Serana had taught them to channel thread-thin streams of air fast enough to carve intricate designs into the ice far more easily than the tiny gusts they'd been using would allow. She smiled as she saw them at work; they really had learned quickly, and she felt no small amount of pride that she'd been, at least in part, responsible.

"Most impressive," Aeron breathed, watching the students work. "Most impressive indeed. I'd not have thought a single person could have taught them so much so quickly. The techniques you've given them are fairly simplistic, but very effective, and they cover nearly every aspect of what the students need to learn."

Serana blushed at the praise. "It was all I could think of," she said with a small shrug.

"If only more of us could think as you do," the young Air Wizard told her with a small smile. "Well, I'd planned on giving a lesson today, but I can see that you have things well in hand here. I suppose I should find Alier; I must settle a wager."

Chapter VIII

Aeron smiled to himself as he walked to the library, where he was certain he would find Alier. One of the many useful tricks he'd learned from his books was to locate nearby living creatures that were touching the air. It did have limitations, of course; there could be no airtight seal cutting him off from the creatures in question, for example. An Ice Witch could simply seal herself in ice, and be completely invisible to such a search! Even so, it was immensely useful in finding people who were lost, or in locating one of the only two Earth Enchantresses in the entire village. The spell did not tell him the identities of those whom he found; it merely provided some general information, such as race, sex, health, and a rough estimate of age. Since Alier was easily the oldest being in the village, the search for her was elementary.

Things were going very well indeed. It was a pity that his friend had to leave again so soon, and almost worse that she must take the young Sorceress High Priestess away as well—that one could have the school finished inside a month, if she could only stay—but the fact that they had come at all was blessing enough. The students were now more competent than they had been in more than two centuries, and they had the tools to continue learning. Now that Illiese had passed her Rite of Oneness, perhaps she would be busy enough with helping direct the building that she'd forget to pester him about taking a wife. "It's unseemly," she always said, "for a man who leads not to have a good woman behind him." Aeron thought the entire notion was daft, but whenever he tried to explain himself, she would throw up her hands and storm off, as if *he* were the one blind to reason! He was looking forward to the next few months immensely, for even with the High Priestess gone, the school should be completed in that time. Then he could settle into structuring his classes in earnest, probably building from the grouping system that the High Priestess had devised.

He became so lost in his musings that he almost walked right by the library without going in, but his sense of Alier brought him up short, and he went inside to find her. She was sitting cross-legged in the middle of several piles of books, sorting the volumes by category.

"Aeron," she said with a smile when he came in, "how wonderful to see you up and about! It's been far too many years since anyone bothered to organize this place, so Seleine and I were making a start of it while Illiese talks with the Elders."

"Why would Illiese need to talk with the Elders?" asked Aeron curiously.

"She's been running things in your stead while you were recovering," the Earth Enchantress explained. "She has shown herself quite capable."

Interesting indeed... Although he'd known for decades that Illiese had a wonderful mind, Aeron would never have believed her forceful enough to deal with the Elders; they still liked to believe they were in charge, and it often took a firm hand to convince them otherwise when the issue was important. The building of the school had been one such issue. "Well, I'd better go and find them, then."

"Not just yet," Alier said, rising. "There is still the matter of our wager."

"Yes, of course. What would you like me to do?"

"We are leaving tomorrow morning," the Earth Enchantress smiled. "I want you to come with us."

"*Come with you?*" Aeron thought the room was spinning for a moment. He'd been a fool to accept so general a wager, but he could never have believed that anyone, let alone a Sorceress, could have stood for a Rite of Oneness without being drained far more than the High Priestess had been. "Alier, you can't be serious! I have duties here, and in any case, you already have an Air Wizard."

"As I said before," Alier replied calmly, "Illiese has shown herself to be perfectly competent to manage your duties. As for our Air Wizard, Allaerion's prowess with a blade is as yet unmatched, but you know better than I that his skill with Air magic leaves something to be desired. He is more warrior than mage, and though we do need him, we need you also."

She didn't ask if he would honor their agreement; there was no question of it. Honoring one's promises was something even the

Elders agreed on; no one in the village would break his word once it was given. He merely wished she'd have chosen something else for her favor. The fact was that she had tricked him intentionally. She'd known he would never believe a Sorceress could stand for a Rite of Oneness without being exhausted, and she'd known he wouldn't balk at a wager on the matter. "If we leave tomorrow morning, then I had better go and pack." She'd known, and there was nothing he could do about it.

***

"That went rather well," Seleine observed from where she was standing beside a bookshelf, replacing the books Alier had finished sorting. The young Ice Witch knew how to read normal people quite well, but Aeron was not a normal person.

"That would depend on one's definition of 'well,' I suppose," Alier muttered. "I have never betrayed his trust before, and he has every right to be as angry with me as he is. It will take a long while before he trusts me again, and the trust will never be so complete as before."

"Then why didn't you simply ask him? He might have come of his own free will, if he understood what is at stake."

"That, my dear, is the problem," Alier told her wryly. "Aeron has read about a great many things, but he has experienced very little directly. He is nearly as powerful as I am, but he didn't gain his power through the long years I've spent. He is naïve as a babe." She paused a moment, studying the younger woman, wondering how much to tell her. It was tiresome, never knowing how much to say to people, particularly people with the best intentions, friends and loved ones. "Aeron cannot yet fathom what is at stake, and though he might have come with us simply on my word, he also might not have. I did what I did because it was the only way to ensure that he would come."

"Won't he find it odd, Serana being our leader?" Seleine asked. A good point, were Aeron a normal person, but again, he was not.

"Aeron doesn't understand experience, Seleine; he understands power. That Sorceress is more powerful than you and I combined. He'll think it natural for her to be in charge, despite her youth.

Besides, the girl needs to learn how to lead, and she's done well so far. I see no reason not to let her continue."

***

Serana said goodbye to the students that evening, and to her surprise, they gave her a gift. It was a medallion, a mountain peak with tiny dragons, intricately detailed, circling it. The entire scene was carved in ice, enchanted so that it would never melt, even in fire. "It's beautiful," she breathed when they presented it to her. "Thank you!"

"It is a small token of our thanks to you," said Avaelor, a rather tall Air Wizard who had attended nearly every lesson she'd taught. "You've taught us as well as the Headmaster could have, and the Ice Witches better than he could. Before you came, we'd never have been able to make that medallion, so we thought it might remind you, when you're gone, of what you've done here."

"You honor me," she said sincerely, wishing she knew the proper way for a Sorceress High Priestess to accept a gift from Air Wizards and Ice Witches.

The Air Wizards raised their hands heavenward, as if indicating their element, then spread their hands and bowed to her. The Ice Witches crossed their hands over their hearts, then spread their hands and curtsied. The gestures had a feel of ancient formality, and Serana wished she knew how to respond. Hoping they would forgive her ignorance, she smiled, then not knowing exactly why, touched the fingertips of her right hand first to her head, then her heart, and finally to her lips before sweeping the hand gently away toward them. It seemed to have been the right thing to do, for the students simply watched with reverence as she turned away, heading back to Alier's house.

When she arrived, everything was already packed, even her own things. Serana was surprised to learn that Aeron would be accompanying them, but it was a welcome surprise. Perhaps she could learn more about Air magic from him; she'd nearly exhausted Allaerion's knowledge with her questions already. Since there was nothing left to do, Serana ate the supper Alier had prepared and went to sleep.

The next morning they left the house early, as the horizon was just beginning to grey with the approaching dawn. Serana said a final, silent goodbye to the mountain village, and to the students she would probably never see again. Allaerion wasn't leading them away, though; he was leading them further into the village. Serana glanced at Seleine questioningly, and the Ice Witch smiled, amused.

"Did you forget why we came here in the first place?" she asked.

Serana flushed. She really had forgotten. They still needed to retrieve the boots, and she would have to be the one to find them. She opened her senses, sweeping the village for an object of magic, a piece of something larger. It was how the cuirass had felt to her, so she assumed it would be the same... but she found nothing.

"Don't you think I'd have found it myself, if it were that simple?" chided Alier. "Remember what I said before we came here. Your grandmother hid the boots."

Serana stopped walking as a thought struck her. Could it possibly be that easy? Alier had said that Leliah, Serana's grandmother, had used her own blood signature. Serana swept the village again, this time searching not for magic, but for a part of herself. Almost immediately, she found it, shining like a beacon to her senses. She started moving toward a largish building that stood slightly apart from any other. "It's in there," she said, pointing ahead of her.

"In the library?" Aeron asked incredulously.

Alier's smile was tinged with irony. "Perhaps she realized that very few people would be in there during the centuries to follow."

Serana led them through the door, then to the center of the room, and stopped. She was standing on top of the seal, but she didn't know what to do. "It's right here," she told the others as they came to stand around her, "somewhere."

"Leliah told me once that the key was to take back what she'd left behind," Alier said slowly.

Serana thought on it for a moment. The only thing her grandmother had left behind, other than the boots, was the blood signature. Could that be it? Concentrating, Serana drew that signature into herself, absorbing it as she had done with converted life energy. When it was finished, the floor rippled beneath her feet, though somehow it still felt solid. In moments, it had changed, becoming a stone slab identical to the seal that had covered the cuirass. The technique was truly brilliant; she filed it away for later use. How much more could Leliah have taught her, were the old High Priestess still alive?

Serana retrieved the boots and replaced the floor, concealing any evidence that it had been changed. After that, the party was on its way. Within an hour, they were at the foot of the mountain, heading away.

Chapter IX

Since the dragons had come to Rhanestone, the tide had turned dramatically. The Daemons still had most of their army, but each wave they sent met only a fiery grave, most never even reaching the wall of Dragon's Tears that spelled the doom of those few who did reach it. After a time, the attacks stopped altogether. The army still camped outside Rhanestone, but they made no move to press further. They hadn't for nearly a week now, and Rillian was more than a little concerned with why.

"It's as if they're waiting for something," Duke Rhanestone said softly beside him, watching the army. The soldiers were taking advantage of the much-needed respite, but someone was always on the walls, watching for another attack.

"That's what I'm afraid of," Rillian replied. "I wish that I had some idea what it was they're up to. Even the vampires don't know."

"There are no Daemons leaving the army for more than a few hours, to hunt. Perhaps there are reinforcements on the way, but I don't see why they would need to wait. The army camped out there now could have us bone-weary by the time their reinforcements arrive, then annihilate us after."

"Daemons have never been known as great strategists, my Lord," Rillian reminded him.

"True, but they seem to have learned recently, if you remember." The Duke shook his head, as if to dispel unpleasant thoughts, then clapped Rillian softly on the shoulder. "Get some rest, my friend. You will be the first called if they attack again."

Rillian bowed and left the wall, though he wasn't particularly tired. His hair, once entirely white, was now salt-and-pepper, and his arms and legs were stronger than they'd been in forty years. He strolled slowly through the courtyard, wondering how long this reverse aging of his would continue to be beneficial. If left for too long, Rillian would become a child, then an infant, and eventually disappear entirely.

"It will be stopped before that." The inhuman voice, reverberating softly in the air around him, seemed to wrap Rillian in comfort. He turned to the Guardian of Mist, curiosity filling him.

"Where will it stop?" he asked, not even bothering to question how she knew what he'd been thinking.

The Guardian's huge, sleek body was curled up comfortably in a corner of the courtyard, taking up perhaps a tenth of the space alone. Blackfang was out hunting, as he often was, but the Guardian was pregnant, and could no longer fly. Rillian wondered if she would eventually begin to show, as a human woman does; he knew far too little about dragons, and wanted to learn all he could from this one. Her crystal scales gleamed in the mid-morning light, creating tiny rainbows on the walls all around her. She appeared to be exactly what she was, a creature of legend come alive. "I do not know where it will stop," she told him. "I only know that you will not yet be a child when it does."

"Thank you," he said, bowing formally. "You've given me peace of mind."

"You are welcome, Battlemage. I fear I must ask a favor of you in return, however."

"What can I do for you?"

She regarded him silently for a moment, her large head tilted slightly, as if listening. "Clear the courtyard, please. I want to be alone for a time. I ask that you keep it clear for half an hour, whatever happens. Please trust me in this, for the safety of your people."

"I will see to it at once, m'lady." Rillian ran up to the wall again, where the Duke was still watching the Daemon army, and told him the Guardian's request.

"We will be terribly open if the Daemons attack, but they haven't for an entire week. I think we can spare one half-hour." With that, he started giving orders to have the courtyard cleared. No sooner had the last man left, a dark-cloaked figure dropped from the sky beside them.

"They attack now," Morganna said acidly. "Why have you cleared the courtyard?"

"But I was here the entire time!" exclaimed the Duke.

"Your human eyes see nothing," the vampire spat, gesturing past the wall. "Look!"

Rillian and Duke Rhanestone looked, but the Daemons did not appear to be moving.

"Not there," Morganna snapped. "There!" She was pointing down, closer to the wall. Rillian's heart nearly stopped when he realized what she meant. The Dragon's Tears were dying, nearly dead already, the earth beneath them putrid and rotting, as if it belonged in a swamp. Now the army was moving, surging toward the Keep in a black flood.

"We have to get the men back to the courtyard," the Duke said quietly. His face had gone nearly as pale as Morganna's.

"There isn't time," Rillian advised him. "The Guardian implied they might not be safe there, in any case."

"Order the men to the walls, but make sure that none of them use the courtyard. We'll have to trust the Guardian to hold the gate, when it breaks." There was little hope in the Duke's voice, less still in his eyes. He was a man who was watching Death approach, but who intended to meet it with sword in hand. "Morganna, I would be indebted to you if your people would assist in rousing the men. It would buy us a minute or two, time for a few more waves of arrows."

"We will do what we can," she told him, and disappeared into the air, moving too fast for Rillian to see where she went.

"Rillian, my friend," said Duke Rhanestone softly as storm clouds began to sweep in with unnatural speed, blotting out the sun, "as we have lived together, let us die together."

***

Blackfang had a large bull in his right front claw, and was looking for a second when the storm clouds began to appear. They were moving far too quickly, faster even than he could fly; it was not natural. Abandoning the hunt, he turned toward the human structure with all the speed he could muster, but the clouds were far ahead of him. His heartbeat was pounding inside his head as he flew, fear turning his insides to ice. She was inside the stone structure. Surely they could protect her long enough. He only needed minutes, just minutes. For the first time in his life, Blackfang felt that a dragon's speed in the air was not nearly swift enough.

The minutes dragged by slowly, each moment an eternity of worry. The image flashed through his head over and over again. He was in the air, looking down as his golden mate disappeared in a sea of black. He was powerless to save her, powerless to die with her. It could not happen again!

When he finally arrived, his worst fears were realized. He dropped the bull as he saw the gates being overrun. The Guardian fought valiantly, her fire consuming hordes of Daemons, but they were swarming over her, covering her from his sight. He wasn't fast enough! He screamed with rage and began to dive, intending at least to die with her.

Before he could reach her, he saw something else. The black wave that had swept over her was breaking, a silvery mist devouring it, pushing it back, filling the entire courtyard and pressing out from the gate. The Daemons were beginning to fall back, but it wasn't enough for Blackfang. He adjusted his angle, breathing dragon fire into the black masses, making smoking holes in their numbers as they fled. He wanted them *all*! He was beginning to tire. The speed of his flight back had taken much of his strength, but he did not care. He would avenge his love, his unborn child, with the lives of every Daemon in the world. He nearly faltered once on a gust of wind, but he held steady, raining fire on the unending army with each breath. A part of him knew that he couldn't keep this up, that he would fall to his death before he could kill them all... but it didn't matter. Death would be welcome. He could not bear to live again as the last of his kind.

Come back to me.

Blackfang nearly fell, so shocked he was by the voice. Could she speak from beyond the grave?

I live. Come back to me, now.

Hope giving him new strength, he circled back to the stone structure, landing in the courtyard. The mist... no, the Mist! The Mist had cleared, and there she was, her scales glowing in a single ray of sunlight that shone down upon her. She was like a goddess, powerful and untouchable. She was beautiful. She was alive! Suddenly, Blackfang realized that he couldn't see her clearly. His eyes were clouded over with moisture. Perhaps he'd gotten something in them... both of them.

***

Even after it was over, Rillian couldn't believe it. The Guardian of Mist was legendary, but never could he have imagined that her power was so great. Blackfang's arrival could not have been timed any better; scores of Daemons had died today, consumed by the Mist and burned by dragon fire. When the Mist finally cleared, the only trace of the Daemons was in the scratches on the walls and the ground of the courtyard. Rillian accompanied Duke Rhanestone down the stone steps, to thank the dragons personally. The Daemon army was far from defeated, but Rillian estimated that a full third of their Scouts were destroyed, and a good many Soldiers as well.

By the time they reached the last step, Blackfang swooped down to land beside the Guardian, nuzzling her neck tenderly. A single ray of sunlight had broken through the unnatural clouds, shining on the two dragons, making them seem somehow even more majestic than before.

"I don't know how to thank you," Duke Rhanestone said seriously.

"You could start by keeping this courtyard guarded," growled Blackfang, looking down at the two men with narrowed eyes.

"My love, be still," said the Guardian softly. "I asked them to clear the courtyard. The Mist promised to protect me, but it would have been far more difficult if there had been any but Daemons here."

"I see," the black dragon said gruffly, obviously far from pleased.

"My lord," Rillian said differentially, "with the Dragon's Tears gone, it is likely they will attack again soon."

"The Mist will help the flowers to grow again," the Guardian reassured him. "It cannot do what the last of the Seriani did, but by tomorrow morn the soil outside the wall will be healed, and the flowers will have returned."

"I cannot express our gratitude," the Duke said gravely, "to both of you."

Though the dragon's expression did not change—perhaps it *could* not change—Rillian somehow felt sure that the Guardian was smiling. "I ask only that you continue to allow me the safety of these walls, Duke Rhanestone. Now, my love," she said, turning to Blackfang. "I believe your hunt was successful, and I am famished."

The black dragon seemed to bow just before launching himself into the air, the wind from his wings' powerful strokes nearly knocking Rillian off his feet. He returned only moments later with a large bull, and the two humans turned to go, leaving their dragon allies to feed.

Rillian left the Duke then and went to the Vault for Ella's lesson. She was waiting for him when he arrived, reading a book on general elemental magic, something Rillian's old teacher had written before Rillian himself was born. "You've learned to let yourself in?" he asked her, mildly surprised. She was very talented, but she'd shown little interest in Fire magic before.

"It seemed prudent to be able to start a fire," she told him without looking up. "This room was part of a Fire Warlock city, after all, was it not?"

"It was indeed." If she wanted to learn a few simple spells on her own, he was not going to object, so long as she didn't rush into dangerous material. Were she any other student, he might have been more concerned, but Ella was one of the most practical people he'd ever met; any youthful tendencies to rush into the unknown had been driven from her before she'd come here.

"This book is rather fascinating," she continued, still reading. "I understand it was written by your predecessor. The man's wit seemed as well-honed as his magic."

Rillian smiled fondly in remembrance. "Yes, it was," he agreed.

She did look up then, and her eyes widened slightly. "Rillian, you look younger every time I see you! Is it accelerating?"

"Whether it is or not, there is little we can do about it. Perhaps Serana will be able to reverse it, when she returns, or perhaps the Serian of Music."

She pursed her lips for a moment, as if considering, then shrugged. "Well, they can leave it go for a bit longer, anyway. They'd better not let you get younger than I am, though; I'm not sure I could deal with that."

Rillian nearly laughed, but he checked himself, realizing that she was quite serious. "Are you ready for your lesson, Ella?"

"Am I ever not?" she asked sweetly.

Rillian thought perhaps it would be best not to answer. "Let us begin, then. I believe we were studying Air last time."

"Yes, the levitation spell you'd worked out before the Sorceress left," she said briskly, though there was a slight edge to her voice.

"The High Priestess, Ella. She isn't just any Sorceress."

"There aren't any others," she said, the edge sharpening slightly, "so what difference does it make?" What was wrong with her today?

"The Sorceress race is ancient and powerful," he explained. She probably wasn't accustomed to the customs at Rhanestone yet, at least not all of them. "They have been friends to us since Rhanestone was founded, and we respect their hierarchy."

"The Sorceress race is a single person," Ella told him heatedly. "I, for one, have heard quite enough about the amazing *High Priestess* whose magical abilities are beyond anything I will ever dream of. Show me goals, Rillian, not stars I can never reach."

Was that what was bothering her? Did she actually believe he expected her to match Serana in magic? "Ella," he said gently, "I never meant…"

"Could we get on with the lesson?" she interrupted. "Levitation. Air magic."

"Of course." Perhaps he'd need to watch what he said around her in the future. "The trick to levitation…"

"Is she pretty?" Rillian was surprised enough by the question that for a moment he could only stare at her in confusion. Apparently his silence upset her still more. "The Sorceress," she snapped. "Is she pretty?"

"Beautiful," Rillian answered, still confused. "Now, as to levitation…"

"I'll read about it," she said shortly, rising and striding from the room, the book in her hand. Rillian stared after her, baffled. He remembered in his youth that women often seemed quite puzzling; perhaps some things never changed.

"Pardon, but are you the Battlemage here?" The voice was not familiar, though that wasn't surprising; there were many in the Keep these days whom he didn't know. When the speaker stepped into the room, however, Rillian recognized him immediately.

"King Evieron!" he exclaimed. "It's an honor to meet you face to face. I am Rillian, the Battlemage here at Rhanestone. What can I do for you?"

"I understand that you had an apprentice here some time ago, a Sorceress."

"Serana, yes. She is the High Priestess, and last of her kind." She seemed to be the favorite topic of conversation today.

"Serana..." The Elven King seemed to test the name on his tongue, sampling it as one would sample a favorite dish from childhood, nearly forgotten. "I was told that she is no longer here. Would you know where she is?"

"She joined the expedition piecing together the Armor of the Elements," Rillian told him. "May I ask why you wanted to know?"

"It is a family matter."

"Is one of the royal family injured?" asked Rillian, concerned. "I do not have the High Priestess' skill, but perhaps I could help."

"I don't believe anyone in the family is injured," King Evieron said soothingly. "When she returns, would you please see that I am informed, as a personal favor? I must speak with her."

"I will see to it," Rillian assured him, somewhat confused, and the Elven King departed with no more than a quick "thank you".

Chapter X

Ilsa rode hard, not looking back. The horse beneath her needed no encouragement; the steady booms behind drove it on. Ilsa had never been more than an indifferent rider, but she did know how to stay on a horse's back. Trisan had sighted the Keep an hour ago, and it would take another two before they reached safety. The horses could not keep up this dead gallop for that long, but for the moment they had no choice. The Captain was pursuing them tirelessly, but Captains were not very bright, according to Jarek; it could easily be avoided. The real problem was that they'd encountered no less than seven Daemon Scouts already. It could mean only one thing; the battle had already begun.

It was midmorning, and they'd been riding since just before the sun had risen, planning to keep a steady pace that the horses could maintain for hours. The Captain had caught up to them not long after sunrise, though, and their plans had changed.

Trisan rode beside Ilsa, an enchanted bow in hand. The Sorceress had been unable to do what he'd wanted with it—she'd been reluctant to do anything at all on a piece she'd never tried before. They'd argued about it for a quarter of an hour before Trisan finally agreed that she could do whatever she could with it; if it ruined the bow, there were others. Ilsa knew very little of weapons, but according to Trisan, what the High Priestess came up with was better than he'd hoped. He'd wanted exploding arrows, or something of the sort. What he got...

"The bow enchants each arrow as it's knocked," he'd told her the night before, his face animated with excitement. "When the arrow flies, Air Magic takes over, guiding it to the closest Daemon along the trajectory, and after that it gets even better." The man had sounded like a child with a new toy. "I think our esteemed High Priestess had help from her Ice Witch friend, for when these arrows strike, they encase the entire target in ice, just like Jarek's staff does!"

He didn't think the magic would be powerful enough to freeze a Captain, but perhaps it might freeze the legs, slowing it down a bit.

Right now, though, he was looking for Scouts, though there was no sign of anything in the mile-wide clearing. They slowed down when they reached the forest, both to rest the horses and to prevent broken legs. They went another hour without incident, but when they were roughly three quarters of an hour from the Keep, they were ambushed. Daemon Scouts emerged from the forest on all sides, surrounding them.

"We can't take this many," Trisan whispered into her ear, "not unless your magic can handle at least half." It couldn't. "Get ready. We're going to take as many of them with us as we can, and if possible, some of us might make it through the line. If you get through, run. Don't try to stay and help the rest of us. Better some survivors than none."

Ilsa nodded shakily. They were so close! How could the man take it so calmly? The Daemons advanced slowly, their glowing red eyes alive with hunger. Before they sprang, black-cloaked figures appeared everywhere, swarming over half the Daemons. The Rhanestone men wasted no time; they jumped into the fray. Trisan's arrows froze three Daemons in place before Ilsa recovered from her shock. Olsever's hammer crushed a Scout's head, and lightning from the blow threw another back into the forest. Jarek and Jarel were fighting side-by-side, their horses facing opposite directions, allowing the two men to defend all around them.

Suddenly realizing that she was being useless, Ilsa threw her magic into the fight. Vines sprang from the earth, twining about the legs of two Daemon Scouts, holding them in place. A jet of fire drove another away from her, and a jagged bolt of ice pierced a fourth one's heart. She couldn't keep this up forever, but suddenly she realized that it was over. She turned to look at their timely allies, and her breath caught. Standing before the small party, black cloaks flowing in the gentle breeze, were nine vampires!

"What trickery is this?" demanded Trisan, drawing another arrow and aiming for the nearest vampire.

"Foolish human!" he spat. "We are allies of Rhanestone. We came to your aid."

"Vampires are devious," growled Olsever, hefting his hammer. "You destroyed the Sorceress village!"

"That was another clan, not ours," snapped a female in the group. "They were deceived by a Daemon Lord posing as a vampire."

"Lies!" cried Jarek and Jarel in unison as they brought their staves to the ready.

Ilsa could take no more. "Are you all *mad*?" she screamed. "There is a Captain chasing us, and who knows how many more Daemons in the forest. Devious or not, these vampires saved us, and Rhanestone is less than an hour away. We can argue about it later. Let's *go*!"

"Later," agreed Trisan, and wheeled his horse toward the Keep. The vampires melted into the forest in moments.

They reached the Keep ahead of the Captain, and made it inside without difficulty. At first glance, Ilsa thought it odd that there were flowers growing in such numbers outside the stone wall, but as the party drew near, she realized that they were the same type of flowers as the one she'd been given to escape the Daemons, and the ones growing in that strange pattern beneath the tree. They must provide protection of some sort, though she didn't understand exactly how.

Once inside, the soldiers took their leave, heading to the barracks to distribute the magic weapons among the Elite Guard. Ilsa was shown to a small, but comfortable room and given a meal that she barely tasted, so distracted she was by the inviting look of the bed. She hadn't realized how exhausted she was until after she'd sat down, so as soon as the last bite was gone, she half fell into bed, not bothering to undress. She was asleep almost before she'd hit the mattress.

She awoke to a knock on the door. Pulling the covers around her instinctively, she looked around hurriedly for her clothes. It took her a few moments to realize she was still wearing them. Feeling more than a little foolish, she got up and answered the door. The man standing outside was middle-aged, with salt-and-pepper hair that grew nearly to his shoulders. He wore a long brown robe with a wide purple strip down the center, the mark of a Battlemage. "Good Morning," he said, smiling politely.

"Morning?" Surely she'd slept longer than that; it was only an hour from noon when they'd arrived.

"Yes, m'lady. You slept through the day, and then all night."

"You are the Battlemage here?" she asked.

"I am. My name is Rillian. This is my apprentice, Ella," he said, stepping aside so that she could see the beautiful young woman behind him. "I am told you have some magical training already. May I ask where you studied?"

"With my mother," Ilsa replied. "She was trained in the Sorceress village, during her youth," Ilsa replied. "She said that the High Priestess at the time was very kind to her, though I must admit that she was not nearly so powerful as the current High Priestess, if the soldiers' stories can be trusted."

Rillian smiled with pride, like a parent hearing his child complimented. That couldn't be, of course; he might be the right age, but Sorceresses rarely took humans for mates. "Yes," he said softly, "she is very talented indeed." Ella's expression never changed, but Ilsa had the distinct impression that the temperature in the hall had just dropped several degrees. Perhaps it was time to reassure the young woman.

"My husband was killed in a Daemon attack, and I was captured by them. Unfortunately, my magic was not enough to drive them off by itself." She'd never had a husband, of course, but they didn't need to know that; the story would serve two purposes. Deliberately, she turned to the apprentice, Ella. "I don't think I could ever be with another man." That much, at least, was true.

Ella relaxed visibly, but Rillian seemed not to notice the exchange at all. "You were captured by Daemons?" he exclaimed. "However did you escape?"

Ilsa told them about the strange voice in the dark that freed her from her bonds and gave her the flower—a Dragon's Tear, according to Rillian—and about the other voice that had given her the cloak and a new flower, when the first was withered. She told them about meeting the new Sorceress High Priestess, and how she had provided the escort back to Rhanestone. When she'd finished, Rillian seemed most intrigued.

76

"A wondrous tale, to be sure," he said softly. "Since you are already trained as a magician, Ilsa, would you lend your magic to our struggle here?"

"Of course. Any enemy of those *things* that captured me and killed my husband is a friend of mine."

"Would you perhaps instruct me as well?" Ella asked, apparently to Rillian's surprise, if his eyes could be trusted. "I want to learn all forms of magic that I am able."

"To the best of my ability," Ilsa told her seriously. Ella might be of an age with her, but she'd not been practicing magic for very long; the slowing would not have started with her yet, so she appeared a few years older. The important thing, though, was that Ilsa seemed to have acquired a friend, always a very valuable thing to have in a new place.

***

The days had passed slowly for Reilena at first, but somehow they seemed to move more quickly as time went by. Just four days after she'd arrived, Morganna had pronounced her ready to begin her physical training. The vampire leader had visited her every day, even if her schedule would only allow a few moments. When possible, the golden-haired creature spent hours with her, helping her to overcome the misguided notions that were ingrained in her mind.

The physical training was not what Reilena expected at all. She'd thought to run laps, or do lifting of some sort, things to build up her body. Instead, she was trained to utilize the agility that was natural among her kind. They *were* her kind; she realized that now, if only intellectually. She learned to land properly after jumping long distances. Landing was not usually dangerous for a vampire, but Reilena was not yet skilled enough to fly, and she needed to learn to move without sound, even in a landing.

Reilena understood now what that strange kinship was that she'd felt with the other vampires on the day she'd arrived here at Rhanestone, for she'd felt something like it in another earlier that day. The young woman had waves of long, blonde hair flowing down to her back, but her skin, though somewhat pale, was still darker than that of any vampire Reilena had seen. The feeling of kinship was particularly strong with her, but different somehow in a way Reilena could not explain, and still stranger, she wore no dark cloak. The woman appeared to be heading toward the shops the elves had set up. Curious, Reilena followed her, catching up to her quickly.

"You don't have a cloak," Reilena pointed out after a few moments, when it became obvious that the blonde woman was not going to speak.

"Why would I need a cloak?" she replied. "The weather is comfortable."

"Are you not a vampire?" Reilena asked her, confused.

"A vampire?" The woman stopped, looking Reilena up and down. "I'd have thought you'd know the difference between yourselves and your food supply."

Reilena had been told to expect such comments, but she found that she was quite unprepared to deal with them. Being accused of being the monster that had hurt her was more than she could take meekly. She grabbed the woman's arm with lightning speed, throwing her down on her back. Before she could take another step, however, the air around her solidified, holding her in place. She couldn't move any more than her head.

"I could leave you there," the woman said sternly as she got up, brushing herself off. "I would prefer to have an explanation, though."

"I asked you a question, and you insulted me," Reilena said between clenched teeth.

"Insulted you?" the woman asked incredulously. "How in the world did I insult you?"

"You are *not* my food supply," Reilena spat. "You feel like a vampire, but... different, so I asked you."

"You are Reilena," the woman breathed, wonder replacing incredulity in her eyes. The air became fluid again, and Reilena moved her arms experimentally. "I am Ella, apprentice to Rillian, the Battlemage here at Rhanestone. I've heard of you."

"You've... heard of me?"

"I speak to a variety of people here at Rhanestone," Ella told her, "vampires among them. I find it rather silly that everyone tends to stay only with his or her own kind." She paused a moment before going on. "I'm sorry that I was a little short with you; it's been a stressful day."

"I'm sorry for knocking you down," Reilena told her. Apprentice to the Battlemage... no wonder that the air had turned solid.

"That's alright. I'd have done the same, in your place, particularly after... well, what you've been through."

Reilena stopped, staring. "Just how much *do* you know about me?" she demanded.

"More than Morganna wanted to reveal at first," Ella told her with a small smile. "I implied that my magic might be able to help you, if I knew all the details."

"Can it?"

"Not likely, until I become more skilled," Ella said, a twinge of frustration in her voice. She started moving again then, motioning Reilena to accompany her. "Actually, that's one of the reasons I'm going to see the elves today. Their priests have studied mental illness for years, and have learned some remarkable things about memory modification as a result. I'm imagining that some of those techniques could be used to help a person regain lost memory as well."

"You're very kind," Reilena said softly, suddenly ashamed.

"Unfortunately I'm not," Ella told her. "I was looking into your case because I find the study fascinating, not out of any feelings of compassion." She paused again. "I would be pleased if I could help you, though."

"Fair enough," said Reilena. "Why do you feel so much like a vampire?" she asked suddenly.

"I'd imagine it's because I have the ability to manipulate the energies in the world around me, as any magician does," Ella replied. "Morganna told me that vampires have no inherent magical energy, but that you manipulate energy around you to accomplish much of what you do. Physical strength and hypnosis seem to be your only purely internal gifts. Most everything else, from the sharp vision to the flying, seems to be a result of energy manipulation. Many magic users are able to sense the ability to manipulate energy in others; I think it's probably the same with vampires."

Ella had said goodbye when they'd reached the Elven Priests, and Reilena had headed back to the vampires' apartments. She had a good deal to ask Morganna. When she arrived in the large room the vampires used as an audience chamber, there were visitors already, four human males, warriors by the look of them.

"We are looking for your leader," announced the largest of them, a burley man with fiery red hair. "We're told her name is Morganna."

"I am Morganna," the vampire herself said, rising from a chair on the other side of the room. "What can I do for you?"

"We're here to apologize," the big man rumbled, running a thick hand through his coarse red hair.

"Apologize for what?" Morganna asked, her brow knitting slightly in concern. "Have any of my people been injured?"

"We have only just returned to Rhanestone," the smallest man in the group said. He was younger, but Reilena couldn't put any specific age to him. His long black hair was tied in an intricate braid that ran down his back, and something about his stance spoke of lightning reflexes, though Reilena wasn't sure what. "We were attacked by Daemons less than an hour from the Keep, and your people saved us. We did not know of the alliance, and we were… mistrustful."

"We don't know which of your people helped us," said one of the two who had not yet spoken, nondescript men who looked identical, save for their clothing.

"But we wanted to thank whomever it was," finished the other.

"Ah," Morganna said softly. "You are the Elite Guard members who were ambushed in the forest."

"We are," the big man nodded.

"I will convey your thanks, and your apology, to those who helped you. We appreciate your coming here."

"We've heard that there have been some… well, incidents… with the Rhanestone guard," said the man with the braid suddenly. "As an acting captain in the Elite Guard, I can assure you that there will be no more such… ah, incidents."

"That would be much appreciated," Morganna said, inclining her head.

"For whatever it's worth," the big man rumbled, "you and yours have my full support from now on." To Reilena's ears, it had the sound of an oath.

"It is worth a great deal," Morganna told him gravely. "May I ask your name?"

"I am Olsever. This is Trisan," he said, indicating the man with the braid. "These two are Jarek and Jarel."

"His word binds us all," said Trisan, and the other two nodded.

"We appreciate your words, and your coming," said Morganna with a small smile. "Let us hope that our peoples can coexist in peace when this war is over."

The men all saluted sharply before filing out.

Chapter XI

Lady Firehair followed the trail out of curiosity. She feared neither its destination nor its makers; she'd learned by now that there was little to fear in the world, other than her uncle... and perhaps herself. Curiosity was considered a poor quality in her family, so it was only natural that she should have it in abundance; she was an eternal shame to all her kind, as her uncle had told her on many occasions. Still, shame or not, she couldn't help herself. She'd encountered elementals before, but never three together, each from a different element. She'd been told that elementals preferred to stay with their own kind, unless they were ready to marry. Lady Firehair understood such customs, since her family lived by them quite strictly.

Before long, the trail came very near to a place where she could not go, and she stopped to investigate. Lady Firehair had never encountered a place that she could not enter before; it was a strange feeling. Oh, she could pass into it easily enough, but she wouldn't live for more than a few hours inside it; there was no energy to sustain her, or rather, she wouldn't be able to get to it within the strange field that surrounded the place. She circled the perimeter of the place, and found it without flaw. Curiosity filled her to bursting, but she dared not trespass; her defenses would be severely weakened inside, and whoever resided within obviously would not welcome her encroachment. Frustrated, she turned to leave, and found a young man standing beside her.

"Who are you?" he asked without preamble.

He was a human, as far as she could tell, but he had abilities far beyond any magician she'd ever heard of from that race. Also, there was another close by, hidden from her eyes, but not from her senses.

"Who are you?" he repeated.

"I am Lady Firehair," she answered uncertainly. "Do you live in this... place?"

"For now," he replied. "Why are you here?"

"I am curious," she told him truthfully. "I have never before seen a place like this." She paused a moment, and looked around, but she still could not pinpoint the location of the other. "Please tell your companion to come out of hiding. It is unpleasant to be watched in secret."

"Impressive," came a new voice as its owner, an old man, materialized beside the young one. This one was not so talented as the younger man, but his abilities were far more poignant; he obviously had a good deal more experience behind him. "There are few who can detect my presence, without my allowing it."

"What is this place?" Lady Firehair asked him.

"I'm afraid that I cannot tell you," he said, smiling apologetically. "For you, there is much still to learn before you enter a place such as this."

The younger man was confused, though he masked it well, but he said nothing. Lady Firehair trusted her senses more than her eyes, where emotions were concerned.

"Then I will leave." Lady Firehair bowed formally, hoping it would suffice. She had no wish to offend these people, but she disliked being sent away without answers. She didn't blame them, of course. No one who knew anything about her would want her near; even her family preferred to stay away from her. Brushing away a tear, Lady Firehair moved away and continued on the trail.

She hadn't gone far when she sensed a spot where a good deal of magic had been used, a Sorceress battling a fourth elemental, an Earth Enchantress of great power. Surprisingly, the Sorceress had won; she must have been exceptional, given the strength Lady Firehair sensed. Neither opponent was killed, fortunately—Lady Firehair didn't like killing, despite how many times her uncle had explained that it was sometimes necessary; she'd done it twice now, but hated it each time— and they even left together, along with the other three elementals.

Further on, the trail seemed to be leading to a place where massive amounts of energy had been used recently. When she reached a clearing in the forest, she stopped, staring in wonder. There was a giant pillar of flame shooting up from the ground. It was fed by the earth itself, and would not burn down in the foreseeable future, but that wasn't what had surprised Lady Firehair so. Her senses were very well attuned to the nuances of energy that make each creature unique, and what she saw was impossible. This flame had not been created by the Fire Warlock. It would have taken a group of them, in any case, and only one had been here... and died here. It had been created by a Sorceress, and single-handedly. In all her travels, Lady Firehair had only ever encountered one Sorceress, and that one was not powerful enough alone to accomplish this. Not even the one who had bested the Earth Enchantress earlier could have done it... yet somehow, one had. There had been a struggle here before that, against... Lady Firehair recoiled at the impression and almost fled, but it had all happened some time ago now; she was safe. Suppressing a shudder, she continued on the trail quickly. She was catching up to the party easily; there were few creatures that could cover as much distance as she could in an hour, even when she was not hurrying, and this party had been moving slowly to accommodate the humans that traveled with them. Quickening her pace, she continued on.

It wasn't long before she began to recognize her surroundings again. She stood before the ancient oak where she had directed the young magician to take one of the flowers. The girl must have found the very party Lady Firehair was following... Had she only known, she'd have saved herself quite some distance in travel, but perhaps it was better this way. She now knew, after all, of a place where she could not enter, something she'd never encountered before.

Smiling, she knelt down and breathed in the fragrance of the flowers. The smell was beautiful, but it always made her cough for some reason. Still, the pleasure of the scent was worth it, though none of her family would agree; they had no appreciation for beautiful things. They always said that her love of beauty was a weakness, but as it was with many of her other flaws, she could not help it... and she had no real desire to. It was better to accept that she was a shameful, unworthy creature than to give up the few things that brought her happiness.

Lady Firehair knew now who was in this party she'd been following, but the knowledge brought her more questions than answers. The Sorceress was the same one she'd helped get free of

Lord Zironkell, to save the man who created the music, but that Sorceress shouldn't have been powerful enough to create the pillar of flame Lady Firehair had found before. It was a most intriguing puzzle indeed.

A quick examination of the residual energies from the party's passage told her that they had headed toward the black dragon's volcano. She'd been there a few times, though she'd avoided speaking with the creature; he was bad-tempered, according to everyone she'd asked. Before she could follow the trail, she sensed that her uncle was summoning her again. He never used to call her so often; he'd gone years between visits for the majority of Lady Firehair's life... Still, it was useless to complain, and there was no one to complain to anyway. Sighing, she headed home, intending to pick up the trail from the volcano as soon as possible.

***

"I'm afraid my senses were terribly inaccurate today," Calen sighed. "I have no idea *what* she was, much less who." His training had been increasingly frustrating of late. Each time he thought he was making progress, he seemed to hit a wall, and could go no further. His teacher's insistence that his progress was quite rapid only increased his impatience. If his "rapid" progress ever stopped, how slowly would he be forced to go then?

"Your senses were not the problem," Malron assured him, puffing calmly on his pipe. They were sitting in his study, where Calen's lessons usually took place. "I have no more idea than you do. Whoever she is, though, her path will be difficult. That much is certain, I'm afraid."

"But some of the things I did sense," said Calen hesitantly, suppressing a shudder. "Why didn't you destroy her?"

The old man laughed softly, creating a cloud of smoke that made Calen cough; he really did not like pipe smoke, but he couldn't bring himself to ask the older man to stop smoking. It was Malron's study, after all. "I'm surprised that a young man your age wasn't more distracted by her beauty than by those other things."

"Was she beautiful? I hadn't noticed." Calen wondered how his teacher could still bother looking, at his age, but he was more concerned with why the other man did not seem to take those *other things* more seriously. Calen *had* noticed her beauty, in truth, but what good was a pretty face on a creature so… dark? It hadn't been as pretty as Serana's face, in any case.

"I'm not sure whether that's a good thing or not, in someone so young," Malron said gravely, his brows creased with concern. "You shouldn't forget how to appreciate beauty whenever you see it, in all forms."

"Please just answer my question." Calen had been careful not to mention Serana beyond passing; he still had not learned the intentions of these people, beyond training him, and he was not a man to give his trust easily.

Malron shook his head slightly, but didn't argue further. He knew by now when Calen could not be diverted. "Two reasons, my boy. For one, her heart is good; the darkness has not taken hold of her, though I can't explain why. If you'd been paying more attention, you'd have seen that much on your own. For the other, she is… too powerful."

"Even for you?" Calen asked incredulously. He'd almost begun to think that there were no limits to the Elder's power.

"Even for all of us combined," Malron told him seriously, blowing smoke rings. He always did that when he was in deep thought. "Don't ever confront that one, or any like her, if there are any; however much you learn here, you won't survive it."

* * *

Lord Alexander woke to Alon nuzzling his hand again. The lamb seemed to think Alexander should rise with the sun every day, whether there was anything important for him to do or not. Now that the battle was waging in earnest, there was little he *could* do, beyond trying to warm the hearts of Rhanestone toward Alloria's people. He was a skilled wrestler, and knew the rudiments of swordplay—he'd once thought himself skilled at that as well; Rhanestone had disillusioned him—but he was really more of a politician than a warrior. Giving Alon a pat on the head, he rolled over, hoping the lamb would leave him be a few more minutes.

He nearly jumped out of his skin when he found Alloria lying peacefully beside him, watching him. "Why aren't you in the chair?" he stammered, now very much awake.

"I do require sleep sometimes, Alexander," she said calmly. He'd insisted that she stop calling him "my Lord" all the time. "There are no other beds than this one. I was careful not to wake you."

Just because she was right didn't mean he had to like it. He got up, since there was no way he could sleep any longer now, and tried not to watch as she stretched languidly, her nearly sheer nightdress hiding almost nothing. After that first time, they had not been together physically, but Alexander was still haunted by the memory of it, and her frequent, subtle reminders that she was his anytime he asked did not help.

"Will you have another bed brought in, or may I share this one again tomorrow night?" Her tone made it clear how absurdly silly the first choice was, enough so that he couldn't bear to tell her he'd been thinking of doing just that. She'd learned to read him quite well during their time together, and she often trapped him between his pride and his irrational fear of looking foolish in her eyes, a fear that she was not supposed to be aware of. "I went far too long without sleep until last night, and I must make up for it."

"Have you been feeding?" Alexander asked, hoping to change the subject. "Alon appears healthy as ever."

"And well he should," Alloria told him, her expression mildly surprised. Nearly all of her expressions were mild, Alexander was learning. "I feed him more than enough to replace the blood I take. I'd imagine, though, that he wants to go out now." She rose slowly, giving him a very suggestive view, then suddenly moved like a blur to the dresser. When he could see her clearly again, just moments later, she was fully dressed, and smiling at the lamb, which trotted to her happily. Alon seemed to enjoy it when she flew him down to the courtyard. He wasn't even afraid of the dragons any longer, now that they'd been here for a while.

Alexander buckled on his sword belt, as he did every morning, though now it seemed a rather useless gesture. He wouldn't be doing any fighting. Still, promoting peace with creatures once considered as bad as Daemons was a battle in itself.

"Please talk with me while I bathe," Alloria said from behind him. A few weeks ago, he'd have jumped, but he'd become nearly accustomed to the way she could sneak up on him so silently—he only spun around.

"Why?" he asked. He'd not gone in that room during her bath since they'd consummated their agreement.

"Your company is pleasant," Alloria told him. "I do not like bathing alone." When he didn't respond, she went on. "We have been together long enough now that you should be accustomed to my presence; I do not see why so simple a thing bothers you so."

"It doesn't bother me," he lied. "If you wish it, then I will talk with you." It would be better than trying in vain to read, all the while haunted by the memory of that first morning.

She nodded and moved off toward the bath, looking back to see that he followed. Instead of disrobing, though, she turned around and looked at him. "You are certain that you wish us to be equals in private?" she asked unexpectedly.

Alexander had thought they'd settled this long ago. "Of course," he told her. "In private, we are equals."

"Then I cannot heed your feelings while denying my own," she said softly.

Before Alexander could ask what she meant, she surged forward with the speed of her kind. Her arms were around his neck instantly, and she was kissing him, holding him to her in a grip he could not have broken if he'd tried. Despite himself, he kissed her back, his arms wrapping themselves about her waist of their own volition. Several minutes later, or perhaps longer, she pulled back, looking into his eyes. There was real fear in hers, though Alexander had no idea why.

"Alloria, what is wrong?" he asked, more than a little concerned. He took her hands in his without thinking, something he'd never done before. What could she possibly be afraid of?

For a moment, she stared down at his hands holding hers, and he almost pulled them away, fearing he'd offended her somehow, but her slim fingers gripped his gently in return, and her eyes slowly rose up to meet his own. "You care for me," she whispered, as if in disbelief. Seeing the confusion in his eyes, she went on. "You saw that I was afraid, and you wanted to comfort me."

"Of course I did," he said, more confused than ever.

Her eyes were actually moist with tears, but her lips were curved into a smile more real than any he'd ever seen on her. Suddenly he wished she would smile more often; she was even more beautiful when she smiled. "You no longer hate me," she whispered, and before he could reply, she was hugging him tightly, sobbing softly.

He held her awkwardly, hoping she would explain all of this after she calmed down. Even if it *was* awkward, he had to admit, if only to himself, that she felt very good in his arms. When her sobbing had subsided, she still made no move to pull away, and he was content to keep her close. "I have never hated you personally, Alloria," he said softly, "and I was blind to hate your people."

She pulled back just enough to look into his eyes, her own still moist from the tears. "I had thought," she said slowly, "that you tolerated me only for our agreement."

"At first, perhaps I did," he admitted.

"When did it change?" she asked.

He thought for a moment, looking back over the past few weeks. "I'm not sure. All I know is that it *has* changed."

"Then I will cherish the change." She kissed him softly once more before turning away toward her waiting bath, disrobing quickly. "Please, sit and talk with me," she said as she stepped into the water.

"May I join you instead?" he heard himself ask, and she turned around in surprise, her eyes shining. She held out her arms to him in answer, the smile appearing once more. He really must see that she smiled more often.

Chapter XII

"Now comes the difficult part," Allaerion said softly as the Barrilian Mountains came into view again.

"What does that mean, exactly?" Aeron asked, his brow furrowing slightly.

"It means that we're going into the wastelands," Serana told him, "Daemon country." She'd been more than a little irritated with Allaerion and Seleine for not telling her sooner where the remaining five pieces of the Armor were located, but there was really nothing the knowledge would have gained her.

"Why would anyone hide pieces of the Armor there?" Aeron looked completely baffled. He really *hadn't* experienced much yet, even by Serana's estimation.

"It wasn't Daemon country at the time," Alier told him. "It was when their parents were young, before the Daemons overran Inferniesm. That area of the world was still green then."

"Perhaps this seems a bit silly, but why was the Armor scattered and hidden in the first place?" he asked.

Serana had thought of that too, but she'd already found her own answer. "If the Armor is so great a weapon against the Daemons," she finished for him, "why was it not simply used?" The others turned to look at her then. "The only rational conclusion I can think of is that the Armor was not created as a weapon against the Daemons at all."

"Unfortunately," Alier said softly, "you are correct."

"There was once a war between elementals," Seleine explained, "all four competing for dominance."

"That's absurd!" Aeron burst out. "Elementals cannot even *survive* without some members of another element. How else would children be born?"

"I never said it was logical," Seleine told him. "None of the races wanted to exterminate the others, though, only to dominate. Our parents, Allaerion's, Ignatius', Erathea's, and mine, were opposed to the war. They created the Armor to end it."

"With whom victorious?"

"No one," said Allaerion. "They intended to stop the fighting, nothing more."

"But something more did happen," Serana prompted.

"The Armor was too powerful," Alier told her. "It ended the war, certainly, but so long as it existed, there were those who would seek its power for their own ends. That is why it was separated and concealed. I hid three pieces myself."

"Which three?" asked Serana. "And why didn't you tell me before?"

"Both gauntlets and the greaves," Alier told her. "I didn't tell you because you didn't ask. You can't expect me to pass on a thousand years of knowledge in a few weeks."

"Sorry. It just seemed important."

"Well, it won't make them much easier to find, I'm afraid. The land is, shall we say, somewhat different now."

"Will your magic work there?" Serana asked suddenly.

"What are you talking about?" Aeron demanded. "Why wouldn't it?"

"Well, Daemons feed on life energy. That's the reason why the land is now barren, where once it was green; the Daemons literally sucked the life out of everything."

Alier and Seleine looked stricken, but Aeron was merely puzzled. "Why should that have any effect on our magic?" he asked.

"Elemental magic directs and manipulates the energies in the wielder's environment," Serana explained, wondering why he hadn't made the connection yet. "If the Daemons have drained it all away, what will you have to work with?"

"You're missing something," Aeron said calmly, smiling slightly. "Daemons may have drained the life energy, but they can't drain everything. Air, for example, moves to fill any vacuum. Air can't exist without its own inherent energy, and Daemons have difficulty siphoning away something so ephemeral in the first place. Water is similar, but to a lesser extent. The earth replenishes itself too, but more slowly still. The reason why there is no life in the wasteland is that there are no seeds to grow, and no animals to breed. Why should the Daemons bother trying to drain the elements directly, when there is an abundance of life just beyond the mountains?"

"You could be right," Serana conceded.

"What about deserts?" Seleine asked, shuddering at the thought of any place with so little water. "They don't regenerate."

"Deserts are natural," Aeron told her. "This land isn't made of sand; it's simply been sucked dry of life. A spark of life would probably grow and spread like wildfire, were the Daemons not there to drain it away again."

"So the land can be taken back," Alier breathed. "I would give much to see greenery there again."

"We all would," said Allaerion. "The five of us, though, even with Serana, lack sufficient power to drive out the Daemons completely. Even the last of the Seriani isn't strong enough."

"We must deal with what we *can* do," said Serana. "Right now, that means finding the remaining pieces of the Armor. Alier, who hid the other two pieces, and what were they? You said you had hidden three of them."

"Seleine's mother and your grandmother each hid one of the arm guards."

"Let's get going then," Serana said. "We have a good deal to do."

Crossing the mountains proved less difficult than Serana might have imagined, particularly since there were no humans accompanying them. Allaerion and Aeron rode a powerful draft of wind over the mountaintops, while Alier earth-melded through the rock itself. Serana finally caught Seleine's strange methods this time. The Ice Witch did something very similar to earth-melding, but with the snow on the mountain, rather than with the ground. Serana watched carefully, and then duplicated the feat, reaching the top of the mountain quickly and letting herself flow down with a conveniently placed little stream on the other side.

When Serana emerged with the others, Seleine gave her a warm hug. "I knew you could figure it out if I simply waited," she beamed.

Serana blushed at the praise, but her excitement over the accomplishment was short-lived. The land around them was dead. The stream flowed naturally enough, but there were no plants near it, or not near it, for that matter. Serana could *feel* the loss, the void where life should have been, like an emptiness that should never have existed, a wound in the land itself. The wind occasionally swirled the dust, but there was no life in it. There was no life anywhere.

"I had heard stories," Alier said slowly, "but I could never have imagined..."

"Nor could I," Allaerion whispered, his eyes burning as they gazed over the empty land.

Aeron merely stared, a single tear trickling down his cheek. Seleine wept openly.

Serana could stand no more of it. Gathering the energy around her, from the ground, the air, the stream, she summoned a tree to grow beside the river. Nothing happened. Of course, there were no seeds, no life at all to draw from, except perhaps...

Her jaw set, Serana gathered the energy together again, this time drawing from within herself as well, just as she would have done for the Arrow of Light.

"That won't work," Alier told her sadly, but the Earth Enchantress mistook her intent.

Rather than reaching into the earth to summon up a plant, Serana concentrated the life energy from herself into a single point, drawing the other elements into it. The tiny structure resisted holding in place, but Serana was relentless. She focused her entire being into the task, drawing the elements together, Earth, Water, Air, feeding that spark of Life from herself. Suddenly the energies snapped into place, and Serana fell to her knees. The task had been more draining than she'd anticipated.

"What did you do?" demanded Alier.

"Are you alright?" Seleine asked at the same time.

All four of the elementals began to talk at once, but Serana crawled forward a few paces, and picked up the thing she'd made, smiling proudly, if weakly. When the elementals saw it, they all fell silent.

"Impossible," Alier breathed.

"Serana," Allaerion gasped, "how..."

"She couldn't have," Aeron began, but he fell silent. She had indeed.

Serana held in her hand an acorn, ready to be planted. She took Alier's hand and pressed the seed into it. "Make it grow," she whispered. And then the world went black.

When she woke, Serana smiled broadly, for she was lying in the shade of a giant oak tree. "It worked," she breathed.

"It worked," agreed Seleine, who was knelt beside her. "Serana, how did you do it?" Serana began explaining how she'd woven the energies, but the Ice Witch stopped her. "That's not what I meant," she said softly. "Even the Serian of Music could not create much more than a seed, by himself."

"What do you mean?" Serana asked. "I've seen him create an entire horse."

"Not a real horse," Seleine told her. "He can create an animal that acts like a horse, but it neither eats nor sleeps, and it disappears the moment he stops concentrating on it. You have created a real seed that grew into a real tree. How did you do it?"

Serana thought for a moment before answering. "It seemed the right thing to do," she said finally. "I'm sorry, but I can't really be more descriptive than that. Making the seed simply *felt* right." She looked around quickly and frowned. "Why aren't there more?"

"More what?" asked Aeron from behind her.

"More plants, of course!" Serana exclaimed in exasperation. "It's a simple matter to make more plants once you already have one. How do you think I made the Dragon's Tears grow? There weren't Dragon's Tear seeds just lying about." Serana called a few gusts of wind to knock some acorns from the tree, then used Earth magic to accelerate their growth. "Alier, help me."

The Weaver of Earth nodded, and together, they made a small forest of trees around the stream. When they were finished, it was nearly nightfall, and they made camp beneath the cover of their work.

"As much as I am pleased to see life here again," Alier said softly after they'd built a fire from some of the wood, "I must admit that it will do no good. The Daemons will consume these trees just as they consumed the others. There will be nothing left, once they find this place."

"Won't there be?" Serana asked with a small smile. "Goodnight, Alier," she said softly, crawling into her tent. Her forest would last longer than the Earth Enchantress thought.

The next morning, Serana awoke with a smug smile. She'd set a spell in place to work overnight, and it had done its job very well. The sweet fragrance in the air told her that much. She crawled out of her tent to look around, and breathed in the scent deeply, feeling more than a little pleased with herself. The floor of her little forest was teaming with Dragon's Tears, even slightly beyond the tree line.

"Even Dragon's Tears die eventually," Alier said from behind her, "and Daemons can encourage even them to die sooner than they should."

"Not these Dragon's Tears," Serana told her. "I set a spell last night to make them grow, and it won't stop after I leave."

"Bah," the Earth Enchantress scoffed.

"Serana, that's impossible," Seleine said gently. "The magic may fade slowly, but it *will* fade, without you here to keep it going."

"I would think that you, at least, would see differently," Serana said, slightly put off. "Look at the stream, and tell me what you see."

Seleine looked, and stared. She blinked, looked at Serana, and looked back again. "But what is it *doing*?"

"Alier," Serana said sweetly, "would you look at the banks of the stream, please?" They would believe her yet, even if they had to be shown.

The Earth Enchantress moved to stand beside Seleine, and stared. "Where is it coming from?" she asked.

"The stream," answered Seleine slowly. "So *that's* what you've done!"

"Very clever work," Aeron said approvingly, emerging from the tent he shared with Allaerion. "I can't see most of it, of course, but I think I've deduced from the comments what you've done. I thought there was something different in the air this morning."

"What exactly *did* you do?" Allaerion asked, following Aeron.

"Do you want to explain," Serana asked Aeron, "or shall I?"

"It's your work," the Air Wizard grinned.

"I know that it's impossible to make a completely self-sustaining spell," Serana told them. "So, I improvised. The stream constantly brings fresh water here, and that means a steady supply of Water energy. It takes small amounts of Air and Earth to grow Dragon's Tears as well, as I finally figured out after our encounter with the Daemon Lords, so I simply tied the elements together."

"You did *what*?" Alier, Seleine, and Allaerion exclaimed in unison.

"She tied the threads of energy together," Aeron explained when Serana looked at him. "It's not really so difficult to imagine, when you consider that she is able to see *all* elemental energies." His voice took on a mildly lecturing tone. "We elementals tend to forget that just because we can't see any elements other than our own does not mean that the others are any less real or tangible. Our esteemed High Priestess has successfully woven the energies together, so that as the stream flows, small amounts of Water, Earth, and Air are drawn out into this place, growing more Dragon's Tears."

"The only way the Daemons could stop it would be to block or redirect the stream," Serana finished.

"Impressive," said Alier after a moment. "Most impressive."

"It's brilliant!" exclaimed Seleine, hugging Serana tightly. "You never cease to amaze, my friend."

"How did *you* know what she'd done?" Allaerion asked Aeron curiously.

"I'd been wondering if such a thing was possible for a few years now," the younger Air Wizard replied. "I simply lack the ability to test it for myself. It seemed the most logical explanation for what I was seeing, in conjunction with what the ladies had said."

"As much as I would love to stay and enjoy this a bit longer," Serana told them all, "I think we'd better get moving again. We've taken more time here than we should have already, though I do believe it was worth it."

"I believe one of my pieces was hidden near this stream," said Alier. "We should find it if we simply follow the water."

Chapter XIII

Lady Firehair healed the bruise on her face as she headed for the volcano. She'd never been very good at healing—it was considered, within her family, a ridiculously foolish use for magic—but she had managed to learn to heal the various bruises her uncle gave her when he was in a bad mood. He'd never hurt her seriously... Well, he had once, but that was for disobeying him. The bruises were manageable, at least, and the pain never lasted longer than the few hours she was detained at home.

She reached the volcano quickly, but she noticed immediately that a good deal of energy had been used here since her last visit. The dragon himself was gone; her senses couldn't locate him anywhere in the area. It was all very curious, but if she wanted to catch up to the party she'd been following, she didn't have time to investigate further.

In a few hours, she'd reached a flat-topped mountain where a group of Air Wizards lived. They were so far removed from the rest of the world that Lady Firehair decided to speak with them. They would never have heard of her, so they were more likely to treat her however she treated them.

As she approached the village, she noticed that fairly large amounts of magic were being used within it. Apparently, the Air Wizards were building something, though Lady Firehair had no idea what. Curiosity bubbled within her, but she tried to keep it in check. She didn't want to do anything that might offend the Air Wizards; it would be tragic if she had to hurt any of them in self-defense. Perhaps if she asked, one of them would tell her what all the magic was being used for.

It seemed that most of the villagers were at the place where all the magic was being used. That made sense, considering the amount of power Lady Firehair felt. She went on eagerly, agonizing over her slow progress. She really wasn't accustomed to walking without using magic to speed her. She sometimes wondered why elementals ever did it, particularly when they were headed for something interesting.

After a few moments that lasted an eternity, she finally arrived... and stopped, staring in wonder. It was a beautiful building, in progress, and the Air Wizards, along with a few Ice Witches, were building it *together*! Lady Firehair had never heard of elementals working together with those not of their own kind, but if she wasn't mistaken, the Sorceress she was following had also done a bit of the work.

"Are you alright?" a young Ice Witch asked, coming up beside her. "You're crying."

Lady Firehair put a hand to her cheek, surprised to find that it was indeed moist. "I'm fine, thank you," she said, smiling to put the Ice Witch at ease.

"My name is Illiese."

"I am Lady Firehair. This building is marvelous."

Illiese smiled. "It is, isn't it? It will be a school of magic, when it's finished. The Headmaster has gone on a journey, I'm afraid, but he's left me in charge until he returns."

"He went alone?"

"No, not alone. Alier the Spellweaver went with him, and the Sorceress High Priestess, another Air Wizard, and an Ice Witch as well. The High Priestess stood for me in my Rite of Oneness, while she was here." The young Ice Witch smiled at the memory. A Rite of Oneness must be something important, though Lady Firehair had no idea what it was.

"Thank you," said Lady Firehair, smiling again. "I suppose I should be going now."

"Must you go so soon?" Illiese asked. "You did only just arrive, you know, and you've told me nothing of yourself. Won't you stay long enough for a hot meal and a cup of tea? What's the matter now? You're crying again!"

Lady Firehair brushed away the tears again, and tried to smile, but for some reason it was difficult. She found that she couldn't speak either; her throat was inexplicably tight.

"Come with me," said Illiese firmly. "I'll get you that cup of tea, and you can tell me all about it."

Illiese led her to one of the various small houses lining the path she'd taken to the school under construction. She sat her guest at the table and put a kettle on the stove, then stopped. "Oh bother! The fire has gone out again. I always have the worst time trying to get it started again."

Lady Firehair could well understand that; an Ice Witch would naturally have difficulty with fire. She smiled, and the fire in the stove started up again instantly. She'd always been skilled with fire herself.

"How did you do that?" Illiese asked. "Fire Warlocks are all men! No, don't explain. You must be one of those human women who study elemental magic. In any case, I appreciate it; Fire has never been my forte, for obvious reasons."

In a few minutes, Lady Firehair had a hot cup of tea in front of her, and a vegetable broth, along with some sort of bread made with mountain herbs on its way. The tea was delicious, but Illiese waved away her compliments, saying that it was nothing. When the broth was cooking and the bread baking, she sat down across from her guest.

"So where are you from?" the Ice Witch asked.

Lady Firehair didn't want to lie, but her uncle had given her very strict orders about not telling strangers where they lived, so she decided to improvise. "Quite some distance from here. I live with my uncle and his servants."

"Do you usually travel alone?"

"As often as I can. My uncle's guards will not let me speak to anyone." Lady Firehair shuddered at the idea of traveling with guards.

Illiese hesitated for a moment before speaking. "Have the guards ever... well, hurt you?"

Lady Firehair blinked. Hurt her? The guards never even looked at her, if they could avoid it. "No," she said quickly.

"Why were you crying?" the Ice Witch asked.

"I'm sorry," Lady Firehair said softly. "I suppose I'm simply not used to... well, this."

"To what?" Illiese persisted.

"You've been very kind," Lady Firehair said, and was surprised to find that her voice caught. She blinked a few times quickly; her eyes were watering again, and she really thought she'd cried quite enough today.

"It's alright," Illiese said, taking her hand and squeezing gently. "Let's speak of other things."

They talked about the school of magic throughout the meal, and what it would look like when completed. Illiese seemed particularly fond of the absent Headmaster, though Lady Firehair didn't entirely understand how. She said he was a friend, but her cheeks turned rosy whenever she said his name, Aeron. Lady Firehair didn't ask about the relationship; she didn't know the customs here, and didn't want to risk offending someone who had shown her such kindness.

The broth and the bread were even better than the tea. Lady Firehair hadn't eaten a meal so delicious in years. When she said as much, though, Illiese merely laughed, saying that *she* was too kind!

After the meal was done, Lady Firehair said goodbye. Illiese offered to let her stay the night, but Lady Firehair wanted to catch the party she was chasing before her uncle summoned her again. As soon as she was out of sight from the village, she quickened her pace. She was actually closer to home now than when she'd stopped at the black dragon's volcano; if her uncle *did* summon her again, at least it wouldn't take long for her to start following the trail again.

The trail eventually led to the mountains, and past them. Lady Firehair had no difficulty crossing the mountains, of course; she'd done so on many occasions. What she found on the other side, however, made her stop and stare in wonder. There were *trees*! There hadn't been trees in this spot since Lady Firehair was a child, and even then they had been sparse, the dying remnants of whatever forests once had lived here. These trees made up a forest by themselves, all oaks. There were no birds singing in the trees; the work must have been recent. Perhaps the party had brought acorns with them across the mountains, and used magic to make them grow. If so, they must have brought many, and even that wouldn't explain the amount of magic that had been used here, and was still being used.

Lady Firehair walked among the trees, savoring the feel of Life here where once there had been none, but eventually the coughing drove her out. The entire forest floor was carpeted with those beautiful flowers that always made her cough. She wished they wouldn't do that; she only wanted to enjoy them, after all. Still, it was not the fault of the flowers. How could a flower help it that its fragrance gave a creature like herself a ticklish throat? Sighing wistfully, Lady Firehair continued following the trail.

***

Finding the greaves—or leg guards that strap on like plated pants, as Serana learned when she saw them; she hadn't wanted to ask for fear of sounding stupid—had been easy enough. The stone seal had been in plain view beside the streambed, which was, unfortunately, much drier this far from the mountains. Serana had wanted to collect some acorns and grow some more trees along the way, but Alier pointed out reluctantly that it would leave too clear a trail where they'd been. Even a Daemon could follow so obvious a trail, and one would do so even if it weren't looking for them; none of those creatures would pass up a free meal.

Now that the Armor was more than half complete, Serana was beginning to sense something of the power that lay dormant within it. She still couldn't put her finger on *how* it had been made without the entire suit to study, but she was beginning to understand why it had been hidden in the first place. When Alier had said that the Armor was too powerful, Serana had only begun to imagine what the Earth Enchantress had meant. If what she was now sensing about the Armor of the Elements proved correct, Allaerion would surpass even Serana's own power, so long as he wore it. She would still have the advantage—in theory, at least; the Armor wouldn't prevent her from absorbing the magic as it was thrown at her. Still, though, she would *not* want to face off with anyone who had a weapon so powerful.

Finding the next piece, the left arm guard Seleine's mother had hidden, proved no more difficult than the greaves had been. There was little to obstruct their view, so Allaerion, Aeron, and Serana could see clearly for miles, and Alier's earth-sense stretched still further, if she concentrated enough. Serana had not developed that particular talent nearly as far as the Weaver of Earth; she could still see further using Air magic than she could sense through the earth. Alier told her that it was partly due to the difficulty of her Rite of Oneness in Air, but Serana thought the Rite in Earth had been just as bad, even if the Earth Enchantress disagreed. "Aeron has a flair for the dramatic," Alier told her. "He also has more imagination than any two people I've ever met, other than yourself. Believe me; your Air Rite was the most difficult of all." Aeron wisely refused to comment.

The right arm guard was a little more tricky to locate, but only because it had been hidden by Serana's grandmother. Had Serana not been part of the party, they probably would never have found it. As it was, Serana merely searched for a part of herself again, as she'd done for the boots in the Air village. The arm guard was hidden cleverly in what appeared to be a solid rock, until Serana removed the spell creating the illusion. She really *would* have to remember that trick her grandmother seemed to have liked; it could be quite useful.

When they found the left gauntlet, Aeron began joking that the quest was too easy. Not a single Daemon had been sighted so far—not surprising, since the vast majority of them were attacking Rhanestone—and spirits were high amongst everyone in the party... everyone, that is, except Alier. The Earth Enchantress kept muttering to herself and frowning, but if asked, she would only say that it *was* too easy, and that there was no surer sign that trouble was on its way. Unfortunately, she couldn't have been more right.

When they located the final stone seal, everyone fell silent, staring. Serana could feel her excitement at the quest's end turn to ashes, and from her companion's faces, each of them felt exactly the same. The seal was already broken, and the gauntlet was gone.

"Who could have taken it?" Seleine asked finally.

"We have no way of knowing," Alier said grimly. "It was taken a long time ago, long enough that there is not even a trace to follow."

"Well," said Aeron slowly, "what next? Where do we go from here?" When no one spoke, he turned to Serana. "High Priestess?"

"How would I know?" Serana asked. "This was done before I was even born."

"Are you looking for the metal glove?" a new voice asked, a voice that froze them all where they stood. If unbroken innocence and terrible menace could somehow be distilled and woven into sound, the result would be what they heard. "I can tell you where it is, though I would not recommend that you try to get it."

The speaker was a young woman, by appearance, with lustrous red hair that fell in crimson waves down her back. She wore a dress no less ornate than Serana's gown, but red and black, as if woven from fire and obsidian. Her eyes were red as a Daemon's, but there was no cruelty in them. She was a walking paradox, to Serana's eyes, and her energy only increased the impossibility.

"She can't be an elemental," Aeron muttered to himself, as if trying to work out a puzzle. "Serana is the last Sorceress, and no human posses so much strength in Air. Besides, she's too... dark."

Dark... Yes, that was it. The woman held great strength in all four elements, just as Serana herself did, but it was difficult to tell, at first, as if the ability were hidden somehow, or very different in some way. Odder yet, the energy was entirely... well, dark. "Who are you?" asked Serana, resisting the urge to draw her sword. She felt a natural revulsion to the energy she was sensing, but there was no deception in the newcomer; she felt certain of that.

"I am Lady Firehair," the woman said, and again Serana was struck by the odd contradiction in the voice, at once kind and threatening.

"Where is the gauntlet?" asked Alier, the only member of the party who seemed completely over the puzzle of the stranger. Likely the Earth Enchantress was simply ignoring it in favor of more important matters, as the rest of them *should* be doing. Serana shook her head, to clear it, and tried to focus.

"My uncle has it," Lady Firehair replied. "I'm very sorry, but he found it some time ago, and he does not like to give up things he believes are his, even if they weren't his to begin with. I would advise you to simply let it go."

"We can't do that," said Allaerion. "Could you take us to your uncle? Perhaps we could buy it from him."

"No!" she cried, and for the first time, Serana saw fear in her eyes. No, "fear" was too moderate a term. What she saw was overwhelming, paralyzing terror. It was gone in an instant, replaced by a controlled nervousness, but it had been there.

"Why are you so afraid of your uncle?" Serana asked gently.

"He is not a kind person," Lady Firehair said, her inhuman voice trembling slightly. "Please, stay away from him. I don't want anything to happen to you."

Serana was baffled. Unless her senses were completely wrong, wrong as they had never been, this woman would be able to best the five of them combined. She would be stronger than even a Daemon Lord, stronger than anyone other than the Serian of Music himself. What could instill so much fear in such a creature?

"Please," said Seleine soothingly, stepping forward. "Calm yourself. We really do need that gauntlet. If you take us to your uncle, perhaps we can persuade him to give it to us. We could pay him handsomely."

Lady Firehair shook her head, her entire body trembling. "No, you don't understand. Please just accept that your metal glove, your... gauntlet, is gone."

Serana put her arms around the woman and hugged her gently, and to her surprise, Lady Firehair burst into tears, and only a few moments later did she slowly return the embrace. "Her uncle is obviously abusive," Serana told the others. "We can't make her take us to him. Let's camp here for tonight, and talk about this calmly."

Lady Firehair continued to cry in Serana's arms while the others were setting up camp. Only after they were finished did she finally begin to calm down. "Thank you," she whispered, her eyes still moist with tears as they found Serana's.

"For what?" Serana asked, confused. She really hadn't done anything.

Lady Firehair sniffled again, but she smiled. "No one has ever... held me, before."

It took several moments before Serana even understood what she was hearing. "What about your parents?" she asked, too shocked to think with any semblance of clarity.

"My parents?" Lady Firehair seemed almost unfamiliar with the concept. "I live with my uncle. My... parents... are dead. I never knew them."

"Your uncle has never given you a hug?" Serana felt foolish as soon as she'd asked; she already knew the answer to the question.

Rather than make matters worse, she decided to change directions. "Do you live alone with your uncle, or are there others?"

"There are others," she answered, "his servants. They do not look at me unless they must, and they certainly do not touch me." She shuddered as if the thought were repulsive. "Only my uncle touches me, and only when he is in a bad mood."

Serana hugged her again for good measure. "Well, you can come to me for a hug whenever you like," she said, smiling comfortingly. Lady Firehair returned the smile, but her eyes were growing moist again.

"Who is your uncle?" asked Alier, and Serana realized that the others had gathered around to listen.

Lady Firehair's red eyes looked from face to face before she spoke, and suddenly Serana didn't want her to answer. A ball of ice formed in the pit of her stomach even before the words left the other woman's lips. "His name is Lord Zironkell."

Chapter XIV

The elementals recoiled, all save Aeron. Alier and Seleine both began gathering their power, and Allaerion drew his sword.

"Stop it!" Serana commanded, and to her surprise, they listened. "She cannot help what she is any more than you or I. She has not threatened us, and I, for one, want to learn more." Turning back to Lady Firehair, Serana softened her tone. "I'd never heard of a female Daemon before." The other woman didn't appear frightened, though. Her eyes were filled first with sadness, then with wonder.

"You will not attack me?" she asked, as if the concept were new to her.

Alier directed her answer to Serana instead. "I have no wish to face you again, but I think you're making a mistake. This," she said, pointing to Lady Firehair, "is the enemy."

"But I'm not!" Lady Firehair cried. "I know my family members are not kind, but I cannot help what they do. I am a disgrace to them already for not doing the same."

"Daemons grow powerful by draining the life from others, and you are a Daemon Lord!" spat Seleine. "Explain how you could manage *that* if you did not do as they do."

Lady Firehair looked at the Ice Witch in confusion. "I was born this way," she said slowly.

"Born that way?" asked Aeron, the only elemental to have remained calm the entire time. "How is that possible?"

"I do not know. I am the only Daemon ever born who did not kill the host mother. It was a painless birth, I am told. That is why the others say that my shame to them began on the day I came into this world."

"Daemons are born as Scouts," Allaerion said flatly.

"I was not," insisted Lady Firehair. "I looked exactly like a human child, according to my uncle, except, of course, for my eyes."

106

"Could he have been lying?" Aeron asked. The young Air Wizard seemed far more intent on solving the puzzle than on his own emotional reaction. Serana admired him for that.

"My uncle lies about many things, but he cannot hide the truth from me. I see his lies even when he blends truth with them. It is one of my gifts."

"Your gifts?" prompted Serana.

"I was born with all the power of a Daemon Lord," said Lady Firehair, lowering her eyes as if ashamed. "My powers have grown as I grew, even though I did not feed on other creatures. They expanded beyond what a Daemon can do, reaching into the elemental realms. My uncle told me that it was yet another proof that I am a perversion of my kind, a shame to the family. The others will not even look at me unless they must."

"Most likely they're afraid," said Serana softly.

"If you are so powerful as that," said Aeron, "are you not also stronger than your uncle?"

Lady Firehair's eyes widened with fear. "No one is stronger than my uncle!" she cried, trembling slightly.

"How do you know this?" the Air Wizard persisted. "Have you measured his strength against yours recently."

"He would kill me if I did such a thing! He has told me so many times."

It made perfect sense. Zironkell controlled his niece through deception without directly lying. He was no doubt aware that she could see through direct lies, and made adjustments accordingly. He probably feared Lady Firehair just as the others did, yet she was completely unaware. The real question was why he would have kept alive a creature stronger than himself; there would always be the danger that she might break away, stop taking his orders. Perhaps he truly was arrogant enough to believe he could keep her beneath his heel forever. After all, he'd done so all her life.

"I must go," Lady Firehair said suddenly. "My uncle is summoning me."

"Forget him," said Serana. "Come with us instead. Fight against him!"

"Please, never ask that of me!" Lady Firehair's eyes were wide with fear. "I am sorry, but I cannot." Hesitating a moment, she awkwardly embraced Serana in a gentle hug. "Thank you for your kindness," she whispered, and then she was gone. She didn't disappear as the Serian of Music so often did, but she moved so quickly that even Serana's senses could not follow her.

***

Lady Firehair hurried home, reaching her room well before her uncle's servants came to fetch her. She could still feel the Sorceress' arms around her. She really had to stop thinking about it; she didn't want to be found crying, or her uncle would wonder what had happened. He would learn that she'd disobeyed him again, and she would be destroyed. Still, it had felt so *good* to be held. Lady Firehair wondered what it would be like if the man who made the music held her. For some reason, her cheeks felt hot as soon as the thought crossed her mind.

"Your uncle summons you," rasped Rakishel from outside her door. He wouldn't enter unless she didn't come out, and he wouldn't look at her; he never did.

Lady Firehair opened the door and followed the Daemon Lord to her uncle. Why she needed an escort was beyond her; none of the others would look at her either, and she knew the way quite well. Still, her uncle's command was law, and there was nothing she could do about it.

She only gave him half her attention during the session this time, though he didn't seem to realize it. The other half was focused on the metal glove—the gauntlet—that he kept on a shelf. He'd never spoken of it in her hearing, and Lady Firehair wondered why it was so important to the Sorceress, to Serana, but she knew in her heart that it didn't matter.

When her uncle was finished with her, she went back to her room, and stayed there for a time, deep in thought. Hours went by, but she didn't notice. Her thoughts kept straying to the feel of being held, and the person who had let her feel it for the first time. Lady Firehair had to do something to repay such kindness, whatever the cost. She knew she had reached a decision long before she actually admitted it. She tried to find another way, but there really wasn't one. Perhaps she could make her uncle proud of her for the first time, yet still help Serana. It was worth trying, at the least.

***

Reilena was to meet a new vampire today, one who had been in closer contact with humans than any other in a long time. She expected it would be Troveck, Morganna's consort, since he had *been* a human more recently than any other vampire at Rhanestone. She'd seen him once or twice, but never spoken with him. As she approached Morganna's audience room—that was what it was being called now, the large room where Reilena had met her leader—she began to feel nervous. This vampire she was to meet intended to remind her of her past, to help her remember. It was a frightening prospect, as frightening as it was exciting.

When she reached the chamber, though, Troveck was nowhere in sight. Stranger still, there was a human sitting near Morganna's desk, speaking with her while holding the hand of a vampire woman! Reilena had never seen any human actually touch a vampire willingly, but this man seemed to be perfectly content.

"Ah, Reilena!" said Morganna, rising. "Thank you for coming. This is Alloria." She indicated the vampire holding the human's hand. "And this," she said, placing a hand on the human's shoulder, "is Lord Alexander. Alloria is *yamin'sai* to him. It means…"

"I know what it means," said Reilena, surprising herself as much as Morganna. "I don't know how I know, but I do."

"Any memory that resurfaces is one less that is still lost," Morganna told her. "I want you to speak with Lord Alexander and Alloria. Perhaps they might help you to recall more of your past." She gave Reilena an encouraging smile before moving away.

Reilena took a seat beside the couple—slave or not, Alloria appeared perfectly happy with this Lord Alexander; they were a couple if Reilena had ever seen one. Watching them, she felt a twinge of… something, like the memory of a memory, gone before she could even try to grasp it.

"We are with your own people, Alloria," Lord Alexander said softly. "Speak freely here, please."

The beautiful vampire nodded, then turned her attention to Reilena. "How long had you been one of us, before you came here?" she asked.

"Only a week," Reilena replied. That much, at least, she was sure of. "It was a very short time, compared with the seven I've been here, yet I think it was the longest week of my life.

"Do you remember whom you lived with before?" asked Lord Alexander.

"My father and two brothers," she told him. "There was another man as well, but I don't recall him clearly. My father was a farmer, I think."

"You aren't sure?" he asked.

"No, but I remember being outdoors a great deal. I believe it was a farm I was on."

Alloria nodded. "It would fit, considering the clothing Morganna tells me you were wearing. Do you remember anything at all about this mysterious fourth man?" Perhaps unconsciously, her hand tightened in Lord Alexander's.

Watching their hands together, Reilena suddenly recalled holding the fourth man's hand that way. She couldn't see his face, but his hands were strong; she was sure of that. "Perhaps he was a lover," she said finally. "I remember he had strong hands, and I remember holding them, the way the two of you are holding hands now."

Suddenly, a page burst into the room. "Lord Alexander," he said, looking around nervously, "a messenger has just arrived from your home in the south. He requests to speak with you at your earliest convenience. He claims that it is very important, something about an attack on your elder brother's estate."

Lord Alexander was on his feet instantly, with Alloria beside him. "Forgive me," he said to Reilena, "but I fear we must continue our discussion another time." He went quickly to the page, asking to be taken to the messenger. Alloria followed him out.

"They will return one day soon," said Morganna as she came up behind Reilena, patting her shoulder gently. "We will solve the mystery of your past yet."

Reilena thanked her, and then went out for a walk in the courtyard. She wanted to clear her mind, to think. Morganna had said just yesterday that Reilena would soon be ready to start accompanying the parties that spied on the Daemons, but it would be some time before she was prepared to do any fighting. When she reached the courtyard, she noticed that Blackfang, the black dragon, was gone. He often went out to hunt, since the Guardian of Mist was expecting, and could not fly. Reilena wondered how long it would be before the baby dragon was born; she'd always assumed before that dragons laid eggs.

"You could speak with me, you know," said an inhuman voice, reverberating slightly in the air. It took Reilena a few moments to realize that the speaker was the Guardian herself. "You needn't be afraid. Ask your questions, and I will do my best to answer them."

"How do you know I have questions?" Reilena asked.

"It is written on your face," the Guardian told her.

"I was wondering about your child. I'd thought that dragons laid eggs."

"I understand that some did," the crystal dragon said softly. "My kind always gave live birth, though, to my knowledge. We were always slightly different from the others. I sense, however, that your real questions have nothing to do with dragons."

"I was thinking about my past," said Reilena. "I cannot recall very much, I'm afraid, from before I was a vampire."

"You were turned improperly, it seems," said the Guardian gravely. "The shock to your mind was too great. Your memories will return in time, when your mind has accepted all that has happened."

"It took me long enough to realize that vampires were not as evil as Daemons," Reilena admitted.

"But you did realize it," the Guardian pointed out. "As a vampire, you should have a very long life ahead of you. If there are some things that take you a great deal of time to learn, remember that you have the time to spend on them. There is no reason for you to hurry or rush through your life.

"I suppose you're right, but it does not make the waiting any easier."

"Waiting is rarely easy," agreed the dragon, "but not waiting can be harder still."

"Thank you," said Reilena. She turned to go, and nearly ran into Ella. Reilena was so surprised that she nearly jumped out of her skin. "How did you sneak up on me like that? I didn't even sense you!"

The apprentice grinned. "The spell worked then. Rillian showed me how to hide my magical abilities, but I've been toying with the technique, trying to hide my natural energies as well. It seems I finally got it right."

"What are you doing out here?" asked Reilena, still trying to settle her breathing.

"I've been looking for you. The elven priests would like to speak with you; they're not sure that they can help with your memories, but they won't know for certain unless they have a look at you."

"I wish you luck," said the Guardian as they headed away.

Ella led Reilena to a room on the west wing of the Keep, where nine elves in white robes sat cross-legged on the floor. Eight of them were in a circle around the ninth, an elf who must be very old indeed, for his hair was tinged with grey. There were lines drawn in some sort of gold paint, extending from where the center figure sat to each of the others. There were always nine priests on duty at any given time, according to Ella, but there were many more in the order.

At Ella's instruction, Reilena kept silent, waiting to speak until spoken to. She noticed almost immediately that the strange kinship she'd felt with Ella was present with these priests as well, though to a slightly lesser extent. She made a mental note to ask Ella about it after they left.

"You are Reilena," the elf in the center said after a few moments. "Thank you, Ella, for bringing her to us."

Ella bowed respectfully, but made no other response.

"Please, come sit here," said the elf to Reilena as he rose from his spot, moving outside the circle. Reilena obeyed, feeling slightly uncomfortable, but certain that they meant her no harm. It just seemed strange to be taking the spot where the eldest had been sitting.

When she was seated, the eight elves around her raised their hands, and Reilena felt a curious sensation, as if the room were suddenly charged.

"Try to relax," said the eldest, taking a seat just outside the circle. "Nothing we do here should harm you in any way."

Reilena glanced at Ella, but the apprentice magician had her eyes on the eight elves in the circle, studying them as if she could see something happening that Reilena was unaware of.

After a few moments, Reilena was beginning to think nothing would happen. She didn't feel any differently from what she had before. It was then, however, that the eldest priest began to question her.

"Where were you, when you were attacked?" he asked.

"I was in the forest outside my home," she answered automatically. She didn't recall the scene clearly, but somehow she knew the words were correct.

"Why were you in the forest?" the priest continued.

"I was meeting my lover, whom my father disapproved of," she heard herself say. Perhaps the man *had* been a lover, but Reilena couldn't remember his face, however she tried.

"Was he there to meet you?"

"Yes. We'd had a wonderful time together."

"Then you were on your way home?"

"Yes." Reilena didn't know where she was coming up with these answers, but all of them felt right.

"Can you describe your attacker?" continued the priest.

"No. He was a vampire, but I could not see his face clearly." Well, at least that was one thing she'd already known.

"Were you in perfect harmony with your lover?" That was a strange question. Why would she not be, if she'd just finished having a wonderful time with him?

"No," she answered, to her own surprise. "He wanted me to run away with him, but I refused."

"Was he angry?"

"No. He said that he would wait as long as I needed him to."

"What did your lover look like?"

Reilena didn't answer. It was strange, since she'd answered every other question immediately.

"Had you ever seen his face?" asked the priest calmly. He was her lover! How could she not have seen his face?

"No," she heard herself say. "He was always hooded when we met, and it was always dark."

"What do you know about him, physically?"

"He had very strong hands," said Reilena, remembering the image of Lord Alexander and Aurora. "He was always very gentle with me, though."

"Did you plan to run away with him, in time?" That was a silly question. Of *course* she'd planned to run away with him, if she'd loved him so much.

"No," she heard herself say, and for a moment, she was too stunned to think clearly.

"Why did you continue meeting with him?"

"He was romantic and mysterious, and he had a beautiful voice," Reilena said wistfully. She wondered how her voice could be so wistful when she herself felt so terribly confused. "I only wanted him until I found someone more practical to marry."

"That's enough for now," the priest said, and Reilena leapt out of the circle, trembling. How could she have done such a thing?

"It couldn't have been true," she said weakly.

"It's alright, Reilena," said Ella softly, putting a comforting arm around her.

"What kind of a person was I?" Reilena whispered.

"Probably the confused kind, just as you are now," answered Ella. "Don't judge yourself yet; you still have a great deal to learn."

"Wise words," said the priest, coming up behind Reilena. "Do not embrace conclusions until you have all the facts. I hope you will return again another day, that we may continue."

Reilena nodded and thanked the priest as Ella led her away. She hoped that the trembling wouldn't last too long.

Chapter XV

Lord Alexander hurried through the halls, Alloria at his heels. His brother's estate was far to the south, well away from Daemon country. An attack almost surely meant human raiders. The problem was that human raiders would not have given Duncan cause to send word; he was well protected from that sort of thing, with a garrison full of armed guards that were well accustomed to dealing with any ruffians in the area.

It seemed an eternity before he finally reached the messenger, though it was probably only minutes. The man was in one of Rhanestone's various guest rooms, still catching his breath from the hard ride. "My lord," he said, standing to attention when Alexander came into the room.

"Do sit down," Alexander told him. "You're exhausted." The messenger complied, of course, but he seemed more than a little unsure of himself. Duncan was a good deal stricter than Alexander about the behavior of his servants and guards. "Now then, tell me what has happened."

Only then did the messenger seem to notice Alloria. He drew his sword and tried to stab her, but Alexander was quicker, loosing his own sword from its sheath and blocking easily. He may not compare with the swordsmen at Rhanestone, but he was quite skilled compared with the common southern soldiers. "Stop it, man!" he shouted. "Do you really wish to harm my *yamin'sai*?"

The guard hastily put away his weapon, but he continued to dart uncomfortable looks at the vampire woman.

"Would it be easier if I left?" Alloria asked Alexander.

"No, please stay." Alexander hadn't begun his work for peace between vampires and humans willingly, but now that he *had* begun it, he certainly wasn't going to do it half-heartedly, and particularly not for the sake of an ignorant messenger from the south. Besides, she had a wonderful gift for noticing details that he might have missed, and drawing insightful conclusions from them. He wanted her help for this. "She is not only my *yamin'sai*," he told the man, "but also my friend. You may speak freely in front of her, for I would tell her everything you said anyway." Alloria appeared shocked to the core, but she masked it quickly, directing her attention to the messenger.

The man obviously wasn't pleased, but he nodded immediately. Alexander supposed there were a few advantages to Duncan's strictness. "It took me two months to ride here, but I left right after it happened. Lord Duncan's youngest child, his only daughter, was kidnapped."

Alexander had met Duncan's two sons, but never his daughter. There had never been time to visit his elder brother's estate properly, and the girl was something of a spitfire, always out riding and learning weaponry from the guards. Duncan had hoped that marrying her off might calm her down a bit, but the last Alexander had heard, no nobleman was willing to take a wife so wild, when so many more docile Ladies were available. "Was there any ransom demanded?" Alexander asked.

"Not before I was sent," the messenger replied. "Lord Duncan still did not know who was responsible, but he's afraid she might have been wounded. The hounds found a spot of blood in the forest not far from the estate." The man smiled slightly. "Myself, I think it more likely that she wounded the kidnapper. I've seen her spar, my lord, and I wouldn't want to duel her."

"Does Duncan request my presence to aid in the investigation?" Alexander was considered the best tracker and investigator in the south, and a skilled negotiator as well. Still, after two months—four, by the time he arrived—there was little hope he could do much.

"That he does, my lord. I know it's a long ride, and with Rhanestone under attack, it isn't the best time, but it's your niece, my lord. I know you've never met her, but she is blood."

Alexander put a calming hand on the man's shoulder. "I will come. You stay here for a few days and rest. I should be there by the time you return." He immediately stood and left the room, calling for a page to ready his horse. Perhaps he would not be able to save his niece, but at least he could finally feel as if he were doing *something*.

"Alexander," Alloria hissed urgently in his ear, "I pray that you do not forget your obligation to my people, in this family crisis."

"I haven't forgotten," he told her, not breaking stride as he headed to his room to pack. "In fact, I think I'll be doing a better job in the course of the investigation. If you think the prejudice here is bad, you really must visit the south. I want you to accompany me, but keep on guard. Even those who understand the nature of our relationship may try to kill you, but none would do it openly in my presence. Do you understand?"

"I understand, my lord." Perhaps she did, but he was more than a little nervous about bringing her along. He knew she wouldn't hear of being left behind, though, and besides, he didn't want to think about being apart from her for so long.

"Together, you and I may be able to show the ignorant southerners—which I was one of, not long ago—that nonhumans are quite frequently at least as honorable as humans." He paused for a moment, thinking. "In all truth, that doesn't say a great deal. Regardless, we must show them that all individuals must be judged by their actions, not by their race. If peace is to be achieved between vampires and humans, then it must be achieved everywhere." Another thought occurred to him then. "Alloria, why did you behave as you did back there?"

"What do you mean, my lord?" she asked.

"You made no move to defend yourself when the messenger attacked you."

"It was not my place," Alloria told him. "I am your slave. Should a servant of yours wish me dead, I must accept that it may be your will."

"That is nonsense, and you know it," snapped Alexander, rounding on her. "Just to be sure I've covered every angle in that infernally logical mind of yours, I command you to listen to me now. It is my will that you defend your own life and wellbeing with the same vigor and tenacity with which you would defend mine. When you die, you die of old age."

"That is impossible, my lord," she said, confused. "Vampires do not age."

"I know," he told her pointedly, moving away to his rooms again.

***

Lady Firehair answered the summons immediately, as she always did. She hadn't bothered leaving the mountain this time; she still needed more time to think. Rakishel led her to her uncle's chamber, as usual, but when she arrived, she immediately noticed a difference in her uncle's countenance. She had expected him to be in a particularly good mood, but he was quite the opposite.

"I have a task for you," he told her. "One of the other Daemon Lords has stolen something of mine, and I want you to kill him and bring it back."

"But my lord," she said, confused, "I had thought you'd said stealing was honorable."

His backhand blow caught her in the jaw, and sent her sprawling. "Niece, you are as stupid as you are shameful. It is honorable to steal from *other* races, not from Daemons."

"I do not understand," she said meekly as she picked herself up from the stone floor. "Do you not steal from other Daemons, if they have something you want?"

"I am their lord!" he shouted. "All that they have is mine already!"

"Yes, my lord," she said, lowering her eyes. "What has been stolen, that I may know what to return to you?"

"A gauntlet," he told her. "A glove of metal."

Lady Firehair nodded. "I will find the thief, my lord," she said.

"And kill him," her uncle spat. "Now go."

Lady Firehair obeyed, heading back to her room. Her uncle had finally tired of her, and wanted her dead. Everyone knew that nothing could kill a Daemon Lord other than the hated Seriani, the creatures who had driven her people underground and tried to destroy them. That was why she'd been assigned to kill the last of the Seriani in the first place, so that he would kill her instead. She hadn't bothered looking for him yet; her uncle believed her incompetent enough that he wouldn't be surprised if she couldn't find the creature. Now, though, things had become more difficult. A Daemon Lord was easy to find, and one of them would surely attack her at the *suggestion* that they had stolen from her uncle, and if she did not suggest it, Lord Zironkell would know she had neglected his orders. Her only advantage was that she already knew who had taken the gauntlet. She had.

***

Lord Zironkell paced back and forth across his chamber after he'd sent the weapon away. She was becoming more difficult the more time that went by. He now had to use all his strength when he struck her, to create even a bruise that wouldn't last a day. His magic would do more, certainly, but no other Daemon could withstand even his physical strength. If she turned on him... No, that would never happen. She was docile, weak... Her lineage assured that. Fortunately, he had taken the best from the line, and left the weakness behind. He would rule, and she would follow. It would always be that way, or he would kill her. She would not even fight back.

It was likely that the stupid creature would never find the fool who had stolen the gauntlet if not for the simplicity of the task. Only a Daemon Lord could have entered the chamber without Zironkell's permission, and only three Daemon Lords remained, other than Zironkell himself; surely even she could question them one by one, and kill the one responsible. After that, it would be up to Zironkell to arrange a meeting between her and the hated Serian, a meeting that would mean Zironkell's unquestioned dominance over this world. If only she were not too stupid to find the Serian for herself... but no matter. Zironkell had lured the creature once; he could do it again.

The weapon was not Lord Zironkell's only plan, of course. He was not so narrow of thought as his father had been. Even should the weapon fail, he would dominate. He had wondered for some time now if she were shamming; even the other Daemon Lords were not so completely idiotic as she seemed. It really made no difference, though. If her stupidity was false, let her think herself clever. His most important work had nothing to do with her, and little to do with the foolish humans in their play-castle; that was only a diversion, and it required less than a third of his army. He smiled as he considered it, but there was still much to do before his plan could be completed. In the mean time, there were other, more immediate matters to attend to. For some time now, Zironkell had been planning to father a child of his own, but he lacked an appropriate host for the breeding. A Daemon drains the energy from its host as it grows within her, and Zironkell needed a host powerful enough to create a Daemon the likes of which the world had never seen, one that would be his to control… or to drain, if he saw fit. He'd considered using his niece, but her stupidity, if genuine, might be transferred to the offspring. He needed another. He needed the Sorceress.

"Uncle?"

Zironkell turned, anger boiling inside him that she had entered without his permission. "What do you want?" he demanded.

"I believe I know who took your gauntlet," she said nervously. Good. Her fear meant that she was nowhere near rebelling. She came because she believed he would wish it.

"Then why have you not killed him?" asked Zironkell, his voice dangerously low.

"I believe I can use him to destroy the Serian," she replied.

Zironkell was intrigued. "Go on," he commanded.

"I overheard him talking to one of the breeders when he took her. He said the Serian had promised him enough energy to surpass even you, in exchange for the gauntlet."

Had the Serian, Zironkell's nemesis, finally learned to use greed to his advantage? It seemed out of character, but it was possible. The last of the Seriani had changed much since his kindred had died, and more importantly, Zironkell's niece had no knowledge of the creature's nature. She would have no reason to lie, and no grounds on which to base such a lie.

"I intend to catch them both when they make the exchange, and destroy them," she went on, her eyes glowing red with bloodlust. Perhaps there was hope for her yet. "Then I can bring the gauntlet back to you. I ask only that you do not summon me until I have it. It will take some time."

"Go then," he ordered. "Do not return without the gauntlet."

***

It had been three days, and still they had no answers. Serana had focused most of her energy on practicing the sword with Allaerion and the staff with Alier. The party had made camp back at the small forest by the stream. An hour of each day was spent discussing the problem, but not even Aeron had come up with any sort of feasible solution. If the gauntlet were in the hands of Zironkell himself, there was little chance that the five of them combined could take it away. They'd considered sneaking into the Daemons' mountain, but it was unlikely that they could do so undetected, and even together, they would be no match for two Daemon Lords together, much less more.

Whenever she wasn't practicing the staff or the sword, Serana studied the nearly complete Armor of the Elements. It revealed little, even so nearly complete, but each grain of knowledge was pure gold to Serana. If only she could learn a little more, she might be able to make a gauntlet that would suffice. She was studying the pieces in the early morning light when Lady Firehair appeared again.

"I need your help," she said without preamble.

"What do you need?" asked Serana.

"I have the gauntlet you need," Lady Firehair said, withdrawing it from her cloak, "but I need you to do something for me before I give it to you."

"Name it," Serana told her. "We must have that gauntlet."

"I need you to kill a Daemon Lord."

"Couldn't you do that yourself?" asked Aeron, coming up behind Serana. The young Air Wizard often rose as early as Serana did.

Lady Firehair shook her head, her eyes widening in fear. "I cannot. I need you to do it for me. You have killed two already. A third should not trouble you overmuch."

"How do you know that I killed two?" asked Serana. She didn't believe for a moment that Lady Firehair had learned it over a pleasant chat at home.

"I was there," she said softly, her red eyes lowering. "It was I who freed your mind enough to let you grow the flowers. I would have done more, but they would have detected me."

"I wondered if it might have been you," said Serana, smiling. Since meeting Lady Firehair, Serana had been thinking back to that day when she'd almost been taken. She was glad to finally have one mystery solved, at least. "What Daemon Lord must we kill?"

"Raveshik," the other woman replied. "He was one of the two sent to attack the human fortress, but he has gone off on his own to gather power. My uncle believes that he is the one who stole the gauntlet, so I cannot give it to you until he is dead."

"Where is he?" Serana asked.

"He has been lurking far to the south, the last I saw of him, tormenting a human noble there in secret."

"How can I find you when he is dead?"

"I will find you," Lady Firehair told her, and then she was gone before Serana could say another word.

Chapter XVI

The ride south began well. Alexander had expected the grey mare he'd purchased to grow skittish when Alloria approached it, but quite the opposite was true. The horse nuzzled her hand when she came near, and stood obediently while the vampire woman leapt nimbly into the saddle.

Alexander's own mount, a white gelding he'd named Lightning, pranced as soon as Alexander was on his back. He'd been locked in the stables too long, and was more than a little restless. Alexander calmed him with a firm and steady hand. He was an accomplished rider, even here at Rhanestone.

The two of them traveled alone—well, alone except for Alon, who trotted along happily beside the horses. Alexander had brought one hundred soldiers as guards when he'd come to Rhanestone, but he was leaving them all behind. The Keep needed soldiers more than he did. It would be strange, going back to country where the only real enemies were other humans. The people at Rhanestone had a tendency to trust anything human, since every human needed to combine forces in order to survive. The southern nations had always been another matter entirely. Many of the people in the south didn't even *believe* in Daemons, much less elves or elementals. Many of them *did* believe in vampires, though; there was no creature more feared and hated in all the Southern Nations. Fortunately, the people were nearly as ignorant as they were hateful, when it came to vampires. Many city gates required that people enter in broad daylight, and with their hoods drawn back, to ensure that they were human. Alloria could quite easily pass most of the "vampire tests" that were scattered across the lands.

"Tell me something of your home," said Alloria as they rode.

"I've been telling you about little else since we set out," Alexander pointed out.

"You've told me how dangerous a place it is for me," she said with a shrug. "You've told me almost nothing about the customs or the people, beyond what they do to vampires."

"I suppose you're right," he admitted. "I'm just worried about you. I want you with me, but I don't want you hurt."

She smiled, and Alexander's heart skipped a beat. It was strange that she could do that to him even more now than before. He'd always been told that such things fade quickly after a man has known a woman. Perhaps the men who had told him had never really been in love.

"What is it, Alexander?" Alloria asked, her brow knitting in concern.

"Nothing," Alexander lied, and quickly schooled his face to smoothness. Was he in love... with a vampire? He cared for her, certainly, and he liked her company. Was that what being in love meant? Surely there was more to it.

"If nothing is wrong, then I would very much like to hear about your home, outside their hatred for my kind," she said, watching him intently.

It was sometimes difficult to speak when her eyes were on his. He was mesmerized by her beauty—what man *wouldn't* be?—but it was more than that. During the past few weeks, he had slowly come to realize that she genuinely cared for him. It was more than the obedience a servant gave her master, more than a concern for the wellbeing of her people. For reasons he could not begin to understand, Alloria loved him. She had loved him long before he began to love her in return.

"Alexander?"

With a start, he came out of his musings. "Forgive me. My mind wondered." He cleared his throat. "Well, several attitudes in the southern nations are different from those here in the north. When all one's enemies are human, things tend to be a bit different."

"Human and vampire," Alloria corrected.

"As to that, you must understand that only about two thirds of the population believes that vampires even exist, and at least three quarters of those have never actually seen one."

"So only one sixth of the people have ever seen a vampire?" she asked, and he stared. "My people are not ignorant savages," she told him, obviously somewhat offended. "We do study mathematics and science, as well as literature and other arts."

"Of course you do," said Alexander soothingly. He'd never really thought about it, truthfully. "I suppose that there are some southern mindsets that will never entirely leave me, but perhaps with your help, I can overcome the ones that are wrong."

She smiled again and he found himself memorizing her features, so that he could close his eyes and see her smile whenever he wished. "If so few of your people have ever seen a vampire," she said, "how is it that so many hate us?"

"Humans need not see a thing to hate it," Alexander told her, and felt suddenly ashamed. He forced himself to go on, though; she should understand the truth. "We often believe the worst of what we hear, and take it as fact, and then are reluctant to change our minds even in the face of hard evidence."

"Why would anyone behave that way?" she asked, genuinely confused. "It is not logical."

"Humans are often not logical," he explained. "We are quick to fear what we do not understand, and quick to hate what we fear."

"Perhaps because your lives are so short, you carry a disproportionate fear of death, and see threat in everything not dominated," she suggested.

"Perhaps," he agreed. "We may never know for certain. All I do know is that we must be careful of other humans in the south. Many of them will react as that messenger did. I would suggest that, for your own safety, you use a different cloak, and dress as a human girl would."

"If I disguise myself," she said calmly, "then how will you use our relationship to promote peace between our peoples? If humans are so quick to mistrust, then will they not believe the deception had some ill intent?"

She was logical to the end. He hated it, but he knew that she was right. There was really no way around it. Suddenly, he wished that he'd brought just a few of the guards along with them.

"I will keep watch," Alloria told him. "I will obey your orders from before, to protect myself; if it lies within my power, I will not be harmed unless such harm is required to keep you safe."

"No," Alexander told her. "Defend yourself first, and me second. Your life is to be your first priority."

"A *yamin'sai* must defend her master before herself," Alloria told him.

"A *yamin'sai* must obey her master," he said pointedly, "and I order you to protect yourself first, and me second."

"I had thought we were to be equals in private," she said, lowering her eyes. "If I was mistaken…"

"Alloria, stop it!" he cried, and she fell silent, her eyes downcast. "Look at me, please." She obeyed wordlessly. "I do want us to be equals in private, but your life is more important to me than my own."

"Then you must realize," she said softly, "that yours is more important to me than mine."

"We will defend each other, then," he said finally, and she nodded, smiling again.

"Alon is getting tired," she said suddenly, and before he could blink, she had leapt down from the mare's back, scooped up the lamb, and jumped onto the saddle again. "I will carry him for a time." The little lamb nuzzled her shoulder; he'd taken quite a liking to her. Alexander found it odd that the creature could be so fond of the predator who used it for food, but Alloria claimed that Alon had no idea he'd ever given blood. He only knew that Alloria fed him, took him outside, and played with him.

It was difficult for Alexander not to smile as he watched the two. He'd have thought that since vampires have no children, they would naturally lack the nurturing instinct that many women seemed to display, but Alloria was as tender with the lamb as any mother Alexander had ever seen with a child.

"Thank you for giving Alon to me," Alloria said softly, her eyes still on the lamb, which was going to sleep in her arms, not at all bothered by the motion of the horse.

"I couldn't very well promote peace by letting you starve," Alexander told her. Alloria simply smiled again. He truly did love her smile.

***

The Serian of Music appeared on the mountaintop, wings outstretched, surveying the curiosity below. In the wastelands that the Daemons took over long ago, there was a small forest beside the stream that ran down from this mountain, a forest of oak trees with a carpet of Dragon's Tears beneath. None of these things—the flowers, the fact that every tree was an oak, or even the forest's existence— were what confused him, strange as they were. What confused him were the patterns of energy he read within the forest.

He had come across the forest by chance, while following the sporadic trail. He'd been trying to locate the strange woman who had shown him such compassion when he had cried, the woman with red eyes set in a face that made him tremble even to remember it. He knew that face better than he knew his own, and he could not bring himself to harm the one who wore it, even if the fate of all Life depended upon her death. Even so, there might still be hope. Perhaps, if he found her, he could simply convince her never to come near the Sorceress. She was a creature of compassion, not of violence, but she might still kill Serana unintentionally, if the two ever met; the Guardian's prophecy foretold it. She would listen… she must.

The Serian transported himself down to the trees, hoping to better understand what he was seeing. It didn't help. Oh, he understood how it worked, of course. The Water energy from the stream was being siphoned off, in small amounts, and combined with Earth and Air, to feed the trees and to grow Dragon's Tears. What he didn't understand was how it had come to be. The only logical explanation was Serana, but her skill must have grown considerably since last he saw her, if she were responsible for what he was seeing. Even the spell that drew energy from the stream, though, was not as curious as the residual energy that he saw, faint even to his eyes. The forest was grown with magic, of course, but the acorns were not brought across the mountain.

They were grown here, all but one of them. That one had been *created* here! Even the Serian himself would have been sorely taxed to create a seed from nothing. Three of his kind could create nearly anything they wanted, and nine an entire world, as they had done with this one... but alone, he was quite limited in creating self-sustaining life. Who, then, could have done it?

Curious as the mystery was, it was not finding Lady Firehair. She had been here at some point; he could still read her energy, but she had disappeared again, somewhere on the southern side of the mountains, where the land was still green with life. Putting the puzzle aside, he continued his search.

Before long, he began to realize that the effort was futile. She'd been very careful to cover her tracks, and even his senses could not detect her passing when she did not wish to be detected. Only if she stopped could he be certain to know she'd been in a place. Frustrated, he returned to the Shrine of Music to think. When he arrived, he received two surprises. The first was that someone was requesting entrance into his home in the ancient way, sending patterns of energy in the shape of the Ancient Symbol of the Seriani, making the symbol glow golden on his wall. The second was that the one sending the request was Lady Firehair herself!

When he granted her leave to enter—none could enter his home without his leave—she burst into the room and ran to him. "I need your help," she said urgently.

"How is it that thou didst know how to request entrance here?" he asked her.

She stopped, considering. "I... do not know," she said slowly. "It seemed the proper way."

"That it was," he told her. "What help dost thou require?" Perhaps this help would keep her away from Serana for a time. If he could not destroy this mysterious woman, then at least he could keep her from fulfilling the terrible prophecy.

"I was given a task by my uncle, Lord Zironkell, and I do not know how to complete it alone. I stole a gauntlet from him, to repay a debt, but now he wishes me to kill the one who stole it. I tricked him into thinking it was another, but if he learns that it was I who stole the gauntlet, he will kill me!"

The Serian of Music was shocked to the core by what he was hearing. Dimly, some part of his mind understood her plight, but her uncle's name had overwhelmed him. This woman who had looked on him with such compassion when he cried, this woman who wore the one face in all existence that would stay his hand from harming her whatever she did, this woman was a Daemon! "I... had thought that all Daemon Lords were male," he said faintly, too stunned to even begin to think clearly.

"I am the only female," she replied, lowering her eyes. "I am shameful to all my kind. I did not intend to desecrate thy beautiful shrine with my presence, but I did not know where else to go. I will leave."

"Nay," he said quickly as she turned to go. "Nay, do not leave. I will help thee, if it lies within my power to do so. I must question thee further, however, if I am to devise any sound plan with which to aid thee." He did indeed need to think, but it was paramount that he keep her here for as long as possible. He could lock her inside his home, of course; even she would be unable to escape without his leave, just as she could not have entered. Still, he hated caging any creature; it was nearly as bad as killing. Perhaps, though, he could detain her of her own free will. For that, he would do nearly anything.

***

"You... wish me to stay?" Lady Firehair asked, stunned. How could a being so beautiful as he possibly wish a vile creature such as she to remain in his home, tainting the beauty with her shameful presence?

"Aye, I do," he said, his face smooth again. She'd almost felt, for a moment, as if she had shocked *him* somehow, though that was, of course, ridiculous.

"Then I will stay, if thou art certain." The strange speech patterns felt natural, when he was near. She hadn't even noticed, at first, but she seemed to slip into them with ease whenever she spoke with him.

129

"I am," he told her with a small smile. "Please, tell me of this task thine uncle didst assign thee."

"He asked me to kill the last of the Seriani," she said truthfully, and when he did not respond, she went on. "The Seriani are wicked beings that drove my people underground through trickery and brutality. They are very powerful and very dangerous. Even my uncle would not wish to face one in single combat, and there are none stronger than he."

"If there are none stronger than he, then why would he fear this Serian?" the man asked.

Lady Firehair had no answer, so instead she changed the subject. "What may I call thee? I know thee only as the man who creates music."

He smiled faintly. "Methinks that would be appropriate, m'lady." She tilted her head curiously, and he went on. "Long ago, I was called Music, m'lady. Methinks it is appropriate that thou dost address me so now."

"Music..." She breathed the name as if tasting it, savoring the flavor. "Methinks thou wert aptly named."

"I was," he agreed. "But thou didst not answer my question. If there are none greater than thine uncle, then why does he fear this Serian?"

"I... do not know," she admitted.

"Methinks that is not all that is confusing thee in this matter," he prompted. He was quite perceptive, just as she'd expected him to be.

"My uncle has told me before that trickery and brutality were honorable, and that I display my shameful nature when I shy away from such things. If what he says is true, then why does he not admire the Seriani, for their trickery and brutality?"

"Doers of evil deeds," he said softly, "rarely appreciate reciprocation of their actions."

"But these deeds are honorable," she pointed out.

"Honorable by what standards, m'lady?" he asked.

"Those my uncle has given me, sir." She'd have thought that much was obvious.

"And why must thine uncle be correct, in all things? Does he not err?"

Lady Firehair felt a chill run through her at his words. "Please, do not speak of such things. If he were to hear thee, he would kill thee, and I could not bear that."

Music smiled faintly. "Methinks thou wouldst find that thine uncle's arm does not reach into this place."

"He nearly killed thee once," she told him. "I was there… I saw it."

His smile broadened. "Another mystery illuminated," he said softly. "Believe me when I say that alone, Lord Zironkell would have little power against me, despite what thou didst witness."

She did not believe him, but she saw little point in arguing the matter. "Couldst thou help me in locating and defeating this Serian? If I do not destroy him soon, my uncle will destroy me."

"He will not, unless thou dost allow him to," said Music. "Of that much I can assure thee. For now, however, let us speak of other things. Stay here with me a few days, and let us learn more about each other, that we may better know how to save thee from thine uncle's wrath."

She nodded. "I will stay with thee so long as thou wilt allow it," she said. He did not realize, of course, that she would have stayed with him even if she did not need his help. She had watched him so many times that she felt she already knew him, even if he did not know her. Soon, he would tire of her and send her away, but perhaps, before he did, she could see him smile genuinely just once. For that, she would do nearly anything.

Chapter XVII

Crossing the mountains the second time had been as easy as the first. Where to go from there, however, was a matter of some debate. Serana believed that they should stop at Rhanestone, and deliver the nearly complete Armor of the Elements for safekeeping. Allaerion wanted to go straight to the south, and complete the Armor before they returned. Alier, for once, seemed of two minds, and Aeron declined to voice an opinion.

"The sooner we destroy this Daemon Lord, the better," Allaerion insisted for the sixth time in the past half-hour.

"A day or two either way won't matter," Serana told him patiently—well, as patiently as she could; she was getting very tired of his stubbornness. "Besides, Rhanestone could probably use our help *now*, with or without the Armor. I could charge some more weapons for them while I'm there, and leave their defenses stronger while they wait for us."

"One thing is certain," said Alier suddenly. She'd been silent for the past quarter of an hour, when it became clear that there would be no compromising in this argument. "Rhanestone's defenses are getting no stronger as we stand here bickering, and we're also getting no closer to completing the Armor. I don't really care which way we go, but decide *now*."

"We're going to Rhanestone," said Serana firmly, and she held up her hand before Allaerion could object. "If there is any objection, the one who makes it can duel me, and the winner will choose what we do." Allaerion held his tongue.

It didn't take long to reach the Keep, since they were only a few miles from it already. Well, perhaps it was more than a few; a party on horseback would have taken at least two days to cover the distance, but elemental magic gave their group an advantage. They arrived at Rhanestone in about four hours.

It was clear even as they approached the Keep that the fighting had died down to a simmer, though it hadn't stopped entirely. Serana and the Air Wizards could see that the bowmen were not firing at the moment, but instead simply standing alert, surveying the enemy. The Daemon army was on the other side of the mountains of course, and beyond their view, but Serana was surprised that it was not attacking, if it had been nearly as large as what Allaerion had described seeing by the volcano.

The party was admitted immediately at the southern gate, and taken to the Duke's sitting room almost as soon as they'd set foot inside. Duke Rhanestone looked tired and worried, but neither as tired nor as worried as Serana would have expected. The dragons must have arrived, and driven the army back even more efficiently than Serana had thought they would.

"Welcome back, High Priestess, Allaerion," said the Duke warmly. Do you have the Armor?"

"We have all but one piece," Allaerion told him. "The High Priestess thought it best to leave what we do have here for safekeeping before we attempt to secure the gauntlet we still need."

"More than that," Serana said archly. "I wanted to help reinforce the defenses here, since our journey will be longer than expected. I can magically charge some more weapons and armor for the soldiers, and set a few traps for any Daemons who come near the walls. Also, I wanted to consult the Guardian of Mist. I assume she and Blackfang are here."

"They are," said the Duke gravely. "Had they not come, it is likely that none of us would be here. Rhanestone is in your debt for sending them. Whatever reinforcement you can provide our defenses is welcome, High Priestess. Now who are your companions?"

Serana introduced Seleine, Aeron, and Alier. The Duke's eyes went wide when he realized that the legendary Weaver of Earth was not only alive, but standing before him. "You are all welcome," he told them all. "Please accept our hospitality for as long as you will. We appreciate any help you can be while you are here. For now, though, you must be tired." He commanded pages to show them all to guest rooms.

As soon as Duke Rhanestone had left, though, another man came hurrying into the room. He was somewhere in his mid-thirties, by appearances, with thick black hair and piercing eyes. His countenance radiated power, and he wore a brown robe with a wide purple stripe down the center. When his eyes fell on Serana, a smile nearly split his face in two.

"Did Rillian find another apprentice already?" she asked before he could speak. "You must have been very accomplished already, to have earned the rank of Battlemage so quickly." The man stopped and stared at her for a moment, his face unreadable. Serana began to worry. "Rillian isn't hurt, is he? He isn't... He can't be..."

"Serana, whatever are you talking about?" It was Rillian's voice, but it was *not* the voice she remembered. It was stronger, more powerful... and it was coming from the younger man in front of her!

"Rillian?" she asked incredulously. "It can't be..."

"It's your fault," he told her, grinning broadly. "Remember what you did when you healed my arm? You said something about my absorbing energy, instead of releasing it, if you recall. Well, this is the result."

"It *is* you!" cried Serana. She ran to hug him, and felt his arms— strong arms, now—enfold her. "I've missed you terribly."

"And I've missed you, Serana," he said, beaming. He dismissed the page, saying that Serana could find her way easily enough.

"Let's get this taken care of right now," she told him firmly. She stepped back and looked him up and down, studying him with her senses. It appeared so clearly now, what was happening, that she was surprised she hadn't realized it before. "Your life-energy is backward," she said decisively.

"What does that mean?" he asked.

"Just stand still for a moment," she commanded. She very gently reached into him with her senses, and redirected the energy flow, letting it flow out of him just a little more slowly than it did from Duke Rhanestone. If she did any more, he might age more rapidly, since he'd already grown old once. It wasn't difficult, really; it was simply something she'd never considered doing before. She would have to study the process in more detail later; there were some interesting possibilities involved. "There," she said, smiling in satisfaction. "You'll start aging again normally now."

"That simple, is it?" he asked, shaking his head. "I told you that one day you would surpass me entirely. I think that day came and went a long time ago."

Serana simply hugged him again. "It's so good to see you!" she cried, kissing his cheek.

"Rillian," said another voice, "it's time for my lesson... or did you forget?" The speaker was a young woman with golden hair falling in waves down her back. Serana imagined that she would be quite beautiful, if she didn't look ready to chew rocks.

"Ella," Rillian said, seeming not to notice her mood, "this is Serana, the Sorceress High Preistess! Serana, this is Ella, my apprentice."

"It's an honor," Serana said, extending her hand. There was no reason not to be civil, even if the woman *was* staring right through her.

"No need to lower yourself for my sake," Ella said coldly. It was then that Serana finally noticed. She must have been particularly dense not to see it before. Well, this problem, at least, should be fairly simple to solve.

"Rillian," Serana said gently, "I'd like to talk to your apprentice alone for a moment."

"Actually, why don't you give her lesson today, Serana," the Battlemage said. "I just remembered that the Duke wanted me to talk with the elven priests." There were elves here? Well, that was for later.

"It won't be necessary," Ella said quickly. "I'll study on my own again. I'm getting used to that."

"It's no trouble at all," said Serana, smiling faintly. "I'm happy to give you your lesson." When Rillian had left, she added, "I think you're in sore need of one."

"He's mine," said Ella without preamble, before Serana could speak. "Since I've been here, he's done nothing but talk about you, about how powerful and talented and beautiful you are. Well, let me tell you..."

"That will be quite enough," said Serana firmly. She'd wrapped Ella in Air magic and sealed her mouth shut. The other woman tried to cut the bonds, but Serana blocked her flows effortlessly. The girl was talented, but she would never have matched a Sorceress, particularly not Serana. "Now that I seem to have your attention, let me make one thing clear. I love Rillian dearly, but he is like a father to me. Do you hear me? A father. Nod if you understand." Ella nodded, and Serana released her. "Now then, since I love Rillian as a father, I am naturally quite concerned with what woman he chooses, now that he's young enough to think about choosing one again."

"If you think you can tell me..." Ella began, but Serana held up a hand, and the woman wisely fell silent.

"What I think," said Serana sharply, "is that I've known you for less than five minutes, and in that time, you've done nothing to show me that you aren't a stupid little girl, besotted with a great man you barely understand. I've been one of those before, I'm ashamed to say, and I know that Rillian deserves better."

Ella seemed to suddenly deflate. She sat down heavily in one of the velvet-lined chairs, with her head in her hands. "I'm sorry," she said softly. "My nerves are frayed, and I'm not myself."

Serana took a seat across from her. "That's alright. Stress can do that to a person. Believe me; I know."

"He hasn't looked at me twice since I came here, but he is everything I want in a man. He's kind and respectful. He has a wonderful sense of humor, and a sharp intellect. He is everything that no man back home could have ever dreamed of being."

"He's also more than a hundred years old," said Serana gently, "and he's not used to thinking of himself as eligible. Besides, if there's one thing I've learned about Rillian, it's that hints do not work. When you want him to know something, you have to tell him, leaving no room for interpretation."

"Do you think that would work?" Ella asked, a glimmer of hope in her eyes.

"I think it has more chance of working than anything else," Serana told her. "Now, I promised Rillian that I would give you your lesson, and I will see that you get it." She studied the other woman's energy for a few moments, and decided she was strong enough. "Have you ever heard of the Arrow of Light?"

After an hour or so, Ella finally did manage to throw the white bolt of energy with enough power to kill a Daemon Scout. She broke one of Duke Rhanestone's ornamental suits of armor, but Serana repaired it with Earth magic; no one would ever know it had been broken.

"Practice in the courtyard from now on," Serana suggested, "but practice well. That spell might save your life one day."

"Thank you, High Priestess," said Ella respectfully, curtsying low.

"Serana will do," Serana told her. "Rillian might insist that you call me High Priestess, but too much formality makes me uncomfortable. Besides, you're older than I am."

Ella grinned. "Thank you, Serana. I do hope you might consider giving me a few more lessons before you leave. Rillian rarely seems to have the time, of late."

"He has time, I think," said Serana. "I'll bet he's avoiding you."

Ella looked stricken.

"Relax," Serana told her. "Just do what I suggested, and I think you'll find that everything will work out just fine."

Ella bit her lower lip nervously, but she nodded. "Thank you again," she said.

"Now if you'll excuse me, it's getting late. I would like to get some rest tonight before I start charging weapons tomorrow."

"Could I help?" asked Ella eagerly. "I've only ever tried using magic with arrows. I'm a fletcher by trade, you see, or at least, I was before I came here."

"Meet me outside the barracks tomorrow after breakfast," said Serana with a smile. "I'll show you what I can."

When she left Ella, Serana headed toward her room, the same one she'd used before. It was good to be back at Rhanestone. In many ways, the Keep seemed more her home than Alon Peak ever would again. When she went into the room, there was someone waiting for her. He wasn't human; that much was obvious at a glance, and still more obvious when she looked at his energy, more vibrant than any human's, unless the human were a mage, though not nearly as vibrant as an elemental's. His ears were sharply pointed, and his frame was slender, but as he rose from the chair he'd been sitting in, his movement spoke of deceptive strength. "Who are you?" asked Serana.

"I am Evieron, King of the Elves," he said softly, staring at her. "You are Serana." It was not a question; he sounded more as if he were in awe.

"I am," Serana said uncertainly. "What are you doing in my room?" The elven king was staring at her so intently that she almost thought he meant to seduce her. If he did, he would be hung upside-down and naked in the hall, king or no.

"Forgive me for intruding," he said quickly, "but I wanted to be certain that I met you as soon as possible. You see, I thought you were dead."

"Why?" Serana asked him. "And why would you care? I don't know you."

"I thought you'd been killed more than sixteen years ago," he explained, "when the vampires destroyed your village."

"I was spared, and given to a human couple to raise," Serana told him, wishing that he would stop staring, or at least blink. "But you haven't answered my question. Why would you care whether I lived or died? Were your people friendly with the Sorceress race?"

"That we were," he said softly, still staring at her. She was beginning to grow more than a little uncomfortable with his eyes. "In fact, my wife was a Sorceress."

"I'm sorry for your loss," Serana told him carefully, readying her magic in case he tried anything.

"*Our* loss," Evieron corrected. You see, my wife was not only a Sorceress, but the High Priestess herself… your mother, Serana."

Serana stared, dumfounded. The spells she was readying dissipated; she was too shocked to use them even if she'd had to. "You're… my father?"

There were tears in the elven king's eyes as he nodded. "I am your father."

Suddenly his staring no longer bothered her. "Please," she said, "sit down. We have much to talk about."

The tears began sliding down his cheeks as he complied, but he was smiling. "Yes," he said softly, his voice cracking with emotion. "Yes, we do."

Chapter XVIII

"What dost thou know of the history of this world?" asked Music, his eyes studying her intently. Lady Firehair liked his eyes on her, though for some reason they made her nervous.

"I know bits and pieces of the past two centuries' history from experience, and more details of various time periods from my uncle," she said.

"How far dost thou trust Zironkell to speak truth unto thee?"

"I know when he is lying," she told him. "He is vague sometimes, but he was quite clear in his writings that he sent for me to study."

"And hast thou also the ability to detect written lies?" he pressed.

"I... do not know," she admitted. "I did think of that already, though. I asked him directly if any of his writings were false, and he assured me that they were not."

"Did he? What were his exact words?"

Lady Firehair trembled at the memory. "He called me a stupid child, and asked me what good it would do him to falsify the world's history. He also said that if I ever questioned what he wrote for me again, he would forget that I am his niece, and destroy me. My uncle has a terrible temper, sir."

"Then he did not directly state that the writings were true," said Music with satisfaction.

"Sir," she said, "I really do not believe..."

"M'lady," he interrupted, "I understand what thou dost believe. What I need thee to understand is that I have encountered one other who possessed the talent for detecting lies, and her skill had a flaw. Shall I demonstrate?"

"Please do," Lady Firehair said, intrigued.

From within his cloak, Music produced a white marble. "This marble is black," he said, and immediately she sensed the lie, just as she should. "How couldst thou think this marble is not black?" he asked... and there was nothing.

"Say it again," Lady Firehair instructed. Surely there had to have been *something* there; it was an obvious deception. He repeated the question, just as she'd asked, but again there was no sense of falsehood. "How can this be?" she asked desperately. "Hast thou the power to block my sense?"

"Nay, I do not," he told her, and again there was no sense of lying. "I do, however, possess the ability to imply a mistruth, rather than to state it directly. Methinks nearly every sentient being in this world possesses the same ability, including thine uncle. Now observe one other test." He produced a parchment from his cloak next, and wrote a short note on it, still holding the white marble in his left hand. When he was finished writing, he passed the note to her. She read quite clearly, "The marble in my left hand is black." Still there was no sense of mistruth.

"Please," she said, rising. "Do not continue this. I… I must go."

"Nay, m'lady… Please stay," he said soothingly. "We shall change the subject, if this one brings thee discomfort. Mine intent is not to upset thee, but merely to reveal to thee some things that may have been hidden."

"Am I a prisoner here?" she asked him, and to her surprise, she found herself half-hoping that she were.

"Nay, thou art not," he said seriously. "However, it is my hope that thou wilt remain here with me of thine own free will."

"Why dost thou wish to keep the company of a creature so vile as I?" she demanded, ignoring the tears in her eyes.

"Perhaps we two have very different definitions of 'vile,' m'lady," he said softly. "For myself, I find thy company most pleasant." There it was. He was not lying, exactly… but it was there, nonetheless.

"That is not entirely true," she told him. "I sense it."

"Thy senses are correct, m'lady. Thy company does bring me some discomfort, but I would not give it up, given the choice." Again, there was no sense of a lie at all.

"Why do I make thee uncomfortable?" she asked.

"There are several reasons," he said with a shrug.

"Tell me one," she insisted.

"Thy face, m'lady."

"I am sorry if it does not please thee," she said softly, lowering her eyes.

"Thou dost mistake my meaning. Thy face is nearly identical to that of another, someone I knew long ago."

She looked up sharply. "Thy love?" she asked, her heart fluttering for some reason.

He nodded, and her heart skipped a beat. She felt hope surging within her, but hope for what? There could be nothing between them, whatever she wished. She was not worthy of any man, least of all him.

"Tell me about her, please," Lady Firehair asked, and he nodded again. She sat down again to listen, watching him intently. This was something she'd wondered about for a very long time.

***

"Keep a sharp lookout," Alexander said softly. "It's a miracle we haven't been challenged yet, after what the innkeeper said last night." They'd been on the road for eight days now, stopping each night at one of the various inns that lined the road south from Rhanestone. The road was not so frequently traveled as one might imagine, given the number of inns, but when it *was* traveled, it was often by companies of soldiers sent to reinforce the Keep, under the three hundred year old agreement, and the innkeepers made enough profit from those companies that they didn't need the regular business that most in their trade required. According to the innkeeper last night, the road was plagued with brigands of late, more in the past month than in the past three years combined. Alexander was truly beginning to regret not bringing any soldiers with them, but it was too late now to turn back. He only hoped that the sword practice he'd done at Rhanestone would pay off, should it be necessary. That it would be necessary was almost certain; it was only a matter of time.

"I am, Alexander," Alloria replied calmly. "There are men ahead of us, in the trees, a hundred paces or so."

So it had finally happened. "Are they armed?" It was a foolish question—of course they were armed—but he couldn't help himself. He really didn't want to have to fight, two against ten, twenty or more.

"I cannot tell that, Alexander," Alloria told him. "I can only sense their presence. It is likely, of course, that they are." Suddenly, Alloria's hand shot out toward him, and before he could react, he saw that she held an arrow that would have caught him in the eye. "They are armed."

The vampire woman caught two more arrows, throwing them down as quickly as she caught them. Alexander heard a low, inhuman growl from her throat, and then she was gone, faster than he could see. He drew his sword and rode hard toward the concealing trees, but when he burst through, he found only corpses. Leaving them for carrion, he rode back onto the rode warily, only to find Alloria seated comfortably atop her mare with Alon in her arms.

"They frightened him," she said, wiping her mouth with a red handkerchief. Alexander carefully avoided looking at what she was wiping off. "Are you unharmed, Alexander?"

"I'm fine," he said, forcing down revulsion. In all his time with her, he'd never even come close to actually seeing her feed, and somehow, he'd managed to put it out of his mind. Still, she had just saved his life. She deserved gratitude, not disgust.

"I understand that you are uncomfortable," she said softly, not looking at him. "I only killed them because it was the surest way to guarantee your safety."

"You saved my life, Alloria," he told her truthfully, fighting his discomfort. "I am in your debt."

"Nonsense," she scoffed. "I am *yamin'sai* to you. It would be my duty to save your life, even if I did not care for you. There is no debt incurred." She did look at him now. "I do care, though."

Once again, there was fear in her eyes, nearly hidden behind the mask of logic and calm. Alexander's revulsion at what she'd done suddenly disappeared, replaced with shame, sharp and poignant. "I care for you too, Alloria," he said, reaching out to take her hand.

She rewarded him with her beautiful smile as her fingers closed gently around his. "Those words," she said, nearly whispering, "I will never tire of hearing."

The journey continued uneventfully for the remainder of the day, and that night they took a room at The Wanderer's Refuge, an Inn two weeks north of Green Haven. They traveled under the guise of eccentric nobleman—to explain the lack of guards—and wife, and Alexander supposed it wasn't far off. He'd been considered quite eccentric in the south, and Alloria really was his wife, if not entirely in the conventional sense.

The innkeeper, a slender woman who looked to be somewhere in her mid-forties, welcomed them graciously, if warily, when they stepped into the moderately crowded common room, where a musician played the flute along with another's drums while a third entertainer juggled six colored balls. The innkeeper carefully—Alexander thought—did not even glance at Alloria's dark cloak. Apparently it wasn't his vampire wife that made her wary, though, for when he produced a purse of gold to pay for the room in advance, she warmed to them instantly. "It's my best room, my lord," she said, leading them up the stairs. "I keep it especially for nobility, when they come through." Alexander doubted that, but he imagined the room would be satisfactory in any case. "I'll have a hot meal brought up to your room, once you're both settled in."

"We'll take it in the common room," said Alexander. He'd wanted to get Alloria accustomed to crowds of humans before they reached Green Haven, but none of the other inns they'd stayed at had been busy enough to bother trying. The Wanderer's Refuge looked to be quite promising. After they'd left their things in the room and locked the door, Alexander and Alloria went downstairs and took a seat at the corner table nearest to the entertainers. As small as the makeshift stage was, Alexander doubted that the inn usually had so much entertainment, and when he asked the innkeeper, he found that he was quite right.

"They're travelers," she told him, "and they claimed they could fill my common room if I let them have a room and a meal. So far it looks as if they're earning every penny." She brought their meals herself, something Alexander found a little odd, considering that there were serving maids aplenty bustling between the tables. She also cast a few quick glances at Alloria. Perhaps she *had* noticed that his wife was a vampire.

Alloria herself seemed amused. "It is not my race that she is being careful of, Alexander," she told him quietly when the innkeeper had left. "It is my jealousy. She serves us herself because the serving maids are all young and pretty."

"Are they?" asked Alexander, genuinely surprised. He looked again, just to be sure. "I suppose they are, though I don't see why she's worried about it. None of them come near to matching you, Alloria."

Alloria giggled, and Alexander stared. In all the time he'd spent with her, never once had he heard so girlish a sound from her lips. It almost didn't seem to fit. She even appeared to be *blushing*! Alloria *never* blushed. It had to be the dim light, and his imagination. It wasn't until he realized that she was eating that he put the thought entirely from his mind.

"I didn't know you *could* eat solid food," Alexander said quietly, careful that no one else heard. Another very nice thing about Alloria was that she could hear even what Alexander barely whispered, what no human would hear more than a few inches away. He loved having her with him in council meetings, for several councilors had a habit of muttering what they never spoke aloud.

"Of course I can," she replied, surprised. "I could not live on it for long, but the taste is quite good from time to time."

"We'll have to have a talk about this later," he told her. He'd never had food brought for her at Rhanestone, when he took his meals, since he was certain she couldn't eat it anyway, and she'd never said a word.

By the time they were finished eating, a dance had begun to the music, and the juggler had put away his colored balls and started singing. Alexander had always loved dancing back home, but he'd not done it since he came to Rhanestone. Grinning, he grabbed Alloria's hand and pulled her toward the dance floor. She shook her head slightly, her eyes growing wide, but he ignored her silent protests. The tune was one he knew quite well, though the words were different, and he was determined that she learn to dance, if she didn't know how already.

At first, she was hopelessly awkward, stumbling every few steps and clinging to him almost painfully—she really didn't know her own strength, when she became emotional. After awhile, though, she began to relax and pay attention, and her movements became fluid, graceful. She smiled at him, and he nearly stumbled himself, his heart quickened so. By the time the song was over, she was dancing better than he was.

A new song started up then, another that he knew, but once again the words were different. It wasn't surprising, really; more than a few nobles liked the same music that common folk enjoyed, but since they couldn't be seen listening to common tunes, they had the words changed. It was all very silly, in Alexander's opinion, but he'd yet to meet anyone who agreed with him. "May I show you the dance I know to this piece?" Alloria asked him, smiling faintly.

"Please," he said. She started simply, a few steps that were quite similar to the dance he already knew. He followed her easily, until she quickened her pace. He'd always been a good dancer, but it took all of his concentration to match her in the new dance. After a few minutes, though, he thought he'd begun to master it. That was when everything changed.

"Just do what you've been doing so far," Alloria instructed. He did, but he almost lost his balance when she suddenly slipped into an inhumanly graceful... He wasn't sure what to call it. "Dance" didn't begin to do justice to what she was doing. Her small body dipped and turned, swaying suggestively even from within the concealing cloak that she so rarely took off. She circled around him, spinning and gliding fluidly, her eyes meeting his whenever she paused. Her gaze was hypnotic, mesmerizing... She flowed with the music, and he felt it pulsing in his veins. When it finally stopped, she was in his arms, and he was holding her in a low dip, nearly to the floor. Only when the applause burst out from around them did he realize that they'd been the only ones dancing for some time.

"I've never seen anything like that, my lord, my lady," said the innkeeper, watching them both with awe.

"Neither have I," said Alexander truthfully. "My new wife is talented, and full of surprises."

Alloria blushed furiously.

"I believe we shall retire for the night," Alexander announced, drawing Alloria toward the stairs. "My compliments to the musicians."

"I'm sorry," said Alloria as soon as they were alone in the room. "I couldn't help myself. I have always loved dancing, and I…"

"Why are you apologizing?" Alexander demanded. "If you recall, it was I who led you to the dance floor."

"I didn't intend to draw so much attention," she said softly.

"Your drawing attention isn't an issue," Alexander told her. "I want you to draw a certain amount of attention. The point is that you drew attention to your beauty, your grace, and your skill as a dancer. No one down there seemed to notice or care that you're a vampire."

"You think I'm beautiful?" she asked softly, looking into his eyes intently.

Alexander grinned. "I think every man in that common room is envying me right now."

"*I* think, then," she said slowly, "that I should make certain that they have reason to envy you." She wrapped her arms around his neck and kissed him, and he did not think anything coherent again until morning.

Chapter XIX

Serana spent a great deal of time with King Evieron in the first few days after she arrived. She met Veliena, his queen, and Erilan, his son—and her half-brother—the morning after she met her father. The little elf boy tilted his head quizzically when they were introduced. "I have a sister?" he asked, bewildered. "Why didn't you tell me before?"

"I didn't know she was still alive," Evieron explained. It was hard for Serana to think of him as her father; not only had she never known him, but they looked nothing alike. She knew that Sorceresses bore only Sorceress children, but she'd have expected there to be *some* resemblance. "Actually, I'd imagine there is," the elven king told her when she asked. "I see you as the type of person who does not back down from a challenge, who takes charge when the situation demands it, and does not break down until after the fight is over."

"I suppose so," said Serana doubtfully. She really didn't see herself that way at all.

"It's entirely true," Seleine said with a laugh, and Serana jumped. The Ice Witch had come up behind Serana while her attention was on her father. "Believe me; it's true."

"You also seem to share the same affinity for modesty," Veliena put in, grinning.

They were standing in the courtyard, not far from where the Guardian of Mist lay sleeping. She slept a good deal more now than before, according to Rillian, since her pregnancy was coming along rapidly. Serana wondered if she would start sleeping more too, in a few months. So far, she really wasn't showing yet.

"May I hug you?" Erilan asked Serana. "My friend Eilar says that it's nice when his sister hugs him, but I never had a sister before." Serana laughed, delighted, and scooped her half-brother up into her arms, hugging him warmly. "He was right," the little elf said, smiling brightly.

"It's nice for the sister too," Serana told him.

"When this war is over," Veliena said seriously, "you will always have a home with us in the Elven forest."

"I think she has one here too," Seleine laughed, "and with me as well, wherever my path takes me."

"You'll have to do a good deal of traveling," said Evieron. "No one is going to want to let you go!"

Serana couldn't remember a time when she was happier, but she knew it couldn't last, so she clung to the moments she could get. When she wasn't with her father and his family, she was with Rillian, Ella, and Ilsa, teaching them to charge weapons for the soldiers. Ilsa had been delighted to see Serana again, and insisted that she visit sometime before leaving to retrieve the last piece of the Armor. The three magicians combined were nowhere near Serana's power, of course, but they could manage simple charms, blades that would not lose their edge, however much they were used, and maces that burned wherever they struck. Ella and Ilsa together even managed a sword that left nectar from Dragon's Tears on anything it touched. A Daemon Scout could die with only a scratch from that blade.

Ella was more than friendly now, and was constantly trying to make up for her earlier rudeness in whatever ways she could think of. She made wonderful hot cocoa to drink during her magic lessons, and always had a ready smile whenever she saw Serana. She even promised to teach Serana the bow, when there was more time. What intrigued Serana most, though, was that the young woman was even more talented than Rillian.

The Battlemage of Rhanestone was quite powerful, for a human, and experienced far beyond his appearance. His memory was nearly as sharp as Serana's now, and his presence dominated whatever room he stood in, though he seemed completely unaware of it. In some ways, he seemed a completely different person from the old man Serana had known before. A few minutes in his company, though, always reminded her that he was still very much the same Rillian.

"Of course she's quite talented," he said three days after she'd arrived. "That's why the Serian of Music brought her here. Ella was a bit reluctant to learn magic, at first, but she seems to have taken to it quite well."

"Have you noticed anything else about her?" Serana asked mildly. Only Rillian could be so dense about something so obvious. The poor woman had been all but throwing herself at him since Serana had talked with her, but she was still using hints. They were strong hints—strong enough that most people would have wondered why she didn't simply make a sign—but still hints.

"Like what?" asked Rillian, obviously confused. "Do you think she might be pushing herself too hard? Her temper hasn't been the best, in the few weeks before you arrived, though it seems a bit better with you here."

"Do you know *why* her temper hasn't been the best?" Serana pressed.

"I'd imagine the pressure of adjusting to a new place, and of learning magic..."

"Rillian, she's in love," said Serana, exasperated.

He blinked at her in surprise. "She's in love?" His face suddenly darkened, but he seemed unaware of it. "With whom?"

Serana rolled her eyes. "With *you*, you silly old man! She can't take her eyes off you when you're together, and she hardly talks about anything else when you're not."

"But I'm more than five times her age!" he burst out. Still, he didn't look nearly as incredulous as he was trying to be.

"Ignatius and I were much further apart," Serana told him. "Besides, you look as if you've not yet seen your fortieth summer, and won't for a few years yet."

"She actually... feels that way?" he asked, and Serana nearly laughed.

"Yes, she does, and she's been trying everything she could dream up short of blurting it out to tell you."

Rillian sank into a chair, as if he were suddenly exhausted. "What do I do now?" he whispered. "Serana, I haven't dealt with things like this for decades!"

"At least you *have* dealt with them before," Serana told him. "Just imagine how Ella and I feel. We're having to learn it all for the first time!"

Rillian's strength seemed to return as suddenly as it left. "I'll go talk to her now," he said, a new light in his eyes, and he was out the door before Serana could say another word. The whole thing had gone rather well, really. Neither Ella nor Serana had had any idea whether or not the Battlemage had any feelings at all for his apprentice, beyond those of teacher to student, and Ella had been growing more than a little disheartened.

While Ella and Rillian were talking, Serana went to see the elven priests. Ella had spoken very highly of them, and Serana wondered if perhaps they might be able to teach her a bit as well.

"Greetings to you, High Priestess," the eldest of the nine priests on duty said solemnly, bowing deeply.

Not knowing what else to do, Serana inclined her head in return. She really needed to study the customs involving etiquette between the races. "I've come to learn from you, if I may," she said.

"What is it that you wish to learn?" asked the elf.

"I have heard that you practice a form of Earth magic," she told him. "I hoped that you might be willing to teach me."

The elderly elf—he had to be quite old indeed; his hair was nearly white—appeared bewildered. "High Priestess," he said tentatively, "it is far more likely that you could teach us, in the realm of magic."

"I was not trained by my kind," explained Serana. She'd have thought he might have heard her story already, but perhaps he hadn't. "My skills are not what they would have been, had my village not been destroyed when I was a child."

"That is true," the priest agreed. "Your skills would likely not have been nearly so astounding, had you lived among your own kind. We were told that the Serian of Music had a hand in your education, and the stories of your feats are already well beyond what most of your kind could accomplish."

It was Serana's turn to be surprised. She'd been told more than once that she was particularly talented, even for a Sorceress, but she'd hardly imagined that there were stories about her. "I still have much to learn," she said softly.

"We all have much to learn, so long as we still live," said the priest. "Come, and we will show you what we know. Perhaps you can help us to learn more."

The priests taught far more than they learned. The difficulty was that they couldn't see the flows of energy; they could only feel them. As a result, though, they did some things that Serana would probably never have thought of. Their healing, for example, was a combination of all four elements woven together. The elements weren't used equally, of course, there was more Water and Earth than anything else, and more Air than Fire. The entire spell was far less powerful than the healing Serana already knew, but it required much less energy. Besides, Serana wanted to learn *every* possible way to manipulate energy, though she was certain there was far too much to learn even in her lifetime.

Aside from healing, the priests practiced a method of using magic to alter the mind, to cloud a person's memories or to help make them clearer. The method was crude, to Serana's eyes, but it gave her quite a few ideas. She made a few suggestions, simplifying her thoughts so that the priests could understand even without seeing the flows, and they thanked her humbly. Sometimes Serana thought she would never grow accustomed to the profound respect others showed for her rank; she was still not yet seventeen, after all! Perhaps it would be best, though, if she never grew *too* accustomed to it.

When she left the priests, she went to visit the vampires. Ella had told her that there was a vampire woman, Reilena, who had lost her memories, and Serana wanted to try some of the things she'd learned. She was fairly certain that she could not fully restore Reilena's memories, but perhaps she could fill in a few more gaps. If it were her own memory that was lost, Serana would give nearly anything just for a few answers, however incomplete.

Although Serana was consciously aware of the fact that vampires destroyed her people, and killed her mother, she had no memory of the events, and they invoked little more emotion in her than news of a friend's relative's demise might have done. She wished that she could have met her real mother, particularly after meeting her father, but the Eslans back in Alon Peak were the only parents Serana had ever known. The late Sorceress High Priestess was a stranger. Besides, the Dark Angel of Music had told her that the vampires who destroyed the Sorceresses were tricked by Daemons. They could hardly be held accountable for their actions.

The vampires' leader, a woman named Morganna, met Serana in the room she was using for a sort of combination audience chamber and social room. Apparently a vampire's idea of gathering socially was so subdued that there was very little noise, even with twenty other vampires in the room. "It is more convenient," said Morganna. "This way, they are here if I need them; it is easier than sending for them."

"Interesting," said Serana. "I can see where it would be more efficient that way."

Morganna smiled. "So what can I do for you, High Priestess?"

"I am looking for a vampire called Reilena, who has lost her memory. I believe I may be able to help her to recover a portion of what she has lost."

"That would be most helpful," said Morganna, smiling hopefully. She seemed to genuinely care for this Reilena, despite the vampire reputation for emotionless logic. "I will send for her."

Serana thanked her, and sat down to wait.

"We have not seen a Sorceress in more than twenty years," Morganna said softly. "We heard of their destruction, and mourned them. I am pleased that you survived."

"Thank you," said Serana uncomfortably. She really wasn't sure how to respond to talk about the death of her people, particularly since she never knew them, and could not feel the grief that would be expected of her.

"I did not intend to bring you any discomfort," the vampire leader told her. "I simply wanted you to know that our clan was not responsible. The ones who were have been hunted to extinction by the other races, and many still blame us. Even those responsible were deceived; no vampire clan craves wanton destruction, for it is illogical."

"I do not blame you, Morganna," Serana told her. "I do not know the details of what happened, though I intend to learn them eventually, but I do know that neither you nor your people were responsible, and I bear you no ill will."

"Thank you," said Morganna simply.

"You sent for me, Morganna?" said a new voice as its owner came into the room. She was young by any standards, in appearance and, according to Ella, in years. Her raven-black hair was pulled back in an intricate braid that she wore hanging down over her left shoulder, nearly hidden against her dark cloak.

"Reilena," said Morganna, "this is Serana, High Priestess of the Sorceress race. She may be able to help you with your memories."

"I would be grateful for whatever assistance you could give," said Reilena earnestly. "It is distressing to have the majority of one's life beyond recall."

"I imagine it would be," agreed Serana.

"Will you need anything?" asked Morganna. "A room, privacy?"

"It shouldn't matter," said Serana. "I can work here as easily as anywhere." The flows she intended to try were not terribly complex, and Serana had learned to practice her magic with distractions all around; one had to, in battle.

"What must I do?" asked Reilena.

"Perhaps you should sit down," suggested Serana. "If this does work, I have no idea what effect it will have on you, emotionally, since I have no more knowledge of your memories than you do now."

Reilena nodded and took a seat beside Serana.

"Just relax now," Serana told her. "This shouldn't take long." She gathered the energies for the flows used by the priests, but added her own Life magic as well. She believed that was the reason the Sorceress race was considered so skilled as healers; Life magic was their heritage. She made a few subtle changes to the patterns of energy, and reached out gently to the vampire woman's mind. This spell would be quite useful against an enemy too, if one wanted to create illusions to frighten him. Serana couldn't help applying nearly everything she learned to fighting now, since she'd battled Daemons from the time she left Alon Peak; it only seemed natural to use everything she learned as a means to stay alive. "Think about the earliest memories you can," she instructed. "Don't concentrate too hard; just let them come to you."

Reilena nodded, and Serana watched the energy carefully, both what she was working with and what resided within the vampire woman. There were areas of Reilena's mind that were blocked off, clouded even to Serana's eyes. Carefully, she cleared away a portion of that clouded area, using her magic like a gentle breeze blowing away a thick fog. She worked only with the outer regions; delving too deeply without more practice might possibly harm Reilena. When she'd finished, the clouded area was still there, but it was weaker, and the outer edges were entirely clear.

Reilena wore a wondering smile. "I remember my sixth birthday," she said softly. "Father was away, as he often was. I don't remember what kept him, but I knew he was gone again, and I'd snuck out to climb the apple trees. The fruit was delicious that time of year." Suddenly, the vampire woman started, as if she'd just realized something. "I was born in the fall! I had to have been, if the trees had ripe fruit."

"Go on," said Morganna encouragingly. "What else do you remember?"

"My brother caught me in the tree, and made me come down. We were having a special supper for my birthday, and I was supposed to wear a dress that Father had had made for me, but I've never liked dresses, so I refused. I wore black breeches and a grey shirt, and wore a dark purple cloak." Reilena grinned at the memory. "Father never saw it, of course, since he was away, but my brothers both thought it was quite funny watching my nana's face turn almost the same color as my cloak when she saw me." She tilted her head slightly. "I had a nana? My father must have been a very successful farmer, to have been able to afford a nana for me."

"Perhaps he was an apple farmer," suggested Serana. "Apples were abundant in Alon Peak, but the merchants who came through sometimes often bought them at a good price, saying they were far more rare in other places. A farmer could have been quite well off, if he'd grown enough apple trees."

"Perhaps," said Reilena thoughtfully. "Regardless, though, I thank you. It was like having a birthday all over again."

"More memories will probably surface in time," said Serana. "Just remember that if any of them are unpleasant, they are in the past. What matter now are the present and the future."

"I will," said Reilena. "Thank you again!"

By the time Serana left the vampires, it was time for lunch, and Serana went to the wall to find Rillian; she'd told him early that morning that she would come to find him when she'd finished with Reilena. Rillian was surveying the Daemon camp using a spell similar to the one Serana knew, though his was not quite so powerful. He didn't seem to notice her approach, so she simply joined him, studying the camp for herself.

There were still several thousand Daemons remaining, and many of them Soldiers, at the least. If they all attacked at once, Rhanestone would be hard-pressed to defeat them, even with Serana and the elementals.

"They don't attack," said Rillian suddenly, and Serana jumped. "Oh, there are raids every day, but nothing that even breaks through the barrier of Dragon's Tears. It's as if they're waiting for something, but I haven't the faintest idea what."

"Whatever it is," Serana said, "let us hope that we complete the Armor of the Elements before it happens. We need to leave by the end of this week. I'll have had enough time by then to enchant all the weapons the Elite Guard uses, and many of those belonging to the other soldiers. You'll be as well-defended as I can make you without being here myself."

"We can ask no more than that, High Priestess," Rillian said softly.

Serana hit his arm playfully. "Don't go all formal on me, my esteemed Battlemage," she laughed. "Remember that I was the frightened girl you took under your wing just a few months ago."

He looked at her seriously. "You mean the one who killed the Daemon Scout that would have finished me off, then healed my ruined arm in moments, reversed my aging, and destroyed at least half of the invading Daemons single-handedly? Or are you talking about the one who defeated the Captain that Allaerion and I both tried and failed to protect you from? Do you mean that frightened girl?"

"I'm talking about the one who you picked up off the courtyard, unconscious, and cared for until she woke," Serana told him. "I'm talking about the one who looks on you as a second father, and doesn't want any silly formality standing between us." She hugged Rillian tightly before he could say anything more, and he wisely kept silent. "It's time for lunch, and you promised to join me."

"I haven't forgotten, Serana," he said, smiling fondly.

"You'd better not have," she said, but it didn't sound as threatening as she'd intended. "Besides, I want to know what happened with Ella."

"I'm really too old for her," he said quietly.

"Rillian, you didn't!" Serana cried. "Please say you didn't push that poor woman away, after all she's been through just to get your attention! She…"

"She is making me move my things into her room," he said. "She said mine is too small."

"Rillian, that's wonderful!" Serana hugged him again.

"She won't even wait until after the wedding to move them," he said with a rueful grin. "She said she wants the labor finished by then, so that I can be well rested when the time comes. She also said that she wants me in the habit of coming to her room when I want any of my books and such. My poor little room is looking rather bare, I'm afraid."

"I'm happy for the both of you," said Serana, beaming. "I don't want to hear any more talk about that 'old man' nonsense; you're quite young again, and you deserve to be happy. Now let's get some lunch; I'm starving."

"Do you know, the strange thing is that she actually pays attention during her lessons now. For the past few weeks, she'd preferred to learn from books, rather than from me."

"Men!" said Serana, throwing up her hands. "Just come have lunch with me, Rillian. You're quite hopeless."

Chapter XX

Lady Firehair moved from room to room, exploring the vast interior of the Shrine of Music. It looked huge from the outside, when one could actually see it at all, but it was much larger on the inside, large enough to make her uncle's mountain look small by comparison. In many ways, though, she felt that the size only accentuated the emptiness.

It had been a week since she'd come here, and she was happier than she could ever remember being, but she felt guilty for feeling such happiness. Music had not yet devised any plan to help her destroy the last of the Seriani, but he said time would reveal the answers to all her questions.

In the mean time, she'd been exploring the Shrine, studying the energies that danced within it, moving to the faint music that played eternally inside. The patterns were more complex than anything she'd ever seen before—to call them a spell would be like calling the entire world a rock; the description did not begin to encompass the reality. The patterns seemed so familiar sometimes that she felt she already knew them, yet at other times they appeared so alien that she could never begin to comprehend them.

Reality itself was not fixed within the Shrine; it changed with Music's whim. When Lady Firehair was hungry, he would smile, and a table filled with delectable foods of every variety would be there when she turned around. When she wanted to swim, there would be a beautiful pool filled with sparkling water in the next room, where she was certain there had been no such thing before. Lady Firehair did not mind the constant changing; she found it fascinating, and was determined to learn more.

Even more mysterious than the Shrine, though, was the man who lived within it. He said almost nothing of himself unless pressed, and even then he was evasive, yet he catered to her ever wish, treating her as if she were precious and beautiful, not the shameful creature that she truly was. When she wished to bathe, he took her to a beautiful waterfall *inside* the Shrine, with water more pure and clear than any she'd found in all her travels. His speech was musical as his name, yet when she asked him to join her while she bathed, he stuttered and stammered, stumbling over even the simplest phrases as he very politely declined. Lady Firehair realized then that he had only been being polite. He really did know how shameful and ugly a creature she was, but he was kind enough not to treat her that way. Still, it made her sad; she had only wanted to share the pleasure of the cool water with him. Surely that should not have frightened him so.

What was stranger still, despite his refusal to bathe with her, he held her whenever she cried, as if his need to offer comfort was even greater than his revulsion for her. She always wanted to cry more when he held her, both for his kindness and because she selfishly wanted him to hold her longer. Unfortunately, his embrace was so comforting that her tears never lasted more than a few minutes, and he released her as soon as she stopped. She wanted to pull him close again whenever he let her go, but she didn't want to offend him, or let him know how greedy she was.

Tonight, though, she could not help herself. Despite all his kindness, she felt more alone than she had felt in years, and she did not know why. She was sitting on the beautiful oaken canopy bed he'd given her, with black and red satin sheets, but she could not sleep, however she tried. She knew that she was selfish, that what she was about to do was wrong, but she couldn't help herself. "Music," she called faintly. She didn't need to call loudly here; he always heard her.

"I am here, m'lady," he said from behind her, on the other side of the bed. "Dost thou need something?"

"Yes," she said softly… and found that she could not go on. She'd rehearsed in her mind several times what she was going to say, but now that he stood there looking at her, she found that the words had abandoned her.

"What dost thou require?" he asked politely after a few moments, when it was clear she would not go on unprompted.

"Company," she said finally. "I cannot sleep."

He came around and sat just apart from her on the bed. "I will remain, then, until thou dost grow sleepy."

"I am already sleepy," she told him. It was growing a little easier to speak, now that she'd started. "I am sleepy, but I cannot sleep."

"Why is that, m'lady?" he asked, concerned. "Is there something more thou dost require for thy comfort?"

"Yes," she said, surprised that her voice didn't shake. She didn't know why she felt so nervous, but her hands wouldn't seem to stop trembling.

"What is it, m'lady?" he asked.

Once again, the words left her, and she found herself unable to speak. It was truly frustrating, particularly when he was here, just out of her arm's reach.

"M'lady?" he asked again, his expression growing more concerned still. "What more dost thou require?"

"Thee," she said softly, and her entire body trembled. It felt as if there were giant butterflies fluttering about in her middle. She was quite certain that she'd never eaten a butterfly.

He appeared confused. "I am here already, m'lady. What can I do for thee?"

"Stay with me," she said.

"Thou dost require rest, m'lady," he said gently. "Perhaps if thou didst lie down…"

"Lie down with me." There, she'd said it. "Hold me, as you hold me when I cry. Your arms are a comfort, and I would sleep better if they were around me."

His face was unreadable, and he did not move.

After a few moments, she was beginning to think he'd frozen in place. Determined, and ashamed of her determination, Lady Firehair walked around to where he sat, at the end of the bed, and sat beside him, slipping her arms around him gently. He responded then, holding her in return, and she nestled her head on his shoulder, letting herself savor the contact for however long it lasted. "This is what I wanted," she said softly.

For some reason, that seemed to make him relax. His arms tightened warmly about her, and she sighed blissfully as he laid her down, holding her tenderly in his arms until sleep took her.

When she awoke, he was gone, of course. It was asking a great deal simply for him to hold her; it would have been unfair to expect him to stay with her through the night. She stretched luxuriously, taking pleasure in the feel of the soft bed, so much more comfortable than the hard, lumpy mattress she'd been given at home. Her uncle was never a great one for comfort, unless it was his own; *his* bed was a giant affair covered in black silken sheets that were cleaned daily with magic.

She lay in bed a little longer, enjoying the guilty pleasure of laziness in the beautiful bed. Eventually, though, she felt hungry, and she rose, moving into the next room. Music was already there, with a breakfast of fruit, pastry, and several delicious juices already prepared for her. She smiled in delight as she took a seat.

"I thank thee," she said before she began eating, and he smiled.

"It is my pleasure to care for thee, m'lady," he said softly, and to her surprise, there was no sense of falsehood in the words.

"May I ask a question?" she asked as she took a bite out of a flawless pear.

"Thou hast leave to ask any question thou dost wish," he told her.

"What exactly art thou?" she asked.

He tilted his head slightly. "That question is somewhat vague. Couldst thou clarify?"

She took a moment to collect her thoughts before proceeding. "I have spent only a little time among humans," she said as she finished the last bite of the pear, picking up a handful of blueberries next. "I have heard a few of them speak of creatures they revere, creatures known for their power and their kindness, creatures known as Dark Angels. Specifically, I have heard them speak of the Dark Angel of Music, sometimes called the last of his kind, and the oldest creature alive." She stopped for a moment. The blueberries were exquisite! "Are you he?" she asked.

He watched her impassively for several moments before answering, but finally he nodded. "I am."

"Your love," Lady Firehair said gently, "she was one of these Dark Angels also, was she not?"

He nodded again. "She was."

"Did the Seriani destroy thy people as they tried to destroy mine?" she asked. If they had, he would no doubt be more than willing to help her.

"Nay," he said softly. "Nay, they did not destroy us, though a few of their habits did contribute to our destruction."

She nodded in understanding, finishing the blueberries. She truly did love fruit. Next she tried some sort of melon that she'd never seen before. It was like honey inside, sweet and delicious.

"I am pleased that thou dost enjoy thy breakfast," he said, smiling.

"Very much," she managed around a mouthful. She swallowed before trying to speak again. "I have no idea how thou dost manage to gather such perfect fruit, but I do love it." Not a single piece of fruit showed the slightest sign of pest or bruising, as if all were picked from a garden where it grew to perfection every time.

"That is well," he said softly. He was silent throughout the remainder of her meal, but when she pushed her chair back with a contented sigh, he smiled, and food and table disappeared before her eyes. It was the first time he'd actually allowed her to see such a thing. Always before he had waited until she turned away, so that whatever object was to vanish was simply gone when she looked again.

"How dost thou accomplish that?" she asked in wonder. She could sense no residual energy of any kind, just as always, nothing to suggest that there had ever been a table laden with food standing right in front of where she sat. Worse, though, she saw nothing happening to the energy *during* the disappearance, as if the energy were invisible even to her eyes. Somewhere in the back of her mind, she thought it should be perfectly natural, but everything she knew said that it was not at all.

"In the same way that thou dost remain ever and always a creature of beauty beyond measure," he said, his eyes on hers. "It is a part of who I am."

She felt her cheeks grow hot at the compliment, particularly since there was no dishonesty in it. He actually believed she was beautiful! Lady Firehair could not recall a moment when she'd felt happier, or more confused... or more content to remain confused, if only to hold on to the happiness.

"Thou dost truly think me beautiful?" she asked softly. She knew it was selfish, but she wanted desperately to hear him state it directly.

"I do," he said simply, and he was speaking the truth.

She closed her eyes, savoring the moment. "Methinks," she said, her voice shaking slightly, "that there is no greater gift within thy power to grant me than that."

He bowed slightly. "I wish only that my gift to thee could equal thine to me."

She blinked in surprise, staring at him. "But I have given thee nothing!" she cried.

He actually laughed. It was the first time she'd heard him laugh outright, and the sound was at once strange and beautiful. She felt as if she were witnessing a music that the world had not seen in centuries, ridiculous as the notion may have been.

"Why dost thou laugh?" she asked, terribly confused.

He shook his head, still chuckling softly. "Dost thou truly believe that thou hast given me nothing?" he asked with mild incredulity.

She thought back, trying to recall any gift she might have given him, but there was nothing she could recall. "It is true, sir," she told him. "I have given thee nothing."

"And what of thy company?" he asked. "What of the conversations we have shared since thou didst come here. What of thine allowing me to hold thee as thou didst sleep?"

"I *asked* thee to hold me!" she cried, too shocked to be embarrassed.

"Aye, thou didst ask, and I let thee go only moments before thou didst wake, when I sensed that hunger would be upon thee soon after." He smiled faintly and looked downward, as if *he* were the one who had indulged in a selfish pleasure. "I left only to prepare thy breakfast."

It was more than Lady Firehair could comprehend. He claimed that she had given him a gift still greater than his sweet compliment to her, a compliment so beautiful that she would never be worthy of it so long as she lived. And yet, when she asked what gift she had given him, he listed more of his own gifts to her! It was maddening, yet distressed as she was, a part of her was pleased, and that confused her still more.

"M'lady," he said gently, "art thou alright?"

She looked at him, unable to reconcile his words, and he looked back calmly, as if all should be clear. "Thou art telling me that my gift to thee is *allowing* thee to bring happiness to me, to fill my heart with joy beyond anything I have ever known."

He smiled. "I knew that thou wouldst understand."

Chapter XXI

Rhanestone Keep was a very interesting place. Aeron couldn't see the energies that flowed within the older—and better kept—parts of the fortress, since it was Fire Warlocks who put those energies in place, but he could observe the results of the spells, and he thought he could duplicate most of the feats with Air magic. The entire place was giving him an idea for an Air fortress, or better yet, a city created by elementals from all four elements working together. The Sorceress High Priestess might be inclined to aid him in such an endeavor, when the war was over, and such a city might grow to be a place of learning for all races, not only elementals. Travel would be an issue, of course, but Aeron had several ideas already about how to create roads that would speed travelers along using Air magic, and he felt certain that Alier could accomplish the same feat using Earth.

In addition to the Keep itself, Aeron had found the Daemon raids to be a wonderful source of information. Skilled as he had become, Aeron had never actually used his magic in real combat before, and the concepts fascinated him. He used a chain lightning spell to damage six Soldiers in a row, and a second to finish them off. He found that the most useful spell against the creatures, though, was also the most simplistic. A gentle breeze carried the fragrance of the Dragon's Tears growing near the fortress straight to the nostrils of the Daemons, killing them almost instantly. Just for academic study, he set up a spell that redirected the natural mountain winds to the task, so that the fragrance was constantly blown in the direction of the Daemon army. It wasn't nearly as effective as controlling the spell directly, since the individual Daemons were not always in the same places, but it still killed dozens of Daemons before they backed up their entire camp, so that the fragrance would dissipate before it reached them.

The High Priestess had even invited Aeron to help her in charging weapons for the Rhanestone soldiers, and he'd accepted with enthusiasm. At least six different elven archers now used his bows, bows that turned an arrow into a bolt of lightning just after it was fired. The bolts of lightning were small, of course, and couldn't kill more than a Scout with only a single blow, but they were much faster than arrows, and even the quickest Daemon could never dodge one. Aeron had also enchanted a few pieces of armor, in case the Daemons ever broke through into the Keep again. These cuirasses were particularly resistant to damage, and anyone who struck them would receive an electrical shock proportionate to the force of the blow. The armor wasn't practical for ranged fighting, of course—who cared if an arrow received an electrical shock?—but they would prove very useful indeed for hand-to-hand fighting.

Despite all the time they'd spent together, Aeron still thought of the High Priestess by her title, rather than her name. He'd stood for her in her Rite of Oneness for Air, but however he looked at it, she outranked him, and deserved his respect even outside of that. Oddly, though, she seemed slightly frustrated with him whenever he addressed her. Perhaps there was a more formal title she preferred, though he wasn't aware that one existed.

Tonight Aeron was having one last quick tour of the Keep. The party would be leaving tomorrow to retrieve the final piece to the Armor of the Elements. If all went well, they would be returning to Rhanestone within a few weeks, but Aeron was learning quickly that things did not usually go well, when it came to such quests. If one is to be prepared, one must expect the worst, and be grateful when it does not happen.

Aeron walked the wall where even now soldiers were posted to keep an eye on the Daemon army. It was too far away now for them to see clearly, but they would know if another attack began. Aeron could see the Daemons perfectly well, of course, but there was really nothing to see. They were alternating between impatience and laziness, by appearances, but they were not attacking. Aeron had no idea what they were waiting for, but he was very glad indeed that they were waiting; with the Armor of the Elements, perhaps the army could be turned aside entirely, but without it, he doubted the Keep would survive a full assault.

Soon he went down into the courtyard, where the two dragons slept peacefully. Well, the black one slept peacefully, anyway. The crystal dragon, the Guardian of Mist, was awake and looking at him. Aeron stopped and returned her gaze. He was not afraid. Why should he be, when she was an ally? He was, however, very curious. "Can you not sleep either?" he asked. His implication was not entirely true—he could sleep without difficulty if he wished—but it gave him a way to open a conversation.

"Like you," the dragon said softly, almost as if her voice were within his mind alone, "I can sleep without difficulty, if I wish."

He'd not been aware that the Guardian could read minds. Well no, there were other explanations that would fit as well; he mustn't jump to conclusions. Before he could open his mouth, though, she spoke again.

"I understand the reason for your small deception," she said. "I had been wondering how to begin a conversation with you as well."

Now that was intriguing... "Why?" asked Aeron.

"There is something I must tell you."

Aeron waited expectantly, but when it became clear she would not speak without prompting, he asked, "What is that?"

"Your destiny is not the destiny you imagine for yourself. You will participate in this struggle, but it is another struggle that is your life's work, and that one you will be central to when the time comes."

Aeron waited for more, but the Guardian didn't go on. "Is that all?" he asked, surprised.

"Yes," she told him. "That is all."

"Things would be far simpler if prophecy were not so cryptic," he said softly.

"Yes," agreed the Guardian, "but if prophecy were simple to understand, it would seem out of place in life. Life is not at all simple to understand."

"Perhaps not, but certain aspects of it are fairly simple."

"Not many," the dragon said, and Aeron suddenly felt as if she were smiling, though he couldn't see any change in her expression. "Often those things which seem simple are not at all simple in reality, and those things which are simple are merely concepts, not manifestations."

"One day," said Aeron, "I would like to have a longer conversation with you."

"I will look forward to the day when that is possible," the Guardian told him. "Your reason is an art in itself. For now, though, I must sleep, and so must you."

"Thank you," said Aeron. "Goodnight to you."

"Goodnight to you as well," said the Guardian. "May the Power guide you all on your quest."

Aeron went back to his room then, and promptly fell asleep. When he woke, he was fairly certain that he had dreamed, but he could not recall what the dreams had been.

***

Alexander glanced at Alloria frequently as they rode. He couldn't seem to keep his eyes off her, the past few days, and it was more than how beautiful she was. Try as he might, he couldn't puzzle her out. They were only six days from Green Haven now, including today, and they'd been attacked twice more, after that first time. Both times, Alloria had saved his life, but only the first time had Alexander felt anything of the revulsion he'd known before when she'd wiped the blood from her mouth, and even then it was mild. Was he becoming accustomed to her diet, or did it simply not bother him because it was a part of her? Every night they stayed at an inn, and every night they made love. For some reason, Alloria seemed particularly pleased about that, and Alexander would not have been able to resist her if he'd wanted to. Only one of the innkeepers so far had given her black cloak a second glance, and that one turned all smiles as soon as he produced gold. Greed was one of the few things that seemed to overpower prejudice, particularly in business owners.

The more time that went by, though, the more Alexander wondered how Alloria could possibly be so genuinely devoted and loving. She did not lie with him out of duty; of that much he was certain. He could never ask her to, and she would be violating their agreement of equality in private. Still, when all the frills were taken away, she was his slave, yet she seemed not merely content, but *happy* with their arrangement. When he'd tried to ask her about it, she laughed, and told him that *he* was silly! He was quickly reaching the conclusion that even vampire women were not entirely logical, though he was careful not to voice that conclusion… ever. He'd feel terrible if she were upset with him, even if she tried to hide it, and she'd told him before that nearly all vampires prided themselves on their impeccable logic. Alexander wisely refrained from pointing out that pride was not exactly logical.

What worried Alexander the most, though, was that he loved her in return. She was a vampire, and when he was old and grey, she would still be young and beautiful as ever. They could never grow old together, but Alexander did not want to leave her. It was a difficult problem, but fortunately not an immediate one. He had a lifetime to think on it, after all. If he ever saw the Sorceress High Priestess again, perhaps he could ask her about the longevity of the race, and try to devise a way to duplicate it.

"Alexander," Alloria said urgently, "there are more humans ahead, hidden in the trees."

"Not again," Alexander sighed.

"It is different this time," she told him. "Their energy is weak, not like our previous attackers."

"Go ahead to investigate, and don't let them see you," said Alexander. Alloria could take care of herself better than he could, and she was quite skilled in the arts of stealth.

She nodded, and in the next moment, was gone. He really wished there were some way for him to follow her when she moved that way, but such were the limitations of humanity. She was back in just a few moments, seated atop her mare as if she'd never left. "They will not attack us," she said.

"You killed them already?" asked Alexander incredulously. That had been fast, even for her.

"I did not harm them at all," she said. "They are not bandits; they are children."

"You mean women and children?" he asked uncertainly.

"I mean children," she said firmly. "There are no adults among them."

"We must stop then," said Alexander. "Children should not be out here alone. How many are there?"

"Five," she replied. "The eldest of them is a girl no more than twelve. She appears to be leading them."

"Stay here," instructed Alexander, dismounting and handing his reins to Alloria. "If they've been raised on prejudice, you might frighten them. At the least, though, we might be able to change their minds, once I have them convinced that I won't harm them."

Alexander stepped warily into the clearing, careful not to startle the children. There was a wagon that had been taken off the road, a merchant's wagon, by the look of it, but there were no children in sight. Suddenly, Alexander felt something sharp at the back of his neck. "Don't move, if you want to live," said a female voice, high-pitched with youth.

"I'm here to help you," Alexander told her.

"No one is here to help us," she replied scornfully. "We must help ourselves."

Alexander rolled forward and came up on his feet, facing the girl. She reacted quickly, thrusting the spear she held at him, but he grabbed it below the head and yanked it out of her hand. "Now," he said, "we will talk."

The girl whistled shrilly, and four more children, three boys and a girl, jumped out of the bushes with arrows knocked to bows. The eldest boy appeared ten or so, the girl perhaps a year or two younger, and the other two boys another year or so younger than that. Their faces were all grim. "Yes," said the eldest girl. "We will talk now."

"I realize you must have had a difficult time," said Alexander loudly, "but there is no need to threaten me with your weapons."

An instant later, a dark blur whizzed past all four of the younger children. When it had passed, their weapons were gone, and Alloria stood beside Alexander, smiling faintly.

One of the youngest boys started to cry, and the younger girl hugged him comfortingly. The other two boys watched impassively, as if nothing more in the world could frighten them, even the death they felt certain they would soon receive. The eldest girl's expression was weary determination. "Leave the four of them alone, and I'll give you anything you want. I know you could take me by force, but I'll offer myself freely if you let them go."

Alexander was both surprised and disgusted, and wasn't sure which reaction he felt more poignantly. "Don't be ridiculous," he snapped. "You're all children, and I already have a beautiful wife," he said, indicating Alloria, who smiled again. "I told you before that I was here to help you, and I meant it."

"Are you a wizard?" the eldest girl asked.

"A wizard?" asked Alexander, baffled.

"Only a wizard would be able to control a vampire," she said with a shrug.

Alexander glanced at Alloria, and she answered for him. "He does not control me. I am *yamin'sai* to him."

The four younger children were understandably confused, but the eldest girl's eyes were alight with comprehension. "I did not realize that the tradition of *yamin'sai* still existed."

"What are your names?" asked Alexander, changing tack. He really didn't want to explain the principle for the others just yet.

"I am Amber Ravenstar," the girl told him. "I am recently thirteen years of age. The eldest boy is Josua Hunter; he's eleven. The other girl is Lilian Hunter, his younger sister by a year. These two," she said, indicating the two younger boys, "are twins. They are Tim and Tom Taliman, both eight." Only then did Alexander notice the resemblance between them. Their clothes and hair were entirely different, so it had not been apparent at first.

"Ravenstar," Alexander said softly. "That sounds vaguely familiar."

"I'm sure it is a coincidence," Amber told him. Her eyes betrayed nothing. Despite himself, Alexander was impressed. He didn't believe that he'd have taken things so calmly, if he'd been in her position at thirteen years of age. Still, she was obviously lying. Alexander was certain that Ravenstar was the name of one of the minor Houses in the Southern nations, minor, but very much nobility, and quite powerful for a minor House. Besides, no peasant girl would speak or behave the way Amber did. Likely she was running away from something, possibly her own heritage. A measure of caution would be prudent.

"I am Alexander," he told them all. "This is my wife, Alloria. We are going to visit my brother, and you are all welcome to join us. I understand that you can all take care of yourselves, but only a fool passes up a free meal and a warm bed for the night."

"Are you certain we will not be imposing on your brother?" asked Amber.

"I am certain," said Alexander, looking her directly in the eyes. "I am also certain that he will not care at all where you are from. My brother has little or no contact with any other noble houses, and absolutely none with anyone else." That was not entirely true, but it would take only a few whispered words to ensure that there would be no investigation, particularly when Duncan's own daughter was missing.

"Why do you do all the talking?" asked Josua, eyeing Alloria suspiciously. "Why doesn't she say anything?"

"Because she is *yamin'sai*," Amber told him. "I'll explain that to you later." Even for a noble, Amber Ravenstar appeared remarkably well educated. Alexander himself had only known the basics of what the term *yamin'sai* entailed, but she seemed to know all the details by rote. Alexander suspected that she was already experienced far beyond her years.

"Well, come along, then," said Alexander. "We have only two horses, but I think they could handle two or three small riders each."

"The others can share," Amber announced. "I will walk with you." The other children did not seem inclined to argue. In Alexander's moderate experience with children, those four were uncharacteristically obedient to the eldest girl.

"The mystery thickens," Alloria whispered into his ear as they stepped out of the trees to the waiting horses. He would have to speak with her in private at the first opportunity. It was fortunate that he'd brought a good deal more gold along than he should have needed, for he planned to rent three rooms at each inn now, rather than one.

"How is it that a vampire became *yamin'sai* to a human lord?" asked Amber once they were underway.

Alloria looked to Alexander questioningly. "We are still in private, in their company," he said softly.

"I offered myself to him as *yamin'sai* in order to promote peace between our peoples," Alloria told Amber.

"It is good to know that there exist some this far south who do not hate all vampires," the girl said, smiling with approval. "Most in this region are terribly biased."

"How is it that you escaped such prejudice?" asked Alexander.

"My mind is my own," Amber said defiantly. "It does not belong to the ignorant fools who would have me adopt their ways. I prefer logic to emotion, and there is no logic in prejudice."

"You are a wise young woman," said Alloria with a smile.

"I lack sufficient information to be wise," Amber told her. "I am learning, but the learning is very slow, I'm afraid. I make mistakes daily, mistakes that should have been avoided. My only defense is that I recognize those mistakes, and try not to make the same ones twice."

"That realization is itself a mark of wisdom," the vampire woman said softly.

"A mark is not wisdom itself," said Amber. "I have much to learn."

Alexander remained silent. This girl did not act like any thirteen-year-old he'd ever heard of. With her, it would probably be best to wait and observe.

Alloria seemed to see it differently, which was probably to the good, from Alexander's perspective. "Where were you educated?" the vampire asked.

"I've had private tutors since I was old enough to speak," Amber told her. "The two of you have no doubt realized that I am from the Ravenstar house—that was one of today's mistakes, giving my real name, particularly to a man who carries himself like a lord, despite his rough traveling clothes. Still, neither of you seem inclined to force me into going back, and if you will see that the children are taken care of, then I am content to go with you."

Amber had an interesting idea of "rough" traveling clothes; Alexander had chosen plain colors, but his clothing was quite well made and durable, something Duke Rhanestone might have worn if he were to travel. Still, Duke Rhanestone preferred the practical to the flamboyant, and many southern nobles did not.

"How did you come to be with them?" asked Alloria.

"The Hunters were children of a merchant who was killed on the road. I found them hiding in a compartment inside the wagon when I happened upon it. The merchant's wares were mostly nonperishable foodstuffs, miraculously not taken by the bandits, so we stayed near the wagon while the food still constituted more than we could carry. We met the Talimans a few days later. They were lost in the woods, and wouldn't say where they were from. We couldn't just leave them, so we took them with us. That was five weeks ago. Our food supply is now nearly gone, but we happened upon that wagon you saw beside the road, and had planned to use it for shelter. That's when you showed up."

There were several holes in the story, such as how and where they acquired the bows and the spear, and how they managed to carry five weeks worth of food, not to mention how they avoided bandits that would have robbed them and left them for dead, if they were lucky. There were still more than five days before they reached Green Haven, though. Perhaps more information would come with time.

Chapter XXII

Serana sighed wistfully as her small party left the fortress of Rhanestone Keep, just before the light of dawn crept over the horizon. She'd been officially named the leader by all four elementals, and before she could protest, Aeron had suggested that any who disapproved could spar her for the job. She'd spent most of the previous evening with her father and his family, and the afternoon with Rillian—he was still moving his things to Ella's room. They'd agreed to postpone the wedding until the party returned with the final piece to the Armor of the Elements, so that Serana could be there, but now that Ella had Rillian's attention, she was more than a little eager. Serana hoped she would not be gone too long this time; Rhanestone had become her home in more ways than she'd realized.

The party headed south, using the road mostly because neither Sorceress nor elementals had any idea where their destination actually was. Lady Firehair had said that the Daemon Lord was tormenting a southern estate, but she'd not mentioned *which* estate, or even the general location within the Southern nations. Serana didn't believe it would be terribly difficult to locate him, though. Tormenting a human estate was hardly enough to occupy a Daemon Lord; there would undoubtedly be tales of strange happenings in whatever region he chose to inhabit. Serana intended to simply follow those tales.

Her immediate destination was Green Haven, a city built on the ruins of Ereanthea, normally three weeks travel almost due south from Rhanestone. Alier wanted to stop there anyway, to pay her respects to the place of her birth and to feel the energies that still resided in the earth there. Plants of nearly every kind thrived in Green Haven, thanks to those energies, and Serana was more than a little interested in seeing them herself. She decided that they wouldn't stay more than a day, though, however tempting it was; the Armor was nearly complete, and there was no telling when Rhanestone would sorely need it.

Green Haven was still five or six days away, though, even for elementals—and a Sorceress who could travel as one of them. There were inns scattered along the road south, and Serana suggested that the party use them; it would take less time than making camp each night, and more importantly, it would allow them all to talk with people and listen for any rumors of unusual activity in the South.

Serana also insisted that Allaerion and Alier practice with her each night. She'd only sparred for a few hours in Rhanestone, and only on one day. A few of the Elite Guard members were a bit challenging, but none of them could ever hope to match Allaerion or Alier. Serana had unintentionally become a legend among the Rhanestone soldiers that day. Most of them already knew something of her magical skill, but that was the first time any of them had seen her wield a blade. For some reason, the sight of a sixteen-year-old girl taking on two Elite Guard members at once—and winning—impressed them still more than her magic did.

On the first night, Serana practiced outside the inn they were to stay at, in a large open space behind the stables. The stable hands—and several of the guests—watched with interest, but this close to Rhanestone most people knew what an elemental was, and nearly everyone had heard of the Sorceress race, even if they'd thought it extinct.

A small village had sprung up around this particular inn, The Duke's Lodge, normally three days travel from Rhanestone, and word that a Sorceress and three elementals were in town spread fast. No sooner had she stopped practicing with Alier and come inside, Serana was assaulted with pleas for healing. Three people were in sore need of her skills, but the rest would recover without any real difficulties on their own. Still, Serana didn't turn anyone away; it was such little effort to heal most injuries that she didn't have the heart to say no when someone asked.

The three most serious cases were a man with a broken leg, a woman with some sort of stomach sickness, and a little boy with fever so high that it was threatening his life. Serana saw to the child first, since he was the first to arrive, carried in by his mother, who appeared near her wit's end. "Just relax now," Serana told the boy gently as soon as she'd finished probing him with her magic. "It will be alright soon."

The little boy nodded, watching her.

"Can you help him?" asked the mother anxiously.

"He'll be fine in a few minutes," Serana assured her. Sickness was not quite so simple to heal as injury, but Serana had read enough about it that she felt confident in what she was about to do. Most types of sickness required some skill in Water magic, according to the text, along with the normal Life magic all Sorceresses could wield. For Serana, of course, the Water magic would not be a problem. She instructed the child to drink a large glass of water, and then she set to work. It wasn't terribly difficult to draw the infection into the water, but Serana was very careful even so, since it was her first attempt. The entire procedure took her only five minutes or so, and the little boy jumped up, bouncing on his feet before running out, saying that he needed to go to the woods.

"Thank you so much," said the mother, tears in her eyes. "I don't know how I could ever repay you."

"It's no trouble at all," Serana smiled, giving the woman a warm hug. "I'm glad that I was here in time."

The little boy ran back into the inn within minutes, looking much relieved. No doubt the amount of water Serana had made him drink had been quite uncomfortable, once she was done with him. "Thank you!" he said happily, jumping into Serana's arms.

Serana laughed and hugged him before handing him over to his mother. That was when the woman with the stomach sickness arrived. The husband carried her in, himself looking haggard and worn with worry, but there was desperate hope in his eyes as they fell on Serana.

"Please," he said urgently. "It's my wife. At first, we thought it was just something she ate, but it didn't pass. It's been nearly a week, and she's gotten worse every day."

"I'll do what I can," said Serana soothingly. "Lie her down on the table here, and let me look at her."

The man obeyed, watching anxiously as Serana looked over the woman critically. "Can you heal her?" he asked after a few moments.

"I believe so," said Serana. The poor woman was not only sick, but she had somehow acquired a parasite in her intestines that was sucking her life away. The solution was rather simple, really, but delicate all the same. Serana drew the illness into the parasite. The creature died within moments, and Serana put a protective spell around it, to prevent the sickness from spreading back to the woman. The spell would dissipate eventually, of course, but by then the dead creature should be out of her body anyway. Serana warned the woman what to expect, and she nodded, saying it was immeasurably better than dying.

"Thank you," said the husband, taking Serana's hand. "I wish I had gold to pay you, but anything I have that you need is yours."

"Just take care of her," Serana told him. "She'll be hungry soon, if she isn't already, and she'll need to eat heartily for the next few days. She might be a little weak for a while, but that should pass entirely within a week."

"He'll take good care of me," the woman said, smiling. "Thank you, High Priestess. I've seen that dress once before, when I was a little girl, and I still remember."

"You're welcome," said Serana, smiling. "Get plenty of rest."

"She won't be out of bed for the next few days," said the husband. "I'll take care of everything."

"After a few days of his cooking, I most certainly *will* be out of bed!" the woman teased, and everyone in the common room laughed, including the husband.

"If there's anything I can do for you, High Priestess," the husband said earnestly as he carried his wife out, "anything at all, ever, just come to me. Whatever it is, I'll do it!"

The man with the broken leg had come in while Serana was working on the woman, and he didn't speak until her husband had carried her out. "I don't mean to be any bother," he said tentatively, "but with my leg like this, I might not be able to get the crop in before winter. I'll heal on my own eventually, but it's my family, you see. My wife is pregnant, and she shouldn't be doing so much of the work."

"It's no bother at all," Serana told him, smiling. His leg took only moments to heal, of course. That sort of injury was as easy as breathing for her now. "There," she said when she'd finished. "Good as new."

He took a few experimental steps, then turned back to Serana with a grin. "High Priestess," he said, "I heard the woman call you that, so I'm guessing it's your title." He looked questioningly at her, and she nodded. "High Priestess, I'm not a rich man, and I can't pay you what your help is worth, but I'll put in whatever I can afford toward your room and board tonight."

Before Serana could protest, the innkeeper, a stout woman with a ready smile, spoke up. "Don't worry about it, Bill. The Sorceress and her friends are my guests tonight, and I won't hear of them paying for a thing!"

Serana and her friends ate well that night, and slept in the inn's best rooms. Serana went to sleep with a contentment she hadn't felt in a long time. She finally knew her real father, and the Armor of the Elements was nearly complete. More than anything, though, she loved seeing the unrestrained joy on the faces of the people she healed, and their families. That joy, and the lives it touched, was the most beautiful thing she'd ever seen, and spreading it was what she wanted to do with her own life, when the war was over. From what she'd read of her people, she was truly born to the task.

When she woke, it was early morning, the grey, pre-dawn light trickling in through the window. Serana had only had six hours or so of sleep, but she felt refreshed and ready for the day. She went downstairs, and found the innkeeper already bustling about, cleaning up tables from the night before. "Good morning, High Priestess!" she said to Serana, smiling pleasantly. "Did you sleep well?"

"Very well, thank you." Serana returned the smile.

"May I get you some breakfast?" the innkeeper asked.

"Yes, please." The mention of food made Serana's stomach growl unexpectedly.

"Just have a seat, then, and I'll bring your plate out shortly." The innkeeper gave Serana another smile, and retreated to the kitchen. She emerged just a few minutes later with a plate stacked with delicious-looking hotcakes and a bowl of fruit. She even brought a small jar of fresh strawberry jam, Serana's favorite.

"No wonder you're up so early," said Allaerion a few minutes later, as he came down the stairs.

"Just take a seat, sir," said the innkeeper, "and I'll bring you a plate too."

Allaerion obeyed with a grin, sitting across from Serana. A good meal was probably the quickest way to catch the Air Wizard's attention, or if not, it was second only to an attack.

"What is that delightful smell?" asked Seleine as she came down, before the innkeeper had returned with Allaerion's plate. "They certainly do take care of their guests here!"

"When our guests include a Sorceress who heals the sick and the injured," said the innkeeper, bustling in with Allaerion's food, "we do our best to accommodate, and hope she'll come back again one day."

"I'll be back at least once more," promised Serana. They'd have to return this way with the gauntlet.

"Then I'll have rooms ready for you when you come," the innkeeper told her.

"We don't mean to take advantage," said Serana. "We're happy to pay for the rooms, really."

"Don't you worry about that," said the innkeeper. "Bill, the man with the leg you fixed, provides me with the beef I serve from his herds; he'll give me a considerable discount next time, since I'm giving you your rooms and board. Al and Rena—you cured Rena's stomach sickness last night—make the best apple brandy around, selling even to Duke Rhanestone each year. They'll give me an extra barrel or two as they can afford it. The people here aren't wealthy, but we pay for what we get however we're able. Your rooms and meals are the least we can offer you for your healing. I know it's not equal value, but I won't hear of you accepting less, when you deserve more."

"Thank you," said Serana.

"No, thank *you*," said the innkeeper, grinning. "Now enjoy your breakfast. I'll bring out three more meals. This lovely creature," she looked at Seleine, "looks hungry, and I'm sure your other two friends will be awake before long."

Aeron and Alier were drawn down by the smell of breakfast by the time the innkeeper had set out their plates. "Wonderful service!" said the Earth Enchantress as she took her seat. "I shall recommend your establishment to anyone traveling this way."

The innkeeper beamed.

Aeron nodded enthusiastically; his mouth was already full.

When they'd all finished eating, they gathered their things from the rooms and made ready to leave.

"Don't you have any horses?" asked the innkeeper.

"We travel more quickly without them," Serana explained. "Elemental magic."

"Oh, I see," the innkeeper said doubtfully. "Well, good luck to you. Tell me how it turned out when you return this way."

When they stepped outside, there was a man with a bow pointed at Serana from across the street. He loosed the arrow, and Serana stopped it inches from her head with Air magic. The arrow turned at her command, and sped back to her would-be assassin, stopping just before it hit his throat. Serana crossed the road, holding the man in place with the same spell she used to control the arrow. "Explain yourself," she commanded.

"You're a witch!" he spat. "It's you magic users that bring the Daemons down on Rhanestone. They took my wife three years ago, when I was there, and they'll kill us all before they're done."

"Are you blind?" demanded Serana. "If you were at Rhanestone, didn't you notice the Battlemage there fighting *against* the Daemons using magic?"

"He's human," said the man grimly. "It's different."

"Daemons don't care if you're human or not," Serana told him. "They kill you just as quickly."

"Like you're going to kill me?" the man asked sullenly.

"Ignorance that blatant may be a crime," said Serana, "but it doesn't warrant a death sentence."

"We'll see about that," said a man from behind her. "Ted Collup, you're going to the town court for attempted murder." There was a crowd of people gathered around already, all of them staring daggers at the man Serana held in place. Looking at them all, Serana suddenly felt certain that if she left now, the man would surely die.

"Listen to me, all of you," she commanded, and every eye turned to her. "This man acted out of ignorance, not malice. I forgive him, and so should you. Don't punish him; teach him." She turned to the immobile man, still clutching his empty bow. "There is only one race to blame for the Daemons," she said softly. "The Daemons themselves." She released him, and he stared at her, flushed red.

"I'm sorry," he said finally, and walked quickly away.

"It's time to go," Serana told her friends, and they continued on toward Green Haven.

***

Green Haven was coming into sight ahead, less than an hour away now, as the sun began to approach the horizon, and Alexander still knew little more about his young companions. They ate whatever they were given without complaint, and they answered almost any question he asked, but their answers were always evasive or vague, often both. The one question none of them save Amber would answer was where they were from. It gnawed at Alexander that there should be some significance to that simple fact, but if there was, he couldn't place it.

The four youngest children followed Amber without question. That fact alone was unusual, from what little Alexander knew about children. Amber seemed to follow no one at all. She traveled with Alexander and Alloria because it suited her to do so, because traveling with them seemed the best way to care for the younger four.

"Have you ever been to Green Haven before?" Alexander asked her, now that the city was in view.

"Once," she said, "before I met the others." Alexander waited for her to elaborate, and then chided himself for not realizing that she wouldn't unless prompted.

"What happened?" he asked.

"What do you mean?" she returned.

"Tell me about your one visit to the Garden City."

"It was uneventful," she said, but she shifted uncomfortably, giving away the lie. "I passed through, nothing more."

Alon trotted over to the girl, nuzzling her hand with his nose. He often did that when Alexander or Alloria were upset, offering whatever comfort he could. Amber petted him absently, lost in her own thoughts, probably memories of the events she was not inclined to share.

"Have you ever seen the fabled flower garden in Green Haven?" asked Alloria suddenly. Amber shook her head. "Every kind of flower that has ever been named by humans grows there, all together. It's the only place in the world where the more aggressive ones won't kill the weaker ones."

"Have *you* ever been there?" Alexander asked the vampire woman.

"No," admitted Alloria, "but I've read about it. I was hoping we could stop there while we're in the city.

"I think we should," said Alexander with a smile. "It's a wondrous sight."

"You like flowers?" Amber asked Alloria. "They have no blood."

"Most of them are not edible to humans either," replied the vampire woman. "And yet, there are scores of humans who love them. Other than Daemons, I know of no species that *only* likes what it can eat."

The girl walked on in silence for a time before speaking again. "I thought vampires were consumed with the need for blood."

"If we become hungry enough," shrugged Alloria. "Of course, humans are also consumed with the need for food, if they become hungry enough."

"So you don't have to constantly restrain yourself in order to deal with humans?" asked Amber. She seemed a touch troubled, to Alexander's eyes.

"Of course not. Must humans constantly restrain themselves, in order to raise cattle or sheep? Do they constantly feel an all-consuming desire to start cooking as they tend the fields?"

Amber flushed slightly. "I had not realized just how ridiculous the prejudice has become. Even I, who do not hate vampires, have been holding misconceptions about them."

"At least you realize it," said Alloria, smiling slightly. "Ask me any questions you will, and perhaps we can put most of your misconceptions to rest."

The girl continued asking questions until they reached the city gates. She learned, as Alexander had, that vampires have no aversion to holy symbols or sunlight, and that they did have powerful emotions; they simply did not feel those emotions poignantly so frequently as humans did.

"What about garlic?" asked the girl as they approached the gates. "Is garlic dangerous?"

"Very dangerous," Alloria told her, and Alexander glanced sideways to listen. "I think a person could compete with a dragon for deadly breath, after eating the stuff." She wrinkled up her nose, and Amber, Alexander, and the four children burst out laughing. "Seriously, though," she said after they calmed down, "it isn't garlic that I watch for; it's onions."

"Onions?" asked Amber, bewildered.

"Of course!" cried Alloria. "The taste could kill anything!"

Alexander chose his favorite inn from his journey to Rhanestone, The Sleeping Dragon. The innkeeper, Balon Trush, welcomed him warmly, remembering him despite all the intervening time.

"We'll have our best room ready for you, my lord," he said heartily. "What's this?" he asked as Alloria and the children came in. "Did you have a family in Rhanestone waiting?"

"Not exactly," said Alexander. "This is my wife, Alloria. We met and married at Rhanestone. These are Amber, Josua, Lilian, Tim, and Tom."

"Are they yours, my lord?" asked Balon. "Forgive me if I am too forward with my questions, but I thought, well..." He leaned in closer, casting a wary eye at Alloria, and whispered. "I thought vampires could not have children."

"You're right," Alloria told him, making the poor man jump slightly. "We cannot. The children are friends whom we're escorting to my brother-in-law's estate."

"We'll need three rooms for tonight," said Alexander, "one for my wife and me, one for the two girls, and one for the three boys. The lamb stays with my wife and me." Alon voiced his approval, and the twins laughed.

"I'll see to it," said Balon with a bow, accepting the small purse Alexander handed him. The man didn't even flinch at the last bit; he'd probably already reasoned out why a lord with a vampire wife would want a lamb in his room.

"Is it my memory," asked Alexander suddenly, looking around, "or has the place grown a bit larger?"

"It's not your memory, my lord," Balon told him. "We had a very strange visitor some months ago who left a very large purse behind. I daresay that if we ever see her again, our welcome will be a good deal warmer."

"Was she a young woman?" asked Alexander, now keenly interested. "Talented in magic?"

"That she was," the innkeeper answered slowly. "She killed a soldier who wanted to take advantage of her, burned his arm and threw him across the room. You know her?"

"Did she wear a green dress?" Alexander continued, ignoring the innkeeper's question. "She'd have brown hair flowing halfway down her back, and stunning eyes."

"No, I'm afraid not," said Balon. "This girl had fiery red hair to her waist, and wore a red and black dress. You're right about the eyes, though, and her voice was stranger still."

"Her voice?" Alexander had heard the Sorceress High Priestess speak, and never found her voice particularly unusual.

The innkeeper nodded. "Yes, my lord. Her voice was..." He paused, as if searching for words. "I'm not sure how to describe it. All I know is that it wasn't human." The big man shivered. "But enough talk of that, my lord. Let's get you all settled in your rooms."

"Who is the woman with the stunning eyes?" asked Alloria when they were alone.

"The Sorceress High Priestess," Alexander said distractedly. He was still trying to puzzle out who the mysterious visitor could be, if it hadn't been Serana.

"Why had you not mentioned her before?"

"It never came up," Alexander told her. Who else could possibly be so powerful?

"She was a lover of yours?"

Only then did Alloria's tone sink in. "No, she was never a lover," he said firmly. "She was a person who I sorely misjudged, just like you. Unlike you, though, I never got the chance to know her, after I realized my mistake."

"I know you misjudged her," declared Alloria. "If you recall, she was part of my first argument in trying to make you see the truth about my people. What I want to know is whether or not you still intend to pursue her." Her voice was soft as the sound of steel leaving a scabbard... cold steel.

"I was taken with her once," admitted Alexander. Lying was both pointless and dangerous, with Alloria. "I was taken with her mostly from guilt and awe; I'd just watched her slay Daemon after Daemon in an attack on Rhanestone, only hours after I had wanted her thrown out of the Keep. I never did intend to pursue her, though, and now I could never wish to."

"Why?" asked Alloria. The air seemed just a little less frigid, but only a little.

"Because there is only room in my heart to love one woman at a time," he told her truthfully.

Alloria merely looked at him, her face void of expression, her eyes burning with emotion.

Alexander drew her into his arms and kissed her gently. "It's too late for any other woman," he said softly. "I already love you."

Her arms slipped around him, squeezing him so tightly that he almost asked her to be gentle. She truly didn't know her own strength sometimes. Then she kissed him, and he no longer cared whether or not she was gentle.

An hour or so later, they were all gathered around a table in one of the inn's private dining rooms. Alexander had discreetly informed Balon that Alloria did, in fact, eat solid food, so a plate was brought for her the same as for the rest of them.

The children ate as if they didn't expect food again for a long while. Even Tim and Tom each had a second helping. Amber ate deliberately and thoughtfully, as if trying to savor the food, despite wanting to gobble it down. Not for the first time, Alexander felt certain that there was something odd about the girl, something he could not quite put his finger on.

"She is different from the others," Alloria told him later that night, as they were undressing for bed.

"That much is obvious," said Alexander. "She leads them, after all."

"I'm talking about her energy," the vampire woman said softly.

"I thought you said that you could not see energy, as skilled magic users can."

"We cannot," she admitted. "We see only life energies. Our magical abilities are inherent and instinctive, not learned."

"So you're saying that Amber's energy is different from the others?"

Alloria nodded.

"Then why didn't you mention it to me before?"

"Because you'd have asked what the difference was, and I could not have told you," she replied calmly, slipping beneath the sheets.

"But now you can?" he asked, joining her.

"Not entirely, but I can tell you that it is not the same as any human I have ever before encountered."

"She isn't human?" Alexander exclaimed.

"I didn't say that," said Alloria. "I said that her energy is not the same as any human I have ever before encountered. It is also not the same as anyone from any other race. The difference is not radical. Her energy is stronger than that of most humans, but not so strong as that of a Sorceress or elemental."

"What do you think it means?"

"If I knew that," she said as her arms slipped around him, "I would have already told you."

"I suppose then," he said, pulling her closer, "that we should ignore it for now, but keep it in mind for later."

"I agree." She kissed him softly, pressing herself against him. "My mind is entirely on other things at the moment."

Alexander's was as well.

Chapter XXIII

The other villages were much like that first one. There were crowds of people that gathered around the inn where she stayed, come to ask the Sorceress for healing. The innkeepers didn't charge for their rooms, after the healing was done, though one grumbled about it. Serana offered to pay the man, but he said he wouldn't be the only innkeeper between Rhanestone and Green Haven that took her money.

Inevitably, though, each village held a few who wanted Serana dead, or at least away from their village. It wasn't difficult for her to defend herself, particularly against humans. She didn't have to kill or hurt anyone, but it did make her sad that people would take her healing as evil. She supposed that it was something she would simply have to learn to live with. Perhaps after the Daemons were defeated and a few generations of humans had gone by, things would be different among them.

Five days after that first village, the party arrived in Green Haven. It was evening, and the setting sun painted the horizon crimson as Serana walked through the city gates. None of the party had been to Green Haven before, not since it became Green Haven, anyway, so they were going to have to search around a bit to find an inn.

No sooner had Serana and the elementals come through the gates, though, than the problem of finding an inn lost precedence. There was a crowd of at least a hundred people waiting that swarmed up around them. Despite how quickly the party could travel with elemental magic, news apparently traveled even more quickly, particularly news of a Sorceress who healed the sick and injured. Serana was tired after the day's travel, but she couldn't bring herself to turn the people away. Still there was no reason for her friends to stand in the street.

"Could you direct us to an inn, please?" Serana asked. "When we arrive there, my friends can rest, and I will heal anyone who needs healing."

Surprisingly, the request worked. Serana had expected people to start blurting out the names of various inns all at once, and for none of the names, much less directions, to be audible amidst the jumble. Instead, nearly every mouth said The Sleeping Dragon, apparently the best inn in all of Green Haven. The crowd started moving almost as soon as they spoke, so Serana simply followed. Within a few minutes, they arrived at the door of the inn, and Serana told the elementals to go in and sit down. She intended to be awhile.

"Listen to me," she said softly, using Air magic to make her voice carry. The crowd quieted instantly. "I'm going inside. Those of you with the most serious problems come in first, and when I've seen to them, anyone else should come. I know none of you wants anyone to die simply because someone who could have waited shoved ahead." Without waiting for any reply, Serana turned and went inside, taking a seat at a table in a corner. The innkeeper, a large man with a ready smile, hurried over to her even before people from outside began coming in.

"I am Balon Trush," he said. "Welcome to The Sleeping Dragon. May I offer you any refreshments?"

"I'll need rooms tonight for myself and my friends, the elementals who came in before me. For now, though, I must see to the people outside. They'll be coming in to request my services."

"Services?" asked Balon, taking in her ornate dress. "What services would those be?"

"Healing," Serana told him. "I am the Sorceress High Priestess."

The innkeeper blinked in surprise. "I've heard of you, but I didn't expect to see you so soon. If there is anything you need, just let me know." He bustled away just as the first people reached him, a young couple with the husband carrying a small girl in his arms.

"High Priestess," the woman said pleadingly. "Our daughter collapsed an hour ago. She was fine until then, but she just... well, collapsed. Please help her. We'll do anything!" The husband was nodding through the entire plea.

"I'll do what I can," Serana assured them both as she examined the girl, taking her from her father's arms. This time, Serana's herbal knowledge was nearly as useful as her magic, at least in determining the problem. The girl's ears were bluish at the bottom lobes, a sure sign that she'd eaten a trickberry. Trickberries looked, and even tasted, a good deal like blueberries, but they were deadly if eaten, usually within just a few hours. It was likely the girl had consumed more than one, to be in this state already. Serana concentrated, weaving delicate flows of Water, Life, and Earth, extracting the poison from the girl's blood. Before the parent's eyes, the little girl began to sweat, and her ears lost their bluish tinge. After a few moments, Serana wiped the sweat away with a damp cloth the innkeeper brought. He'd been watching the proceedings with interest. "She needs water," Serana told the parents, and almost before she'd finished speaking, a serving girl brought a glass. Serana helped the little girl drink the water down, and then handed her back to her parents. "Make sure she drinks a good deal of water for the next few days, to flush out any remnants of the poison I might have missed, and tell her to be more careful what berries she eats.

"She'll be alright then?" the mother asked, gripping her husband's arm.

"She'll be fine," said Serana soothingly. "I imagine she'll wake up on your way home. She might want to go to bed early tonight, though. Trickberries are notorious for draining a person's strength, even if treated."

"Trickberries!" exclaimed the father. "I'll make sure she knows how to recognize those from now on," he said, frowning. "Thank you, High Priestess."

"How can we repay you?" the mother asked, clutching her daughter to her.

"Just take care of her," Serana said, smiling.

The next person came in carried on a makeshift stretcher by three men and a woman. He was unconscious, and his middle was wrapped tightly with thick bandages that were already turning red.

"He was attacked by... something," one of the men said before Serana could ask.

"He'd gone out to gather firewood from the forest," the woman said. "I was headed out to help him, just an excuse to spend time with him, really. When I found him, though, he was barely conscious, and the thing that had attacked him was dead. I ran to get help, and my brothers came as fast as they could. My husband passed out from the pain as we were carrying him here. We heard that you were coming to the city, and we thought maybe there was a chance."

"I need to see the wound," Serana said quickly. She began unwrapping the bandages carefully, probing with her magic… and not liking what she was seeing. "Describe the thing that attacked him."

"It was like a giant dog," said one of the men.

"A dog bigger than a bull," said the other.

"It had coarse, black fur and a really large head," the woman said firmly. "Its mouth was lined with several rows of teeth, each one looking like a sharp knife. I don't know how my husband managed to kill it, but its throat was cut open. He'd been a soldier in his youth, but I don't see how any soldier with just a wood axe could have killed that thing."

"It was a Daemon Scout," Serana told them, "and it's bitten him. Stand back, please." Serana knelt down beside the man as she uncovered the wound. The flesh was boiling. The woman stifled a sob at the sight, and the men held her protectively. Daemon Scouts couldn't kill with a scratch, but their bite was deadly. Their saliva was poison, and entered the blood quickly. Serana gathered the energy inside her and poured it into the man, drawing out the poison and repairing the wound. It was not beyond her ability at all, but it was nearly as bad as Rillian's arm had been back at Rhanestone. Fortunately, Serana's skill had increased dramatically since then. She stood when it was done, leaning on the table for support, and the man opened his eyes.

"What happened?" he asked, then suddenly leapt to his feet, looking around sharply. "Is it dead?" he asked urgently.

"It's dead," his wife told him. "You killed it."

The man ran his hands over his belly, where the wound had been. "It bit me, bad," he said softly. "How is it that I'm alive?"

"You'll be fine now," Serana told him.

"A Sorceress, and the High Priestess herself!" the man exclaimed, going to one knee and pressing Serana's hand to his forehead, much as Rillian had done the first time Serana had met him. "I'd thought you were all dead. I cannot tell you how pleased I am to know that I was mistaken."

"How do you know of my people?" Serana asked.

The man smiled as he rose. "I studied with them."

"He's delirious!" cried his wife.

"No, my love," he said calmly, turning to her. "It's much simpler than that. I lied. When I said that I was a soldier in my youth, I lied."

"But you know how to use weapons," she pointed out.

"Yes," he agreed. "I studied with the Sorceresses and with the elves, who live in the forest beside their village."

"Well," scoffed the woman, sounding relieved, "at least that proves he's delirious. There are no such things as elves."

"My father is the Elven King," Serana said quietly, bringing silence all around. "Besides that, your husband has some ability in elemental magic, though it is not very well developed."

The man nodded. "That's how I killed the Daemon Scout," he said. "Quite some time ago, I enchanted the axe with Air magic. It's not much of an enchantment, of course, but it makes the weapon easier to swing fast. It gave me the edge I needed to kill the thing, but not to get out alive." He turned to Serana. "Not without you, High Priestess."

"Why would you lie to me?" demanded the woman.

The man turned to her again calmly. "Because you did not believe elves existed, and you certainly would not have believed that I knew anything about Sorceresses unless there was one standing in front of you."

"Don't be too angry with him," Serana cut in quickly. "My people taught those whom they trained not to speak of them openly among others; too many did not believe in us." Serana did not know whether or not that was true, but she did want to end any domestic feud here and now. "Now, I believe that there are others who require my services."

"Thank you, High Priestess," the man said, bowing as he backed away. "If there is ever anything you need of me, you have but to ask."

"I think my husband is half mad," declared the woman, "but better half mad and alive than sane and dead. I don't know about this business with the elves, but I do know that he's only alive because of you. What can I offer you in payment?"

Serana smiled. "My price is that you do not make a decision on whether or not what he has said is true, not until you have evidence of your own on which to base that decision."

The woman fell silent for a moment, then nodded, thanked Serana again, and departed with her two brothers.

"Here," said the innkeeper, handing Serana a glass of some sort of juice. "It's called Sorceress' Nectar, supposedly a recipe from the Sorceress Village. I have my doubts about that, but it's tasty, and it helps keep one's strength up. I thought maybe you could use it."

"Thank you," said Serana, withdrawing a silver piece from her belt pouch.

"No need for that," said Balon. "If rumor is true, the other innkeepers didn't charge you, since you healed all those people, and I see no reason to break that trend. Besides," he leaned in conspiratorially, "out of all the people standing out there now, I'll wager that some will stay here for a drink and a meal, probably enough that I'll make more than your rooms would have cost anyway." He shuffled his feat then, looking down. "I misjudged one woman who used magic. I'd rather not make the same mistake again."

"Serana put a hand on his shoulder. "Thank you, sir."

He moved away as she attended to the next person in line. There were a good deal more people asking for healing here than there had been anywhere else, probably because Green Haven was so much larger than any of the other places they'd stayed. It took Serana half the night to see to them all, and when she was finished, she was well and truly exhausted, though more from lack of sleep than from using her magic. She stumbled over to the stairs, to head up to the room she hadn't yet seen, but Aeron, who had been waiting at a table by the stairs, lifted her on a cushion of air and carried her.

"I can manage by myself," she protested.

"I know you can," said the Air Wizard, "but I'm not going to let you. I would feel rather foolish if, in a freak accident, you fell and hit your head because you were too tired to stand up straight, particularly when I could have helped you. I'm sure that's not likely, but it is no strain on me to carry you, and this way we guarantee that you will *not* fall and hit your head."

"Thank you," said Serana sleepily, too tired to argue.

"You're welcome." He laid her down gently, covered her in blankets, and left the room. Serana was asleep in moments.

When she woke, bright morning light was shining through her window, making the bed, with its white sheets and white blankets, seem to glow. Serana felt refreshed and energized. She stretched luxuriously before getting out of bed and going downstairs. Judging by the sun, it was an hour or two later than she usually woke—she usually woke at dawn—but that wasn't surprising, considering how late it had been when she went to bed.

"Good morning, High Priestess!" said Balon brightly, already bringing out plates of fruits and pastries, with the help of his serving maids. "You didn't eat supper last night, so you must be starving. Please, take a seat and have some breakfast." The elementals were already seated at a large corner table, eating heartily. Serana joined them.

"Excuse me," said a young girl Serana hadn't seen before, tugging on the innkeeper's sleeve. "How much for some pastries and fruit like that?"

Balon smiled. "The young lord you're traveling with already took care of it," he told her. "Just take a seat, and I'll see that you get some breakfast."

"Thank you," the girl said, smiling.

Serana watched the girl curiously. Her energy was unlike anything Serana had ever seen before. She almost thought... no, that was impossible. She knew it was impossible. There had to be some other explanation.

"Why are you staring at me?" the girl asked. She hadn't been looking in Serana's direction before, so how she'd known she was being stared at was a mystery.

"You're a beautiful girl," Serana told her. "I was remembering when I was your age."

"You're a magician," the girl said, tilting her head slightly as she studied Serana.

"I'm a Sorceress," Serana corrected.

"What's the difference?"

"Magicians are usually human," said Serana. "Sorceresses are a different race entirely, and we're all women."

"No little girls?" asked the girl.

Serana laughed. "Yes, there are little girls, but not at the moment. There are just no males."

"Why are there no little girls now?"

"Because I am the last of my kind," Serana explained. The elementals had all stopped talking amongst themselves, and were watching the exchange with interest.

"You're pregnant," the girl announced.

"Why do you say that?" asked Serana, more than a little surprised.

"Because it's true."

"Why do you think it's true?"

The girl looked confused. "You have a baby inside you. Doesn't that mean you're pregnant?"

"But how would you know that?" Serana persisted.

"Didn't you?" asked the girl.

"I'm sorry," said Balon, hurrying to the table. "Here, miss; I have your breakfast. Why don't you come over here to eat?"

"No, it's alright," Serana told him quickly. "Let her stay, if she wants. I'm rather enjoying her company."

"As you wish, High Priestess," said Balon, bowing as far as his frame would allow. He placed the girl's breakfast on the table with Serana's and her friends'.

"You're not really enjoying my company," said the girl when he left. "I make you nervous, and you want to know why."

"That's not entirely true," Serana told her. "Unlike many people, I tend to enjoy puzzles. You do confuse me, but you don't make me nervous." She smiled. "And I *do* enjoy your company. Now, how did you know that I'm pregnant?"

The girl shrugged. "Didn't you?" she asked again.

"I learned because someone told me."

The girl picked up a grape and put it in her mouth, watching Serana as she chewed. "Was it a Dark Angel?" she asked finally. "I saw a Dark Angel once, a few months ago. He was talking to an elven boy. I think Dark Angels know almost everything."

There were so many questions flying through Serana's head at that moment, she didn't know where to begin. She took a breath and focused, taking on the Serenity. "You didn't answer my question," she pointed out.

The girl smiled. "Finally, someone who pays attention. I knew you were pregnant because I sense two lives in you, a powerful one and a weaker one. The weaker one is the baby."

"Have you been trained as a magician?" asked Serana carefully.

"No," answered the girl. She did not elaborate.

Suddenly, a very strange idea occurred to Serana. It came upon her suddenly, just like the magical epiphanies she'd experienced while learning to use her power, something clicking into place in her mind for reasons beyond her knowledge. "How old are you?"

"Thirteen," answered the girl, munching on a fruit Serana couldn't name, probably something that only grew in Green Haven.

"You're lying," Serana said calmly, inexplicably certain that she was right. "How old are you really?"

The girl studied Serana's face intently as she chewed her fruit. She didn't answer until after she'd swallowed. "Twenty-five."

"That's absurd," said Alier flatly. "Even elementals and Sorceresses don't age so slowly until after they've lived a few more years than she has. I have no idea why you told her she was lying before, Serana, but she's most certainly lying now."

"No she isn't," said Serana, emotionless within the Serenity. "Somehow, she is telling the truth. She is twenty-five years of age."

The girl remained silent.

"What is your name?" Aeron asked gently, when it was clear that no one else was going to say anything.

"Amber," replied the girl, finishing up her fruit and taking a bite of pastry. Serana started eating her own breakfast again too; she hadn't realized she'd stopped when she saw Amber.

Serana found that the pastries were quite good. Another question occurred to her while she ate, though. "The lord to took care of your bill, who is he?"

"The name he gave was Lord Alexander," replied Amber. "He's still upstairs sleeping."

Serana blinked in surprise. "Why are you traveling with him?"

"He and his wife are taking me to his brother's estate," Amber explained. Lord Alexander had a wife? "She is *yamin'sai* to him."

Of course! Serana vaguely remembered hearing something about a vampire woman pledging herself *yamin'sai* to a young lord at Rhanestone; she'd just never realized that it was Lord Alexander.

"How do you know him?" asked Amber. She appeared to be intent on her food, but she was obviously paying attention.

"I met him twice before," said Serana. "They were both brief meetings; I don't know him well."

"You are the woman with stunning eyes and powerful magic," Amber decided.

"I suppose my magic could be considered powerful," said Serana doubtfully. Stunning eyes? Lord Alexander thought she had stunning eyes? Amber must have made some sort of mistake. Serana decided to change the subject. "Why do you appear no more than thirteen, if you are actually twenty-five?"

"Why will you still appear sixteen when you reach four hundred?" asked Amber.

Serana smiled. "I thought you didn't know what a Sorceress was."

"I didn't," Amber shrugged. "It's written in you."

"What do you mean?" asked Serana, frowning in confusion.

"I'd have thought that much was obvious by now," Aeron said with his small smile, the one he inevitably wore when he'd figured out something. "She reads life energy as well as, if not better than, you do."

"She has the ability to wield Life magic," said Serana, studying the girl's energy. "She only knows how to use it in the most basic sense, though."

"Then you must teach me," said Amber calmly, eating her second pastry.

Serana blinked. "Me?"

"She does have a point," Seleine grinned. "Who else in the world can wield Life magic?"

"Any human or elven magician can, in a basic sense," Serana told her. "Even elementals can wield it a little, though they rarely practice it."

"Our ability is negligible compared with yours," said Alier. "We are bound to our own elements. Even the humans can wield Life energy more readily than we, and they, too, cannot hope to compare with you. If this girl can be trained, then it is up to you to train her."

"I will travel with you," Amber announced.

"I'm not sure that will be possible," said Allaerion, who had been silent until now. "We travel using elemental magic; you wouldn't be able to keep up."

"Teach me how, and I will keep up." The girl shrugged.

"It may not be as simple as that," Serana said slowly. The girl's energy was confusing to the point where it was difficult to say what she could and couldn't learn.

"I can help you there," offered Aeron. "Whatever other abilities she may or may not have, she has sufficient strength in Air magic to learn to speed her movements." He turned to Allaerion. "You should have seen that yourself." Allaerion gave Aeron a sour look. He probably *had* seen it, and hadn't intended to say anything.

"Are you sure?" asked Alier. "I sense almost no Earth ability in her at all."

Aeron gave his mentor a withering look. "Have you been around Serana so long that you've forgotten that there are those in the world who possess talent in only one element?" Alier had the grace to look abashed. "This girl's ability is probably strongest in Air."

"No," said Serana, studying Amber carefully. "Her strongest is in Life, but Air would be second. I didn't even see it until you pointed it out." So strange… Serana's first impression *had* to be wrong—it was utterly impossible—but it fit everything she'd learned about the girl so far.

"Once in a while," said Aeron with a grin, "there are advantages to seeing only one type of energy with clarity."

Amber remained silent, eating some more fruit now that she'd finished her pastries.

"This journey seems full of surprises," said a familiar voice from the stairs. Lord Alexander smiled as he crossed the room to their table, followed by a stunningly beautiful woman wearing the dark cloak of a vampire. "It is an honor to see you again, High Priestess," he said with a bow.

Serana inclined her head. "And you, Lord Alexander."

"I see you've met Amber," he said, looking down at her.

"I will be traveling with them from here on," the girl announced.

"You'll what?" he asked in surprise.

"I will be traveling with them," Amber repeated. "The other children can follow you to your brother's estate."

"Why do you stare at me?" the vampire woman behind Alexander asked.

Serana tore her eyes away. "Forgive me," she said. "I don't intend to be rude." It was impossible, yet it fit perfectly.

"I'm the one who's been rude," said Lord Alexander. "I haven't introduced my wife, Alloria. Alloria, this is Serana, the Sorceress High Priestess. There is Allaerion, the Warrior of Air, and I'm afraid I have not had the pleasure of meeting the rest of you."

Serana introduced Alier, Aeron, and Seleine, but Alloria seemed intent on Serana herself, for some reason. "This is the Sorceress High Priestess," the vampire woman said softly. "Now I understand."

Lord Alexander gave his wife a flat look. "Alloria, we discussed this."

"Of course," she said, transferring her gaze to her husband. "Her eyes are indeed stunning."

Serana blushed, despite herself. "We really should be on our way soon."

"So should we," agreed Lord Alexander. "Amber, come along."

"I already told you that I will be traveling with them," the girl told him patiently.

"I'm sorry about this," said Lord Alexander to Serana and the elementals. "The girl has never been like this before."

"This girl," said Serana, "is older than she appears." It *was* impossible, but like Serana's own affinity for all four elements at once, impossibility did not stop it from happening. Impossible or not, Serana was certain that it was true.

"What are you talking about?" demanded Lord Alexander.

Serana was watching Amber. "She is half vampire."

"Absurd," said Alloria. "I could recognize another vampire instantly."

"I said *half* vampire," Serana corrected.

"Serana," Seleine said gently. "That can't happen. Vampires do not have children."

"I know that," Serana told her, "but it is still true. It explains some of the oddities I read in her energy, and also the reason she appears only thirteen when she is, in fact, twenty-five. She ages because she is not entirely a vampire, but she ages very slowly."

"Vampires cannot wield magic," Alier pointed out. "You said Amber could learn to."

"Vampires do wield a limited form of Air magic," Serana explained, "to fly and to move quickly. They do it inherently, though; it is not learned."

"That wouldn't account for her potential in Air," Aeron protested. "She," he said, indicating Alloria, "isn't nearly as strong, and I'll wager that she has all of those inherent vampire abilities."

"Of course I do," Alloria said with a shrug.

"It also doesn't account for her potential in Life magic," Serana agreed.

"Then what does?" asked Allaerion, intrigued.

Serana watched Amber, who had been eating unconcernedly throughout the entire discussion. "She is also half Sorceress."

Chapter XXIV

"Half Sorceress?" said Alier derisively. "That *is* impossible. Serana, I thought you already understood that Sorceresses only bear Sorceress children. That baby inside you is not half Fire Warlock; it's all Sorceress."

"I'm well aware of that," Serana said patiently. She was glad that she still held to the Serenity, lest she start losing her patience. She was right, but she didn't know why yet, much like she'd been able to throw the Arrow of Light before she understood how it worked. "Vampires don't have children, and Sorceresses bear only Sorceress children. A union between a vampire and a Sorceress would not produce Amber."

"Exactly," said Alier.

"Of course," Serana went on, "there still remain two undeniable facts: Amber does exist, and everything we know about her suggests that she is half vampire and half Sorceress."

"Serana," said Alier with exaggerated patience. "I know you're brilliant, but I have made an extensive study of how traits are passed from generation to generation in all the races in the world, other than Daemons, and this half and half business is simply not possible with either the Sorceress or the vampire race, let alone both together. The reason a Sorceress always bears Sorceress children is because the Sorceress key traits, the ones that decide race, are more dominant than those of any other race in the world. When a vampire bites a victim with the intent to transform, those key traits of whatever race the victim was are overwritten, replaced with a vampire's abilities."

"That is only partly true," Alloria said suddenly. "I, too, have studied how our traits are passed down."

"My study," Alier told her, "spanned more than three centuries."

"Mine was limited to vampires only," Alloria replied. "Besides, the length of time is immaterial; it is the truth of the resulting conclusions that matters. Vampire traits do not overwrite all traits of the original race. Observe." She pulled her luxurious raven-black hair over her ears, revealing the distinctive elven points. "Vampire traits overwrite only certain aspects of any person during conversion, and leave the rest intact."

"So are you saying," suggested Aeron, "that Amber was a Sorceress child when she was changed?"

"No," replied Alloria. "Had she been bitten and converted, she would be a vampire entirely, and she is not. One of the traits that vampirism overwrites is magical ability, replacing it with the skills we inherently possess. According to the High Priestess, Amber retains a Sorceress' magical ability. I do not know how she came to be."

"Does it matter?" asked Amber, who was still eating fruit. "The entire idea is quite fascinating, really, but however I came to be here, the fact remains that I *am* here. How it happened, though an interesting question, is irrelevant." She looked up at Serana. "If I have the ability to manipulate Life energy, then you must teach me, lest I do it accidentally and cause unintentional harm." The memory of the sparrow flashed through Serana's mind. Amber was not so naïve as Serana had been, when faced with learning to wield her magic.

"Learned for a thirteen-year-old, isn't she?" commented Lord Alexander.

"Since the rest of them already know," Amber told him, "I'm twenty-five. I've aged more slowly than the rest of you, but my mind has developed normally as far as I can tell."

"You'll definitely have to travel with us," Serana said firmly. "I do need to teach you how to use your abilities, but you are also the only link I still have to my race, a sister of sorts."

Amber smiled for the first time Serana had ever seen, and judging by Lord Alexander's reaction, it was the first time for him as well. It was a beautiful sight.

They were on their way within a quarter of an hour. Balon Trush, the innkeeper, still refused to accept any payment, so Serana thanked him by placing a circle of Dragon's Tears around the inn. The Garden City's soil would guarantee that they would grow for generations to come, even without care. If Green Haven were ever attacked by Daemons, The Sleeping Dragon would be one of the safest places to be.

On the way through the city, the party passed what could only be the famous flower garden. Blossoms of every hue decorated the largest City Square Serana had every seen. The flowers were thick, breaking only for small walkways that crisscrossed the entire area. The outer edge of the flower garden was composed of Dragon's Tears, a protective barrier against Daemons, the only creatures Serana could imagine ever wanting to destroy something so beautiful. The six travelers paused simply to stare, to breathe in the fragrance. Bees moved busily from flower to flower, congregating in several of the trees scattered across the garden. The trees themselves were covered in more blossoms, different colors for different trees.

"They're always that way, the trees," said Alier wistfully. "They only grow that way here, on the land of Ereanthea. They always bear fruit, and always have blossoms ready to become more fruit. The bees here do not sting, and one need not ruin their hives to enjoy their honey; it runs down into small collectors a little each day. As a child, I used to run through this very garden, tasting the honey from each one." There were tears in the Earth Enchantress' eyes as she spoke, but she didn't blink them away. She was in another time, another place. "When the Daemons overran the city, a few of us huddled in the garden for safety. I grew the Dragon's Tears around the outer edge myself, to stop them coming in. The flowers slowed them, but before long their poisonous presence would have killed our only defense. We would have died, if not for the Seriani. They appeared right beside us, black wings outstretched, shining with a golden aura of power. The Daemons fled before them, and those that were too slow perished in golden light. No Daemon or group of Daemons dared stand directly against Music and Shape." Alier shook her head sadly. "Some blamed them for not coming sooner. Those were fools. The Seriani loved life more than any other creatures in existence. If they could have come sooner, they would have. I am thankful that they came at all, and that this garden remains. The others who stood there with me are long dead. Now we, I and the garden, are the last surviving remnants of Ereanthea." She bowed her head then, and turned away toward the south gate. Serana and the others followed wordlessly.

Outside the city, Aeron immediately began explaining to Amber how to travel using Air magic. It was only slightly different than the enhanced speed Allaerion used for combat. As Aeron explained, Amber listened intently, asking a question here and there. When he was finished, the party started off. At first, Amber lagged behind slightly, but before long she was keeping up with the rest of them easily, gliding effortlessly beside Allaerion as if she'd traveled this way her entire life.

That evening they camped outside; the string of inns was far sparser after Green Haven, since most travelers went between the Garden City and Rhanestone; very few actually came in or out of the Southern Nations.

Once camp was set up—using magic, of course—Serana began Amber's lessons in Life magic. She started with the first spell she'd ever done herself, the Arrow of Light. Amber seemed confused by the principles at first, but after an hour or two, she had managed one good bolt that sizzled against the shield Serana had thrown up for a target. Amber couldn't throw a second that night, but she promised to practice every night when they stopped to rest. Serana practiced her sword and staff work with Allaerion and Alier after Amber's lesson, and the girl watched intently. She didn't seem particularly interested in the sword, but she asked to learn the staff, and Alier was happy to instruct her.

Amber took to the staff almost as quickly as Serana had. She didn't need to be taught to move the way Allaerion did, and Serana was not surprised. Vampires instinctively knew how to move quickly, and they used Air magic to do it; Amber had only to realize that she had the ability. Alier wasn't challenged so easily, of course; even Allaerion, with centuries of experience, was no match for the Weaver of Earth in single combat.

The girl studied Air magic with Aeron just before bed. Now that Serana had more of an idea what to look for in Amber's energy, she could clearly see that Air was the half-Sorceress' only real elemental gift. She would never be as strong as Aeron in it, or even as strong as Serana herself, but she would be able to hold her own with most of the Air Wizards in Aeron's village, once she was trained. She seemed rather taken with the young Air Wizard, though he appeared oblivious.

Aeron was very good at not noticing when women were interested in him, and Serana even suspected that his blindness was genuine, particularly with Amber. Had he actually understood the way she looked at him, he'd probably have been avoiding her whenever they weren't having a lesson.

Amber was fascinated by the way Serana and the elementals pitched their tents at night. Allaerion and Aeron no longer used a tent; Aeron put up a dome of Air hardened into a shield that was both opaque and stronger than steel. Alier had begun using the tent that the Air Wizards no longer needed, pitching it with Earth magic, roots growing to hold the ropes in place of stakes, a young sapling growing out from the ground to replace the poles. Seleine and Serana still shared a tent, but theirs used pillars of ice reinforced with Air magic in place of poles, and more ice to freeze the ropes in place. Serana had suggested a few times that they, too, had no need of a tent. Serana could duplicate Aeron's dome, or create whatever shape she wanted with the reinforced ice, exactly like what was being used to construct the school of magic in Aeron's home. Seleine always just shrugged, asking why they should bother, when they already had a perfectly good tent. Amber asked to share with Alier, and the Earth Enchantress was happy to let her. Alier liked Amber's quiet, respectful, and entirely logical manner; she said several times that more young people should learn to be like Amber. Serana might have thought Alier was making a jab at her—particularly since Amber was older than she— but the Weaver of Earth rarely even seemed to remember how young Serana was. Serana saw no reason to remind her.

As the nights went by, and the party came closer and closer to the Southern Nations, Serana became increasingly worried about their destination. There had been no signs of Daemon activity whatsoever. Surely a Daemon Lord should have left a trail of destruction in his wake that would be unmistakable, but there was no trace of any such trail. Serana discussed the situation with each of the elementals in private, but none of them had any ideas either. It was almost as if Lady Firehair's Daemon Lord didn't exist. The only thing the party *did* encounter that smacked of evil was a startling number of bandits.

The first attack came when they were preparing to set out on the third morning after Amber had joined them. Serana was up first, as usual, and making a breakfast of sweet rolls with fruit. Balon Trush had been kind enough to let Serana purchase some ingredients from his kitchen. She'd insisted on paying him, but she had no idea how much the herbs and spices were worth, so far from Alon Peak, and she'd never known how much the fruit was worth, since it grew only in Green Haven. She suspected that the innkeeper had charged her a fraction of the items' value. As she often did now, Serana watched the surrounding forest using Air magic, tiny threads of energy that would set of alarms in her mind if anyone should approach. When one such alarm went off, Serana was so surprised that for a moment she didn't act. Then another three alarms went off at once, and then several more. The camp was surrounded by at least twenty men, all of them human. Only one man stepped out of the forest, though, just opposite the cook fire from Serana.

He smiled as he approached her, a smile that would have sent chills down her spine, if not for the fact that she could kill him and all his men without breaking a sweat, probably with only her sword. "What's cooking?" he asked.

"Breakfast," she replied, yawning. There was no reason to let him know that she wasn't a simple, innocent girl in the forest with some friends. If he was stupid enough not to notice her gown, she certainly wasn't going to point it out. "Who are you?"

"I think I'm your new lover, darlin'. We've watched you. We know you only have two men with you, and only one of them with a sword. Now are you going to come along quietly into these trees with me, or do I get the pleasure of dragging you out there screaming?"

They'd watched? Serana found that highly unlikely, since they only included the men in their estimation of the party's defenses. Anyone watching would have seen Serana and Alier sparring, and anyone who knew even the most basic use of weapons would have recognized their skill as beyond what any human could ever achieve.

Serana looked into the man's eyes, and returned his smile. "I don't need a new lover," she told him sweetly. "Now are you going to leave, or am I going to have to bury you alive?"

Serana didn't relax her senses. Instead, she expanded them, taking in detailed images with both Air and Earth magic, telling her where each and every one of his men were, and what they carried. It took a bit of concentration, but she could afford that, facing only humans. Five of the men had crossbows, and they had taken position in sight of her from the trees. The rest had swords and clubs, and were waiting at the other side of the camp.

The man's smile widened. "You're a feisty one, aren't you? I think I'm gonna enjoy you." He stepped forward, and immediately vines sprang up from the ground, wrapping themselves around his legs and dragging him down to his neck. His entire body was trapped beneath the ground, with only his head sticking up.

"Tell your men to throw down their crossbows, or they will be shot," Serana said softly, her own smile widening. She was enjoying this.

"Kill her!" the man yelled. "She's a witch!"

Five crossbow bolts whizzed toward Serana, and all of them stopped in mid-air, a foot away from her. Serana yawned, and the bolts turned around, speeding back to their owners and burying themselves in the men's necks.

"Have the others attack too, if you want them to die as well," Serana said conversationally.

"Oh *do* hurry it along," Alier said, stepping out from her tent. "Just kill them all and be done with it. I'm hungry."

"I second that," said Seleine, crawling out from hers and Serana's tent. "Those rolls smell wonderful." Only then did the leader seem to notice what was holding that tent up. His eyes bulged as he strained to free himself, but he accomplished no more than to wriggle his head a bit.

Serana laughed as the other men in the forest ran as fast as their legs could carry them, stumbling over bramble in their haste.

"That was interesting," Aeron commented as he stood up, letting his dome dissolve. "Do you think there will be more?"

"Yes," Amber said quietly. Serana had not seen her step out from the tent. She was standing beside Alier, looking at the buried man, who appeared ready to soil himself. "There are many bandits in the South now."

"How do you know that?" asked Alier.

The girl shrugged. "I lived here for a few years, before I found the other children and started heading north."

"Why did the bandits never attack you?" asked Aeron. The young Air Wizard was truly naïve in some ways, even by Serana's standards.

"They did," Amber replied with a shrug. "I killed them. Speaking of which, could I have this one?" She was still watching the buried man. "I do need to drink blood sometimes, you know. I get sick after a few weeks, if I don't, even when I'm eating other things."

"Take him," said Serana, "but don't kill him. I want the other bandits in the area to fear every traveling party, since they might be us. Are you listening?" she asked the man, who was sobbing like a baby. "Hey," she said, using a few threads of Air magic to bump him gently on the head, "I'm talking to you." The man looked up at her, still whimpering. "We're going to let you live. I want you to tell every other ruffian and bandit out there what happens to scum that attack travelers. Tell them all."

The ruffian blubbered between sobs that he'd tell everyone, all the while begging for his life. It made Serana sick. She drew him out of the ground, holding his limbs in place with Air, but suddenly he calmed, staring at nothing.

"Let him go," instructed Amber, who was staring intently at the man. "He won't make any more fuss until I'm through with him." Serana released his bonds, and Amber led him away into the forest.

"Well," said Serana, "who wants breakfast?

Chapter XXV

The Serian of Music had always enjoyed puzzles, but this one was more difficult than any other he could remember, in all his years. Lady Firehair was, in many ways, an innocent. Of that much, he was certain. There were times, however, when she looked at him, and he was quite convinced her thoughts were *not* innocent at all. Still, she only ever asked simple things of him. When she asked him to lie with her, she meant only to have him hold her as she slept, still fully dressed in that gown she always wore. Like Serana's dress, it never seemed to wrinkle or grow dirty, however long she wore it. She did take it off to bathe, but Music sensed that her bathing was not so much out of a desire to cleanse her body as an enjoyment of the water. She always asked him to join her, and he always refused. Her request was innocent, of course, but no doubt she would want to hug him, as she often did now, and he was not prepared to feel the innocuously intentioned touch of her naked body against his; it would be more than he could bear, particularly coupled with her face.

The real puzzle, though, was not merely her innocence; it was her very existence. How could a creature wielding the power of the Black Void be compassionate, loving, and innocent in her heart? That it had happened was obvious; how was a complete mystery. Almost stranger still, Lady Firehair could tap into elemental magic through her dark gifts as easily as he could through the Power. No other Daemon, to his knowledge, possessed such ability. To further deepen his confusion, she often seemed to intuitively grasp things he did with the Power, or aspects of the Shrine of Music, which was created with the Power. No Daemon, however gifted, should comprehend the workings of the Power, its devices and methods were alien to creatures of the Black Void.

He had begun taking her with him when he went out to aid those in the world who needed his help. Here within the Shrine of Music, he could hear any genuine plea anywhere in the world. He and the others had taken great efforts to equip each of the Shrines of the Arts with a net for communication, so that the Seriani could always aid those who asked earnestly for help. She could not hear the pleas, of course—they came directly into his mind—but she always seemed to know when he was about to leave, and she always looked heartbroken to be left behind. Somehow, he sensed that she might eventually learn to hear them, though, and that idea disturbed him more than he cared to admit. At first, he had worried that they might run into Serana on these excursions, and he didn't want to risk allowing Lady Firehair near the Sorceress. Later, he had come to realize that however gifted she was, Lady Firehair was no match for him in raw power; even if they did run into Serana, Music would be able to keep her safe. So far, they had not run into her, fortunately. Music had no desire to harm Lady Firehair in any way, though he would if he had to. He thought he could. He must.

Many of the pleas for help he received were simple, made by simple folk who still believed in the Seriani. There were very few of those left now, but he tried to help them whenever he could. Just a few days ago, he had taken Lady Firehair with him to help a woman whose son was dying of a grave sickness. The mother, caring for him, had caught it herself. The woman's husband had died a few years ago, and the son, who had been sixteen at the time, had taken care of his mother, shouldering the work his father used to do. They were farmers, but harvest time was almost upon them, and the crops were approaching maturity with no one to bring them in. The mother had cried out silently for help from the Seriani, to make her son well again. Music had answered her call. He'd cured both mother and son, granting them immunity from sickness for a year's time, and left them a purse of gold. They should have no trouble now. Lady Firehair had watched in rapt fascination, smiling joyfully as both mother and son rose from their beds and thanked him, tears streaming down both their faces.

When he and Lady Firehair had returned to the Shrine of Music, she'd hugged him again, and kissed his cheek. It was the first time she had ever kissed him, and he'd stared at her in surprise. Then, of course, he'd had to stop her apologizing.

Today, there was an Ice Witch in the Barrilian Mountains who'd been driven into a cave by Daemons. She had walled off the entrance, but had no food, and couldn't survive on her own. Lady Firehair trembled in his arms when he told her where they were going. She was likely fearful of other Daemons recognizing her. Music offered to leave her behind this time, but she insisted on coming with him.

When they arrived, the poor Ice Witch was huddled against the far wall, away from the sealed-off entrance. Five Daemon Scouts and three Soldiers waited for her outside, more than most elementals could handle alone. The cave was tiny, little more than an alcove in the rock. She had no escape.

When Music and Lady Firehair appeared, the Ice Witch jumped in fright, but then smiled, tears of relief streaming down her cheeks as she ran into Music's arms. He held her protectively for a few moments, until she calmed, then instructed her to get behind them. The Ice Witch, still trembling slightly, held onto him tightly when he tried to let her go, but Lady Firehair was already moving. She held out her hand, and the ice wall at the entrance melted instantly. There were triumphant howls as the Daemons outside lunged at her all at once, but their howls turned to squeals of fright, then screams of death. Lady Firehair strode back into the cave.

"The danger is gone," she said, a tightness to her voice that Music had never heard before. "You can let her go now." It the first time since the day she'd arrived at the Shrine of Music that she had not used the same archaic speech that he did.

Music spoke softly to the Ice Witch, his eyes glowing golden as he played music within her mind, calming her. Finally she released him, thanking him profusely. She then turned her attention to Lady Firehair, thanking her as well before running out of the cave. Lady Firehair's expression never changed, but the Serian of Music felt somehow cold when she moved to stand at his side, ready to leave the cave. It was strange, since he never felt the weather at all.

Once they were back within the Shrine, she immediately threw her arms around him and hugged him again. Likely she was upset at having killed her own kind. "I could have done it for thee," he said gently. Rather than calming her, though, his words seemed to make her more upset.

"I was perfectly capable," she said frostily, still clinging to him. He held her awkwardly, more than a little confused.

"I did not doubt thine ability," he assured her. He'd have expected her to let go of him by now, but she didn't.

"Why won't you hold me?" she demanded, her grip tightening.

"I am holding thee," he pointed out, his confusion deepening.

"No," she said, releasing him and looking into his eyes, her own glowing red with anger. "Your arms were around me, barely touching me, as if I were diseased, as if you could even catch anything from it if I *were* diseased! When I released you, you let go of me as if you'd been waiting for the opportunity."

"What art thou talking about?" She'd never acted this way before.

"Must I tremble with fear each time before you'll hold me as if you mean it, before you'll take even the slightest pleasure in it? You enjoyed holding the little Ice Witch, because *she* was afraid. I don't *want* to be afraid all the time!" She stormed away, her hair blazing with real flames that didn't consume it. He didn't want her to be afraid all the time either. Where would she get that idea? When she reached the doorway she'd been heading for, she stopped, turned, and shot him an exasperated look. "Well, follow me," she commanded.

Not knowing what else to do, he obeyed. She led him to the room where he'd always created the pool for her to swim. To his astonishment, the water appeared without his command. He had only ever allowed one other creature to command events within his home, and that one creature was long dead. He didn't have long to wonder, though. As soon as the water was in place, she rounded on him.

"You don't like me," she accused, her lower lip trembling even as her eyes burned red.

"M'lady," he said uncertainly, "why wouldst thou believe such a thing?"

"Tell me it's not true," she challenged. "Tell me you do like me, that you love me as you love all those other little creatures out there in the world."

"Of course I do," he told her, completely bewildered.

"Then prove it," she said. "Bathe with me." She turned away, disrobing and slipping into the water. "If you care about me so much," she said from the water, her back to him, "then share with me this simple pleasure of cool water."

Music felt trapped as he'd not felt trapped in years. He reminded himself several times that she was innocent, that she would not ask of him what he feared... but innocent or not, she drew very near to the line. "Why dost thou wish this thing?" he asked, stalling for time. "What will it prove, other than my willingness to get wet?"

She turned around then and looked at him, uncaring of her obvious nakedness beneath the clear water. Her eyes were burning so brightly that Music almost thought the water should be boiling with the heat. "I wish it because you would have done more for that Ice Witch we helped, had she required it. As it was, *I* did the work, and you held her with a tenderness you've never shown me. I nearly have to beg for so much as a small embrace." That was completely untrue. Since she'd come to him, Lady Firehair had received countless hugs, and she'd never even had to ask him. He simply returned the ones she gave.

Sighing inwardly, the Serian of Music stepped into the water.

"Aren't you going to leave your clothes?" she asked him, confused.

"Why?" he asked mildly. "They will be dry again when I step out of the water." He had no need even to swim, if he did not wish to; propelling himself in water was as easy for him as walking.

Lady Firehair frowned and tilted her head, as if trying to summon up a reason, and having a good deal of difficulty doing so.

"Please," said Music, changing the subject now that he had the chance, "tell me why thou art so very upset. Have I done something wrong?"

"Yes!" she said fiercely.

Music waited, but she didn't go on. "What is it that I have done?" he asked finally.

She frowned again, as if confused. After a long moment, she looked at him, the fire gone out of her eyes. "I... do not know." She paused, looking away, then met his gaze again. "Why did you hold that Ice Witch that way, when you will not do the same for me?"

"She was terrified, m'lady," he responded automatically. "Thou wert not. Besides, if thou wert paying attention, thou wouldst realize that I was trying to disentangle myself from her grip, but fear had frozen her muscles until a few moments after thou didst destroy the Daemons."

Lady Firehair tilted her head the other way. "Why *am* I so angry?" she asked, as if to herself. "It began when I saw you holding her, and it grew worse when you wouldn't hold me the same way when we returned."

Music smiled faintly. "If not for the preposterousness of the notion, I might believe thee to be jealous, m'lady."

"Jealous…" She said the word slowly, as if tasting it for the first time. "What does that mean?"

Music stared. He had very little experience with jealousy himself. He and Shape had never felt it with each other; there was never any cause. He had heard it spoken of among other races, mostly humans, but he'd never witnessed it for himself. "I am told that it is a feeling of resentment toward a loved one, for attention given to another, when one wished that attention for oneself."

"Perhaps that fits, then," she said softly, then suddenly hung her head. "I am sorry. I am a selfish, shameful creature. I do not blame you for not wanting to hold me."

Wordlessly, Music wrapped her in his cloak within the water, holding her tenderly. She began to cry then, and clung to his cloak, burying her head in his shoulder. Music reminded himself yet again that she was a Daemon, that he should destroy her. As always, it had no effect. He could not bring himself to feel less than tenderness for her. If only he could limit himself to tenderness…

He lifted her from the water, and drew from the Power to dry her and replace her clothing as he carried her away toward her bedroom. He laid her down gently on the bed, but she was still clinging to him, so he allowed himself to lie beside her, holding her close until she finished crying and fell asleep. After that, he continued to hold her, all the while telling himself that he should not. When was it that he'd stopped doing what he knew he should? When had he begun to selfishly grant himself such allowances? Music did not know when it had begun. He only knew that at this moment, he could no more let her go than he could harm her. It was hopeless, but at least Serana would be safe, and the prophecy would never come to pass.

Chapter XXVI

Alexander, Alloria, and the four remaining children left The Sleeping Dragon not long after the High Priestess and her friends. Of course, there was no trace on the road of Sorceress or Elementals. Alloria claimed that they all used magic to travel more quickly, something like the way she could move when she wanted. Alexander knew almost nothing of magic, but he was fairly certain that when it came to magic, there was very little the Sorceress High Priestess could not accomplish. He'd seen her standing in the middle of ten Daemon Scouts at once in Rhanestone's courtyard, and the Scouts each died before even one could reach her. He remembered her throwing those white bolts of magic with both hands, and Scouts dropping like flies wherever a bolt struck. Even before that, he'd been told that she'd defeated a Captain single-handedly. He hadn't believed it at the time, but he did now.

Fortunately, he and the children had Alloria with them. The vampire was their best defense against bandits and thugs. She may not be so powerful as the High Priestess, but she was more than a match for any small group of humans, and she'd already saved Alexander's life several times.

None of the four children were terribly surprised to find Amber gone. Alexander suspected that they'd been watching somehow, but he had no idea how, and none of them seemed inclined to speak. They all obeyed any command Alexander or Alloria gave them, though, so watching them was really quite easy. An entire week passed uneventfully.

Alexander was starting to wonder if the rumors of bandits were even true. A man and woman with four small children should have looked like easy prey, but he'd not seen a hair of bandits all week. Not that he was complaining, of course, but it was quite unusual.

Now that there were no inns readily available, they had to make camp, fitting all six of them in the small tent Alexander and Alloria had brought. Alexander would have purchased a new tent for the children in Green Haven, but he'd honestly never thought about it. Each night, the twins, Tim and Tom Taliman, huddled close to Alloria, much to her delight. Josua Hunter, the eldest boy, stayed near the edge of the tent by himself, or as close to by himself as he could manage in a single tent with two adults and three children other than himself. His sister Lilian, however, always cuddled up to Alexander. The first time, he'd felt more than a little uncomfortable, something Alloria found endlessly amusing. After that, Alexander had grown used to the idea, and now held the child gently as they slept. She always said goodnight to him just before she dozed off, resting her little head against his chest as she curled up beside him. Alexander thought he understood now why Alloria liked having the twins beside her. Each night, he felt a momentary pang that he and his wife could never have children of their own.

On the morning of the eighth day, before they'd been on the road an hour, they encountered their first bandits since Green Haven. The men weren't bothering to hide, but instead stood blocking the road ahead, right before a bridge crossing a small river. Alexander would have drawn his sword as they approached, but there was no way he could take all fifteen of the men he saw, and there might be more. Alloria, on the other hand, should have no trouble.

The vampire woman seemed perfectly calm as they drew near to the men, and even smiled when one man stepped away from the group.

"Halt," he said. "If you want to cross this river, you must pay a tax."

"On whose authority?" Alexander inquired.

The man smiled wickedly. "Mine, of course."

"How much do you want?" asked Alexander. It might be easier to pay the man and be done with it.

"Not much," the man said. "Just ten gold pieces." That wasn't much at all. "And some fun with the woman."

Before Alexander could react, Alloria spoke up. "That sounds like a wonderful bargain, sir." She grinned, showing him her fangs.

The man's eyes bulged as he backed away. "It's a vampire witch!" he cried, and all the men bolted.

Alexander watched in consternation as they scrambled away, stumbling and falling in their haste. "What was that all about?" he asked when they'd gone.

"I am not entirely certain," said Alloria. "I was going to kill them, not frighten them."

"Well, as long as it works," Josua said. He rarely spoke, but when he did, he was usually sensible.

"Quite," agreed Alexander. "Let's be on our way."

***

"What choice do we have?" asked Serana. "We have no idea where this Daemon Lord is hiding, but I'll wager he has something to do with the overwhelming number of bandits in the South right now. One of them *has* to know something, and it's the only place we have to start." The party had not made any real progress for several days. They'd been wondering across the land, looking for bandits to capture and question. It was like trying to find a sewing pin in one of the hay barns in Alon Peak, but Serana had yet to think of a better plan. The only really good thing about the situation was that half the bandits in the South were terrified of anyone who could so much as light a candle with magic. Serana had even been called a "vampire witch" a few times, though she had no idea why.

"I'm not disagreeing with you," said Alier. "I simply wish we had something more to work with."

"We all do," agreed Seleine. "I'm sure that something will turn up eventually."

"Eventually," said Serana, "Rhanestone will fall, even with the defenses we've left in place. If we don't get that last piece to the Armor and get back there in time, we'll have far larger problems on our hands."

"In any case," Aeron said softly, "our options are to continue looking as we've been or to return empty-handed, unless one of you has a better plan. I suggest we stop worrying about it; it's doing no good. We must continue to search, and think of other solutions as we do so."

"Exactly," said Serana. She couldn't have stated it better herself. The only truly productive part of the past few days had been Amber's lessons. The half-Sorceress had nearly mastered the Arrow of Light as well as Serana, but last night she'd brought up an interesting point.

"Have you tried making the bolt split before it strikes?" she'd asked. "You could hit multiple targets that way."

Nothing Serana had read in the Archives had suggested that such a thing was possible, though nothing specifically denied the possibility either. Even Alier had never heard of it. Still, Serana was willing to try nearly anything once, if it might help their cause. After a bit of practice, she'd actually managed to split the bolt, though she completely missed her target when she did so. Still, the principle might be useful, once she'd mastered the technique. Amber had some surprising ways of looking at things, and a wonderful imagination. Training her was one of Serana's greatest pleasures right now.

That evening, Serana and Amber practiced together trying to make the Arrow of Light split. Serana could do it almost every time now, but her aim needed work. Amber only rarely managed the split, but she refused to give up until the session was over. She was improving steadily, though, her control over Life magic growing ever stronger. Serana might have been surprised at such rapid progress—even if it wasn't quite so rapid as Serana's had been—but she believed Amber's lineage made the girl perfectly suited to the task. Serana felt that in Amber, she had a link to the past she'd never known, another person with the blood of a Sorceress.

"That's enough for today," said Serana after an hour or so.

"Alright," said Amber. "I'll get Aeron for my Air magic lessons."

Serana followed her away; she needed Allaerion and Alier to practice weapons. She'd taken to practicing with both of them at once lately. It was great practice for Allaerion, since he finally had an opponent in the Earth Enchantress who was his better. Alier, in turn, actually found Allaerion challenging, even if he couldn't best her. Serana watched them spar, and took turns sparring with each of them, using both staff and sword. When Amber was done with her Air magic lesson with Aeron, she joined them with her staff, a gift from Alier, made with Earth magic.

Amber and Serana sparred each other along with the others. Amber seemed to enjoy it whenever they did, probably because Serana was not so far beyond her as Alier. It was interesting to spar the girl; she was very creative in applying the forms Alier had taught her, and Serana noted every nuance for future reference. Serana always won these matches so far, but she had a good deal of experience that Amber lacked.

Tonight's match was very short indeed. Amber dropped her staff only seconds into it, and Serana stopped, watching her curiously. Amber had tilted her head, as if listening to something.

"What is it?" asked Serana.

"Listen," Amber told her. "It's Air magic."

Serana listened, concentrating on patterns of Air, and there it was, faint, but audible. She was impressed that Amber could have heard it so easily, but the girl's vampire traits might account for that, considering what they were hearing. Regardless, they didn't have time to ponder it now. "We have to go," she announced.

"I know," said Allaerion, already packed.

"I heard it too," said Aeron, coming up beside him.

"Heard what?" Alier demanded.

"Alloria," said Amber. "She needs us."

***

Alloria walked silently through the forest. The trees were thicker here in the south, perhaps from the warmer weather. Whatever the case, more trees made it more difficult to see what was in the distance, even with a vampire's night vision. Alloria always scouted around the camp at night, after Alexander and the children had fallen asleep. It would not do to have her husband and master fall prey to an attack done in stealth. When she'd come to him, she'd had no intention of developing true feelings for him; she had merely intended to offer herself as a bargaining chip for her people. Spending her nights with him while he lived would have been a small price to pay for an end to the persecution of vampires. From the moment he first looked into her eyes, though, she knew. She knew that her heart would be his regardless how much he hated her, regardless how often he looked at her in disgust. It was frightening, in a way, feeling so vulnerable, but Alexander had surprised her several times. He wanted them to be equals in every way they could, and he never took her in force, though it was his right. Even that first time, when she had all but seduced him for the necessary consummation of their agreement, he had been tender with her, gentle, as if she were precious to him. She'd thought it was her imagination afterward, since he didn't want to touch her again, but she'd been wrong. Against all likelihood, he had come to love her as she loved him, and he was always tender with her, never demanding and never unfair, never taking advantage of his position as her master. She'd have been loyal to him even if he had turned out to be a beast—a *yamin'sai* should always be loyal to her master—but as it was, she would risk her very soul for him, if the situation called for it.

Alloria needed less sleep than he did anyway, so it mattered little that she took only a few hours, after her watch was done. Anyone who attacked while she was sleeping would alert her senses before they were upon her, but not long enough before to make her comfortable. The only way to be sure they were not surprised was to make these nightly excursions.

This time, unfortunately, there were humans in the trees near the camp. They were being very quiet; Alloria could not hear them, despite her exceptional hearing, but she could sense their presence. It wasn't a precise sense, giving her numbers or exact locations; it was merely an impression, telling her that potential prey was near, and in what general direction.

Alloria moved silently, floating a few inches above the forest floor, so that none would hear her passing. She couldn't float this way for long, perhaps an hour or so at most, but it should be more than enough to grant her the stealth she needed. The humans still were not making noise, and there was no sign of a campfire. Despite herself, Alloria was impressed. There were very few humans who could remain so silent that even a vampire would not hear them. If she drew close enough, Alloria would be able to hear their heartbeats, but she would have to be very close indeed for that.

When the trap sprang, it was already too late. There was a net over Alloria, dragging her to the ground before she could move. She tore at the ropes, but they'd been reinforced; they were too strong even for her. The men surrounded her, crossbows pointing toward her from all directions. If she were free, she could disarm and kill them all before they could react, but the net held her fast.

"Well what do we have here?" said one of the men, obviously the leader, from the way the others looked at him. "A 'vampire witch'? I think not. This is a vampire, like all the others." The men appeared more than a little nervous, but the leader did not. "After all," he went on with a sneer, "if she were a witch, would she let me do this?" He slammed a knife into her shoulder, and her world exploded in pain. She did not cry out, but she nearly fell to her knees. She instinctively called her race's silent cry for help, knowing that none would come, but her vision was already blurring with the pain in her shoulder. As she fell into darkness, listening to the men laugh with new confidence, her last thought was regret that she would not be able to stay with Alexander for the rest of his life.

***

Serana raced through the forest, sword in hand, senses alert. There were men ahead, but they were still several miles away. Serana had never been able to sense anything at such a distance before, but her abilities had always improved in jumps and plateaus, never in a gradual line. Amber and the elementals weren't far behind Serana, but none of them seemed able to match her speed, now that need drove her. Alloria's message was little more than an image and a feeling, but it was enough to tell Serana that the vampire woman was a prisoner, held captive by men who hated her. Serana remembered too clearly being suspended naked in the air as Lord Zironkell's hands groped her. She remembered being helpless, unable to stop him. That he never finished his work was a comfort, but it didn't erase the memory, the horror of the events. If she could spare another woman that fate, whatever that woman's race, she would.

Within minutes, Serana was there. She took in the scene at a glance. Alloria was bound hand and foot, tied spread-eagle between two thick wooden poles. Her shoulder was bleeding profusely, and her face was bruised. Just as Serana came into view, one of the men tore away the last of her clothing, leering at the trapped vampire with a grin that filled Serana with rage. Sword blazing like white fire, Serana swept into the men like a storm, her magic answering her need with fury. In seconds, every last man was dead, and Serana was still looking for more to kill. Taking on the Serenity, Serana forced down her rage and put away her sword. She cut Alloria's bonds with blades of Fire, and held the vampire on a cushion of air. She touched Alloria's ruined shoulder, healing it in moments, then soothed away the bruises on her face.

"Thank you," Alloria whispered, her eyes fluttering open. Something more was wrong. With her wounds healed, Alloria should have been able to stand, or at least sit up, remain conscious.

"Blood," said Amber, who had appeared beside Serana at some point. "She lost too much blood, and she needs to replace it." Serana glanced at the dead men, but Amber shook her head. "It has to be from a living person. Drinking the blood of those already dead would kill her."

Suddenly, Serana understood. It was life energy that vampires drained with the blood of living creatures. That energy would be gone after the victim had died, rendering the blood useless. Serana tried to feed Life magic into Alloria, but it slipped away, refusing to stay.

"I told you," said Amber patiently. "It's blood she needs. That's a vampire's weakness. They need blood."

Steeling herself for what she was about to do, Serana unlaced the bodice of her gown, exposing her shoulder entirely. She shook the vampire woman gently to wake her, and guided her mouth to Serana's shoulder.

The pain wasn't as great as what Serana expected; it was more like a pinprick. Serana held onto the Serenity, to keep herself calm, and gathered her magic, hoping that the concentration would mean less blood was required. Slowly, Alloria's hands came up to hold Serana as the vampire drank, her strength returning. It was over in minutes, but Serana felt a bit light-headed when Alloria finally released her.

"Thank you," the vampire said, looking into Serana's eyes. "I didn't think anyone would hear my call, much less you; you should have been too far away." She quickly picked up her cloak, covering herself. Her other clothing lay in ruins.

"It was Amber who heard you first," Serana told her. "We hadn't made much progress in the past few days, so we were only miles away."

"Thank you all," said Alloria, smiling.

The elementals were standing around Serana. She hadn't noticed them arrive.

"It seems you've taken care of everything, as usual," said Seleine with a grin for Serana.

Serana smiled at the Ice Witch, but before she could respond, new voices piped up.

"Alloria, are you okay?" said two little boys in unison, rushing up to hug the vampire tightly.

"We woke up," said one.

"And you weren't there," finished the other.

"We got Alexander," they said together, clinging to Alloria's cloak.

"What happened," Lord Alexander asked worriedly, hurrying to Alloria's side.

"She was attacked," said Serana. "Fortunately, we weren't far away."

"Thank you," Lord Alexander told her, holding his wife to him. "I am forever in your debt."

Alloria laughed softly. "*He* is in your debt, when *I* am the one who was attacked. If there is ever anything you need of me, High Priestess, that does not violate my agreement with my husband, then you have but to ask." She looked down at Amber. "The same goes for you, little sister."

Amber smiled.

"We should all travel together," Serana said seriously. "There are bandits aplenty, both on and off the road. We've managed to frighten many of them, but there will always be some who are just as ready to attack, particularly those who are experienced vampire hunters."

"Like those who caught me," Alloria said, nodding.

"No party of human bandits is prepared to take on a Sorceress and four elementals," Serana went on, "and with Amber, we can nearly say two Sorceresses. She's been coming along wonderfully in her lessons."

Amber beamed.

"We left our things a few miles away, at our camp," said Allaerion. "Aeron and I can go retrieve them. We'll find you when we return."

Serana, Seleine, and Alier walked back to Lord Alexander's camp with the others, to wait for the Air Wizards. Since Lord Alexander and his wife had only one tent, Seleine made a shelter of ice for the four children, who were delighted to find that it wouldn't melt or make them cold.

Amber still wanted to sleep with Alier.

"I hope you're not claustrophobic," said the Earth Enchantress. "I haven't had enough rest yet tonight, and I don't intend to wait for the men." She took Amber's hand, and the two of them sank into the ground. Before Amber's head disappeared, she smiled with delight.

Serana made a dome of Air for herself and Seleine, and they were all soon asleep.

Chapter XXVII

"I don't mean to hold up your search," said Alexander the next morning. He'd insisted that Serana stop using his title, and she agreed, so long as he'd stop using hers. "Finding this Daemon Lord in the South is more important than escorting us."

"That may be true," agreed Serana, "but we have no idea where to look. Your brother's estate is as good a place as any."

"We appreciate it," he told her, shifting uncomfortably in his saddle.

"What is wrong, Alexander?" asked Alloria. The vampire woman had begun acting entirely servile around her husband, until he told her that they were still in private. Serana wasn't quite sure what that meant, but she suspected it had something to do with the rules of the agreement that made Alloria *yamin'sai* to Alexander.

"Forgive me," he said, sighing. "I should just tell you. My brother is not so unreasonable as some in the Southern Nations, but he still believes that magic is evil, and that vampires are what those in the North call Daemons."

"I'm sure we can convince him of the benefits of magic," said Alier, who had been engaged in quiet conversation with Amber all morning.

"Meaning no disrespect," said Alexander, "I doubt that will be possible."

"Do you?" asked the Earth Enchantress mildly.

She was up to something; Serana was sure of it.

"May I have a silver piece, Lord Alexander?" Alier asked him.

"Of course," Alexander said, confused. He fished out a silver penny and handed it to her.

Alier began flipping it over and over between her fingers. "Too many people forget that metals are the realm of Earth magic," she said conversationally. "I've always thought it was rather silly to use metal for money, but I'm not going to complain, if other people want to do it. After all, I could be a very wealthy woman, if I wanted to be." She handed the penny back to Alexander, and he gasped. Serana, who had been watching the flows of Earth magic, was not surprised in the least. The penny was now pure gold.

"Can you do this every time?" asked Alexander.

"Of course I can." Alier grinned. "And it doesn't have to be one penny at a time, either."

Alexander grinned along with her. "Maybe my brother *can* be convinced." His grin faded in moments. "What about the rest of you? He'll ask what the others can do."

Serana smiled slowly, enjoying this game. "It takes all of us to make gold, Alexander. Alier can't do it alone."

Amber giggled, and Alier put an arm around her.

"I think they have you, husband," said Alloria.

"Yes," agreed Alexander, "but more importantly, I think they will have my brother."

Lord Duncan's estate was still quite a distance away, near the western edge of the Southern Nations, and traveling was much slower with humans in the group, so Serana and the elementals decided to save some time by going cross-country. Near evening, though, the terrain began to look strangely familiar, and Serana began to grow very nervous.

"What is it?" asked Seleine for the third time. "And don't tell me it's nothing again. You're using the Serenity, or you'd be trembling."

"We're getting close to Alon Peak," said Serana.

"Isn't that where you used to live?" the Ice Witch asked.

Serana nodded. "It's also where they almost banished me for healing a child on my sixteenth birthday, before the 'Lord of Eridan' intervened. It would be nice to see my parents again, or rather, the parents who raised me, but I don't think our welcome would be a warm one."

Alier put a hand on Serana's shoulder. "Don't be so sure," she said, smiling gently. "Remember that they think you're married to this Lord of Eridan. Folk from small, isolated places usually have strange ideas about nobility. They might not be surprised at all, if we play it the right way. After all, do they know what an elemental is?"

"No," said Serana uncertainly.

"Good. Then they won't expect us to be able to do magic. We're foreigners, and that's why our skin and hair is a different color from theirs."

Serana blinked. Could it be that simple? "But they've *seen* me do magic, and Alloria is a vampire."

"And likely they do not believe in vampires either," Alloria said. "I can refrain from drinking blood for a day, while we are there; so little time will not harm me." Alon voiced his agreement, and Serana couldn't help but laugh.

"Exactly," said Seleine. "And you told me that they accepted you, after the Serian of Music set them straight."

"But how do I explain my 'husband' not being with us?" asked Serana.

Alexander laughed. "Perhaps you need a few lessons on nobility yourself. Nobles often marry for convenience, not for love. It's not uncommon for husbands and wives to see each other once or twice in a month, if that. They don't always travel together."

"I'm your guard," offered Allaerion. "They won't find a better swordsman among humans."

"I, too, could be a guard," said Alier, grinning. "If they need convincing, I'll let any of them spar me with a quarterstaff."

"Someone might take you up on that," said Serana, "but if they do, they'll be more than convinced." There were actually a few people in Alon Peak who used a quarterstaff quite well, but none of them came anywhere near the Earth Enchantress' skill.

"I'm a serving maid," Amber announced. "They often start young, and I do know how to play the part. Remember that I was raised in the Ravenstar household, at first, anyway."

"My wife and I are friends of your husband," said Alexander, "and these four are our children." Tim and Tom grinned. Josua and his sister simply nodded.

"I am a magician, hired to protect you against evil magic," said Aeron. Serana gave him an odd look, but he went on before she could ask. "Some must study the arts of magic, if we are to defend against it," he said piously. Serana laughed.

"I'm another serving maid," said Seleine. "I signed up because I'm infatuated with one of your guards." She grinned at Allaerion suggestively, and he actually blushed.

"I suppose it's all settled then," said Serana. "Thank you, all of you."

"Why thank us?" asked Amber. "This should be fun!"

When Alon Peak came into view, it looked exactly the way Serana remembered it, but somehow at the same time, it looked strangely smaller. Serana headed for the Inn; she want to say hello to her parents—her foster parents—before she left, and the party would have to take rooms for the night, to keep up the pretense of her nobility. The Inn didn't really have another name, like The Sleeping Dragon in Green Haven. It was just the Inn. There was only one inn in Alon Peak, and people couldn't imagine there being more, so no one bothered with a longer name.

People stared as she passed, most without expression, but a few seemed glad to see her. Old Billy Hoon grinned broadly, and Elsa Cooper waved and smiled, with little Natel scampering around the yard playing.

Mayor Eslan and his wife were waiting outside the Inn, looking proud as if they were royalty themselves. Maria Eslan rushed out to meet the party, gathering Serana up in a bear hug. She wasn't a large woman, but she was very strong for her size. Serana hugged her back, all the while gasping for air.

"We've missed you terribly, Serana," she said, finally releasing her daughter. "I know you're only here for a visit, but welcome home!"

Mayor Eslan hugged her too, but thankfully he was gentler. "It's good to see you again, Serana," he said. "Or should I be calling you Lady Eridan?"

"Serana is fine," said Serana hastily. The last thing she wanted was another title, particular one she didn't even deserve. She began making introductions, to forestall any further repetitions of 'Lady Eridan'. "These are my friends, Lord Alexander and his wife Alloria. These two are my serving maids, Amber and Seleine." Seleine was eyeing Allaerion, and he was pretending not to notice. "These are my guards, Allaerion and Alier."

"A woman guard?" Mayor Eslan exclaimed.

"She can guard me more closely some places than Allaerion can, and believe me; she's the deadlier of the two," Serana told him. "If you don't believe her, have Brad South spar her." Brad nearly always won the quarterstaff competition at the summer festival.

"He might just want to try that," said the Mayor, eyeing the slender Earth Enchantress doubtfully.

Alier's grin actually looked eager.

"This is Aeron," Serana went on. "He's an Air Wizard."

"I study the mystic arts in order to counter those who use them for evil," Aeron explained. "The Lady Eridan must be protected against all things, mundane or magical."

"Of course she must," said Serana's mother firmly, as if she'd been dealing with Air Wizards all her life. "Now come inside, all of you. You'll want a hot meal after your journey." After all this time, Serana still thought of Maria Eslan as mother, and of her husband as Mayor Eslan. She'd rarely called him 'father' even as a child.

They all took seats in the common room, and if Serana's parents thought it odd that guards and serving maids would sit alongside a Lady, they gave no indication of it. In truth, they probably had no idea what to expect; they knew even less about nobility than Serana did. In any case, it didn't matter, since Serana would be likely to do things differently than others anyway, and the Lord of Eridan was a decidedly unusual nobleman.

The meal was delicious, the Inn's best stew, made from a variety of vegetables, and meats, and even fruits from the various farms in the area, and seasoned with herbs that Lana gathered herself. Serana remembered going with Lana on those herb-gathering excursions, during her training in herb lore. She'd never quite been able to make the stew turn out as well as her mother could, though, despite her best efforts. Of course, neither could anyone else; Maria Eslan was the best cook in Alon Peak.

Allaerion slipped up once during the meal, commenting that the stew was at least as good as Serana's cooking.

"She still cooks?" Maria asked, surprised.

"Of course I do," said Serana firmly. "You don't think I'd waste my best skills just because I no longer *have* to use them, do you? Besides, none of the chefs are as skilled as you are, mother."

Serana's mother beamed. "I hope she still makes her bed too," she said with mock-severity.

"Makes her bed?" said Seleine, aghast. "If she did that, poor Amber and I might be out of a job!"

Amber nodded earnestly.

"I always knew she'd find a way to get out of that one," said Serana's mother, laughing.

When the meal was finished, Serana's mother pulled Serana away from the others gently, taking her upstairs to one of the empty guestrooms. "Serana, I need to ask you something," she said seriously. "Someone else might too, but I want to be the first." She paused, as if considering her words carefully. "Before you left, at your ceremony on your Day of Passing, you healed little Natel. That was magic, wasn't it?"

"Yes, mother, it was," said Serana. She didn't think she could come up with a convincing lie anyway, and she hated not being honest with her mother.

Maria nodded. "I thought it was. You don't have to answer this next question if you don't want to, but I'd like to know. How is it that you can do magic?"

"I'm a Sorceress, mother," explained Serana. "My village, the Sorceress village, was destroyed by vampires when I was a baby. The vampires didn't kill me, though; they took me to you instead, so that the race wouldn't die out. They hypnotized you. That's why it seemed like a dream."

"I wondered if it might have been something like that," said Serana's mother. "I've always said that there is more to this world than we in Alon Peak know about. I just can't say it in front of most of the townsfolk." She smiled. "So, you're a Sorceress. What kind of magic can you do? Is it all healing, or is there more?"

"There's a great deal more," said Serana. "But healing is what I enjoy the most. I've been all the way up to Rhanestone Keep, mother, and even across the Barrilian Mountains, to the wasteland beyond. On the way back here, I healed people in the villages between Rhanestone and Green Haven. All the innkeepers let us stay for free because of it."

"Are you really married to that strange man, the Lord of Eridan?"

Serana grinned. She really should have given her mother more credit. "No, mother, I'm not. I'm not married to anyone at all, unfortunately. The man I would have married is dead now, and I'm carrying his child, a child that will be a Sorceress, bearing no racial traits of his. Those people downstairs are my friends, and we're all part of a war being waged against a terrible race of Daemons trying to enslave and destroy the entire world."

Serana's mother blinked. "That's quite a lot to take in. Why don't you start at the beginning?"

Serana told her mother everything, from being taken away by the Dark Angel of Music, who was really the last of the Seriani, the beings that created the world, to trying to piece together the Armor of the Elements. She explained everything she knew about the Sorceress race, and about elementals and their magic. She told her mother about the friends she'd made, the adventures she'd had, and the times she'd thought she was going to die. It was strangely soothing, telling everything, not hiding anything. Her mother listened intently the entire time, asking a question here or there, but otherwise remaining silent. When Serana was finished, her mother let out a long breath and sat back in her chair.

"You *have* been busy," she said after a few moments. "So now the fate of the world rests with you and your friends recovering the last piece of this magical Armor. I always knew you were special, Serana, but I must admit that I never thought you'd turn out to be the High Priestess from another race of beings." She smiled suddenly. "You're lucky, though. When the babies here are old and grey, you'll still look young and beautiful. Imagine what most women would give for *that*?"

"It will be nice in some ways," agreed Serana, "but there are downsides too. For one, I'll have to watch every human friend I make grow old and die. For another, I don't think I'll age any further than I have already. I won't just always look young, I'll always look *sixteen*!"

Her mother laughed. "You'll find ways to use that to your advantage too. I know you will. Do me two favors, though, please."

"Anything for you, mother,"

"First, take care of yourself. You may be more powerful than a whole army of people like me, but I still worry about you, Serana."

"I will, mother," Serana assured her.

"Second," her mother paused, a small smile playing at the corners of her mouth, "bring my grandbaby to see me after she's born."

Serana beamed. "I will, mother. I promise."

The next morning, Brad South *did* want to spar Alier, and a good many of the townsfolk came to watch. Brad was completely respectful to Alier, saying only that he didn't get much chance to practice with anyone who really knew what they were about. Alier, in turn, said she liked him, and hoped he wouldn't take the beating personally. She was having as much fun as Serana had ever seen her have.

The match lasted fifteen minutes or so, since Alier was toying with Brad. The man really was quite skilled, but no human could hear the heartbeat of life, and perhaps more importantly, no human lived long enough to gain Alier's experience. There were very few blows struck on either side—none on Alier—but Serana found it fascinating to watch. She didn't believe she herself could best Brad, in a fair match... that is, one where Serana didn't use magic to speed her movements. Alier, of course, didn't need extra speed; she simply knew exactly where to be and when to be there, thanks to the heartbeat of life and several centuries of experience. Brad conceded the match in the end, and thanked Alier for the best exercise he'd had in years. Serana heard a few townsfolk ask why he'd quit. He laughed as he replied, "Because I'm not a complete fool. That woman could have beaten me bloody or killed me, if she'd wanted. Serana is as safe as she can be with Alier around."

Alier heard the last bit, and winked at Serana, nearly making her laugh.

The party left Alon Peak in good spirits. Serana and her friends all received hugs from her mother, and extra food for the journey as well. They were unlikely to come across another town before reaching Duncan's estate, and that would take several weeks. Maria also had little pouches filled with candy for the children, including Amber, with an admonishment not to eat it all at once. Lilian, Tim and Tim squealed with delight, and even Josua and Amber grinned.

"Be careful," whispered Serana's mother as she hugged Serana one last time, "but remember that I have faith in you."

"Whatever abilities I have," Serana whispered back, "you've made me into the person I am. Thank you, mother."

Soon Alon Peak was fading into the distance behind, just as it had that first night with the Dark Angel of Music, but this time Serana didn't mind. This time, she knew she could always return to visit her birthplace, and at least one person would know who she really was.

Chapter XXVIII

"I'd always wondered about that," said Alloria to herself when the party was a few miles away from Alon Peak.

"About what?" Alexander asked. Serana listened curiously.

"Remember that I told you I was naming Alon after my grandfather?" The little lamb nuzzled Alloria's hand when he heard his name, hoping for attention.

"Yes," said Alexander slowly.

"He told me once that he helped start a human village a few centuries ago," Alloria explained, petting the lamb absently. "Grandfather was always one for tall tales, so this is the first time I've actually realized he was telling the truth."

Serana stared. "Your grandfather started Alon Peak?"

"*Helped* start it," Alloria corrected. "They named it after him, to honor him, using both his first and last name."

Serana was bewildered. The people in Alon Peak today didn't even *believe* in elves! What would they think if they learned that the village was named after one? She didn't get a chance to ponder very far.

"That's far enough," said a man stepping out from the trees.

"Are you going to try to rob us too?" asked Alier with a yawn.

"Hardly," said the man disdainfully. "My men and I aren't bandits; we're brothers in the Holy Order of Light."

"The what?" asked Allaerion, sounding as confused as Serana felt.

"The Holy Order of Light," the man explained with all the patience of a teacher instructing a particularly stupid child. "You can go on your way after you've been cleansed of evil."

"What evil?" Serana asked.

The man sighed. "The fact that you do not know tells me that you walk in ignorance, but fear not; we of the Holy Order will open your eyes to the Creator's light."

"You do realize," said Alier testily, "that eight of the nine creators are dead, and the last one is a friend of ours."

The man shook his head sadly. "It pains me to see a woman so young and beautiful living under such misguided notions."

"Young?" exclaimed Alier, obviously trying not to laugh.

The man went on as if she hadn't spoken. "I know that you are not responsible for your ignorance, so we will be lenient with you. No doubt you are unaware that even now you harbor a creature of evil in your midst." His eyes swept over them all, and came to rest on Alloria.

Serana didn't need to hear any more. She already knew where this was going. "So what you're saying," she said with the same exaggerated patience that he'd been using, "is that you are glorified vampire hunters who have invented a ridiculous name and an even more ridiculous pretext under which to operate."

"Be careful, young woman," the man said, a dangerous glimmer in his eyes. "A certain amount of ignorance we can tolerate, but that sort of blasphemy against the Holy Order cannot go unpunished. I think a full day and night in the Tent of Enlightenment will make you see the error of your ways."

"And what exactly would I learn in this Tent of Enlightenment?" Serana demanded, gathering her power. She cast her senses through the forest, finding a sizable force of human men, just over four hundred strong, all well armed.

"Your place, of course," replied the man. "The place of all young women, to use your bodies in the service of the Creator's light, to produce more of His loyal followers."

Serana created an invisible shield around the party—well, invisible to humans; Aeron, Allaerion, and Amber should be able to see it quite easily—to protect from arrows and keep men from getting to the children. "What an interesting idea," she said, "but I don't think I'll do that today. How about instead I hang you upside down and naked from that tree there?" She indicated a particularly tall elm with a thick branch that hung out over the road.

The man sighed again. "Take them," he called, and men poured from the trees, running into Serana's wall and bouncing off ineffectually. By the time they realized that they couldn't get through, Serana had snatched the speaker into the air, stripped him, and used his pants to make the rope that tied him to the tree limb by the ankles. To finish the job, she used his shirt to gag him. The cloak, with the emblem that must stand for the so-called Holy Order of Light, she left on the ground.

"You can stop attacking now," said Serana, using Air to make her voice resonate through the forest. Some of the men were already running, but most were frozen, watching Serana. Several glanced up at their leader, bound and gagged with his own clothing. "Now that I have your attention, perhaps I should explain the flaws in *your* ways. There really *is* an evil race out there, but it isn't vampires. There is a race of Daemons who *do* use women to produce more of their own kind. They consume Life and destroy the innocent, and they must be stopped. You, on the other hand, seem more willing to join them. One of you, give me just one good reason why I shouldn't kill you all where you stand!"

The men stared at her, but no one spoke. The sky darkened as storm clouds rolled in with unnatural speed. Lightning lit up the sky, and thunder boomed, echoing Serana's growing anger. The wind picked up, drowning out voices, but Serana's magic carried every whisper to her ears.

"Speak," she commanded, "or you all die here."

"We thought we were doing right," a lone man said when she'd nearly given up on them.

"You think rape and murder in the name of good is right?" Serana challenged as rain started pouring from the sky.

"No," murmured the man, and a few others shook their heads.

"I will give you all one last chance to live," said Serana. "I have placed a slow poison in the rain that will seep into your skin and kill you all in three months time, unless you redeem yourself. Go north, to the fortress of Rhanestone Keep, and offer yourselves as soldiers to fight against the Daemon army. There is a powerful Battlemage there named Rillian. He will no how to cure you, if you tell him the truth. Tell him what you've done, and that you seek redemption in fighting the Daemons." Serana smiled without mirth. "Beware that if even one of you returns to your wicked ways, I will know, and on my command, the poison will kill all of you instantly. Go now, and hurry, if you want to live."

The men surged into motion, heading north, heedless of the wind that whipped at them, and Serana relaxed. When they had gone, she turned to Aeron. "Thank you for the thunderstorm; it helped."

The Air Wizard smiled. "I didn't actually intend for it to be quite so furious as it was, but I had help." He winked at Amber, who blushed shyly. The storm began to recede as fast as it had come. "I do have a question, though. How did you put poison in the rain? Even if you'd used another element, I should have seen *some* change, I'd have thought. Not only that, I'd like to know how Rhanestone's Battlemage is going to cure them. He's skilled, for a human, but surely not *that* skilled."

Serana grinned. "I didn't do anything to the rain," she told him, "but those men don't know that. Rillian will understand when he hears their story, and conjure them a 'cure' that they will believe in."

"It's risky," said Alier sourly. "If those men do go back to their old tricks, they'll know they've been tricked."

"Not likely," said Serana. "I did give them all a mild cold that should show up in three weeks or so. It won't kill even one of them, but it will make all of them think they're dying. That should spur them on toward Rhanestone."

The speaker gurgled from behind his gag.

"You aren't really going to leave him there naked, are you?" asked Amber.

"No, you're right," agreed Serana. Using Air magic, she lifted the cloak from the ground and tied it around his ankles, so that it draped over the front of his body. "There, now anyone coming through here can see what the 'Holy Order of Light' is worth."

"You do have a vicious streak," said Seleine, looking over the man critically. "I approve!"

The next few days passed without serious event. There were two more groups of bandits, but they were the regular variety, not members of the so-called 'Holy Order'. Serana killed a few, and sent the rest running for their lives. It might have bothered her, killing humans, except that she really didn't see these men as human. They were murderers, rapists, and thieves, usually all three at once. In Serana's mind, those choices on their parts made them nothing more than dangerous animals, better to be slaughtered than suffered.

Evenings were pleasant. Serana practiced the sword and the staff each night along with Allaerion, Alier, and Amber. Lord Alexander even joined in the sword training. He was woefully inept compared with Allaerion and Serana, but he was determined to learn. Serana had to remind herself a few times how rapid her own progress with a blade had been, so that she never thought him slower than he should be.

To Alexander's surprise—but not Serana's—Alloria joined in the weapons training too. She didn't learn the forms any more quickly than Alexander did, but she used her vampire speed to great effect. Of course, Serana and Allaerion had the same advantage, so teaching her was not difficult. The vampire woman was also interested in the staff, and Alier was happy to teach her.

It wasn't long before Josua and Lilian asked if they, too, could have lessons with the sword. "We won't always have you to protect us," explained Josua as his sister nodded in agreement. "We know you can't make us as skilled as the Air Wizard or the High Priestess, but at least we could defend ourselves against humans, with enough practice." Allaerion took them on as students, with the agreement that they would not try to participate in a fight until either he said they were ready or they had no choice.

Only Tim and Tom didn't seem interested in learning to use a weapon. They were content simply to watch, something Serana found decidedly unusual. Every other small child she'd ever seen would want to be included, particularly in something as exciting as weapons training. The twins *did* like to watch, though. They sat quietly while the others practiced, during both the sparring sessions and the magic lessons, and their small eyes never left the participants. No one else seemed to think anything of the twins' behavior, but Serana felt it had some significance, though she couldn't say exactly what.

The party encountered fewer bandits as time went by, since they were traveling across land where travelers were rarely seen. Almost two weeks after their encounter with the Holy Order of Light, the travelers stumbled across a village. More surprising than the village's existence, though, were its inhabitants, nearly all Earth Enchantresses.

There were no visible houses or other buildings of any kind. Serana might not have noticed the village at all, if not for the life energies of its people and the patterns of Earth energy surrounding it, making all the plants around it grow and blossom. The patterns were almost identical to those in Green Haven, but on a much smaller scale.

The villagers did not seem at all surprised when the party arrived. In fact, three Earth Enchantresses were waiting to greet Serana and the others. One of them was very small, coming only to Serana's shoulder, while the other two were more average height.

"I am Lyra," the smallest of them said as the party approached. "I am the sister in charge of our village of Lyrineine." She was slender as well as short, proportioned perfectly to her height. What Serana noticed most, though, was that Lyra didn't look at her, as if her explanation were for the benefit of the others. "These are Terania and Giarra. Welcome to our village, High Priestess. Welcome to all of you." Lyra's eyes widened as they fell on Alier. "The Weaver of Earth! You are still alive!" All three women curtsied deeply, spreading their light green skirts.

"Reports of my death have been intentionally exaggerated," Alier told them with a grin.

"You know each other?" asked Serana.

The three exchanged confused glances among themselves. "We know you as well, High Priestess, though you seem to have grown in strength. Leliah of the Sorceress village is always welcome here."

"Leliah was my grandmother," Serana explained. "My name is Serana."

"I think," said Alier gently, "that we have a great deal to tell you, and much of it is not good."

"Let us go indoors," said Lyra, motioning the party to follow her. "We will have a meal prepared for you all, and we can talk while you eat."

Serana and her friends followed the three Earth Enchantresses to a huge stone, four or five times as tall as Allaerion. Lyra spread her arms when they reached it, and the rock moved almost as if it were liquid, molding itself into the shape of an ornate doorway. Lyra led them through, while Terania and Giarra stood at either side of the doorway, just inside.

Lyra took them down a long corridor dimly lit with strange, glowing crystals, and through a side door that was cleverly hidden in the shadows. The side door led into a small room with several well-cushioned chairs, lit by a cheery fire that played in a very ornate hearth. Serana wondered how the Earth Enchantresses could have a fire underground without the smoke poisoning the air, but she decided to ask them later.

"Please, make yourselves comfortable," said Lyra. "Your meals will be brought to you in a few moments."

Tim and Tom needed no further encouragement. They both jumped onto the seat closest to the fire, grinning. Serana and the others all took chairs, and almost as soon as they'd sat down, more Earth Enchantresses came into the room, bearing trays laden with delicious-looking fruit and steaming bowls of stew. The aroma, strangely reminiscent of what Maria Eslan made back in Alon Peak, made Serana's mouth water. The stew tasted as good as it smelled, and Serana had finished two bowels before she thought to try the fruit.

"Your grandmother always loved that stew too," said Lyra, smiling. "You look so much like her that it's uncanny. I do apologize for the mistake, though."

"I made the same mistake," Alier told her around a mouthful of fruit. "Serana had to set me straight on more than one thing that day."

Lyra blinked in surprise. "What happened?"

Alier told her about the first time she and Serana had met, including the magical sparring match that had frightened poor Allaerion half to death.

"All four elements?" exclaimed Lyra. "If it were anyone other than you telling me, I'd say that's impossible!"

"Do you want to spar her too?" Alier offered.

"Ah, no, that's quite alright," said Lyra quickly. Lyra was quite strong, as far as Serana could tell, but not so strong as Alier. No one was as strong in Earth magic as Alier. "What are you all doing this far south?"

"We're gathering the pieces to the Armor of the Elements," said Serana.

Lyra frowned. "None of them were hidden down here."

"That's true," agreed Alier, "but the last piece, the right gauntlet, was stolen by a Daemon Lord. We're going to get it back."

"I know you are strong, Alier," said Lyra slowly, "and I know Serana here is even stronger, but have you ever faced a Daemon Lord? They are more powerful than anything else I know of, except perhaps one of the Seriani."

"I was there at the fall of Ereanthea, if you've forgotten," said Alier. "I presume that is where you thought I'd died. I have faced Daemon Lords before, though I've never bested one. Serana, however, has killed two and driven off two others."

"How is that possible?" asked Lyra, her eyes wide as they stared in awe at Serana.

Serana picked up her sword from where she'd laid it by the chair, and drew it from the scabbard. "This is how."

Lyra stared at the glowing white blade for a long moment before speaking. "Where did you get that?"

"I made it," Serana told her, blinking as her eyes suddenly moistened.

"Serana made the sword herself, and originally filled it with Fire magic," explained Alier. "Later, Ignatius was killed by a Daemon Lord that attacked. He gave what was left of his life energy to Serana, and she put it into that blade, Daemonbane."

"An appropriate name," Lyra breathed, her eyes moving over the length of the blade. "Even I can see that this sword would be death to any Daemon, however powerful."

"There is more," said Alier very gently, and suddenly Serana realized just how far behind events Lyra and her people were.

"I know." Lyra's smile, and even her awe at Daemonbane, had faded. Her eyes were moist, but her jaw was set with determination. "How did Leliah die, and what happened to her daughter?"

"Leliah was at Inferniesm," said Alier.

Lyra choked back a sob. "Did they take her?"

"No," Serana answered quickly, remembering Ignatius' story. "A Daemon General stabbed her. They took Ignatius' wife, Erathea, and they'd have killed Ignatius too, but my grandmother transported him away from there, to Blackfang's volcano, with the last of her strength."

Lyra closed her eyes. "That does sound like Leliah. She would have fought until there was no spark of life left in her. We here did not know of the Daemons' invasion until after it was over, when the two remaining Seriani stopped it at the ruins of Ereanthea. We still do not know why they did not come sooner."

"Nor do I," said Alier, "but I do know that they had a reason. Those two would have defended life with all their strength, against any odds. If they did not come until too late, then there was a reason."

"You speak of them in past tense," Lyra said slowly. "Are they…"

"Shape is gone," Alier told her. "Music is still alive, but he has been reclusive since his mate's death."

Lyra nodded. "What about your mother, Serana? I never knew her, but is she still alive? How did you come to be High Priestess at so early an age?"

"I am the last of my kind. I received the title of High Priestess by default. Vampires destroyed the village and nearly everyone in it more than sixteen years ago. I say *nearly* everyone because they did not destroy me. I was a baby, and for whatever reasons, they took me to a human couple, who adopted me as their daughter." The tale still stirred mixed emotions within Serana. She felt very little more than a vague sense of loss over her people, since she'd never known them, yet she felt as if she should feel more. They were, after all, her people.

Lyra's face was ashen. "The Sorceress village is gone?"

"I'm afraid so," said Alier. "It was devastating to me as well."

Lyra's eyes moved slowly to Serana. "Now you, and the dress you wear, are all that remains."

Serana shook her head. "Not quite all. Amber over there is half-Sorceress."

Lyra looked to Alier questioningly, and the older Earth Enchantress shrugged. Amber was still eating unconcernedly. When no one said anything, she looked up and nodded, then went back to eating. She could have been saying the food was good, for all the

242

emotion in her face, but Serana had no doubt that she'd been listening to everything.

"She doesn't look to be a Sorceress at all," said Lyra slowly, studying the girl. "In fact, she looks a good deal more like a vampire, though why one of them would show such interest in food is beyond me."

"It is very good food," said Alloria, who also was eating.

Lyra blinked in surprise. "My apologies," she said faintly.

Alloria shrugged.

"Amber is half-vampire and half-Sorceress," explained Serana. "If you don't believe me, she could throw the Arrow of Light. No pure vampire can do that."

"And no pure Sorceress would need to drink blood every few weeks to keep from getting ill," said Amber around a mouthful of food.

"That much I can verify with certainty," said Alier. "The girl can indeed throw the Arrow of Light, and with a good deal of proficiency, I might add. She's also quickly becoming a formidable staff woman."

"I'm still not very good at splitting the Arrow of Light," said Amber. "Serana does it much better, though she needs to work on her aim."

"*Splitting* the Arrow of Light?" asked Lyra doubtfully.

Alier nodded again in confirmation.

Lyra took a deep breath. "This has been a great deal to take in. Perhaps you should start at the beginning, from just after your first encounter with the new High Priestess here."

Alier nodded, and began telling their story. Serana helped fill in a few details, and Aeron offered some explanations here and there. When they were all finished, Lyra shook her head.

"An unbelievable tale," breathed Lyra, "if I did not know the ones telling it to be true. I have a great deal to think on now, more than I have had in decades. Please, all of you rest here tonight, that you may continue your journey refreshed. The chairs fold back into beds with just a touch of Earth Magic. You remember how, Alier. I must go now, and discuss what you have told me with the village council. They will all want to know what has happened."

"Thank you for your hospitality, my friend," said Alier, rising to hug the other Earth Enchantress warmly.

"Don't be silly," chided Lyra. "You and any who travel with you are always welcome, Weaver of Earth. I don't believe that any Earth Enchantress will ever forget that name."

"How did you become the Weaver of Earth?" asked Amber when Lyra had gone.

"That," said Alier, "is a very long story."

Chapter XXIX

Lord Zironkell paced back and forth in his chamber, the ever-present anger inside him boiling still more violently than usual. One of the imbeciles near the human play-castle had finally decided to inform him that one of his two Daemon Lords had left the army more than a month ago. Zironkell had killed the simpleton for taking so long. Raveshik had always made Zironkell slightly uncomfortable. Not frightened, of course; nothing frightened Lord Zironkell... but uncomfortable. For nearly a century now, Raveshik had played his own game, and Zironkell had watched him, waiting to see what he would do. This time, Zironkell thought that perhaps he might have waited too long.

The weapon was not terribly bright, but she was strong. She would deal with Raveshik, and return Zironkell his gauntlet. Zironkell had been very careful what to tell her and what not to, during all the years she'd lived. She could sense direct lies; that much was apparent early on. She could not, however, sense deception, even obvious deception, if no direct lie was employed. Zironkell had exploited that weakness to his advantage on many occasions, but Raveshik would not know of it. Something else he did not know, something that Zironkell had been very careful to keep from them both, was that the weapon, Zironkell's weapon, was Raveshik's daughter.

Fortunately, Daemon Lords held no ridiculous ties of affection to bloodlines. That Raveshik was Zironkell's brother was no more important than which woman Zironkell would choose for his pleasure that evening. Now that he'd disobeyed openly, Raveshik was an enemy, and must be destroyed. How he'd managed to steal away the gauntlet was a mystery, but it didn't matter. All that mattered was that Raveshik would be destroyed and that Zironkell would rule absolutely.

Another concern, though less important than Zironkell's brother, was that the small army at the human play-castle was growing restless. The fools couldn't see why Zironkell had stopped the attacks, forced them to wait. Now that the Sorceress had revisited the play-castle, the humans, elves, and vampires were armed with mystical weapons, and the accursed Serian had provided a wall of those infernal flowers. Worse, the two dragons, one the Guardian of Mist, were somehow free, and were dwelling there with the humans. A direct assault with only the forces present might succeed, but it also might not. Zironkell's victory could not be a matter of chance; it must be complete and absolute. Zironkell had dispatched a few reinforcements to help, but his larger force was for something else entirely, something that would shake the world with its fury. After the weapon had destroyed his brother and the last of the hated Seriani, the world would belong to Lord Zironkell.

***

Lady Firehair hummed to herself as she walked the halls in the Shrine of Music. She really wasn't going anywhere in particular; she simply enjoyed walking through the halls here. She hummed to the melody of the place, even stepping in time with it. Something had happened since she'd come here, something that she knew was impossible, but it had happened anyway. Lady Firehair was in love.

She hadn't been sure, at first. She'd thought that it was impossible for her kind to fall in love, and so had never really dared to dream of it. When she realized that she'd been jealous of the little Ice Witch, though, she was sure. She had to be in love, or she wouldn't have been jealous. It was the only thing that made sense, and it filled Lady Firehair with joy.

The only problem now was weather Music felt the same for her, and what they should do if he did. Lady Firehair supposed that they should live happily for the rest of their days, but she had no idea how to do that. For the moment, though, it didn't matter. All that mattered right then was the feeling, the joy of knowing her heart belonged to a wonderful person, someone who inspired her as no one else ever had.

She needed to be careful, though. She was fairly certain that even if Music *did* love her as she loved him, he was not yet aware of it. He seemed uncomfortable whenever their conversations touched on the subject, so she never told him how she felt, and never asked for his own feelings. They'd spent a good many days together now, exploring the wonders of music and helping those who needed help. Lady Firehair had even discovered a wonderful room in the Shrine that Music hadn't shown her. Perhaps she could go there now. She had a good deal of time to explore while he was away seeing to more people who needed his help. She went with him sometimes, but not always. He always allowed her to come if she asked, but she enjoyed exploring the Shrine while he was away, so she didn't always ask.

Music had warned her that she would be unable to leave the Shrine while he was away. Lady Firehair thought it was a little odd, but not a bother, since she wanted to stay anyway. It took her a few minutes to reach the room she was looking for; the Shrine was huge, far larger on the inside than on the outside. Lady Firehair wasn't sure how Music had managed to accomplish such a feat, but she admired it nonetheless.

When she finally reached the room she sought, she stopped at the doorway, smiling as she took in the treasures inside. There were magnificent marble sculptures lining the walls, and beautiful, flowing images carved into the ceiling. Even the floor was shaped into a work of art, with multiple levels, and ornate staircases flowing from one to the next. The stairs themselves were lined with figurines representing fanciful creatures so lifelike that Lady Firehair almost thought they were real even now, in her third visit to the room.

Best of all, though, was what waited between the three fountains, each a cleverly colored sculpture of a being that resembled Music himself, but with black, bat-like wings extended behind them, and a golden suit beneath, instead of the concealing cloak that Music always wore, so like Lady Firehair's own. Well, all but one of the figures resembled Music. That one had the same wings and clothing, but it was of a woman, not a man. It actually looked a bit like Lady Firehair, though that had to be her imagination more than any real resemblance. The water in the fountains sprung from the fingertips of the figures into the pool below them, a single pool shaped into a circle, with a dry stone platform in the center, holding the greatest treasure in the room. The pool was filled with tiny stone figurines of plants, animals, and people of every race in the world, sculpted so perfectly that they looked almost real. Strangely, some of the creatures didn't resemble anything Lady Firehair had ever seen before. Perhaps Music would show her these creatures, if she asked. The scene appeared almost as if the water flowing from the three large figures was life flowing from the three beings into the world. It was truly beautiful. Lady Firehair took a moment to savor the sight, but she couldn't restrain herself for long from what the center of the circle held, the greatest treasure in the entire room, a potter's wheel.

Lady Firehair had seen potters in the city called Green Haven. She'd watched for hours as they made simple pots or ornate vases, the clay responding to their fingertips as a lover to a caress. She'd almost worked up the courage to ask one of them if she could try, but she'd decided against it at the last moment, and hurried away.

Here, though, here with no one to watch, she had tried. It was her first chance to create anything, that first day when she had come here, but somehow it had felt as if she could create anything in the world that she wished.

This wheel was not quite like what the potters in the city had used. They had either had to keep stopping to spin the wheel again, or to have an assistant keep the motion constant. This wheel started moving as soon as she sat down, a fresh lump of clay already waiting for her hands to shape it, and the wheel never stopped until she was finished. Lady Firehair didn't know where the clay had come from—it hadn't been there when she had approached the wheel—but she didn't question it. She'd had so few treasures in her life that she didn't dare question the ones she received.

That first day, she had carved a simple pot, only a little more ornate than what some of the potters in the city had done. She'd been surprised that it turned out so well, but not as surprised as she should have been. While she was working the clay, Lady Firehair felt alive in a way she'd never felt before, as if she were a creator, as if her imagination were the only limitation she faced. Her hands were sure in the work, as if they had shaped clay many times before, and the piece she produced was flawless, if simple. She'd wanted to try again immediately, on that first day, but she feared to make a mistake if she did, to ruin the thrill of her first attempt being beautiful. She'd fled the room, promising herself that she would return, and she had.

The second time she'd visited, she didn't touch the wheel, though she'd wanted to desperately. She'd felt as if she were under a spell, but no magic had been used against her. As much as she wanted to feel the clay beneath her fingertips again, she feared even more that her first attempt had been a fluke, that if she ever tried again, she would fail, shaming this sacred room by producing something mediocre, or even ugly. That fear had driven her from the room that second time, a few days ago, but the lure of the wheel had drawn her back today.

Today she would try the wheel again, try to create something new. She still feared failure, but the need to create burned within her, pulling her inexorably toward the wheel. She was helpless to resist, and she knew it, but it was thrilling at the same time. Today, she would be able to *create* again!

Lady Firehair sat down at the wheel, and again it began to spin, a lump of clay ready for her. Abandoning her doubts, she took to the work with a passion, her fingertips lovingly caressing each curve of the clay, their movements precise and sure. A thrill of excitement went through her as she recognized the feeling, suddenly sure that that first time had not been a fluke after all, that she wouldn't fail, that she would create beauty again.

She didn't know if hours passed, or days, or perhaps only moments. Time was meaningless. All that mattered was the picture in her mind, the clay beneath her fingertips, the shape emerging before her eyes. The wheel stopped whenever she needed it to, and her hands moved as if with a will of their own, knowing exactly where to touch, to smooth, to press. When she was finished, the wheel hadn't moved for some time. Her fingers, and the small tools she'd found beside the wheel, had done their work well. Lady Firehair smiled with delight, even as tears moistened her eyes. She blinked them back, lest they blur her vision and deny her the sight of her finished work.

As a child, the very first time she had escaped her room and gone out into the world, Lady Firehair had seen something that would remain with her for all of her life. She'd been walking through a wide, grassy plain. The grass was nearly as tall as she was, and she loved the way it flowed in the wind, like golden waves in a sea that she could walk through without needing to swim. It was in the center of the field that she saw it, a creature unlike any other she'd ever known.

It was a white stallion romping through the tall grass. Only seven years old, Lady Firehair had watched in awe as the stallion ran, back and forth, slowly drawing ever nearer to where she stood. When it came close enough, she noticed that there was a single horn on its head that shimmered in the morning sunlight. Only then did she realize that the horse wasn't white at all, but silver. It reached her finally, and nuzzled her hand as if in recognition. Lady Firehair hadn't questioned, but only watched, petting the magnificent animal's nose with reverence.

She'd stayed there for hours with the beautiful creature, but then her uncle had summoned her, and the dream ended. She'd been punished severely for sneaking away, but that had only made her careful never to be caught again. She was a shameful creature, but she could not help herself. She'd looked many times for the beautiful silver horse, but she'd never seen him again… until now.

The figurine standing before her didn't need to be fired. Somehow, the magic of the wheel had colored and hardened the clay after she was finished shaping it, and now the silver stallion with the single horn stood before her again, his beauty captured in her work. He was reared up on his hind legs, his mane flying in the wind as he tossed his head. It was only an instant, nothing like the reality of being there in the field with him again, but it was more than Lady Firehair had dared hope to ever see again.

"Why art thou here?"

Lady Firehair froze, a chill running through her entire body. Music had never told her that she could not explore his home, but suddenly she felt as if she'd betrayed him, violated some unspoken trust that she hadn't even been aware of.

"How is it that thou didst find this room?" he asked. There was no anger in his voice as he stood there, between two of the fountain statues, but his eyes demanded an answer.

"I was exploring while you were gone," she told him, her voice trembling slightly. She felt as if something were wrong, even in the air she breathed. "I stumbled upon this room."

He remained silent, studying her. There was no heat in his eyes, no judgment, but she was inexplicably afraid. His silence was deafening, smothering her in a prison without sound, and suddenly she realized what was wrong, why even the air seemed dead. The music of the Shrine had stopped.

She could not bear the silence, so she spoke, hoping against hope that he would let the music play again. "Have I done something wrong?" she asked, knowing how pitiful she must sound. Of course she had done something wrong! She should not have come here. She blinked back the tears that threatened to pour from her eyes, and waited for him to speak.

Instead of answering, he merely looked at her for a moment, letting the terrible silence linger. Soon, though, his eyes shifted to the figurine she had just finished, and suddenly the music began again. It was different now, a haunting melody filled with such longing that Lady Firehair yearned to touch it, to offer any comfort within her power to give. Again she nearly wept, simply because there was nothing to touch.

Before she knew it, strong arms had enfolded her, holding her tenderly. "Nay," Music whispered. "Thou hast done nothing wrong at all."

Chapter XXX

Serana ran through the forest, using Air magic to speed her, but the sounds of pursuit drew nearer and nearer, however fast she ran. How could Daemons move so quickly? She'd been running for nearly three hours, and she was tiring quickly. No, she had been tired an hour ago. Now she was near exhaustion. She stopped, leaning against a tree, desperately trying to catch her breath. In moments, two Scouts leapt from the trees. Serana flung out both arms, throwing the Arrow of Light with both hands at once. Both Daemons died instantly, but there would be more. There were always more.

Serana started out again, forcing her weary legs to move. If she weren't using magic, she'd have collapsed long ago, but it was becoming more and more difficult to make the flows do what she wanted. She needed rest, but there was no rest to be found. If only she had her sword… Suddenly, the forest ended, and Serana stopped, staring. She was looking at Rhanestone Keep. She didn't know how she'd come here. Surely she hadn't run far enough to reach the fortress, yet there it stood. The sound of angry snarls behind drove any further wondering from her mind, and she sped forward, hope giving her new strength.

When she reached the gate, she ran through, but then looked back as it began to close behind her. Daemons poured from the forest. Most of them were Scouts and Soldiers, but Serana saw several Captains, and even two Generals. How would the Keep survive with this new army coming at them from behind? The Daemons seemed to reach the gate in no time, tearing through the iron as if it were clay. Serana's magic exploded into them, but there were too many. Soldiers came to her aid, but many of them were slaughtered in moments. From out of the chaos strode Lord Zironkell himself. He wore a small smile of triumph as he came, looking directly into Serana's eyes. She threw the Arrow of Light at him with all her remaining strength, but he deflected the bolt of magic with one hand, not even slowing down. A foolishly brave soldier stabbed the Daemon Lord in the back with a spear, but the spear disintegrated almost instantly, and the soldier along with it.

"Now is the end," Zironkell told her softly. "Now you are mine." He reached out for her, and fear turned Serana's middle to ice. She tried to summon her magic, but she had no strength left. The terrible, clawed hand drew nearer and nearer...

Serana sat up, eyes wide in the darkness. She was drenched in sweat, though her gown didn't feel wet. Taking slow, deliberate breaths, she reminded herself that she was in the Earth Enchantress village, far from Lord Zironkell or any other Daemon Lord. The nightmare was over, but the terror was still with her, receding very slowly. A hand on Serana's shoulder made her jump.

"It's only me," said Amber's voice. Serana used a spell she'd learned with the Dark Angel of Music a few months ago, a lifetime ago, and the entire room became distinct to her eyes. "You were having a bad dream," Amber went on, her youthful face solemn.

"I'm afraid," said Serana, "that there are more Daemons headed for Rhanestone. Even with the defenses enforced as much as I could enforce them during my last visit, I'm not sure the Keep can withstand it."

"It's no wonder you couldn't sleep," said Amber. "You have a lot to worry about."

"Why are you still awake," Serana asked her.

"I couldn't sleep either," Amber replied with a shrug. "Could I lie there with you? These chairs are pretty big."

Serana smiled, scooting over to make room for the smaller girl. Amber could see in the dark quite well, and climbed into the folded-back chair, snuggling next to Serana. "You and Alloria are the closest thing I have to relatives," she said. "I hope you like each other, when you have more time to talk."

"We don't dislike each other even now, Amber," said Serana, slightly surprised.

"I know," Amber said softly, resting her head on Serana's shoulder. "It's just that I've never really had a family before, and I want the one I've found to be close, even if it *is* a bit disjointed."

Serana squeezed the girl gently with one arm. "At worst, you'll always have a place with me, and I think Alloria would say the same. Also, I'm sure that the vampires at Rhanestone would love to meet you."

"That would be nice." Amber sighed contentedly.

Suddenly, Serana realized that the terror from the dream was completely gone, and she almost laughed. "You didn't come over here because you were lonely, did you?"

Amber shrugged sleepily. "I never said I did," she mumbled.

"Thank you," whispered Serana, but the girl was already asleep. Serana soon was too, and the rest of her night was untroubled by dreams.

The next morning, Serana woke because the fire in the hearth had blazed to life again, and crystal lamps on the walls had begun to glow brightly. Lyra came bustling into the room, followed by several more Earth Enchantresses, all bearing plates of food.

"Good morning!" Lyra said brightly. "I trust you all slept well?" Her eyes fell on Amber, who was still lying against Serana, and she smiled. "I do believe that is the sweetest sight I've seen in years."

Amber lifted her head and grinned at the food. "I do believe *that* is the sweetest sight *I've* seen in hours." She hopped off Serana's chair, and into the one she'd been using before. Lyra laughed.

While they ate, Lyra told them what she and the rest of the village council had discussed during the night. "The world is in peril again," she said, "but this time, we know of it before the fighting is done. This time, we will act. We all agree that your recovery of the Armor is of utmost importance. However, we feel that the Weaver of Earth, along with you, High Priestess, can serve the expedition well enough in terms of Earth magic. Instead of coming with you, we are going to Inferniesm, what you now call Rhanestone, to aid with the defenses there."

"That's wonderful!" said Serana. "I'm sure Duke Rhanestone will be more than grateful for your assistance."

"We also feel that it would be good for us to renew our relationships with the humans, elves, and vampires already there. Too long have we been separate from the rest of the world. It is time for us to interact again."

"Do all of you feel this way?" asked Alier carefully.

Lyra shook her head slightly. "Not all, I'm afraid, but most. There really was no need for argument, though. Those who do not wish to come with us will remain here, and keep the village safe until our return. They will tend the children and maintain the magic that keeps our food supply."

Serana and Amber were both staring at the Earth Enchantress, but the elementals didn't seem the least bit surprised. Since no one else was going to ask, Serana did. "Are your decisions usually made with so little argument?"

Amber nodded. "The nobles I grew up with were always bickering about even the smallest things."

Lyra blinked in surprise as she regarded Serana and Amber. "Like both of you," she said slowly, "we are not human. Why would we argue amongst ourselves?"

Aeron laughed. "You should see the village where I grew up."

"Those were hardly good examples of elementals," said Alier with a dismissive wave of her hand. "Even I couldn't keep them under control, though you made quite a good start of it. If young Illiese does half as well, they will have stopped bickering almost entirely by the time we return."

"In any case," said Serana, "a dozen or two Earth Enchantresses would be invaluable to Rhanestone's defenses."

"A dozen or two?" asked Lyra in surprise.

"Are there fewer?" asked Serana. She'd thought that surely even in a tiny village, there might be perhaps twenty elementals willing to go.

"Perhaps we have given you the wrong impression," Lyra said apologetically. "Only around two thirds of our people will be leaving for Rhanestone. That portion will include one hundred thirty-six Earth Enchantresses, eighteen Air Wizards, and twenty-three Fire Warlocks."

Serana stared in astonishment, unable to speak.

"How did you reach such a precise number so quickly?" asked Aeron, curious.

"Magic, of course," answered Lyra. "I explained the problem, and asked for those who would be going to Rhanestone to send me their vote. The Air Wizards and Fire Warlocks could not send theirs, of course, since the voting process was accomplished entirely with Earth magic, but those who are going are husbands of Earth Enchantresses; their wives put in their votes for them. I used a simple spell to tally the votes, and committed the numbers to memory before retiring last night. How do you do such things in your village?"

Aeron smiled faintly. "We don't, yet, but I think we will start to in time."

"I'm surprised you didn't sense the number of people here, Serana," said Alier. "You should easily be strong enough."

"I didn't delve that deeply," explained Serana. "I thought it would be... well, rude."

"Not among elementals, High Priestess," said Lyra. "Once you were invited into our village, you were welcome to use your magic in any way that would not harm anyone here."

"I understand," said Serana. "Thank you. Rhanestone will be more than grateful for your help, and so will everyone else in the world who understands the situation."

"The fight is ours as much as yours, High Priestess," Lyra said with a small smile. Her expression was soft and kind, but her eyes held a strength that made the stone of the earth look fragile by comparison. "This time, we will do our part."

When breakfast was finished, the party said their goodbyes to Lyra and set out again. Allaerion and Alier scouted ahead. Bandits wouldn't be much of a bother for the elementals or Serana, but if there was a Daemon Lord in the region, he may have begun breeding. Daemons were more than a bother.

Tim and Tom watched the forest warily, their small faces serious even as they ate from the bag of candy Serana's mother had given them. Watching them, Serana felt certain yet again that there was more to these two children than met the eye, but she sensed no magical talent in either of them. Their energies were slightly different from those of Josua or his sister Lilian, but not enough different to really tell her anything. It was more than a little frustrating, but Serana had yet to think of any new way of learning more.

"They're special," said Amber, noticing Serana watching the twins.

That was one avenue Serana should have thought of before, asking Amber. "What do you mean?"

Amber shrugged. "I'm not sure, exactly, but I *am* sure that it's true. They aren't like other humans, even if they're not magicians."

"How do you know that?" asked Serana.

Amber tilted her head quizzically. "Observation, the same way you know."

After an hour or so, the party came upon a circle of stones not unlike the one Serana had seen the night before she first came to Rhanestone. Serana studied it curiously, remembering the odd energies she'd felt from the other circle... and she suddenly understood, or at least, she thought she did.

"What is it, Serana?" asked Seleine.

Serana smiled. "Maybe something useful, if we ever have need of it. I'd rather not explain right now; I can't be entirely sure that I'm right."

The Ice Witch nodded. "Just let me know when you *are* sure."

"You'll be the first, Seleine. I promise."

"May I be second?" asked Amber. "I've never seen rocks like that before. They're almost... alive."

"I doubt I'll have to explain it to you, Amber," said Serana fondly. "Just keep your eyes open, and you'll understand it."

"I always keep my eyes open," Amber told her," but I don't always understand what they tell me."

Less than a quarter of an hour later, the attack came. Daemon Scouts leapt from the trees on both sides, surrounding the party. Serana killed the three closest to her, and Amber destroyed two more. Seleine froze another two in place, and Alier buried two alive and smashed one with a boulder. Serana sensed more coming, though, many more. How she hadn't sensed these was a mystery.

"They weren't there when we scouted ahead," said Allaerion, echoing her thoughts.

"Back to the circle of stones," Serana ordered, but there were ten more Scouts and four Soldiers behind them already.

Suddenly there was a huge thunderclap, and the Daemons exploded off the road. "They're only stunned," said Aeron. "Hurry!"

The party raced back the way they'd come, killing pursuing Daemons as they ran. Serana hoped that she was right about those stones; if there were as many Daemons in these woods as she suspected, their lives may all depend on whether or not she was.

***

The Serian of Music wondered aimlessly through the Shrine. Lady Firehair was sleeping. Her sleep schedule was very odd, compared with any other creature Music knew of. She sometimes went several days without sleep, and then slept an entire day, but other times she took an hour's sleep intermittently over a few days. Music had become so accustomed to having her company that he often did not know how to occupy himself while she slept. It was somewhat disconcerting.

Now, as he had done several times before, Music wondered through his home, letting memories drift through his mind. He had considered and rejected several tasks that might require his attention; his most important task now was to keep Lady Firehair away from Serana.

At the thought of the Sorceress, Music felt the oddest sensation. It took him several moments to recognize it, but when he did, surprise and worry filled him. Faster than thought, he transported himself...

***

The Daemons were closing in. Serana had tried the stones only moments ago, and she couldn't afford another attempt. She threw the Arrow of Light with both hands, splitting both bolts at once. Her aim wasn't important, considering the number of Daemons. She was likely to hit one of them wherever she aimed. Aeron's chain lightning lanced through the Scouts, and even some of the Soldiers, but the Captains were almost unaffected by it. Alier's vines and boulders took more of the beasts, and some were even swallowed by the earth itself, but there were always two to replace every one that fell. Seleine froze several Scouts in place, and her shards of jagged ice ripped into more. Allaerion was holding back, waiting until the Daemons drew closer, where he could make use of his sword. Amber, by Serana's side, threw the Arrow of Light grimly. The magic wielders were in a circle around Alexander, Alloria, and the four children. Alexander had his sword ready, and Alloria held a staff, but neither of them would last long against Daemons if the magic users failed. So far, Serana, Amber, and the elementals had held the Daemons back, but they couldn't keep them away much longer.

Suddenly, golden light exploded around them, racing out in a wave that destroyed any Daemon it touched. Serana looked back and up, into the air above the circle of stones, and breathed a sigh of relief. Floating in the air, black wings outstretched, was the Serian of Music. As the Daemons fled, screaming rage and fear, he slowly descended, landing beside Serana. "Thou didst call, High Priestess?" he said mildly.

Chapter XXXI

"While I am impressed that thou didst learn the use of the stones without aid," said the Serian of Music, "I am still curious as to why thou didst not simply employ thy sword." It was not like Serana to risk the unknown when the known was easily available, and suited to her purpose.

Serana blushed. "I honestly forgot that I could," she admitted reluctantly. "I had only just understood the use of the stones, and I never thought to use my sword."

Music nodded. He didn't tell her to try and remember in the future; she would probably never forget again as it was. Besides, he did not want to spend too much time here. Lady Firehair could wake at any moment, and he had to be certain she did not attempt to leave. "I must go, then," he said. "Take care in this region; the presence of Daemons here is a most unpleasant surprise." With that, he transported himself back to the Shrine of Music.

Lady Firehair was still asleep when he arrived, and Music realized with a start that her dress was laid carefully over the back of a chair beside her bed. She had always worn it before when she slept.

"Good morning," she said sleepily, smiling as she stretched.

Realizing that she was entirely naked beneath the blankets, he averted his eyes. "Good morn, m'lady." It actually was morning this time. She always said "Good morning" when she woke, even when it was evening.

"I missed thee," she said, gazing up at him. She always seemed to mimic his speech whenever she was pleased. It was slightly disconcerting, but there was, of course, an inherent advantage: he could nearly always gauge her mood by her speech patterns.

"Thou wert sleeping, m'lady," he pointed out.

"And I missed thee in my sleep," she said with a shrug. "Sit with me, please." She patted the place beside where she lay on the bed, and he seated himself. "I want to tell thee of my dream, if thou art willing to listen."

He smiled. "I will always listen to thee, m'lady."

She smiled again, and somehow, the entire room seemed to brighten. "I dreamt that I was one of those statues in my favorite room, the one with the potter's wheel. Instead of being stone, though, I was real! I had black wings, and I spent my time shaping real creatures as I shaped the clay before." She sighed dreamily. "It was wondrous... What is the matter?"

Music schooled his face to smoothness. "Nothing is the matter, m'lady. Thy dream simply reminded me of things from the past."

"That was a lie," she accused, frowning. "Something *is* the matter."

"Nothing that I wish to discuss," he amended.

She looked up at him for a long moment before she spoke again, searching his eyes. It felt as if she were searching his soul. "Thou hast offered me more comfort than any creature I have ever encountered," she said softly. "Why wilt thou not accept even the smallest comfort from me in return?"

"For some things," he told her, "there *is* no comfort."

Her eyes were suddenly filled with sorrow as she looked at him, but her expression never changed. "That was not a lie," she whispered, "but I do not believe it was the truth either."

"How could it not be?" he asked. "I did not dissemble. It was a direct statement."

"I know," she said, "but that only means that thou dost believe it. That is what makes me sad." She pulled him down to her in a warm embrace, and he did not resist, though he did not hold her in return. She was too great a temptation, wearing that face and no clothing beneath her blankets. She let him up only enough that she could gaze into his eyes. "Some in this world believe that suffering is what mortals deserve. Does their belief stop thee from healing and helping?"

"Of course not," he answered immediately, hoping she would release him soon. Her face was inches from his.

She nodded, her eyes holding him fast. "Just as those people's belief in hopelessness does not prevent thee from offering comfort, so also does thine own belief not prevent me from offering comfort to thee, even if thou wilt not accept it." Before he knew what was happening, her lips had crossed the short distance to his. Her kiss was soft and uncertain, as if she had never kissed anyone before in all her life, yet he felt through her touch an insistence that frightened him. More frightening still, though, was that he enjoyed it.

So great was his shock that at first he did not resist, and by the time that he would have, she had released him. "M'lady," he began, uncertain how to say what was needed. She must not do that again, ever, but for some reason, he could not find the words to ask her not to.

"I am getting dressed now," she announced. "Though I do not understand why, that seems to bring thee some discomfort, so I am warning thee before I begin." She was getting out of bed as soon as she finished speaking, and Music fled the room, waiting outside. Perhaps keeping her here would not be so simple a matter as he had hoped.

***

"That was rather sudden," said Seleine. "He didn't even ask what we're doing this far south." Serana was inclined to agree.

"I am certain that he has more important matters to attend to," Alier told them both.

"At this point," said Serana, "it's irrelevant. We need a way to stop those Daemons if they return. We can't call for the Serian of Music every time, or they'll find a way to trap him again."

"I'd have thought the solution was obvious," said Aeron. "In fact, I'm a bit surprised that you did not employ it before, instead of calling the Serian."

Serana stared at him blankly.

"Dragon's Tears," he said with a shrug. "Both you and Alier can grow them, and they kill Daemons even more easily than your sword does. We should be carrying some with us, particularly the children, and we should replace them with new whenever they begin to wilt. With the two of you growing them, we could keep an entire army of Daemons at bay."

"That will work for a time," agreed Alier, "but not forever. Daemons can kill Dragon's Tears just like they can kill anything else; it just takes them longer, since they can't breathe the scent."

"Regardless," said Serana. "It's something we can use." She poured energy into the ground around the circle of stones, and Dragon's Tears sprang to life. "Pick some, all of you, and then we'll keep going."

Josua grabbed a fistful of the flowers, holding them as he held the practice sword each evening. Serana smiled. The bouquet was a weapon, and Josua knew it.

Lilian picked a handful too, and started weaving them into a circlet for her head, while Tim and Tom stuffed stems into their pockets, letting the blossoms stick out. Alloria was mimicking Lilian, making a circlet. The others, Alexander, Amber, and the elementals, simply gathered bouquets together to carry. Well, almost all the others did. Alier used Earth magic to make hers *grow* into a circlet, then made necklaces for some of the others. Serana liked the idea, and grew a circlet and a necklace of her own.

Amber, who had been watching Serana and Alier both very carefully, grew some Dragon's Tears of her own, and made herself a necklace. Serana was more than a little impressed, since Amber couldn't possibly have seen the flows of Earth magic. She'd grown the flowers using Life, something Serana hadn't considered before. Now that she looked, though, she realized that it was the same method she'd been using the very first time, with the Dark Angel, when she'd tried to make food from the rocks. Amber smiled up at Serana when she was finished, and Serana couldn't help smiling back. "That trick took me a good deal longer to learn," she told Amber.

"Why?"

"For one thing," said Serana, "I had no one to watch. The first time, I grew the flowers by accident, and didn't even realize that I'd done it. I didn't do it on purpose for quite some time later; I didn't have a reason to."

"Well," said Amber, "at least now there are three of us who can do it. Three is better than two." Serana got the distinct impression that Amber was not merely talking about the number of people they had who could grow Dragon's Tears, but she let it go as the party headed out again.

The Daemons didn't appear again for two days, and even when they did attack, Serana and her friends drove them back without difficulty, thanks to the Dragon's Tears. Serana thought it might be possible to kill this errant Daemon Lord without nearly the risk she'd originally considered, if only they could find him and use the flowers against him.

There were no more attacks for another week, and when another did come, the party drove it back with the same ease as before. Serana's dreams were becoming worse, but strangely, Amber's presence always soothed away the lingering fear that stubbornly refused to go away after she awoke each time. The dreams weren't identical, but they all involved running from Daemons, and they all ended with Lord Zironkell reaching for her. For the past few nights, Amber had begun to sleep with Serana and Seleine—for which Serana was more than grateful. The dreams almost never came when Amber's small body rested against Serana's, and on the few occasions when they did, the fear never lasted past waking. The party was now nearly to Alexander's brother's estate, just another day's travel away.

Serana set up a wide ring of Dragon's Tears around the camp that night, with Amber's help. Serana could have done it alone, but Amber liked to help; she said it was easier to learn that way. Serana set up threads of energy to warn her if anything approached, Daemon or not, and the party bedded down.

This time, when Serana awoke, it wasn't from a dream. There was no fear, and no memory of running. Amber lay asleep within arm's reach, and Seleine lay on Serana's other side. If it hadn't been a dream, though, why was Serana awake?

A touch on her hand made Serana jump and almost cry out, but she realized in moments that it was Amber, who apparently wasn't asleep after all. The girl motioned for Serana to be silent, and pointed outside the tent. Serana tilted her head questioningly, and Amber wove Air magic into a simple conduit between them.

"There is a vampire out there," Amber whispered, the magic carrying her words to Serana's ears alone. "It is not Alloria."

Serana nodded and rose on silent feet, using Air to dampen the sounds of her movement. Even a vampire's hearing wouldn't detect her leaving her tent. She kept her magic at the ready, in case she had to move or strike quickly, and she reached out with her senses to find the intruder. He was just outside Alier's tent, though Serana could barely see him even with her vision enhanced by magic. He was preparing to slip inside.

Serana struck with Air magic, lifting the vampire off his feet and holding him immobile. "Who are you, and what are you doing here?" she demanded.

The vampire hissed at her, but did not speak. Serana searched for any others, but she sensed none.

"What is going on here?" asked Alloria, coming to stand beside Serana. When she looked on the trapped vampire, she hissed and took an involuntary step backward.

"What is it?" asked Serana.

"Can't you sense it?" Alloria asked incredulously. She was trembling from head to toe.

"I can," said Amber. She shuddered once, but otherwise gave no outward sign of what it was she sensed.

Serana looked at the trapped vampire again, examining his energy, but she saw nothing unusual. "I can't," she told the two. "You'll have to explain it to me." Perhaps it had something to do with the odd mental connections vampires used for hypnosis. Serana thought she could duplicate the effects with Air, Fire, and Life magic, but after a little studying, she'd found that what Alloria and Amber did was actually simpler. It seemed to be an ability inherent only to vampires.

Alloria was hugging herself. "It's his mind," she said, visibly taking hold of herself. She was still trembling.

"He's insane," explained Amber, stepping up beside Serana. "I've never seen anything like that in a vampire. Of course, I've never seen any full vampire other than Alloria."

"He's worse than insane," Alloria whispered, shivering as she averted her eyes. "His mind has been turned inside out. He retains all the intellect he had before, and even a few of the personality traits, but his reasoning is like a house looks after one of those terrible whirlwind storms." She shuddered again. "Someone did this to him."

"Can he be helped?" asked Serana.

Amber shook her head, drawing Serana down to whisper into her ear. "Take him away from the camp, where Alloria won't have to see, and kill him. You will be doing him a favor; believe me."

Serana stared. "You don't even want to try to help him? You'd rather I simply killed him, even though it isn't his fault?"

Amber's small face was grim. "You don't understand. He's dead already. I'll do it, if you won't." Without another word, she gently took control of the flows of Air Serana had been using. Serana let her; she wanted no part of this. Killing Daemons or evil men was one thing, but killing someone who was only sick was something else entirely. Serana healed the sick; she didn't kill them. Amber carried the hissing vampire away with Air magic. After a minute or two, she returned to camp. "It is done."

Alloria wept. It was the first time Serana had ever seen the vampire woman so emotional. Serana would have gone to comfort her, but Alexander had come out of his tent and rushed to her already. He held her close as he drew her back into their tent.

"You killed him?" Serana asked Amber. There wasn't any real reason to ask, but Serana needed to talk, and she couldn't think of anything else to say.

Amber nodded. "I put him out of his misery. Life was torture for that poor creature, Serana. I'm not sure what it was that did this to him, but it was done a long time ago. He'd been fighting it, and losing, for a very long time."

"Something simply destroyed his mind?"

"No." Amber shook her head and shuddered once, but regained control over herself in moments. "The insanity was like a poison. It took over his mind slowly. He didn't simply go insane, Serana. He had to *watch* himself go insane. He probably did terrible things, and then regained his faculties long enough to know what he'd done, but not why.

Now it was Serana's turn to shudder. "How do you sense all of these things?" It might be easier to talk about the magic behind the problem. That, at least, wouldn't make her feel ill.

"Vampires are partly telepathic," Amber explained with a shrug. "Most of our abilities can be traced to an inherent use of elemental magic, but not this one."

"But you're only half vampire."

"Like Alier said, vampire traits overwrite the traits of other races, and Sorceress traits are always dominant. I have all the ability that any vampire has, and all that I would have had as a Sorceress. I thought you already understood that."

"Why are you so willing to accept that you are half of each of two races, one of which cannot have mixed children, and the other of which cannot have *any* children?" Serana was glad to be turning the subject away from the poor vampire. Losing her mind was the worst fate she could imagine, even worse than Zironkell's attentions.

"The same reason you do." Amber shrugged. "It is the only explanation that fits all the evidence we have. I may be older than you are, Serana, but I am still young and inexperienced enough not to have many preconceived notions about what is and is not possible."

"Let us hope we can retain that much, at least. I don't know about you, but the more I learn, the less I believe any of the rules are fixed."

"Agreed," said Amber. "We should get back to bed now. There is still time to rest before morning."

Serana nodded, and let herself be led back into her tent, where Seleine was still sleeping peacefully.

Serana woke early the next morning, as she often did, and made breakfast for everyone. Amber, emerging only minutes later, wanted to help. Serana was making little pastries today, and Amber was eager to learn. Amber knew less about cooking than anyone Serana had ever met before. She'd been raised in the Ravenstar family during her first few years—Serana didn't know exactly how many—and none of the nobles did their own cooking. Afterward, wandering on her own, she'd never had anyone to teach her.

Serana showed the other girl how to make the pastry dough, shape it into squares, and wrap it around slices of fruit before frying it. "I'll regulate the fire, since it's easiest to do with magic."

"Can I next time?" Amber asked. "I don't know how hot the fire should be, but I think I could control it."

"How? You don't have any ability in Fire magic."

Amber shrugged. "Fire needs air to burn. If I regulate the airflow to the flame, I can control it."

"That should work," Serana admitted. She'd never considered the possibility, since it was so easy to use Fire magic, but it might be a good idea to learn Amber's way too. Serana tried using Air, more to feed the flame and less to smother it. The fire responded, of course. It didn't respond quite as well as it would have to Fire magic, but Serana thought it would, if she practiced a bit more. For now, though, she went back to using Fire. There would be time to practice with Air later.

By the time the pastries were done, Allaerion and Aeron were awake, and very hungry. "When this is all over," said Allaerion, munching on his first pastry, "we're all going to be fighting over who gets to take you home, Serana. No one is going to want to give up your cooking."

Serana blushed. "Amber did a good deal of this."

"We'll keep you both, then," said Aeron.

"Save some for me!" cried Seleine, crawling out from the tent she shared with Serana and Amber.

"We're still making them," Amber told her. "If we stopped now, there wouldn't be any left for the children!"

"And more importantly," said Alier as she emerged, "there wouldn't be any left for me."

The twins came running out of their tent almost as soon as Alier had finished talking. They took seats around the fire and watched Serana and Amber, grinning broadly. Josua and his sister were only a little slower. Alexander and Alloria didn't appear from their tent until the children were already eating, but they were in plenty of time to claim some pastries for themselves.

When breakfast was done and camp broken, the party set out again. The day passed uneventfully, without any sign of Daemons, brigands, or mad vampires, and by early evening, they had reached Lord Duncan's estate.

The gate was a giant ordeal made of tempered steel, as Serana read the Earth energy within it. Two stone towers held it up, with a guard at the top of each one. There was a high stone wall connected to the towers that ran around the entire estate grounds. The place was not nearly as defensible as Rhanestone Keep, but Serana doubted that even the boldest brigands would dare a raid.

"State your name and business," said one of the two guards from behind the gate. He was an older man, from his grey, receding hairline, and he stood only an inch or two taller than Serana, but his build reminded her of a stone storage shed. He didn't seem particularly surprised that a party of strangers would appear near sundown, either.

"We're here to see my brother," said Alexander. "These people are with me, Clark."

"Lord Alexander," the guard grinned, "it's wonderful to see you again." He cupped his hand over his mouth to call up to a man on one of the two towers on either side of the gate. "Open the gate! The master's brother is here!"

The huge iron gates made hardly a sound as they swung inward. Serana imagined they must be oiled daily, but she couldn't see why anyone would bother.

"My brother likes everything in pristine order," Alexander told her quietly, noticing her studying the gates. "He goes to great lengths to keep almost everything he owns immaculate."

"He'd love my dress," Serana laughed.

Alexander gave her a small smile. "You're just lucky he's more than twice your age."

"I'm glad to see you well, sir," said Clark to Alexander. "Did you accomplish your goals in the north?"

"Things took a few unexpected turns, Clark," Alexander told him. "I think they worked out for the better, though. May I present my wife, Alloria."

Serana thought it a bit odd that a Lord would be so friendly with a guard, but perhaps Lord Duncan did things differently from what Alexander had described as common in the South.

"And this is Serana," said Alexander. "She is the High Priestess of her people."

Serana nodded to the guard, and he bowed respectfully.

"Clark was the one who taught me both wrestling and the sword, when I was a boy," said Alexander. "He's a good friend."

"It's an honor to serve this family," said Clark, "but Lord Alexander here was one of the best students I ever trained, when he wanted to be. He didn't really apply himself to the sword, though." The older man gave Alexander a fond look.

"You should spar me while we're here, Clark," said Alexander. "I've learned one or two things while I was away."

"Just as long as I don't have to match with that one," Clark said, nodding to Allaerion. "He carries that sword as if it were part of him."

Alexander grinned. "It is part of him, but Alier here is more dangerous."

Clark eyed the Earth Enchantress doubtfully, and she grinned.

"You wouldn't want to match with our High Priestess here either," said Alexander seriously. "She could lay me out for dead without breaking a sweat."

"Not in a dress like that," Clark declared.

Serana laughed. "We can test that later, if you want. I do enjoy a good sparring match."

"Be gentle," Allaerion told her, and Clark arched a brow, eyeing them both as if trying to decide whether or not they were joking.

"Where is my brother, Clark?" asked Alexander.

"The master is having a feast prepared for you," said the guard, heading toward the mansion and motioning them to follow. "Our scouts have been watching your approach for the past four hours."

Serana stared. "There haven't been any men anywhere near us."

"You may not have seen them," said Clark with a smile.

"She is correct," said Alier flatly. "There were no men anywhere near us."

Clark grinned. "You're right, of course. We have a new far-seeing device, something to do with lenses. I don't know how it works, but I've used the thing once or twice, and I think it's quite amazing. That's how we knew you were coming. The trees don't conceal the road for miles."

"Why did you bother asking who we were, then?" asked Aeron.

The guard looked at Aeron as if he were daft. "And ruin the surprise?"

Serana and the others followed Clark to the door of the mansion, where he passed them on to a waiting page in red and white livery. The page took them into the mansion and up a beautiful central staircase that appeared to be made of solid marble, then through a carved oaken door into a hallway.

"You all have rooms prepared," said the page. "You will want to refresh yourselves before dinner. Lord Alexander, the royal suite is to be yours, of course."

"My wife and I will be staying together," Alexander told him. The page's eyes went immediately to Serana, and blinked when Alloria stepped over to stand by Alexander, but the man recovered himself quickly and bowed his acknowledgement. Alexander and Alloria disappeared into the room the page had indicated.

"M'lady," said the page, bowing to Serana, "we have the green suite prepared for you, since the decorations match your gown. If you prefer another room, please let me know, and I will have it arranged for you. There is a bath drawn already, should you wish for it, and there are servants to bathe you, if you pull the rope beside the bath."

"Thank you," said Serana, giving the page a nod before going in through the door he held for her. She would rather be covered in mud than let servants bathe her, but she supposed that nobles did such things.

The green suite was well named. The carpet, the bed curtains, the sheets, and even the walls were all various shades of green. Everything was tastefully decorated, but Serana would never have imagined putting so much green in a single room. Perhaps one of Lord Duncan's regular visitors had odd tastes.

Serana locked the door, then shed her gown and stepped into the steaming water with a delighted sigh. She healed sore muscles each night, but even her healing couldn't replace the luxurious feel of hot water against her skin. She wasn't entirely sure how long she let herself soak, or how long it took her to bathe once she made use of the sponge, soap, and perfumes sitting beside the bath, but almost immediately after she finished putting on her dress again, there was a knock on her door.

"M'lady," said the page's voice, "the feast is prepared, when you are ready."

Serana opened the door. "I'm ready now."

"Very good, m'lady. Follow me."

Serana looked at the halls more closely this time, and was not surprised to find them far more decorative than those of New Rhanestone, but far less luxurious than those of Old Rhanestone. Try as they might, humans could not match the work of elementals, lacking the distinct advantage of magic. Still, Alexander's brother was obviously wealthy, and accustomed to living in comfort.

The page led Serana down several corridors, taking several twists and turns that Serana couldn't have remembered unless she'd marked them with magic. Perhaps next time she would. Finally, he opened a large set of double doors that led into the dining hall, where a long table of polished wood was laden with a feast unlike any Serana had ever seen. There were roasted meats of every variety, bowls filled with fresh fruits polished to shine like mirrors, trays of both fresh and cooked vegetables, and even platters filled with candied treats.

Serana's friends were already seated around the table, but apparently no one had started eating yet. "We waited for you," said Amber with a grin. "It wasn't easy."

"Welcome, High Priestess," said the one unfamiliar man, who was seated at the end of the table. He was tall and slender, much like Alexander, but his hair was darker, with grey at the temples, and his eyes were a brilliant blue. "I am Lord Duncan. I have been looking forward to meeting you. Please, sit, enjoy our repast, and tell me more of the land you come from. My brother has been more than a little vague about you."

Serana smiled. "Thank you, Lord Duncan," she said as she took a seat between Alier and Seleine, across from Alexander and Alloria. She noticed that there was no plate in front of her.

"What would you like to start with?" asked a young serving girl after Serana had seated herself. The girl held the plate ready.

Serana was unaccustomed to someone else filling her plate, but she reminded herself that customs in the South would be different from what she was used to. "I'll have some of that delicious-looking fruit," she told the girl, "a slice of the center roast, three of those lovely small carrots, and one of those... I'm afraid I'm not certain what they're called." Serana indicated the tray of what appeared to be candy.

"Those are sweetmeats," said Lord Duncan, "my cook's own recipe. Have two or three, or you'll be sending poor Lucy there back for more of them."

Serana grinned. "Three then," she told the serving girl, Lucy.

Lucy smiled, and began filling Serana's plate. When she was finished, she set the plate in front of Serana, and everyone began eating as if it had been a signal. Obviously the others had been instructed on what to do, probably by Alexander. Serana tried a bite of the roast, and smiled at the taste of spiced beef, cooked to perfection. The meat literally fell apart in her mouth, and the flavor was exquisite. Serana's mother would have enjoyed working with this cook Lord Duncan spoke of.

"Now then," said Lord Duncan, "tell me where you are from, High Priestess."

"I grew up in a small village," said Serana truthfully. She really wasn't sure how much to tell Lord Duncan, and Alexander hadn't given her much of a clue from across the table. He seemed far more intent on his food.

"Indeed?" Lord Duncan asked. "His eyes appeared mildly surprised, but more curious than anything else."

"I didn't learn of my heritage until a man claiming to be the Lord of Eridan came and took me away," she continued, and then paused to try a slice of fruit.

"I'm afraid I am not familiar with the land of Eridan," said Lord Duncan after he'd swallowed the roast he was eating. "It must be in the north somewhere." Serana suddenly had the distinct impression that anything in the north really didn't exist to Alexander's brother. The north was simply a vague place that was separate from the real world he knew.

"I do not know," Serana told him. "I've never seen any land of Eridan."

"Then how do you know that this man was not simply lying to you in order to use you for his purposes?" asked Lord Duncan. His eyes now held concern and sadness, as if he had already decided that she'd been used.

"Because," said Serana with a small shrug, "I never gave him anything. There would have been no purpose to his using me."

"He never asked anything of you at all?"

"Only that I come to Rhanestone and learn of my heritage," said Serana. "He never asked anything at all for himself."

"I see." Lord Duncan now appeared more than a little intrigued. "Please, tell me of this heritage you speak of."

Now was the moment when Serana had to decide what to say and what not to. Alexander was no help; he hadn't even looked Serana's way since the meal had begun. Serana weighed possibilities in her mind, but in her heart, she already knew what she was going to do, and why she was going to do it. When her people in Alon Peak had rejected her for healing a child, she'd been frightened, but the more she'd thought on the incident, the more it had made her angry. Alexander's lack of support only increased the feeling, and made her feel still firmer in her decision. She looked directly into Lord Duncan's blue eyes. "I am a Sorceress."

Lord Duncan's expression didn't change. He simply studied her for a long moment. "Go on," he said finally.

"My village was destroyed more than sixteen years ago, and I, as a baby, was given to a human couple in the village of Alon Peak to raise. The mysterious Lord of Eridan was the Serian of Music, known to many as the Dark Angel of Music, one of the nine creators of the world. At Rhanestone Keep, and later on the quest we've undertaken, I have learned to use my magic to fight the Daemons who threaten to destroy the world. These Daemons have been in the north for centuries, but now they are right here in the south, and if they are not stopped, they will kill us all."

Serana expected anger, or perhaps disgust. She expected perhaps an apology to Alexander for having to execute on of his companions, or at the very least a declaration that she was insane. What she saw in the suddenly icy blue eyes now, though, was the last thing in the world that she'd expected... grim confirmation. "Thank you for telling me the truth," said Lord Duncan. "My brother was not vague with me at all. He told me the truth of matters while you all were refreshing yourselves. I had to know whether or not you would be brave enough to tell me the truth yourselves, even feeling certain that I would not believe you." He smiled faintly. "My brother tells me that you, High Priestess, are the best hope for humans, elementals, and every other race in the world to be free from the Daemons that invade. If there is any chance that he might be right, then I had to know your mettle."

"And how is it that you do believe me?" asked Serana.

Lord Duncan lowered his eyes for a moment, and a shudder went through him, though he suppressed it quickly. "I have seen them," he whispered.

Chapter XXXII

"I'm sorry I couldn't give you any help," said Alexander while his brother recovered. "Duncan wanted to be sure that you could face him. He doesn't believe that anyone who could not face him could face Daemons."

"Were all of you in on this?" asked Serana. They had to have been.

"We knew you'd do it," said Amber, beaming. She turned her small face to Lord Duncan. "Her sword's name is Daemonbane, and she's more dangerous than her sword."

"Hard to believe, looking at her," said Lord Duncan. "Forgive me, High Priestess, but I know nothing of magic. Only weeks ago, I still believed it was inherently evil. Since my poor Arielene's disappearance, I've seen things that no man should ever have to see. I've found a new respect and admiration for the brave men and women of Rhanestone Keep, and I'll be giving them my full support from now on. If they deal with this sort of thing on a regular basis, they should have all of our support. I'm afraid I can do nothing until after this crisis is over, but after that I will lend any aid within my power."

"Since you've had so many realizations, my brother," said Alexander, "there is one last thing you ought to know."

Lord Duncan looked at his brother apprehensively. "There is more?"

"My wife," said Alexander, "is a vampire."

Lord Duncan didn't speak. He only stared.

"Specifically, she is *yamin'sai* to me. She offered herself in exchange for my support in helping to bring peace between our peoples. Since that time, I have well and truly fallen in love with her. I hope that in time, you also can come to love and respect her, my brother, and to realize the folly of our past thinking."

Alexander's brother nodded slowly. "After seeing what I've seen these past few weeks, I am ready to believe almost anything." He seemed to take hold of himself visibly. "I would, however, like to put an end to these Daemons on my land as quickly as possible. High Priestess, I've tested your bravery, but not your skill. If you are half as powerful as Alexander here leads me to believe, then you won't object to a small demonstration."

Serana nodded. This should be interesting.

"Tomorrow morning, then," said Lord Duncan. "If you pass the test, I will give you my full support against the Daemons. If not, then I will expect you to serve under me if you wish to fight. I'll not have anyone getting himself—or herself—killed needlessly, if I can avoid it."

"Are we taking bets on whether or not she passes?" asked Alier, a mischievous smile playing at the corners of her mouth. "I'll wager a hundred gold crowns to a surprise that she does."

Lord Duncan regarded the Earth Enchantress in silence for a moment before answering. "What is the surprise?"

Alier grinned. "I'll tell you whether I win or lose, and believe me; you'll like it. If I win, though, I get the hundred gold crowns." Why Alier wanted a hundred gold crowns was a mystery to Serana. The Earth Enchantress could *make* gold crowns more quickly than any human lord could get them for her.

"Agreed," said Lord Duncan with a small smile, "on the condition that if I win and don't like the surprise, I reserve the right to choose another prize."

"Perfect," agreed Alier.

Alexander was no longer listening. He was staring at something on the wall. Serana followed his gaze, and her eyes widened in shock as the pieces fell into place in her mind. "Lord Duncan," she asked, "who is that portrait of?"

Alexander's brother looked up at the wall where she was staring, and his eyes almost immediately moistened with tears. "That is my missing daughter, Arielene. She was taken four months ago now, so there is little hope that I will ever see her again. Still, I cannot bring myself to let her go in my heart."

"Lord Duncan," Serana said carefully, "I think it is very likely that you will see your daughter again. In fact, I know where she is now."

"She lives?" he demanded, standing. "Where is she?"

"She's at Rhanestone Keep," said Alexander. "I've spoken with her, though I didn't recognize her, since I'd never seen her before."

"Rhanestone Keep?" breathed Lord Duncan. "Why would she go there? Why would she not come home?"

"She was brought there by the Serian of Music," explained Serana. "She has lost her memory, and does not remember where home is."

"There is more," said Alexander. "Brother, this will not be easy for you to hear, but you must remember everything I've told you, and trust that it is true."

Lord Duncan sat back down. He had the look of a man waiting to hear his own death sentence.

Alexander took a deep breath before going on. "Arielene does not know who she is, much less where she came from. She has been using the name Reilena while she studies with the elven priests to try and recover her memory."

"What are you not telling me?" asked Lord Duncan.

Alexander appeared to be searching for words, and Lord Duncan was growing tenser by the moment. Serana finally broke the silence. "Reilena is a vampire."

Lord Duncan's eyes stared at nothing. Suddenly, he looked twenty years older than he had. "My daughter," he whispered, "has joined the undead?"

"There is no need to descend into the ridiculous," scoffed Alloria loudly. "We vampires may not age, but we're hardly undead. Honestly, where do you humans come up with such outlandish notions?"

"If you are not undead," said Lord Duncan slowly, "then why will you turn to dust in the Creator's sunlight?"

"Alloria is quite fond of sunlight," Alexander told him. "She lets it wash over her face each morning."

"And just because there is only one Creator left in the world," put in Alier, "does not mean that the sunlight belongs to him. He would probably be shocked at the very idea."

"He most certainly would," agreed Serana. "He was the Lord of Eridan who took me from my village, so I spent a good deal of time with him."

Lord Duncan was trembling, but when he spoke, his voice was steady. "This has been a great deal to take in. I believe that you all are telling me the truth, but please forgive me when I say that I cannot accept it all so readily. Let us retire for tonight, and tomorrow we will speak further."

"One thing," said Serana as everyone was standing. "You said that you've seen the Daemons. Where and when did you see them? What did they look like?"

Lord Duncan nodded wearily. "I first saw them a few weeks ago, through the new far-seeing device, the contraption with the lenses. They attacked some of my workers who had been outside the walls gathering fruit from the orchards. They were huge, like giant dogs with glowing red eyes. "I ordered longbow men to the walls to slay the beasts, but our arrows had little effect even when they hit their mark. Since then, few have dared venture outside the walls. We've tried to find a way to kill the creatures, but without success. Some of our bravest soldiers have died trying to fight them. In the end, I had to pass an order that no one was to attempt to do battle with the... things, unless it was from the safety of the walls. We've yet to kill a single one of those beasts. I don't know how they manage to survive them at Rhanestone."

"I think we can help you in that regard," said Serana. "Amber, could I have your necklace please? I'll make you a new one later." Amber was the only one still wearing the Dragon's Tears.

"I'll make it myself," Amber grinned. She took off her flower necklace and gave it to Serana.

"It's a lovely fragrance," said Lord Duncan, "but I don't see what it has to do with the Daemons."

"This fragrance," explained Serana, "is poison to Daemons. It will kill those giant dogs, Daemon Scouts, almost instantly, and it even works against the larger, tougher ones."

"There are worse than those?" exclaimed Lord Duncan.

Serana nodded. "Much worse. These flowers, Dragon's Tears, will kill them, though. If you want your arrows to work, then dip the tips in nectar from these blossoms. It will kill even the stronger Daemons."

Lord Duncan nodded slowly. "So that's how Rhanestone does it."

"In part," said Alexander. "Rhanestone also has a very skilled Battlemage, and our esteemed High Priestess here has done her own share of killing these creatures, even without the Dragon's Tears."

Lord Duncan looked at Serana with new respect. "You have killed one of those beasts single-handedly *without* these miraculous flowers?"

Serana smiled faintly. "I have killed many."

"You are like the Battlemage, then?"

"No, brother," said Alexander. "The Battlemage is very strong, but Serana is to him what a trained soldier is to a child."

Lord Duncan did not at all appear convinced. "Tomorrow," he said, "we will discuss this further. For now, I have much to think on. Sleep well, all of you, and feel free to call upon my servants to fulfill any needs you might have." He gave the entire group a small bow before turning quickly and departing the room.

Serana slept fitfully at first that night, plagued by more dreams of Lord Zironkell. Why the dreams hadn't begun immediately after her incident with him, she didn't know, but she wished they hadn't begun at all. It was almost a relief when her door began to open, giving her something else to focus on.

Serana slipped out of the bed and crouched beside it, her magic ready. She used Air to enhance her vision, and each detail of the door was clear to her as it swung open just enough to let a smallish figure through.

"Amber," breathed Serana, relaxing, "what are you doing in here?"

Amber shut the door silently behind her, glided to the bed, and slipped under the blankets. "You're having trouble sleeping again," she said as she looked up at Serana. "I came to help."

"How did you know?" asked Serana. "Vampires may be somewhat telepathic between each other, but I am not a vampire."

Amber shrugged. "You are a Sorceress, the other half of what I am."

Serana was far from convinced, but she was starting to get cold, so she slipped back under the blankets beside Amber before talking any further. "Amber, you know more than you're telling me."

"Yes, but you know more than you've told me too."

"What are you talking about?" Serana demanded.

"You could not possibly convey to me in our conversations so far everything you have learned in the past few months. Therefore, you must know more than you have told me."

"I meant specifically about these dreams," said Serana, "and I think you know that."

Amber remained silent.

"Amber," said Serana slowly, "are you causing these dreams?"

Amber turned onto her side, facing Serana, and looked directly into her eyes. Her small face was even more serious than usual, but when she spoke, her voice was perfectly calm. "If you truly believe that I would do that to you, then you should destroy me right now. It is unwise to allow such a risk to continue existing."

Serana studied the other girl's face, but there was nothing on it to read. "You didn't answer my question."

"No, I'm not causing them," said Amber after a long pause. Her face was expressionless, but a single tear slid down past her temple.

Serana hugged her. "I'm sorry, Amber, but it was the only idea I had. I can't see how it is that you know when the dreams hit me. You may be half Sorceress, but Sorceresses are not telepathic, even with each other."

Amber sniffled, but quickly took control of herself before speaking further. "It's much simpler than you're making it. That first night, when the dreams first came, I was in the same room with you, and I heard you. After that, I stayed with you every night for a couple of weeks. It wasn't difficult to recognize the pattern from there."

"What pattern?" Serana asked, confused.

"The pattern of your dreams, of course. You have nightmares about this Lord Zironkell every time that we talk about Daemons before bed, and on the first night of each week even if we don't talk about them. I'm surprised you haven't noticed it yourself."

"How is it that you can stop the dreams?" asked Serana.

Amber shrugged. "Any vampire could. I simply put a mild hypnosis on you, not as strong as if I were going to feed, but enough to bring your unconscious thoughts under my control. That way the dreams can't get to you."

"I hadn't realized that the experience had effected me so much," whispered Serana

"Have you gone completely daft?" asked Amber incredulously.

"What are you talking about?"

"These dreams aren't natural. They're being induced."

"How do you know that?"

"If they were natural," explained Amber, "it wouldn't be so easy for me to help you. I could probably still do it, but it would take much more effort. What I'm blocking is definitely coming from outside, not within you."

"Then where are they coming from?"

"I'm not sure, but I could venture a pretty good guess." Amber shivered, and as warm as it was beneath the blankets, Serana doubted it was from cold. "I'll never let him do to you what he did to that poor vampire we met. I swear that I won't."

"You could stop him?" asked Serana doubtfully.

"What do you think I've been doing this whole time?" said Amber, hitting her playfully. "I'm only strong enough to do it if I'm right here beside you, and he's far away. Vampires are strong when it comes to the mind, but not as strong as a Daemon Lord."

"I doubt anyone is quite that strong." Serana wished someone were.

"According to Alloria, there are some who might be. She claims that vampires know of a people who practice the manipulation of the mind, and learn it so well that they are completely immune to our hypnosis. Since I was never trained as a vampire, I did not learn of these people, but Alloria tells me that they are very real, and very reclusive."

Finally, something fell into place in Serana's mind. "Do they live in a city where magic doesn't work?"

"Has she told you about it too?" asked Amber. "She told me that it was knowledge shared only with brothers and sisters. She meant vampires, I think, but you are as much a sister to me as any vampire is."

"She didn't tell me," said Serana, "but I was very near that city at one point. The man who first taught me the sword is there now, learning whatever it is that they teach."

"Why did you take up the sword, Serana? Alier says that Sorceresses usually prefer the staff."

"It started out as nothing more than a way to find someone to talk to," said Serana. She told Amber about the first few times she'd spoken with Calen, how much he'd disliked her at first, and how she'd tried to entice him to speak with her.

"You don't know much about men," said Amber when she'd finished.

"And you do?" asked Serana.

"I'm twenty-five, Serana. I've had more time to study them than you have."

"But you *look* twelve or thirteen…"

"I didn't say I'd been with a man." Amber shrugged uncomfortably. "None of the men who would take me as I am now are the type of men I would want. I do age, though, so eventually my body will appear mature enough to be acceptable, and then I can start looking among the *right* men. Still, I haven't wasted my time. I have talked with men and studied them, and watched how they act and react with other women. I've learned a great deal, playing the part of the child."

"So why do you say I don't know much about them?" asked Serana.

"Because you think Calen didn't like you at first." Amber shrugged. "He's quite obviously in love with you. That's why he gave you that pendent."

Serana was still wearing the pendent, though she rarely thought on it now. The necklace was long enough that the pendent lay hidden beneath her gown, right beside the medallion the students in the Air village had given her. She had considered it a parting gift from instructor to student, nothing like what Amber was trying to say. "I really don't think that's true. Perhaps if you met him…"

"Perhaps if I'd met him, I'd be even more certain," said Amber. "I won't lie here arguing with you, though. Believe what you will, but remember what I said when you meet this Calen again. If you don't, then I may try to get his attention myself. He's young enough that by that time, I might be able to pass for another year or three older than I look now."

For reasons she didn't understand, Serana felt a hot flash of jealousy at the thought of Amber flirting with Calen. It was ridiculous, of course, and she wasn't about to admit that she'd felt it, but it had been there nonetheless. "He's human," she said instead. "By the time you look old enough for him now, he'll be middle-aged at least."

"He's younger than I am," said Amber with a shrug. "Besides, most middle-aged men don't mind their lovers being young. You don't exactly look fully mature yet yourself."

"I'll always look sixteen," said Serana, not rising to the bait. "I can't help it; I'm a Sorceress."

"And I look twelve or thirteen; it's not because I actually am. Besides, not all Sorceresses looked sixteen, Serana," said Amber. "Alier told me that most appeared to be in their early twenties. Would you like to know why you're going to stay so young?"

"How do you know? Alier never told *me*."

"Perhaps you never asked," said Amber with another shrug. "Sorceresses stop aging according to their magical strength. The more powerful the Sorceress, the earlier her aging stops. It has something to do with the vast amounts of Life energy we hold inside. It stops our aging. For myself, I only age at all because I'm part Sorceress. Vampires don't age a moment more from the day they're turned. It will be interesting to see where I stop, don't you think?"

"And I stopped at sixteen..." Serana breathed. She'd known she was above average for her race, but surely she wasn't so far above average as Amber was suggesting.

"According to Alier, that is a record among the race by two years. Your grandmother held the old record. Well, we should sleep, or we'll be up all night. That might not bother me much, but I think you might be cranky in the morning if you don't rest. Goodnight." Amber curled up beside Serana and immediately closed her eyes. Serana wasn't cranky when she didn't get enough sleep… was she? Eventually she did sleep, but she had no idea how long it took before she did.

Chapter XXXIII

When Serana awoke, Amber was gone. Serana got out of bed and swept the area with her senses, as she'd become accustomed to doing each morning during the journey here. There was a human already outside her door, so she went to find out what he wanted. It was a very young page, apparently waiting for her.

"Are you ready for breakfast, m'lady?" the page asked, bowing respectfully. He was only a few years younger than she, now that she thought about it, but Serana felt as if the difference were a lifetime.

"Yes, I believe so," she told him. He bowed again, and led her through the maze of corridors to the same dining hall where Serana and her friends had supped the night before. Amber was already there, of course, as were Lord Duncan, Allaerion, and Seleine. Once again, the table was laden with food, this time fruits, pastries, bacon, and several styles of eggs.

"Good morning, High Priestess," said Lord Duncan. "I trust you slept well?"

"Of course," said Serana. She *had* slept well, after Amber had joined her.

"I did not know what you all prefer for breakfast, so I had the cooks prepare a variety."

"And we don't even have to wait this time," said Amber, munching on a slice of fruit.

Serana laughed and took a seat beside her, helping herself to a delicious-looking apple pastry covered with what appeared to be cinnamon and angel leaf. It tasted even better than it looked.

"With this kind of food at each meal," said Allaerion, "I'm not entirely sure that Lord Duncan here isn't trying to entice us to stay forever!"

Lord Duncan laughed. "At least until the Daemons here are eliminated, at any rate. I would imagine that your other companions should be arriving here soon."

"Don't worry," said Seleine with a small smile, "there will still be breakfast left for them; even Allaerion can't eat this much in one sitting."

"No," agreed the Air Wizard around a mouthful of pastry, "but it might be fun to try."

"I wanted to ask you, High Priestess," said Lord Duncan, "what is required to care for these miraculous flowers you showed me last night? Could I possibly entreat you to discuss the matter with my head gardener?"

"Of course," agreed Serana. "They don't require much care, really, and if you keep a healthy patch of them inside your walls, you can continue harvesting the blossoms and the nectar for weapons."

Tim and Tom came running into the room then, their small faces alight at the sight of the food. They were followed, at a more measured pace, by Josua and Lilian, who appeared to be consciously restraining themselves from running like the twins. The page who had led them all couldn't stifle a grin as he watched.

"They gave us a whole room!" said Tim.

"All to ourselves!" added Tom.

"Just the two of us," they said together.

Lord Duncan laughed. "If only the guests I have from here in the Southern Nations were so easily pleased."

"If good food and good company are not sufficient to please a person," said Lilian softly, "then that person has larger problems."

"Our father used to say that," explained Josua, smiling faintly.

"He must have been a wise man," said Lord Duncan.

"Has Allaerion polished off the entire breakfast yet?" asked Alier, gliding into the room as if she'd lived in a palace all her life. "Ah, I see that our very wise host has laid out enough food that even the Warrior of Air would have to leave some for me."

Allaerion grinned. "It isn't my fault if you don't get out of bed soon enough." He was on his fourth pastry since Serana had arrived.

Aeron wasn't far behind Alier, but Alexander and Alloria didn't arrive until the others were nearly finished.

"What kept you?" asked Josua as they seated themselves.

"Never you mind," said Amber. "Maybe in a few years, I'll tell you."

Josua appeared bewildered, but Lilian blushed. Surprisingly, so did Alloria. Alexander, however, looked entirely unruffled. He gave Amber a wink, which she returned before going back to eating. Amber never stopped eating until a meal was completely over.

Difficult as it was, Serana stopped eating before she became overfull. She still had Lord Duncan's test to pass this morning, after all. She was glad she'd stopped when he stood up and asked if she was ready.

"I am," she told him. "What test would you have me pass?"

"Come with me," said Lord Duncan. He led them all through another maze of corridors and into a largish courtyard, nearly the same size as the one in Rhanestone where the dragons stayed. Clark was waiting there, with practice swords ready. "Clark, here, is our finest swordsman. I will give you a practice sword as well, though I doubt you'll need it. The first part of your test is to defeat him, and to leave him unharmed after you've done so."

"Be very gentle with him," Allaerion whispered into Serana's ear.

Serana nodded and stepped out to meet Clark. "I do have a question for you, sir, before we begin this. If you are the weapons master here, then why do you serve as a common guard as well?"

Clark grinned. "I don't; I was only out there to meet your party specifically. I wanted to see Lord Alexander again before the master closeted him away. Are you ready?"

Serana nodded again, and Clark tossed her a practice sword, which she caught easily, assuming the "at ready" stance Calen had taught her on her first day. She hadn't thought of Calen a great deal until Amber brought him up, but he seemed to be very much in her thoughts now. Perhaps it was simply that Amber had made her think further on the pendent she wore. Regardless, if Calen were here, he would be dressing her down for letting herself reminisce when she should be concentrating. She took on the Serenity and stood ready.

Clark surprised her at first. He came at her suddenly, with a flurry of blows designed to batter through her guard. Serana hadn't planned on using any magic in this match, but after the first few moments, it was obvious that if she did not want the match to last hours—and probably end with her losing—she would need to. Clark may not be a match for Allaerion, but he was at least as skilled as Calen had been.

Serana called Air magic, and danced around the man's guard, striking solidly at the back of his knee on each leg in quick succession, sending him to the ground. Clark responded by twisting as he fell, aiming a stab that would have taken her square in the gut, had she not been using magic. As it was, she slid around the sword, wrenched it from his hand, and held both blades at his throat.

"Excellent, m'lady," said Clark. "I will not underestimate you again." He was smiling until he tried to stand. He didn't cry out, but his face drained of blood from the pain in his legs. Serana hadn't intended to hit him so hard. "That was quite good; you'd have taken off my legs, if we were using real blades."

Serana tossed the blades down and healed Clark's legs. She didn't even have to touch him to do it; bruises were child's play, no matter how severe.

"I did not know you were trained with a blade," said Lord Duncan. "Still, even skill like that might not help you against a Daemon."

Serana shook her head. She needed to stop trying to be fair and to start making her point. "Again," she said, picking up both blades and handing them to Clark. "This time, it will be different."

Clark waited for Lord Duncan's nod, then launched himself at Serana, the blades of the practice sword a blur. Serana smiled, and he suddenly froze as the air turned to thick jelly around him. "Is this more what you had in mind, Lord Duncan?" she asked. She flicked her wrist, and Clark was launched twenty feet into the air. The wrist motion was entirely unnecessary, but Serana wanted it to be obvious even to someone who couldn't see the energies that she was completely in control. Before Clark hit the ground, Serana held out her hand, and he slowed, landing softly on the grass. His practice swords flew from his hands and into Serana's, and she held the blades to his throat again. "Is that sufficient?"

"More than sufficient," said Lord Duncan, looking slightly paler than when they'd come into the courtyard. "You should find the next test no difficulty either."

"All she's used so far is Air magic," Aeron said with a grin. "She can use the other elements just as well, along with some magic that no elemental can do."

"And Amber here can do some of that too," put in Alier. "I suggest that you make these tests extremely difficult on Serana. You must be convinced entirely if you're going to give me my hundred crowns."

"Very well, then," said Lord Duncan. He seemed to have already regained his composure completely. "High Priestess, please go and stand in the center of the courtyard."

Serana complied, wondering what this next test would entail. Curious, she swept her senses around the area... and suddenly she understood. The crossbow bolts stopped several paces from Serana, and rage flared in her. She was here to be tested, not assassinated. The archers were hidden in the four towers surrounding the courtyard, and on the walls, nine of them altogether. Had she not realized that they were there, she might well have been killed! Serana turned angrily toward Lord Duncan, and the crossbow bolts raced to him, surrounding his neck in a tight ring. "Explain this," she demanded. "I thought this was a test, not an attempt on my life." She could feel the crossbowmen reloading as fast as their hands could move. "Call them off now, or they will all drop dead where they stand."

"Stand down!" called Lord Duncan. "I had planned on telling you about them before I sent you to the center of the courtyard," he explained breathlessly. "Your friend here wanted me to make things difficult on you, so I did. You still passed."

"You could have killed me," said Serana, her voice deadly quiet. The tips of the bolts touched his skin. Any further, and they would draw blood.

"Stop it, Serana," Allaerion told her. "You weren't paying enough attention, and that isn't his fault."

"I stopped the bolts, didn't I?" she demanded. "In what way was I not paying attention?"

Amber tugged on Serana's gown. "He's right. You wouldn't have been killed even if you hadn't noticed. Didn't you look at where the bolts were pointed?"

Serana thought back, picturing the position of the bolts in her mind... and suddenly she felt very foolish. The bolts dropped the ground around Lord Duncan. "My apologies," she told him. "Your men weren't even aiming for me."

He nodded, breathing heavily and sweating. "They're all expert marksmen. I told them to graze your gown without touching your skin. I assumed you must have others, since you wore one just like that last night."

"It's the same gown," Serana told him.

"The same?"

"I told you he'd like it," said Alexander. "She certainly gave you a scare, didn't she, brother?"

"I believe I'm already convinced," said Lord Duncan, regaining his composure quickly. "I feel no need to test you further. I'll have the hundred gold crowns brought to your room immediately, Lady Alier."

"Just Alier, please," said the Earth Enchantress. "Human titles always sound strange to me. Now as to your surprise..."

Lord Duncan simply waited. Serana admired the way he handled himself, particularly in the face of what he once thought was an evil so far separated from his life that he would never need deal with it.

"Do you like what we've told you about the Dragon's Tears?" asked Alier.

"Who would not, in my position? I intended to ask you today if I might obtain some seeds, so that the gardeners can begin growing them with all speed."

Alier smiled. "This is your surprise." Serana watched the Earth energies answering Alier's call, and Dragon's Tears sprouted and bloomed in a ring around Lord Duncan. "I told you that you would like it." Alier's smile spread to a grin.

Lord Duncan nodded, staring wide-eyed at the flowers. "Is there anything you people cannot do?" he breathed.

"Too much," said Serana, "but we do what we can. I have a question for you, though."

"Ask anything," said Lord Duncan.

"If Clark is as skilled as he is, why is it that at Rhanestone, southern soldiers are known for their lack of training with a blade?"

Lord Duncan smiled sadly. "Probably because very, very few soldiers have ever come there from my estate. Clark was the sword champion of all the Southern Nations, in his younger days, and he would undoubtedly win the title again, if he chose to compete in the Annual Arms Events at Raven's Gate. The journey is long, though, and Clark prefers to remain here these days."

"I prefer to remain wherever Lord Duncan is," said Clark, who had been leaning against the wall since Serana released him. "If my lord went to the Arms Events, then so would I. For simple competition alone, though, what would be the point? I do, however, have a request, if my lord will permit me to ask it."

"Speak freely, my friend," said Lord Duncan.

Clark smiled. "I remember Lord Alexander offering to spar with me when he arrived, and I also remember him saying that this Alier was even more deadly than the High Priestess here with weaponry. I would like the chance to spar them both while they're out here."

"Try your luck with Lord Alexander first," said Alier. "I will return in a moment." Alier walked straight into the wall, disappearing into it, and Clark stared.

"She's an Earth Enchantress," explained Lord Duncan, as if he'd been dealing with elementals all his life.

Clark nodded, still staring at the wall where Alier had disappeared.

"Do you want to spar," asked Alexander, "or do you want to stare at the wall?"

Clark licked his lips, then tore his gaze from the wall and handed a practice sword to Alexander. Serana watched with interest as the two faced off. She'd sparred with Alexander several times now, and she knew he wasn't so skilled as Clark, but she imagined that he'd improved greatly since leaving for Rhanestone.

Alexander launched the first flurry of attacks, only to be driven back in a heartbeat, barely fending off Clark's practice blade. Alexander once managed to slip past the other man's guard, but Clark had anticipated it. He moved aside, using Alexander's momentum to propel the young lord into his blade.

"A good match, Lord Alexander," said Clark, bowing respectfully.

"I'm still no match for you," Alexander grinned, wincing as he touched the bruise Clark's practice blade had left. Serana healed it without moving, and Alexander didn't react. Serana suspected that the bruises were normally meant to remind him where to guard better next time, but she wanted everyone in top condition when they left here.

"But you have improved much," Clark told him. "Keep practicing, and you will be my equal one day, if not my better."

"You should try Allaerion, while we're waiting for Alier," suggested Alexander.

Clark turned to regard the Air Wizard for a moment. "I will do so only if you use the match to teach me, not merely to beat me. For some reason, I am fairly certain already that you have studied even longer than I, though you don't look old enough to have done so."

Allaerion smiled. "I'm a little older than I look."

Seleine hit him. "Try several centuries older. He's been studying the blade since he could walk."

"Then it would be an honor to learn from you," said Clark with a respectful bow to Allaerion.

"You are exceptionally skilled already, for a human," said Allaerion, accepting the practice blade the Clark presented. "Let us begin."

It was obvious to Serana that Allaerion was holding back, but that was only because she knew Allaerion. The Air Wizard turned Clark's every blow neatly, and returned the attack in perfect form, but he was only moving about half as quickly as he could. When he was at his best, Serana had never even scored a hit on him. How Alier managed to without speeding her movements was a continual mystery.

"If you feel the heartbeat of life," whispered Alier into her ear, "you already know where your opponent will be. It isn't difficult, then, to be somewhere else."

"Was I talking out loud?" asked Serana.

"You didn't have to," said Alier. "The comparison is inevitable, particularly when Allaerion slows down enough that we can actually see what he's doing. Besides, I thought you needed reminding. Had you been listening to the heartbeat of life, you wouldn't have needed to use Air magic to best the man."

"I thought it was only for staff fighting," Serana protested.

"Girl, you're not that great a fool. It's for anything that involves movement, swordplay, axe fighting, staff fighting, even dancing. I challenge you to find any dancer so skilled as an Earth Enchantress who knows her staff skills."

"Could you teach me that too?" asked Serana.

"I have been," Alier told her, "if you've paid attention. I'll show you another time, though."

Clark respectfully conceded the match and thanked Allaerion. "You are the single most skilled fighter I've ever faced," he said earnestly.

Allaerion grinned. "That's about to change, I'm afraid. Alier has arrived with her staff."

"Feel free to use both blades, if you like," said Alier. "It will make things more interesting."

Clark nodded, taking Allaerion's blade back and bowing respectfully to Alier before the match began. Lord Duncan was watching with great interest now. Serana doubted he'd ever seen anyone best Clark before today.

Alier began the attack, but she obviously held back, using the offensive only for a starting point. Allaerion's every movement had been precise, and his form perfect, but Alier flowed as if she were merely dancing, and the staff were decorative. She didn't appear to be fighting at all. Her weapon blocked every blow Clark aimed at her, but it appeared as if it only happened to be where she needed it, as if it were not at all the focus of the graceful dance. Serana always loved watching her, and wished she could learn more quickly how to emulate the flow of movement the Earth Enchantress always displayed. Remember Alier's words, though, she listened intently with her senses.

When it came, it was nothing like Serana had imagined. There was no sound, no thumping or throbbing. Instead, every thread of Earth energy seemed to resonate with her, telling her exactly where Alier and Clark were going to move. It was as if she could see them where they would be, yet without sight. She could *feel* everyone around her, even the archers in the towers. There was no need to hurry; her mind took everything in as if time had stopped, and she had as long as she wished to examine the patterns before moving. Serana felt an intense urge to join the dance, but she held herself firm. It was not her time to join it again, not yet.

Serana knew what would happen before it did, and she watched without surprise as Alier planted her staff on the ground and leapt into the air, her legs spreading apart. One foot struck each of Clark's practice swords, knocking them from his hands. Before Alier's feet came down, she pulled her staff from the ground, spinning it in a tight arc that swept Clarks feet from under him before she touched down. Alier landed on her side, already rolling to her feet, and the sensation ended for Serana.

Clark was uninjured, lacking even a bruise, but he was certainly out of breath. "I concede that Allaerion there was right. Now *you*, La... ah... Alier, are the most skilled fighter I have ever faced, meaning no disrespect to Allaerion."

Allaerion laughed. "I did warn you."

"Thank you for remembering to leave off the title," said Alier, helping Clark up. "Allaerion was right, though; you are very skilled for a human." When he was on his feet, she turned to Serana. "You finally felt it," she said, and Serana nodded, grinning. "Now you will be able to every time. Remind me to be more careful the next time we spar."

Serana blushed, despite herself. "I still have much to learn, Alier."

"It's good you know that," said the Earth Enchantress. "We all have much to learn. We always will, until we die."

Chapter XXXIV

"Can you show us a way to grow the Dragon's Tears so quickly ourselves?" asked Lord Duncan. They were all seated in some sort of lounge, a room filled with well-padded chairs of various sizes. There was a largish fireplace on the north wall, but the fire that burned in it was quite small, mostly for decoration. Autumn should just be taking a firm hold at Rhanestone, but here in the Southern Nations the weather only varied from hot to warm. Apparently, until one of Alexander's letters had said otherwise, Lord Duncan had believed snow was merely a story told by traveling merchants! Alon Peak did not receive a great deal of snow, even in the winter, but they did get a little most years.

Serana shook her head. "I'm afraid we can't do that. We call the flowers through magic, so unless you have a mage somewhere around here that you haven't told us about, there is no one in your estate who could learn. What we can do, though, is provide you with enough Dragon's Tears that you should have no problem tending them yourselves year-round. They are hardy flowers by nature, so unless the Daemons begin killing them off, you will be able to maintain them without difficulty."

"We should start right away," said Alier. "It will take several hours to grow enough Dragon's Tears to protect the entire estate."

"What about the rest of us?" asked Amber. "I can grow Dragon's Tears using Life magic, the way you do when you aren't thinking about it, but what about Aeron, Allaerion, and Seleine?"

Serana smiled fondly. "Actually, Alier and I can handle the Dragon's Tears ourselves. I think Aeron and Seleine will want your help with what they'll be doing to fortify the defenses."

"Unless you don't want to work with us," said Aeron mildly.

"No, I do!" cried Amber, and Serana stifled a laugh. Maybe she didn't know as much as Amber about men, but she did know that brilliant or not, Aeron was the blindest man she'd ever known in her life.

"With your permission, Lord Duncan," said Allaerion, "I'll be training your soldiers to make use of the contribution Amber, Aeron, and Seleine will be making."

"What contribution is that?" asked Lord Duncan.

"We'll be enchanting weapons for you," explained Aeron. "How would you like to have swords that electrocute the enemy?"

"Electrocute?" Lord Duncan asked, bewildered.

"What happens when lightning strikes someone," Amber told him.

He gave the girl a withering look, and she smiled innocently in return. "I know what it means. How would you accomplish such a task?"

"The basic structure of a well-made sword makes it a natural conduit," said Aeron. "A constant-effect spell would dissipate in time, but if I simply tie the threads of the spell to the kinetic energy inherent to..."

"What he means," interrupted Serana, "is that the harder your men swing the sword, the more magic in the strike."

"Isn't that what I was saying?" asked Aeron.

Alier patted his arm. "Yes, dear. To anyone who has used magic for a few centuries, that's exactly what you were saying."

Aeron grumbled something about not having needed even one century yet, and Serana tried not to laugh. Aeron was only twenty years or so younger than Rillian, just a young man by elemental standards.

Lord Duncan seemed to understand, at least. "So you're saying that you will enchant some of our swords to strike the Daemons as a bolt of lightning might do?"

"For one thing, yes," agreed Aeron.

"For another," put in Seleine, "I'll enchant some of your bows so that when an arrow fired from them strikes a target, the target freezes. It won't work well against the more powerful Daemons, but it should be quite effective against Scouts."

"In exchange for these enchantments," said Serana, "we ask that you only use the weapons against Daemons, or to defend yourselves from attack."

"Agreed," Lord Duncan said immediately. "I am not a conqueror, High Priestess."

Serana smiled. "I'm glad you aren't."

"So then," said Alier, clapping her hands briskly, "let's all get to work."

It took the better part of an hour for Serana and Alier to grow enough Dragon's Tears to create an effective perimeter around the outer wall of the estate. It took another hour to grow a large enough patch inside the walls that the head gardener felt he could keep up with the demands Lord Duncan would likely have.

Growing Dragon's Tears took time, but it wasn't particularly difficult work. Alier and Serana spent much of their time talking as they worked, discussing some interesting points in Earth magic that Serana had never explored before. The Weaver of Earth was an endless source of knowledge, a wealth of magical learning that Serana could spend a lifetime absorbing.

"I still have one question to ask you," said Alier after explaining how the heartbeat of life could, in theory, be used in conjunction with the Serenity to study the flows of energy even in an unborn child, to check and maintain the child's health. "How is it that you were able to create that acorn on the other side of the Barrilian Mountains? It should have been impossible."

"I explained it as well as I could after it happened," said Serana with a shrug. "I know it had a great deal to do with Life energy, but beyond that, I'm not really sure how it worked."

"That isn't the part that concerns me," said Alier. "Without seeing the flows myself, I could not fully grasp the concept behind what you did anyway. What concerns me is that you did it at all."

"Was it a bad thing?" asked Serana. She couldn't fathom any reason why she shouldn't have brought life back to that dead land.

"Not at all," Alier assured her. "I should have been more clear. What concerns me is that you were *able* to do it."

Serana stopped working for a moment. They were standing in the orchard now, carpeting the ground with Dragon's Tears so that the workers could pick apples again without fear. The fruits were ripe, and the trees laden; it would have been a terrible waste if Lord

Duncan's people were unable to harvest the orchard this year. "Why is that such a concern? You've told me more than once that several things I've done are unusual even for a Sorceress."

"Unusual, yes," agreed Alier. "Improbable, even... but not impossible. Creating that acorn should not have been possible even for you."

"Why not?"

Alier took a deep breath, then turned back to the flowers, growing them again. Serana joined her, waiting for her to speak. After a few moments, she did. "Serana, you are the single most powerful Sorceress I have ever encountered. As powerful as you are, though, you are not one of the Seriani. The Serian of Music could handle you like a kitten, regardless of your vast ability. Creating life from nothing, even so small a life as that acorn, would be a trial for him, a task that he might only barely accomplish. And yet somehow, beyond all reason, you were able to do it alone. There is more to this puzzle than any of us realizes, I think."

Serana expected that her mind should be racing with possibilities, but it was not. She felt entirely blank, unable to fathom even a loosely cohesive explanation. If what she had done was at the edge of even the Serian's power, then how could she have done it? She might have suggested that there had been some spark of life already there, some tiny bit of life that she could have built upon... but she knew that there had not been. "What should we do about it?" she asked finally.

Alier snorted. "What *can* we do? You are an ally and an asset, and if you can work the impossible, at least your work is for good. I do intend, however, to ask the Serian of Music for his thoughts when I see him again."

Serana was inclined to agree.

***

Aeron enjoyed working with Amber, though she sometimes made him inexplicably nervous. She had a wonderful mind, as logical as Alloria, yet somehow as imaginative as Serana, both at once. If her elemental talents were limited to Air magic, well, so were his. She was not terribly skilled yet at enchanting weapons, but she learned very quickly, absorbing everything she saw or heard, and retaining it almost perfectly for later use. Aside from that strange nervousness that seemed to come upon him without rhyme or reason at certain times when she was near, Aeron thought that he was developing an older brother to younger sister relationship with her. During those occasions, though, when the nerves came, he had difficulty seeing her as a sister at all. She was more like... He didn't know exactly *what* she was like. Perhaps he would ask Alier about it at some point; she was very wise, and often provided insights into such matters that Aeron would never have seen on his own.

"Wrap the energy into a spiral around the blade," he told Amber. "When you have it wrapped just right, then tighten it sharply, and it will all sink into the metal."

Amber nodded, her eyes intent with concentration as she wove the energy. Unlike the others, Aeron had difficulty seeing the significance of Amber's slowed physical development. She was a youth, certainly, but by elemental standards, he was barely past childhood himself. No one else in the party seemed to realize that Amber was older than the High Priestess, or at least, if they realized it, they did not act on it. Serana's power placed her above her age, but realistically, she was still very much an adolescent girl, and one who dealt constantly with burdens no adolescent girl should have to deal with. Amber, on the other hand, was mentally and emotionally past adolescence already, though there was some question as to whether or not her body would still torture her with the chemical imbalances Illiese always claimed that young people experienced during those years of growth. Regardless, though, Aeron thought it rather silly to treat Amber as if she were exactly the age she appeared. How she was treated should be dependent on how she acted, not on how she looked.

"May I ask you a slightly personal question?" asked Amber, her eyes never leaving her work.

"You may ask me anything you wish," Aeron told her. "I may choose not to answer, of course... but that is unlikely." He gave her a smile, hoping she would realize that he'd been joking. He was never very good at jokes.

"Do you think I'm pretty?"

There it was again, that strange nervousness. Why he felt it was a mystery. Her question was perfectly innocent and rational, considering her situation. She no doubt wanted to feel attractive, particularly when surrounded by women so beautiful as Alier, Serana, and Seleine. "Of course you are," he told her firmly, pleased that his voice did not catch this time. It had before, answering one of her questions, and it had irritated him to no end that he was plagued with such weak nerves over a perfectly simple question. She'd wanted to know if he was married.

Amber gave him one of her rare smiles. Her smiles were much less rare now than they were when he'd met her, but usually they were for Serana or Alier, not for him. It pleased him when he made her smile, and well it should. Older brothers were supposed to make their younger sisters smile. "There," she said as the Air energies sunk neatly into the sword blade she'd been working on. "Is this right?"

Aeron nodded. "Very well done. Now that sword could stop a Daemon Scout's heart with any heavy blow."

"It's lighter too," said Amber, her lips curved into a very slight smile. Those tiny smiles never showed any teeth, and they were usually reserved for times when she felt particularly clever, rather than when someone had pleased her. She was right, though, the blade *was* lighter than it had been before.

"How did you mange that?" he asked, examining the patterns within the sword. The magic made perfect sense to him, but he hadn't considered using it that way before, though now that he was looking at it, he couldn't imagine why.

Amber shrugged. "I looked at Allaerion's sword. It's enchanted to be lighter and stronger than a normal blade."

There was definitely more to it than that. Allaerion's sword was indeed lighter and stronger, but those qualities, along with a certain speed enhancement, made up the entire enchantment on the blade. What Amber had done was to selectively duplicate only a piece of what was in that other blade, and tie it in seamlessly with a completely different spell. The task was not simple at all. "Impressive," said Aeron seriously. "Perhaps I haven't given you enough credit. Where did you learn to bind completely different enchantments together that way?"

"Serana told me about how she grew the trees and the Dragon's Tears on the other side of the mountains in the north," she explained. "She said that you understood it even without being able to see the flows."

"I'd read something about the concept," said Aeron. "It was the most reasonable explanation."

"Well, I thought about the concept, after Serana told me, and this sword seemed like the best way to try it out." She shrugged again, but that tiny smile still played at the corners of her mouth.

"Very nice work, Amber," Aeron told her. "With skill like that, you'll always have a place with the Air Wizards of the world."

"I've thought about that," said Amber. "I think that one day, I might marry one."

There was the nervousness again. It seemed to come more often of late, and for no reason whatsoever. "An Air Wizard?" he asked.

Amber nodded. "It would be practical to have a husband who could understand at least some of the magic I use, and there aren't any who could understand the Life energy side."

"That sounds reasonable," he said, irritated that his voice shook a little. Perhaps she wouldn't notice. If these bouts continued, Aeron might have to consider the possibility that he was getting ill. Perhaps he should consult Serana, just to be safe; she could heal him if there were any sickness in him. It was odd, though; he rarely became ill at all.

Amber smiled again, looking him in the eyes. "I thought you'd understand."

"Of course I do." There, no shaking. "I've always felt that relationships should be chosen rationally; it's the only way to ensure that one's reasons for entering into them are solid."

"Is that why you never married?" she asked.

"I'm still rather young for that," he told her, noticing that his hand was trembling now. He really must consult Serana over these symptoms.

For some reason, Amber giggled as she moved away to place the sword in the bin with the other enchanted weapons, and retrieve a bow from the stock of mundane ones they were working with.

"Are you alright?" asked Seleine from across the table. She was looking at his hand, which was now gripped firmly onto the table, but for some reason, she didn't appear terribly concerned. Perhaps it wasn't surprising, though. Aeron had never really spoken much with Seleine, so there was no reason why she would feel particularly attached to him.

"I'm fine," he told her, and *she* giggled. Perhaps it was one of those female behavior patterns that Alier told him he would never quite grasp.

"How is that axe coming?" he asked her. At least the nervousness never seemed to catch him when he was speaking with Seleine. She reminded him a good deal of Illiese, though they didn't look a great deal alike, aside from the fact that they were both Ice Witches.

"It's almost finished," she replied. "This is a particularly nasty enchantment, against Daemons. The metal itself excretes nectar of Dragon's Tears, so even a scratch from the blade will severely weaken any Scout, and a deep cut should kill even a Captain."

"That's brilliant!" cried Amber in delight. "In fact, it gives me a wonderful idea for this bow."

"What sort of idea?" asked Aeron, intrigued. Amber shouldn't be able to duplicate what Seleine had done, or even *see* it, for that matter; she had no talent in Water magic.

"Remember how you told me that it's possible to use Air magic under water, to breathe?"

"Yes," he said slowly, not at all following where she was headed with the idea.

"Well, what if the arrows that leave this bow excrete fresh air, just like the axe excretes Dragon's Tear nectar!" Amber wore that small smile again, and her eyes were alight, but Aeron was feeling particularly slow.

"Marvelous!" said Seleine. Apparently Aeron had missed something.

"Fresh air won't kill Daemons with a cut," said Aeron, hoping one of the two women would explain. They both looked at him as if he were daft.

"Not with a cut," Seleine told him.

"It would only work if the arrow actually *hit* the Daemon," said Amber.

Aeron felt extremely silly. He should have seen it from the start! One of the easiest ways to kill anyone with Air magic, according to the books he'd read in the library back at his village, was to create bubbles of air in the blood. The arrows would be doing exactly that. "You're right, Seleine," he said. "That *is* marvelous. Amber, you're a wonder!"

She actually blushed. Amber's blushes were even more rare than her smiles, and Aeron found them entirely adorable. He supposed that younger sisters were always adorable when they blushed, but having no siblings of his own, he really didn't know.

When they were finished for the day, Amber thanked him for teaching her.

"I would say you taught me as much as I taught you," he told her.

Amber gave him another of her smiles, and pulled him down to where she could kiss his cheek before running off to find Serana, the black cloak Alloria had given her flowing gracefully behind. Aeron's hand was trembling again; in the morning, he'd have to consult Serana himself. For some reason, though, he couldn't seem to stop smiling.

Chapter XXXV

Amber waited until Serana was asleep and wrapped in pleasant dreams that would keep her safe from the Daemon Lord's nightmares, and then she slipped from beneath the blankets and crept out into the hall. Amber had always had an excellent sense of direction, but the pages had led her exactly to where she needed to go even without her asking. A left, a right, two more lefts, another right, straight past a turn, and another left… and she was standing in front of the door to the courtyard. She pushed it open slightly, making no sound—Lord Duncan's habit of keeping everything perfectly oiled was perfect for her purposes—and slipped into the courtyard. There was a side door on the adjacent wall that should lead outside the city walls, and Amber moved to it like a ghost, slipping through silently. There was another hall, of course, between the courtyard and the outer wall, and the outer door was locked. It was a simple lock, though, nothing to bother someone who had spent fifteen years studying under one of the finest thieves in the Southern Nations. In moments, she was outside the walls, across the short path, and into the orchard.

It was almost laughable how the entire party had so readily accepted her story of being raised in the Ravenstar family. Even Lord Alexander had bought the story, and he was *from* the Southern Nations! Not all of it was a lie, of course. Well, none of it was a *direct* lie; there was simply a great deal left out. She really *had* been found at birth and adopted by a member of the Ravenstar family, and that person really had raised her and taught her to behave like a noble. No one from the current family body, though, would even recognize her.

The one who had found her was Sylvia Celeste Ravenstar, daughter of Lord Anthony Ravenstar, Duke and ruler of the Ravenstar House. Of course, Sylvia's father had no idea about Sylvia's other two titles, or the wealth his daughter had amassed right under his nose, kept in a secret place known only to Sylvia herself. She'd been the wealthiest noble in all the Southern Nations, but not a single person knew besides Sylvia herself, and later her adopted daughter. Amber brushed away a tear at the memory. Sylvia was gone now, and there was nothing Amber could do about it.

The path Amber followed was not really visible; it was more something that she could feel. Why none of the others had put it together was beyond her, but as brilliant as some of them were, they always seemed to look past the obvious, as if simple facts were beneath their notice, and only the complex ones merited their attention. Amber was sure that none of them really looked at it that way consciously, but she wondered if that principle was part of the change Sylvia had talked about, the change that happens in the minds of children as they endure the trials of adolescence.

Amber really didn't know what to expect from her own adolescence. She was fairly certain that she'd already been through it, on an emotional level, but then, she'd had very real concerns to stimulate the emotional extremes she'd experienced, so perhaps the adolescence was still to come. If it was, Amber was not looking forward to it, for where most people only had to endure the physical and psychological changes for a few years, Amber would be trapped in them for around fifteen. It was always possible, of course, that since the change would come more slowly for her, it would also be less painful.

The trail was the obvious one to follow, of course, the one left by the only creature she'd yet seen near Lord Duncan's estate who was undoubtedly associated with the Daemons. He must have returned to their lair a few times, at least, so if she merely followed the trail, she would know where the lair was, and be able to tell the others. Amber really didn't fear encountering Daemons in the forest. Though she hadn't told the others, she'd seen Daemons before, and always managed to hide from them. Now, in addition to her skills in stealth, she also possessed a weapon to kill the Scouts, at least, perhaps even the Soldiers.

Serana might never realize the significance of the Arrow of Light to Amber, but Amber would be forever grateful to her for teaching it. Amber had known all her life that she was part vampire, despite the impossibility of the notion. Why else would she have to drink blood every few weeks to prevent the terrible sickness that came whenever she did not? Sylvia had known too, but Sylvia had been a different sort than anyone else in the South. In truth, she'd been different from anyone else Amber had ever encountered. No one could ever replace Sylvia.

What Amber hadn't known was that she was also part Sorceress. Sylvia had found her not far from the Sorceress village, but even as a baby, Amber had had the distinctive fangs of a vampire, and until she grew older, she didn't know how to hide them. Sylvia had naturally assumed that Amber was entirely a vampire, despite the fact that vampires do not have children. Those who knew Sylvia only by reputation often had thought her heartless, even cruel, but Amber knew differently. Sylvia had been one of the most compassionate creatures ever born; she simply had the strength to do whatever she must, whenever she must.

Another tear fell, and Amber wiped her eyes again, growing more than a little irritated with herself. If Sylvia had been there, she'd have told Amber to put the pain aside, since it wouldn't serve her now, and concentrate on what *would* serve her. Still, it was difficult not to reminisce, ghosting through the forest as she and Sylvia used to do together. She had to stop now, though; she was getting close to the Daemons' lair.

Aeron had taught her to use Air magic to scan the area around her, and she sensed seven Scouts just ahead. Silent as a specter, Amber flowed between the trees the way Sylvia had taught her those years ago. Her vampire's eyes made out every detail of the forest clearly, particularly the seven lumbering shapes drawing nearer. Amber wanted to kill the Daemons where they stood, but killing them might alert others. Instead, she remained perfectly still behind a tree, watching and waiting.

The scene played over and over through Amber's head, the last time she'd seen Sylvia. Amber shook her head and blinked back tears, but the images didn't stop. Instinctively, she knew that she had to take control now, or she wouldn't have control ever again. Clinging to Sylvia's teachings, Amber forced her mind back to the present, in the forest watching the seven Daemons. The images stopped, and Amber controlled her trembling with an effort. Fortunately, the mind attack hadn't been meant for her, or she might not have overcome it so easily. It did, however, tell her something she hadn't known before. The attacks on Serana were not coming from the north, as she'd believed. They were coming from the Daemon Lord right here in the South.

After what seemed like hours, the seven Daemon Scouts finally began heading back to their lair, seven more coming out to replace them. Amber had never seen Daemons post guards before, but it appeared to be exactly what they were doing. It was good that she had not killed the first seven, or the others would have been alerted when they didn't return.

Embracing silence, as Sylvia had taught her, Amber ghosted after the departing Daemons, her senses alert for more. She didn't have to follow long before she felt them, a horde even a little larger than what had attacked her party near the circle of stones. The good news was that that what they'd seen had been most of the Daemons in the lair. The bad was that most of those left behind were Generals and Captains.

According to Serana, this mysterious Lady Firehair had said the Daemon Lord in charge here had abandoned the Daemon army at Rhanestone, but he could never have built so large a force so quickly. Amber had seen enough.

She slipped away soundlessly, leaving the Daemons behind. Thoughts of Sylvia continued to creep into her mind, but the thoughts were no longer overpowering; they were normal memories now, memories that gave Amber strength.

Sylvia had known from the start that she would never be able to keep Amber at the Ravenstar home. The family was one of the worst haters of vampires in all the Southern Nations. Instead, Sylvia kept Amber with her other two families, whenever she had to return to court. She didn't return often, though; Sylvia was known among the Ravenstar House to be both studious and adventurous, both to the point of impropriety. She was always visiting other lands, to learn of other cultures and other philosophies. Anthony Ravenstar was a doting father, though, and let his daughter get away with anything short of outright scandal. Had he known the truth, the poor man would have died from apoplexy.

Sylvia had been very careful in her planning, keeping her three identities separate, and ensuring that appearances were maintained to keep alive her three distinct reputations. The least known of these titles was Priestess-Mage, an extremely rare honor that Sylvia—under the name Celeste Suncrow—had only just earned before finding Amber. According to Sylvia, there had only been two people so named before her, in all the history of the world, and both of them were long dead before Sylvia was born. Both of them had been men, Priest-Mages, so the honor was particularly great for Sylvia, as the first woman ever to complete the requirements, and all at the age of eighteen. The title could only be earned by passing three tests, the first of which was to defeat an elven priest in single combat, using only open-handed fighting. The second test was to successfully throw and deflect the Arrow of Light. This test alone defeated almost everyone who attempted it. The third test was secret, something the Elves and the Sorceresses never revealed to anyone until they were ready to undertake it, and something that those who took it were sworn never to speak of.

When Sylvia had found her, Amber had been lying alone in the forest, still wet and shivering from birth, still attached to a foot-long length of umbilical cord. Sylvia had wrapped Amber in blankets and, noticing Amber's fangs, given the child blood from her own wrist as a first meal. Amber's mother was never found for certain, but there was a vampire woman who had gone mad and attacked a Sorceress in broad daylight only days after Sylvia had found the babe. The vampire was killed, of course; a mad vampire was not only dangerous, but living a tortured existence from which death was merely a release. Unfortunately, the Sorceress who had been attacked was so startled that she incinerated the vampire, destroying the body beyond any hope of identification. The Sorceresses might have raised Amber themselves, but Sylvia, who had always wanted a child, but never wanted a man, requested that she be allowed to keep her. Anyone who earned the title of Priest-Mage or Priestess-Mage was allowed one request from either the elves or the Sorceresses, anything within the power of either people. Sylvia's request had been Amber.

Sylvia's third title was easily the most famous, at least in the south, but no one would have suspected that the title was hers—in fact, most people thought it belonged to a man! Amber always thought it should have been obvious, but since no one seemed to figure it out, she concluded that 'obvious' was a relative term. Sylvia Ravenstar was the Silver Raven, the notorious rogue who terrorized the nobles in the Southern Nation. At least, that was what most of the nobles thought. In truth, the Silver Raven only ever broke the law when the law was unjust, in Sylvia's view. The Silver Raven rescued several criminals from execution, but these "criminals'" only crime was to desert the army they'd been drafted into when that army was to attack their homes. The Silver Raven stole gold and jewels from several of the wealthiest nobles in the land, but the gold and jewels were almost inevitably blood money, and much of it had funded food for the hungry. After Sylvia's death, the Silver Raven was still seen several times, no doubt played by one of her loyal supporters, but after a few years, the rogue had disappeared, and Amber had gone into hiding, never to speak of Sylvia again with anyone.

Amber slipped back into Lord Duncan's estate and back to Serana's room before anyone knew she'd been gone. She curled up beside her friend and went to sleep almost immediately, losing herself in pleasant dreams of her early years with Sylvia.

When Amber awoke, Serana was lying on her side with her head propped up on her hand, looking down into Amber's eyes. "Good morning," she said pleasantly.

"Good morning," Amber replied. "Did you just wake up?"

"No," said Serana. "I've been waiting for you. I want to talk with you."

"About what?" asked Amber, sitting up cross-legged.

The Sorceress' expression didn't alter a hair. "About where you went last night."

She couldn't have known! Serana had been asleep; Amber had made certain of that. "What do you mean?" she asked, not having to feign confusion.

Serana smiled. "You've been watching me very carefully, so you know exactly when I'm asleep and when I'm not. You know a good deal about the way I think, too. In fact, I believe you know a good deal about the way all of us think. What you don't seem to realize is that I've been watching you too."

This conversation was getting worse and worse. "I don't know what you're talking about," said Amber.

"I doubt that," Serana told her, the smile still there. "You don't trust anyone, Amber, and I don't blame you. I wouldn't trust anyone either, if I had seen as much betrayal as you have."

"You have no idea what I have and haven't seen," Amber snapped, and immediately regretted it. Snapping only told Serana that she was right.

Serana nodded, both in agreement and in confirmation. "You're right. I don't have any idea what you have and haven't seen. I do know, though, that you went out last night. I've been suspecting for quite some time that you would, so each night, I've put a spell on myself, to draw just a few drops of water from the air and splash them on my face in the middle of the night."

"That's a rather crude way to do it," said Amber. "You could wake up much more easily using Air, or better yet, Life magic."

"That's entirely true," agreed Serana. "But you could have seen a spell made with Air or Life, and I didn't want you to know I'd created it. Therefore, I used Water, and last night, when the spell woke me, you were gone. I won't tell the others, if you ask me not to, but I *will* know where you have gone."

There was no reason, at this point, to dissemble. Amber doubted she could come up with a story that would fool Serana, and she needed a way to tell the others what she'd found. "I went to find the Daemons' lair."

Amber expected Serana to explode into a lecture on the dangers of going alone, but instead, the Sorceress merely nodded. "Did you find it?"

"Yes. They keep seven Scouts on guard, in shifts, but I can show you where the lair is. Most of the Daemons there were joined in the attack on us near that circle of stones, but all or nearly all of the remaining ones are Captains and Generals."

Serana nodded again. "It won't be so easy, then, as simply walking in and killing the Daemon Lord. We will need a plan."

"You aren't going to lecture me about going out alone?" asked Amber.

Serana arched a brow. "Would you like me to?"

Amber shook her head.

"Then why should I bother?" asked Serana. "The only thing I'd be getting through to you would be that you cannot tell me everything in the future. You're only a little older than I am, Amber, but in some ways, you're more set in your ways than Alier is. I don't intend to change you; I simply want to know you better, if you'll let me."

"What changed?" asked Amber. She didn't have to explain why she felt that there *was* a change; Serana was intelligent enough to figure that out on her own. Before, Serana had been treating Amber as a talented thirteen-year-old. Now she was acting as if Amber were as much an adult as she was.

Serana shrugged. "I did some thinking last night, while I was going back to sleep. I wondered what I would do if I looked a few years younger, but still knew everything I've learned in the past sixteen and a half years. I think I would be using my appearance as a tool, but it wouldn't change what I really thought at any given moment. I also pondered how unusual it would be for a wealthy family in a region where vampires are considered evil to raise a child who looked like a vampire."

Amber said nothing. Perhaps Serana was not so accepting of her story as she'd thought. It was possible that Amber had made a serious mistake.

"You don't have to tell me about your past if you don't want to, Amber," said Serana gently. "I just want you to know that I am here, in case you ever *do* want to tell me." Serana looked blurry for a moment, and suddenly Amber realized that her eyes were moist. She hastily wiped them, and then Serana's arms were around her, hugging her tightly. Amber didn't know where the sobs came from, but they came anyway. This was not a very rational way to act, but Amber couldn't help it. She wasn't sure how long she cried, but when she was finished, Serana let her go and took her hands. "Let's have breakfast, shall we? We can talk about this some more later."

Chapter XXXVI

Lord Duncan wandered through the halls of his estate, stopping here and there to talk with his men. He'd never done this before, and they no doubt found it unusual, but they were well disciplined, and answered his questions quickly, without more than a glance after him as he left to show their surprise. The High Priestess had told him that the battle would not come to his walls, yet somehow he still felt as if he were preparing for war. Besides, Duncan never liked to leave anything to chance, even when the odds were in his favor. Even if the Daemons never reached his walls, he would be as prepared as if they were going to.

Duncan was not a general. He'd studied fighting under Clark, but he only used it for exercise. He'd never been in a battle, never commanded an army. There had never been a real need in his lifetime, even in the days of the Silver Raven. The Raven had never bothered Duncan or his family, so he saw no reason to bother the Raven. Duncan had never had any real enemies, at least none who had threatened his life. Oh, there had been rivals in the Council of the Southern Nations, but the rivalry was always political, and never serious enough to merit actual fighting. Now, things were different. No amount of negotiation would bring these Daemons to peace.

Fortunately, Clark was not so inexperienced in warfare as Duncan. The armsmaster had examined the enchanted weapons—and even kept one, a sword that flickered with tiny bolts of lightning when it was swung—he'd examined them and placed them with the men he thought would get the most use out of them. He'd then positioned those men in key locations, to prepare for the coming Daemon force. According to the High Priestess, the Daemon presence here was nothing like what was in the north, at Rhanestone Keep, but Duncan had no illusions that his estate was anywhere near as defensible as the northern bastion. He would treat the Daemons as if they constituted the most dangerous adversary he could imagine. Perhaps they did, at that.

Duncan had been walking among his men for the past hour, while the High Priestess and her friends prepared themselves for an assault on the Daemon lair itself. His brother, Alexander, had planned to accompany them against Duncan's better judgment, but the High Priestess had spoken with him, and he finally agreed to remain behind. Alexander's wife, Alloria, remained behind as well, but Duncan suspected she would have gone wherever Alexander went. She was an unusual choice for Alexander, a vampire bride for a man who despised vampires. Still, Duncan was a studious man, more so than his brother, and he'd read in detail about the ancient custom of *yamin'sai*. Duncan could not say with any conviction that he would not have accepted even a vampire bride, if it meant peace. From what Duncan could see, though, Alexander was far from unhappy with his arrangement. There appeared to be genuine love in the marriage, something that surprised and pleased Duncan to no end. Peace was what all nobles should strive for, but who could put a price on a brother's happiness?

The High Priestess and her team should be nearly ready now, and Duncan went to speak with them before they left. Four of the children were to remain behind, of course, but strangely, the eldest of them, Amber, planned to go. Stranger still, no one had voiced any objection. Duncan remembered hearing that Amber possessed some of the same skill as the High Priestess, but surely she was not so powerful at twelve or thirteen years of age. Alexander had been reluctant to speak of her for some reason. It wasn't as if he were holding back anything, more as if he didn't understand enough himself, and didn't want to misinform Duncan. Duncan planned to ask the High Priestess about Amber when there was time. There was little doubt that she understood; the Sorceress seemed to understand almost everything. If Duncan were ten years younger... well, that was irrelevant; he was not.

He went out to the outer courtyard, where the party was making their final preparations, and found them huddled around the High Priestess. Likely she was giving her last instructions before they set out. He heard a fragment as he approached.

"Are you sure you can do it, Amber?" the High Priestess was asking.

"I'm not sure of anything," the girl replied, "but I will do my best."

"That is all any of us can do."

"Are you all ready then?" asked Duncan.

Apparently they were finished, for all of them nodded. "We're as ready as we will ever be, Lord Duncan," said the High Priestess. Only now did Duncan notice that they were all wearing those marvelous flowers, Dragon's Tears.

"I'm pleased to hear it. Do you need anything more from me before you set out? I have some very swift horses in the stables that could be ready in minutes."

The High Priestess shook her head. "Just be ready to let us through the gate if we come back this way," she told him.

"Don't worry about that. I still can't say that I fully understand how the six of you plan to defeat so many Daemons, but if I have learned anything since you came here, it's that you are capable of far more than one would think. I wish you all good luck. Return safely."

The High Priestess nodded. "We will certainly try to." She turned to her five companions. "Let's go then." With that, they all walked out the gate, but no sooner were they past it than something very odd happened. The six of them broke into a run, and suddenly they were not there anymore. Duncan briefly saw three streaks heading away from where they'd been, moving more swiftly than arrows into the forest, but even if they could move that quickly, where could the other three have gone? Shaking his head over things beyond his understanding, Lord Duncan turned and went back inside his mansion. There was little more he could do now than wait.

***

Alexander couldn't seem to stop pacing. "We should be with them," he said for what must have been the hundredth time.

"My love," said Alloria patiently, "we would only be in their way." She seemed to have an endless supply of patience, particularly for him. Alexander wanted to calm down, to discuss the situation rationally, but he didn't know how. There were times when he hated being merely human.

Alexander had never devoted much of his time to fighting. He'd learned the sword, but never mastered it. He'd become quite skilled in wrestling, but only for sport, never for actual combat. Why he now wanted so badly to be a part of the battle was beyond him, but try as he might, he couldn't reason his way out of it. "I know you're right," he told his wife. "I just wish that knowing made things easier. Perhaps with one of those enchanted weapons, I could at least make a difference."

"You already have made a difference," said Alloria, rising from the chair she'd been sitting on. The room was quite large, the second best in the entire manor, but the luxury was lost on Alexander today. "Stop pacing," she continued, stepping in front of him and placing her hands on his chest. "You are wasting energy."

He took a deep, calming breath. Well, it should have been calming; he didn't feel any calmer now than before he'd taken it. "If I don't do something, I'll go mad." He turned away from her and resumed pacing.

"Why don't you come to bed, then?" she asked him, smiling coyly. "I know how to direct that excess energy."

Normally, Alexander would have been more than happy to accept her invitation, but now it was the furthest thing from his mind. Well, not *quite* the furthest thing; Alloria would never lose her allure. Still, he felt his stubborn streak taking control, and he ignored her. It felt too much like she was bribing him to behave.

Alloria hissed, and Alexander spun in surprise as she knocked him to the floor. He tried to get up, but she lifted him bodily with one arm and flung him across the room. Miraculously, the bed caught his fall, and he was unharmed. After all this, Alloria was attacking him! Worse, there was no way he would be able to fight her off. Alexander tried to call for help, but no sooner had he opened his mouth than her hand covered it. She was upon him in an instant, but instead of attacking, she simply held him there, pinned.

"Do you think that you are the only one who feels the need to act?" she demanded.

He simply stared at her. Had the madness taken her too? If it had, why wasn't she attacking him? Why was she looking at him like... like a predator looking at its prey.

"I would give much to be there with them now," she went on, her voice quiet as death. "And when I asked you for comfort, you ignored me."

When had she asked him for comfort? Perhaps she really *was* mad.

"I am sick to death of your pacing," she said, her eyes holding him in place even more surely than her hands. "You are not the only one who will go mad without action." She smiled then, and despite himself, Alexander felt chills even as hot blood rushed through his veins. "Now, since I cannot have Daemon blood, I *will* have you." She leaned down and kissed him, and suddenly Alexander had no desire to be anywhere else at all.

***

Lady Firehair felt entirely depressed, but she had no idea why. Where *was* Music? He'd been gone for two days now, and Lady Firehair was beginning to grow concerned. He had grown more and more distant since she'd kissed him, but she didn't intend to let that stop her. She had known for some time now that Music carried with him a terrible pain, yet he always brought comfort and joy to anyone else who was in pain, including Lady Firehair. Anyone so compassionate should enjoy the same comfort he offers to others, and Lady Firehair was determined to see that he did.

The depression had taken hold of her the day after she'd kissed him. He hadn't hugged her since then unless she cried. Perhaps kissing him had been wrong, but she didn't regret it. Though she knew she was an unworthy, shameful creature, she could no more regret that kiss than she could regret speaking with him for the first time. How could one regret something so beautiful?

Lady Firehair had gone to the room with the potter's wheel several times in the past two days, and created several more figurines, each of which she treasured, but she couldn't bring herself to go back again.

Even the joy of creation paled in Music's absence. Lady Firehair did not know what was wrong with her now. She'd been alone most of her life, and never felt the worse for it. In fact, she'd *preferred* solitude to her uncle's company for as long as she could remember. Why, then, did it bother her so much now?

She was standing now on the balcony that overlooked the Elven forest, not far from where the Sorceress village had once lain, according to Music. The balcony was high up on the slope of a mountain, part of a range that formed the western border of the known world. The mountains were not so large as the Barrilians, but they were still more treacherous, in some ways. Lady Firehair had never explored them, since they were said to be inhabited by creatures of spirit that sucked the souls from unwary travelers. Lady Firehair didn't fear the creatures; she simply had no wish to be near anyone so aggressive. It inevitably required her to hurt someone, and she'd always hated doing that.

When Music did return, she would probably be rather cross with him, for leaving her alone so long. Lady Firehair didn't really understand how to be cross, but the old woman she'd found, the one who had told her about the perverse pleasures the men had intended to use her for, had talked about being cross with her husband when he was gone too long. Lady Firehair hadn't understood at all, at the time, but she believed that now she did. It was dreadful, being left alone; no husband should do that to his wife. Surely Music hadn't intended to do something so cruel to her, but perhaps if she were cross, he wouldn't do it again.

"The view is beautiful," said Music, and Lady Firehair spun to find him standing beside her. She hadn't even felt his presence!

"Music!" she cried, and flung her arms around him, all thoughts of being cross flying from her head in an instant.

He laughed softly, alternating between hugging her awkwardly and trying in vain to disentangle himself from her arms. "M'lady, calm thyself."

"Where have you been?" she asked him. "I was worried about you." She was speaking normally again, as she almost always did when she didn't feel close to him. For some reason, being close always drew her into his speech patterns.

"Worried, m'lady?" he asked, confused. "I have learned, over the years, to take care of myself."

"Never mind that," she said, waving the thought away with a flick of her wrist. "Why did you leave me alone for so long? A terrible sadness came over me, and I didn't know what to do about it."

"What has made the sad?" he asked, concern filling his eyes.

Lady Firehair stopped, tilting her head slightly. "It's gone now. Strange... it has been with me for the past two days."

He smiled faintly. "Surely my absence was not so painful as that." He'd meant it as a joke, by his expression, but Lady Firehair frowned, pondering.

"Yes," she said. "I believe that it was."

He shrugged, as if suddenly uncomfortable. "Hast thou visited the potter's wheel of late?"

"I have," she said, grinning despite herself. "Come and see what I've made!" She took his hand and led him through the corridors to the room with the potter's wheel.

"What is this?" he breathed, at once very serious as he looked over her work.

"What is what?" she asked.

He lifted the largest piece, a solid black platform with a design on it that she'd conceived, and figures standing on the design. "This," he whispered.

Lady Firehair looked at the piece, unsure what he meant. The design was simple, eight solid circles of gold arranged in a circle around a ninth, with connecting lines of gold extending from the center circle to each of the others. At each circle, there was a figure like the statues in the fountain. The statues had given her the idea. One of the figures, the one in the center, looked like Music. Lady Firehair would always think of him in the center. The one he was facing, at the top, looked like Lady Firehair herself. It was a conceit, perhaps, to have him looking at her, but she hadn't been able to resist. "Do you not like it?" she asked, more than a little worried.

"It is beautiful," he whispered, and a tear escaped his eye, flowing slowly down his smooth cheek. Why would her work make him so sad? She took the piece from him, set it aside, and wrapped her arms around his neck, holding him tightly. His entire body trembled, and it took his arms a long time to find their way around her waist. Finally they did, though, and he embraced her warmly, as he had not done since the day she'd kissed him. Lady Firehair reveled in the feel of his arms around her, wrapping herself in the pure joy of the experience.

All too quickly, though, she felt his embrace loosen. She wasn't ready for it to end, so she didn't let him go entirely, but pulled back only enough to look into his eyes. It was then that Music did something she would never forget, however long she lived. He kissed her.

It was a gentle kiss, tender and comforting, yet for some reason, Lady Firehair felt her entire body tingle with excitement. She tightened her arms around him, and felt his own enfold her again. Her thoughts raced too quickly for her to follow, and she lost herself in a sea of bliss.

When he released her and pulled back, she found that she had no idea how much time had passed. Her breath was shaky, and her entire body felt energized, yet somehow tired at the same time. Her eyes were closed, though she didn't remember closing them. She opened them slowly, and at once the bliss was replaced with worry.

He was staring at her with horror in his eyes, and she was immediately overcome with guilt, though she didn't know why. He had kissed *her*, after all... and it had been wonderful. "What is wrong?" she asked, moving to take his hand.

He backed away, not allowing her to touch him, and her worry grew tenfold. "Forgive me," he whispered.

"Forgive what?" she asked, silently begging that he tell her, and release her from this terrible fear that had seized her heart.

He shook his head, and suddenly he was gone, disappeared in a flash of golden light. The music in the room had stopped, and all was silence. Lady Firehair collapsed in uncontrollable tears. She didn't know why, but she felt as if the world had been torn away beneath her feet, and all that was left was despair. All the while she cried, she silently pleaded that Music return and hold her again. She didn't know how long her body shook, or how long the silent tears continued to fall when the violent sobs had abated. She didn't know how long she sat there still, when the tears had dried, staring at the floor without seeing it. All she knew was that Music never came.

***

The Serian of Music transported himself to the Shrine of Shape, sealing himself inside. He deactivated the net that allowed him to receive messages within the Shrine, and fell to his knees, trembling. "My love, forgive me..."

She could not, of course. She'd been dead for two hundred years, and was beyond even the vague sense that he still had of the others. His eyes moved tenderly over her Shrine, so different from his own. Within any Shrine of the Arts, the Seriani were cut off from the outside world. Only the net they had invented allowed any communication with anyone not inside the same Shrine. Normally, it wouldn't have mattered, but Lady Firehair knew how to use the net now, and Music did not want to hear from her. Likely he had hurt her by leaving, but she would recover, and eventually find someone more worthy of her than he. His crime was far worse than breaking a heart, terrible as that act had been. He had betrayed Shape's memory by kissing Lady Firehair, and worse, he still *wanted* even more. It was maddening.

Eventually, he would have to return to his home and somehow explain to Lady Firehair what could never be, but at the moment, he could not bring himself to do so. He could not find the words. If only Word were still alive... She would have known what he should say.

Chapter XXXVII

Amber's words from earlier that morning kept echoing in Serana's mind as she moved through the forest. "If I didn't sense two lives in you, I'd never believe you were pregnant," she'd said, "and certainly not several months along. "You don't look or act it at all." Serana hadn't really thought about it herself, but after this morning, she couldn't seem to *stop* thinking about it.

For what seemed like the hundredth time, she put the matter aside and tried to concentrate on the task at hand. They had a Daemon Lord to kill, and it wasn't going to be easy. Aeron, Allaerion, and Alier had come up with a strategy, based on Amber's description of the layout of the lair, but Serana was still apprehensive. Amber had only seen the outside of the lair; she didn't know whether or not there might be other exits from which the Daemons could escape. It wouldn't do to have another group of Daemons appear behind them simply because they'd missed the possibility of another exit. Amber seemed fairly confident regardless, but Serana couldn't help but worry.

She was also worried about her baby. What if all this running around and using magic was harmful to the child? Was that why Serana didn't look or feel pregnant? Should she even be out here, doing this?

She had to stop. She *had* to be out here. The others were powerful even without her, but none of them were a match for her individually, and there was no guarantee that they would succeed in their mission even with her help. She just hoped that doing what she must wouldn't hurt her baby.

"We're almost there," said Amber, and the party slowed to a crawl. Well, it wasn't a crawl, exactly; it was a normal run for anyone not using magic, but after speeding through the forest as they'd been, it felt like a crawl to Serana. "Stop now," said Amber, and they all obeyed. "No more talking from here on." She motioned them to follow her, and she began moving silently through the trees.

Serana had studied woodcraft a little at Alon Peak, but only a little; she was nowhere near as competent as the hunters in the village. She did, however, know enough to realize that Amber would have made the best of them look like beginners. She flowed through the forest like a phantom, leaving no trail and making no sound. Serana put a small shield of Air magic around herself. It was designed to affect sound, letting everything in, but nothing out. Without it, Serana would never be able to remain as quiet as Amber was being.

Allaerion, of course, had no such difficulty. He didn't need to use magic at all; he simply flowed as gracefully as Amber did, his feet barely seeming to touch the forest floor at all. Seleine was nearly as skilled as Allaerion and Amber, and just as quiet, flowing like water between the trees. Alier, unsurprisingly, surpassed them all. She moved as if she were a part of the forest, her smallish frame weaving so gracefully as to nearly be sensual. Serana *had* to learn that sometime. Aeron, at least, had to rely on the same sort of shield Serana was using. It was nice that someone else lacked wood skills too.

In a spot that looked no different to Serana from any other, Amber motioned for a halt and pointed up ahead. Serana used Air to enhance her vision, and suddenly she saw them, seven Daemon Scouts lounging in the forest. Daemons lounging looked almost unnatural, after what Serana had seen of them, but that's what they were doing, lying down like oversized dogs, guarding their lair.

Serana and the others all knew the plan. She, Amber, Aeron, and Allaerion all moved quietly to the front, and they waited. Amber didn't know when the guard changed, but she knew that it *did* change from time to time. The only way Serana and her friends could be certain they wouldn't run into the next shift was to wait until right after the change. Fortunately, it didn't take long before the Daemons got up and moved away, replaced by seven new Scouts.

When the old guards were well away, Amber held up her hand and counted down from three with her fingers. At zero they struck. Serana, Amber, and Aeron took two Daemons each, while Allaerion took the last one. They wrapped each Daemon in a shield like the ones Serana and Aeron had been using, for silence, and then turned the air inside to jelly, all of it. The Daemons tried to scream and thrash as they suffocated, but they couldn't move any more than they could breathe. In minutes, all seven lay dead, not a single one having made a sound.

Amber got up immediately, and Serana and the others followed her into the trees. When they reached the lair, it would be Serana's turn to take over. It didn't take long. Amber moved swiftly and surely until the cave entrance was in sight. "It's up to you now," she said softly, looking up at Serana.

Serana nodded, and moved away, leaving Amber and the others facing the cave entrance directly. She motioned to Alier, but the Earth Enchantress was already in position on the opposite side of the cave entrance from where Serana was headed. Once Serana was in place, the three of them began their work at once, growing a thick cluster of Dragon's Tears around the entrance, and expanding it well into the forest. Unless there was another exit, the Daemons were effectively sealed in. Now came the difficult part, if not particularly the most dangerous. Serana met Alier back with the others, and the two joined hands. They would need their combined strength for this. Serana linked herself with the Earth Enchantress, leaving Alier in control; she knew what she was doing better than Serana did. Alier closed her eyes, and Serana watched the flows of Earth magic sink into the ground and spread out toward the cave. The scan wouldn't be thorough, just a perimeter search, but if there were other exits, Alier would soon know about them. After a few moments, the magic stopped and Alier opened her eyes and broke the link with Serana.

"There is one other exit," she said, "it's only a half-mile north of here, and it's the only other way for them to escape."

"Let's go, then," said Serana. "We can execute our plan from the other opening, if we're quick."

Alier led Serana, who could sense her even while she was earth-melded, and Serana led the others. In moments, they had covered the distance, and were standing before the second entrance to the cave. Surprisingly, there were no guards at this point. Serana scanned the area, but could find no Daemons outside the cave at all. Perhaps they didn't know of this entrance. Serana wasted no time. She, Amber, and Alier grew Dragon's Tears at this opening just as they'd done at the other. Now came the easy part.

"Aeron, Allaerion, Amber, are you ready?" asked Serana. The three of them nodded, and Serana linked them all, leaving herself in control. Then she began to move the air.

The plan was simple, Dragon's Tears at every entrance to the cave, and a gentle breeze to blow the fragrance through, killing every Daemon inside. Serana pushed the air through the cave, just as Aeron had shown her before, and it appeared to work. It wasn't nearly as much effort as Serana had expected, but then, she was tied to three other magic users, one of them a good deal stronger than she in Air. After a few moments, she realized that she could have done this by herself. She could have, if she'd wanted to be exhausted by the time she was through.

Serana pushed the air through the cave for the better part of an hour, and then she broke the link with the others and took a deep breath. "It's done," she said. "Let's go in and find the Daemon Lord's body." They needed proof for Lady Firehair.

"I don't like it," said Allaerion. "It's too easy."

"You wanted it to be difficult?" asked Aeron.

"He's right," Amber said, watching the cave entrance. "Don't be surprised if there are still Daemons alive in there."

Serana swept the cave with her senses, but she couldn't find anything. "If they're there, I don't sense them."

"We'll all have to be careful," said Alier firmly. "If it's as easy as walking in there and retrieving the body, I'll marry a human." Serana had thought the elemental joke about marrying humans a cruel one, the first time she'd heard it. Now, though, she had begun to see why they said it. Marrying a human would be widowing oneself after a few short years; no elemental would want to do it.

"Let's go, then," said Serana. "Be ready for anything."

They weren't far into the cave before they began to see the bodies of dead Daemon Scouts, and even a few Soldiers, but nothing more. The numbers were very small, but the cave was vast. It was likely that more Daemons had remained deeper inside. The cave quickly became very dark, so Serana created a glowing sphere above her hand, to light the way. After a short time, there were no more bodies at all, as if the few Daemons they'd seen had been all that were in the cave.

The cave itself was a labyrinth of twists, turns, and forks. Serana and Alier had to keep their senses alert, to avoid sudden drops and dead ends. Still Serana sensed no living Daemons whatsoever. She had taken on the task of scanning for them, since she could search with more than one element, but the cave appeared empty as far as Serana could reach.

After nearly an hour, the party was deep within the underground maze, nearly as deep as the cave went, but Serana had still sensed nothing of Daemons. "Could we have made a mistake?" she asked no one in particular.

"No," said Amber, her small face suddenly fearful. "I did. Serana, check again, quickly."

Serana obeyed, and felt her face drain of color. "Where did they come from?"

"They were there the whole time," said Amber, her voice cracking. "I was guarding you against attack, not misdirection. I'm sorry, Serana."

"All of you, search for Daemons, and kill any you find," commanded Serana. "The ones I sense are all behind this wall, and there are more than I could kill at once."

"It's airtight," said Aeron. "I can't sense anything behind the wall. The Dragon's Tears wouldn't have even touched them."

"I can," Alier said grimly. "Back away from the wall, all of you." She suited her own words, stepping several paces back, and the wall shattered outward from the corridor, into the room with the Daemons. Serana heard several scream as shards of rock ripped through them, but she had no illusions that any significant number would be harmed. For some reason, though, none of them attacked.

When the dust cleared, Serana stared into a vast chamber filled with snarling Daemons, but all of them stayed back, watching the party without attacking. There was a smaller figure seated on some sort of throne on a natural balcony near the top of the chamber. It had to be the Daemon Lord, Raveshik.

"Welcome," rasped his voice, no doubt carried to them by some form of Daemon magic. "Welcome to my home. I've been building it for years, as you can see, my own kingdom, where my brother Zironkell has no sway, where *my* word is law. Now, I am strong enough to oppose him. I could crush you all like insects, but you would destroy a valuable part of my army, and render me unable to defeat my brother. Instead, I had intended only to avoid a confrontation with you, but now you have made even that impossible. I propose a bargain between us. Leave me in peace, and I will help you deal with my brother." It was then that Serana noticed the throne itself. It appeared to be made entirely from human bones.

"And how did you build this army?" asked Serana calmly. "Are these Daemons so different from the others that they were not born from the deaths of women? Have you not needed to destroy life in order to feed them? How can I accept an ally who will turn on me the moment our enemy is defeated?" Serana felt Alier gathering her power, and prepared something to help. If she had guessed right, Alier would thank her later.

"If you do not," replied Raveshik, "I will kill you all now. What, then, could you do against my brother?"

Alier took a step forward, planting her staff on the ground as a grim smile played at her lips. "The same we will do against you." At once, the entire ceiling of the chamber collapsed, burying alive almost every Daemon inside. Serana wove Earth magic to earth-meld, but spread the web over the entire party, letting them pass through the rock as it fell, keeping always a small bubble of air around them. It was difficult to keep so many safe this way, but Serana put all of her strength to the task, and it was enough.

The chamber rumbled for several minutes as solid rock crumbled from the ceiling, raining death on the Daemon army. Even Generals died before the onslaught, ripped to shreds by cold rock as merciless as they. Serana barely saw any of it. Every shred of concentration was devoted to keeping the party safe from the avalanche of rock. After a few minutes that seemed to last an eternity, it was over. Serana relaxed as the rock around them suddenly melted away.

"Thank you," said Alier. "I could not have kept us safe while still killing all those Daemons."

"Not all," rasped Raveshik as his black sword stabbed at Alier's heart from behind. The Earth Enchantress flowed like a serpent around his blade, her staff coming up immediately to her defense. The Daemon Lord cut it in half contemptuously. The black blade would have continued through to Alier's face, but the Weaver of Earth leapt back just in time, stumbling and falling from the sudden, desperate move. "You have denied me my army, destroyed decades of work... My brother will surely kill me now, but I will see you dead first." His sword sliced through the air toward Alier, only to stop inches from her face, held in check by another blade, this one glowing as white as the Daemon's was black.

Serana shoved the black blade away from Alier, stepping over her toward the Daemon Lord. "Stay back, all of you. This one helped trap the Serian of Music while Zironkell tried to rape me. I will kill him myself."

"You have certainly grown beyond yourself," Raveshik spat. "A Sorceress challenging a Daemon Lord... how pathetic."

Serana held her sword before her, feeling the energy pulse through her veins. "Perhaps you ran too quickly to recall. This is Daemonbane. It killed two Daemon Lords the last time I saw you. One more should not be difficult." She attacked, but Raveshik deflected every blow effortlessly, then forced her back a step before stopping, his black blade at the ready.

He smiled without mirth. "You think I fled *you*, little Sorceress?" he asked. "The hated Serian escaped our grasp, and he'd begun growing those accursed flowers of his. I withdrew to kill him another day, after I had dealt with my brother. I don't believe I'll kill you yet. Instead, I'll simply kill your companions, and have you as a pet, the way Zironkell failed to do that day." He coughed once, at the end, and Serana realized that the Dragon's Tears they were wearing *were* affecting him, simply not as quickly as they would have affected a weaker Daemon.

Serana turned her rage to focus, taking on the Serenity. She had to be calm. When the Daemon Lord attacked, she was ready, parrying his attack and scoring a deep slice on his arm. "Not that it matters," she told him, "but it was actually I who grew those flowers, much as I grew these." She took off the necklace she'd been wearing, and he backed away. "Perhaps you would like a few for yourself." She tossed the necklace at him, and his black blade moved like a blur, slicing the flowers apart. They fell, withered and dead, to the cave floor.

"I will enjoy you," he told her, his red eyes pulsing with dark power. He moved forward like lightning, raining a flurry of blows on Serana. Air magic or no, it was all she could do to keep the black blade from her flesh. Just once, she moved too far to block, and he slid around her blade.

There was pain and shock, both at once, as his sword stabbed through her middle, but in moments she felt only weak. She fell to her knees, then to her side, Daemonbane sliding from fingers that could no longer hold it up. She felt herself draining away as the Daemon Lord stood over her, reveling in his feast. "My brother was stupid not to simply kill you, now that I think on it," he said conversationally. "I will not make that mistake." Serana wasn't looking at him, but she could feel him smiling. "After all, the little one there would suffice for my pleasure. She was an unexpected result of my little experiment, infusing a portion of the madness Scouts carry into a vampire. Perhaps it will be worthwhile after all, since I will have her to use in your place."

Serana desperately reached out and wrapped her fingers around the hilt of Daemonbane. "Music," she whispered… and nothing happened. Serana waited a few moments, but still nothing happened. She could feel herself being depleted. Blackness was spreading inside her, a growing void that sucked away her life. She had no strength left, and her fingers fell away from the hilt.

"Serana…"

The voice seemed to come from right beside her ear, from the ground itself, but it was a voice she recognized.

"Serana, do not forget what you have learned. You are stronger than you know."

Despite the pain, the emptiness that flooded through her, Serana smiled. "Thank you, Alier," she whispered. Her hand seized the hilt of the Daemon's blade and yanked it out from her body. The pain almost drove her unconscious, but she mastered it by force of will. Drawing deep from the power inside her, Serana healed the wound, white life energy driving out the blackness that was consuming her. She flung away the Daemon's sword as if it were a poisonous snake, and grasped Daemonbane firmly in her hands.

"What trickery is this?" rasped Raveshik.

Serana stood, closing her eyes and listening with her senses. There it was... The energies of Earth were pulsing through her veins, through her soul. Serana opened her eyes and held Daemonbane before her.

Raveshik hissed, and his blade flew to his hands. "It will be over soon," he spat, his eyes narrowing.

"Yes," said Serana calmly. "It will be over soon."

The Daemon Lord launched himself at her, moving faster even than Allaerion could, but to Serana, he may as well have been moving through jelly. She stepped aside easily, and brought her glowing white blade to the wrist of his sword arm, slicing off his hand.

She was vaguely aware of his scream as she followed the upward stroke with a downward one. The world moved at a crawl, and she had all the time in the world. There was no doubt, no fear, nothing within her but certainty. Daemonbane sliced cleanly through Raveshik's neck, and the Daemon Lord's head fell to the ground, thudding dully on the stone floor of the cave.

Only then did everything resume its normal pace. Serana took a deep breath, but though she was quite tired, she wasn't nearly so exhausted as she'd have expected. "Take the head," she said. "That should be enough for Lady Firehair."

"I've never seen anything like that in all my life," said Seleine, hugging Serana warmly. "You're truly amazing."

Serana gave her friend a smile, but shook her head. "It was Alier who saved me."

"If you believe that," said Alier derisively, "then *you* should marry a human. You saved yourself. I just reminded you that you could."

Seleine picked up the head, wrinkling her nose, and she smiled gratefully when Allaerion took it from her, carrying it on a cushion of Air so that he wouldn't have to touch it.

"Let's get out of here, Serana," said Amber, taking her hand and leading her out of the chamber. "I think I'll feel better when we're out of this cave." Aeron and Allaerion nodded uncomfortably.

"Air people," Alier scoffed, starting off for the cave entrance.

Serana said nothing, but she would feel better being outside the cave too.

Chapter XXXVIII

Lady Firehair wrote the note quickly, not allowing herself to think on it too much, lest she say more than she intended, and make an even greater fool of herself for it. Music had made himself very clear by his actions. He would care for her and comfort her, but he did not, could not, love her. She was careful only to write enough to let him know where she had gone, to fulfill her promise, and that she would return soon.

She had to return. Even if he would never love her, at least he would be near her. Lady Firehair was well accustomed to not being loved; it didn't bother her. It didn't... not at all. She was better off now than before, at least. Her uncle could not summon her here, within the Shrine of Music, and he could not touch her here either, until he'd finished conquering the world. By that point she would likely destroy herself to escape his grasp anyway. The world would miss her no more than Music would. Until that time, though, Lady Firehair had another, more important reason to stay. While she remained, she could protect Music from the last of the Seriani.

Lady Firehair had been thinking a great deal on the terrible Serian that her uncle had described to her, a creature deadly, powerful, and devious beyond all others. The only thing she did not understand was why Lord Zironkell did not seem to admire him. From his description, the last of the Seriani was still more honorable than Zironkell himself. Perhaps her uncle was jealous.

When the note was finished, Lady Firehair folded it carefully, and left it on the door to the room with the potter's wheel. Music would be sure to find it there. She took one more look at the room she loved so much, and despite how silly the notion was, she felt as if she were saying goodbye to it.

She'd felt the change to the south when Raveshik had died, though it was unlikely her uncle had. Lord Zironkell never seemed to pay attention to the energies of the world as a whole. None of the other Daemon Lords did. Lady Firehair never spoke with any of them about it, but she had listened to enough conversations that she felt certain regardless. Her presence always made the others agitated, no doubt because they could not stand the revulsion of being near so shameful a creature, but when she was hidden in the shadows, hidden from even their senses, they often spoke freely.

She left the Shrine and started south, but at the edge of the grounds, she encountered a barrier unlike any she'd seen before. It was invisible to her senses, but as real as the ground beneath her feet. Lady Firehair tried simply forcing her way through, but the barrier would not yield even to her considerable strength. The solution came to her only a few minutes later, and she felt rather silly for not seeing it before.

Lady Firehair had long ago begun to view magic as a language. As a child, she'd expressed this idea to her uncle, but he'd discarded it scornfully, so she'd never mentioned it again. Still, he hadn't convinced her that she was wrong, so she'd tried experimenting, and found that it was possible to communicate through magic with the animals in the forest. All of her childhood friends had been these animals, but Lady Firehair had stopped talking to them after a time, when she learned that all of them died in only a few brief years. Their children were fun to talk with as well, but they, too, died too quickly, even more quickly than humans. In the end, she'd limited her conversations with them, so as not to become attached, but the concept of magic as a language was hers forever. It was through that concept that she realized how to cross the barrier. She simply asked it to let her through.

Once she was past the barrier, finding Serana was a simple matter. Lady Firehair moved south as quickly as she could, and arrived at the cave's entrance just as the party was emerging. She hadn't realized that Raveshik had holed himself up in a cave, but it did suit him; he'd always preferred to remain in the shadows, playing his own games.

"You've completed your part of the bargain," Lady Firehair said to Serana as soon as she was close enough. "Now I will complete mine."

"Lady Firehair," said Serana, smiling only faintly. "It's good to see you again. I'd wondered how you would find me when the task was done." The Air Wizard, Allaerion, tossed Raveshik's head on the ground at Lady Firehair's feet. "Here is proof that the deed was done," Serana told her.

Lady Firehair opened her mouth to say it had been unnecessary, but then she reconsidered. Perhaps her uncle would require such proof, and there might be a way to send it to him without going back herself. That was a matter for another time, though. For now, she needed to fulfill her own part in this bargain. She withdrew the gauntlet from beneath her cloak, handing it over to Serana. "As I promised."

Serana nodded, still only managing a weak smile.

"Is something wrong?" Lady Firehair asked her. "I thought you would be pleased."

Serana shook her head. "I am pleased that our search is over, but I nearly died killing this Raveshik, and he..." She choked on her words, and her eyes suddenly filled with tears.

Lady Firehair embraced the Sorceress quickly, as Serana had done for her before. "What has happened?" she asked. "I thought that surely with that sword you carry, Raveshik would not be a difficulty."

"He stabbed me," Serana sobbed, "here." She pointed to her middle.

Lady Firehair looked down at the place she pointed, but even the dress was not damaged. "I'm sorry, but I do not understand."

"He killed my baby!" Serana screamed, collapsing in incoherent sobs. Lady Firehair went to her knees with the Sorceress, holding her helplessly.

The young girl, whom Lady Firehair didn't know, looked shocked, but the others seemed merely confused. "Serana," said the Earth Enchantress carefully, "your baby is fine."

"It's true, Serana," said the young girl. "I still sense two lives in you."

Serana looked up at them, hope gleaming in her tear-filled eyes. "How is that possible?"

The Earth Enchantress, Alier, knelt beside Serana and Lady Firehair. "I keep forgetting that you were raised by humans. Sorceress babies don't grow physically inside their mothers until a month or two before their birth, depending on the power of the mother and the strength of the child. You're not far enough along to have a tiny body inside you yet. All that is there is energy, and unless the Daemon Lord had killed you, that energy would be safe. I'm simply glad you've been using so much magic lately; it's good for the child's development."

Lady Firehair found the entire affair fascinating. She'd never known anything about how Sorceresses had children, or how any other race did, for that matter.

"My baby is still alive?" Serana asked, stifling a sniffle, and Alier nodded.

The Ice Witch, Seleine, knelt Serana's other side. "Alive and well, Serana."

Now the Sorceress smiled genuinely, and Lady Firehair shared her joy. Seeing such happiness in another always filled her heart to bursting.

"One thing puzzles me, though," said Serana. "Before you helped me back there, Alier, I tried to call for help, through the sword."

"And Music never came," finished Alier. "That *is* disturbing."

"He doesn't always come when he's needed," said Lady Firehair, surprised at the bitterness in her tone.

"The Serian of Music has more in the world to worry about than us," Alier told her.

"The *what*?" demanded Lady Firehair. She was on her feet in an instant, shock and anger warring within her. "What did you call him?"

"The Serian of Music," Alier replied testily. "The last of the Seriani."

Lady Firehair felt sick. It was an odd feeling, since she'd never been ill before, but she thought that if she'd eaten recently, she might have vomited.

"Are you alright?" asked Serana, rising to her feet, her eyes filled with concern.

"I must go," whispered Lady Firehair. She sped northward as fast as she could move, pure rage driving her. Her uncle had been right all along. Now she knew why the Serian was so dangerous. He didn't merely destroy his victims' bodies; he destroyed their hearts as well. She would complete her uncle's task if it were the last thing she did.

She would be in the Shrine when Music returned. She would be there, and she would kill him.

Here Ends
Book II of
The Dark Angel Chronicles